Sapphire Sun

suzi davis

central
avenue
publishing

2013

Central Avenue Publishing Edition

This edition is published by arrangement with Suzi Davis, contact at suzi@authorsuzidavis.com

Central Avenue Publishing - www.centralavenuepublishing.com

First print edition published by Central Avenue Publishing, a division of Central Avenue Marketing Ltd.

SAPPHIRE SUN

ISBN 978-1-926760-84-1

Published in Canada with international distribution.

Cover Design: Michelle Halket

Cover Photography: © Courtesy PhotoXpress ngnightsky

For Jesse.

Love you always and forever.

Sapphire Sun

Chapter One – Under the Moon

EVERYTHING WAS BLACK, EVERYTHING WAS SILENT. IT was the sound of approaching death. It was the inhalation before a scream.

The darkness stretched infinitely around me. It was everywhere. It was inside of me, thick and cloying, choking. It *was* me. I could no longer separate myself from the black void. Time ceased to exist here. Nothing could exist here.

My soul constricted with fear. I tried to blink but my eyes were frozen by the impenetrable shadows. Shrill silence rang in my ears. I couldn't feel my own body, all I knew was darkness. I teetered on the brink of insanity. I was lost and alone.

"You are not alone."

The man's voice came from nowhere and everywhere at once. His words slithered through the darkness, his smooth, oily tones sliding into my ears, poisoning my mind. I wanted to scream but there was no air to breathe. "You are never alone. We are always here in the shadows, waiting… watching… We are coming for you."

I felt something in the darkness move, the shadows around me stirred. His hatred and contempt echoed in my ears, demanding a response.

"I don't understand." The words came out of me as I thought them, my mind's voice small and afraid. "Where am I? Who are you?"

There was a pause. A heavy tension hung in the air as the darkness seemed to thicken. I blinked and my eyes refocused. I could sense my body again, I was aware of myself. I was no longer floating away in this never-ending nothingness. My relief was short-lived. The darkness moved and separated, slowly swirling all around me, trapping me in tendrils of icy black mist. I shivered.

"Who are you?" he whispered right in my ear, throwing the question back at me. My heart began to hammer in my chest, my throat tightened.

"I… I'm…"

Fear gripped me, threatened to overwhelm all my senses. A desperate panic set in as I realized I didn't know who I was! I had a name, I knew I did but what was it? Who was I?

The shadows moved, something flashed past me in a rush of sudden blistering heat. I gasped, staring in bewilderment at the painful, throbbing gash that had appeared in the shadow's wake. The skin across my arm was torn open and dark, sticky blood trickled steadily down to my hand, dripping from my fingertips. My shivers accelerated to a violent trembling, I was losing all control. I hugged myself tightly with my uninjured arm, my hand reaching to my chest, my fingers automatically searching, grasping desperately for reassurance but there was nothing there. My fingertips brushed against my cold, clammy skin with my heart hammering beneath.

"Please, stop! I don't know—"

My pleas were cut off by another disturbance in the shadows around me. Something moved, spinning past me at a speed that defied all reason. There was a quick flash of metal and a searing hot stab of pain. My leg was on fire, my flesh ripped apart and bleeding profusely, the blood pouring down my leg.

"Stop!" I screamed, my voice hoarse with pain and fear. I fell to my knees in a slippery puddle of my own blood, trembling and panting, my eyes wildly searching the darkness. I scrambled in a circle, struggling to focus my eyes on something, anything. "Don't do this. Please."

"I don't want to hear you beg." The man's voice came from behind me now, his words twisted with loathing and disgust. I spun around, clutching at my wounds, blood seeping between my fingers. "I want to watch you die."

As he spoke, something in the darkness caught my eye. There was a flash of silver, a glint of light catching a long curved blade before the shadows swallowed the deadly weapon again. To my right there was another flicker, a brief flash of movement. I didn't turn quickly enough but I thought I might have glimpsed a thin, bony hand holding that wicked knife. My breath caught in my throat as suddenly, directly in front of me, the large, deadly blade cut through the darkness, spinning as it flew straight towards my face. I only had time to close my eyes, wincing as I braced myself for the expected pain but the blade somehow fell short, clattering to the ground at my feet. The sound rang eerily through the pitch black void.

There was no time to think, no point in questioning or asking why. Before I could even reach for the blade, a face began emerging from the darkness straight ahead of me. His black, greasy hair tangled and blended with the shadows, his sallow gray skin was stretched tight over gaunt, protruding cheekbones. His cheeks were hollow and his dark eyes were completely empty, void of all life, glazed over in death.

I tried to move away from him but I slipped and slithered upon the ground, trapped by my own blood and my weak, failing limbs. I briefly thought of the knife on the ground ahead of me but I was too terrified to move any closer to this monster. His face swelled in the darkness as he fed off my fear. His horrifying visage filled my vision until there was no where else to look but at him. His thin, sneering lips moved.

"Do you remember me?" he asked in his oily voice.

"No," I whispered. My heart felt ready to explode as I realized I was about to die. "Please, I don't know who you are. I…"

His bloodless lips twisted into a mirthless smile as he realized at the same time as I did, that I remembered. I gasped as the realization struck me.

"Walter? But you're…"

"Dead," he confirmed. His black eyes flared with sudden life. "And so are you!"

In a silent scream of rage and vengeance, his mouth opened wide to reveal row upon row of demonic, razor-sharp teeth. He dove forwards, filling my vision, ready to tear apart and consume my soul. There was a flash of indescribable, excruciating pain, and then everything went black…

MY EYES FLEW open and I gasped for air. I searched my surroundings, my head tossing wildly from side to side, my eyes struggling desperately to focus. I was trapped within the never-ending darkness still. I could barely tell if my eyes were open or closed. Fear crushed my chest; I couldn't breathe. Where was I?

It took several long seconds for me to get a grip. Reason was slowly returning. As my eyes adjusted, I realized I could make out the faint gray shapes of objects in the inky shadows. There was a small writing desk, an old dresser, the tall four posts surrounding the large canopy bed that I lay in… in the Jensons' guest room, I remembered with a sigh. I collapsed back against the soft pillows. I was safe. It had just been a dream.

I felt much calmer with this realization but was still shivering and trembling uncontrollably. Even though I was tucked in under a thick quilt that Mrs. Jenson had made, I was freezing cold, much too cold even for the chill, late-Autumn night. An icy numbness had set into my bones that for some reason made me think of a cold, dark, underground tomb. The image of the wide pillared cavern from my dreams, full of shadows and flickering torchlight flashed through my mind. It was a place of danger, a place of death, the mysterious scene for many of my nightmares lately. I shuddered and reached for the lamp on my bedside table, trying my best to push the disturbing images away.

I reached for the lamp but when I flicked the switch, nothing happened. Puzzled, I tried it again but still I sat in the cold, strangely eerie darkness. I shivered, telling myself I was just cold and debating pulling the quilt over my head and falling back asleep when out of the corner of my eye, I thought I saw something move. My whole body tensed. I sat perfectly still, barely breathing. I stared into the darkest corner of my bedroom without blinking, straining to see what had caused that one, small, movement. When nothing else happened, I tried to relax. Just my imagination, I told myself but I had the sudden disturbing sense that I was being watched. My skin crawled with the feel of unseen eyes, the fine hairs on my arms stood on end. My heart began beating faster.

Don't be ridiculous, I silently scolded myself. *It was just a dream.*

Rubbing my arms briskly, I tried to warm my icy skin. I couldn't shake the feeling that there was something else there with me in my room, watching me from the shadows… waiting… My eyes widened as ever so slightly, the curtains at my closed window began to sway as if someone had just walked past them…

I jumped out of bed, running from the room and the strange, shifting shadows. I was still haunted by my dreams, unable to escape the fear that still lingered. I was a coward and I fled.

I burst out into the hall and closed my bedroom door firmly behind me. Relief washed over me as the door clicked shut and I gained some distance between myself and my nightmares. I had no idea what time it was, definitely past midnight. It didn't really matter, I'd never be able to get back to sleep now.

The surface of the old hardwood floors felt almost warm beneath my feet as I began tip-toeing down the hall. The peculiar icy numbness that had clung to me seemed to fade with each carefully placed step I took. I crept down the hall quickly, avoiding the creaky floorboards with the ease of someone who had walked this path a hundred times.

A quiet sigh of relief escaped my lips as I reached the other end of the hall and saw the faint light glowing beneath the door. Someone was awake but I wasn't really surprised. I quietly turned the knob and slipped inside.

The room was lit by the warm glow of a lamp. It looked much different in here than it once had. Sebastian's large canopy bed and his writing desk had been moved into my bedroom to make room for the two single beds, one pushed up against each wall, that now filled the space. There was a large dresser beneath the window and only one of Sebastian's bookshelves remained; the other had been moved downstairs to Mr. Jenson's study.

I was surprised to see that both beds were empty, especially when a quick glance at the old clock on the bookshelf told me that it was nearly 4am.

"Are you alright, Grace?"

David's smooth, low voice made me jump, my heart briefly leaping into my throat. He had stood so silently by the window that I almost hadn't noticed him. Disappointment and confusion sank in as I realized Sebastian wasn't there.

"I'm fine," I muttered quickly, taking a small step back. "I was just looking for Sebastian. I…well, I couldn't sleep."

"Neither could we," David sympathized with a half smile. He stepped away from the window, closer to the lamp. It was then that I realized he wasn't wearing a shirt. The lamp's soft light seemed to make his skin glow, highlighting every contour of his athletic, lean frame. A pair of plaid pajama pants hung low on his hips, too low. I dropped my eyes, feeling uncomfortable as he walked right up to me, stopping so close before me that we were almost touching. "Are you sure you're alright?"

I glanced up reluctantly. David's handsome face was full of concern. He was a few years older than Sebastian and I. He had quickly taken on a big brother role, developing a close and easy friendship with Sebastian and always being courteous and kind towards me. For some reason, he always made me feel a little uncomfortable though. Like now, his eyes bore down into mine, so dark and steady, glowing with an intensity that was difficult to look away from. I swallowed nervously.

"I'm fine. Where's Sebastian?"

A smile briefly tugged at David's lips. "He's outside. Like he usually is when he can't sleep." He turned away as he spoke, dropping down onto his bed and stretching out on his back, his hands behind his head.

"Like he usually is?" I repeated uncertainly.

"Yes, but… well, perhaps I shouldn't have said it like that."

"Sebastian hasn't mentioned anything to me about having trouble sleeping."

"It's not every night… he probably just doesn't want you to worry. You know how he is," David dismissed. I slowly nodded my agreement.

"Thanks. I'll go look for him outside."

"It's my pleasure. But wait…" David hopped back up off the bed, brushing past me to reach into the open closet by the door. Heat radiated out from him, I forced myself not to step back. "Here, take this." He wrapped a thick gray coat around my shoulders, stepping in close as he carefully did up the top button so that it wouldn't slip off. His fingertips paused by my throat, lightly brushing against the thin, silver scar left by a piece of shrapnel from the explosion in which we had all been injured, just two months ago in Greece.

"It's so strange," David commented softly, his eyes never moving from my scar, his fingertips lingering near my collarbone. "Almost two months ago to this day, we all could have died; you almost bled to death at the Necromanteion. And now here we are, and all that's left are our missing memories and this tiny scar."

I abruptly stepped back. "I wouldn't exactly say it's tiny," I argued. The scar stretched nearly three inches down the side of my throat. I was almost glad I couldn't remember how I'd gotten it—almost. Lately, it had been bothering me more and more that I couldn't remember, that none of us could. "And we came away with more than just one scar." I glanced down at my arm as I spoke, noticing that the peculiar, silvery scars that had wrapped around my melted and burned skin appeared fainter everyday. I was healing at a remarkable pace, astonishing in fact, we all were.

"Yes, we also have our friendship," David agreed, smiling once more. He smoothly stepped back. "I truly value having met you and Sebastian, and all that you and the Jensons have done for me."

"We're glad to have met you too," I assured him with a quick smile, though I wasn't sure if I was being entirely honest. I liked David, and he and Sebastian had certainly become close friends. I always had fun when the three of us were together but on the rare occasions when it was just me and him… something just didn't feel right. Like there was something a bit "off" about him but I couldn't quite place what it was. I shrugged.

"Thank you for the coat, David. I'm going to look for Sebastian now. Good night."

"Good morning," David replied with a laugh. He sat back down on his bed as I left the room, his eyes never leaving me.

I tried to forget about David as I crept downstairs and quietly slipped into a pair of shoes at the backdoor. The dark and violent nightmare I'd had was fading now, I could barely remember what it had been about—some kind of monster, a haunting sense of death and despair lingered—but I still wanted to see Sebastian before I went back to bed, especially now that I knew he was having trouble sleeping and that he had apparently been hiding it from me.

The back door closed behind me with a soft click as I stepped outside. Though Sebastian was sitting on the far edge of the lawn, he turned immediately at the sound. Beneath the moon's gentle light, I could just make out the surprised smile on his face as he stood to greet me. My heart instantly swelled and settled at the sight of him.

I hurried across the lawn, the dewy grass already soaking into my shoes and dampening the cuffs of my pajama pants.

"Grace, what are you doing out here?" he asked with a smile. "Not that I'm truly unhappy to see you," he added, taking me into his arms and kissing the top of my head.

"I couldn't sleep. I had a bad dream and wanted to see you," I confessed quietly. His muscles tensed around me. "What is it?"

"Nothing. I just… I don't like you having bad dreams," he muttered.

I pulled away and caught him frowning up at the moon, his eyes dark and narrowed. He saw me looking at him and suddenly smiled, his expression instantly brightening.

"So you had a scary dream?" he teased, rocking me slightly in his arms. "Do you want to tell me about it?"

"No. I don't think so. I think I'd rather forget," I answered quickly.

"I might be able to help you with that."

My heart began to race as he bent his head down to mine, his lips easily finding me in the quiet darkness. His cheeks were cold from the chill night air but his lips were warm, and very soft. They brushed against mine gently, teasingly, in a sweet and chaste kiss that only made my passion for him flare. He pulled away much too soon, suddenly looking confused and a little amused.

"Are you wearing David's coat? You smell like his cologne."

"Yes, it's his," I replied, telling myself it was Sebastian's kiss that had made my cheeks glow and not the strange sense of guilt that had crept into my stomach. "He told me you were out here and insisted I wear it. Aren't you cold?" I shivered as I looked over the thin, cotton shirt Sebastian wore and his loose sweat pants, his feet were bare and must have been numb from the cold.

Sebastian shrugged. "It seems like lately I'm always cold."

His words reminded me of the icy numbness I had experienced in my nightmare and that had clung to me upon waking. The frightening images and sensations crept at the edge of my conscious mind but I managed to keep them at bay, for now.

"David said you've been having trouble sleeping lately," I stated hesitantly. Sebastian tensed again for a second, an unexpectedly angry expression passing over his face before he relaxed.

"Did he? Well that's not entirely accurate. It's more that I've been waking and having difficulty falling back asleep. But David is often the same way. He shouldn't have worried you," Sebastian added disapprovingly. He frowned. "It wasn't his place to say anything."

I was surprised. It was the first time I'd ever heard Sebastian say anything even remotely negative about David, besides the fact that he sometimes mumbled in his sleep. Sebastian had sounded almost menacing for a second. I shivered again, dismissing my concerns as just my tired mind playing tricks on me. I tried to focus on the issue at hand.

"But what is it that's waking you? David's snoring?" I teased. Sebastian only faintly smiled. He suddenly looked tired and years older than just 19. Every now and again, his eyes would take on a sudden depth that seemed to stretch back hundreds of years like they were right now—it gave me chills.

"Don't worry about me."

I searched his eyes for the truth and he abruptly looked away.

"You're having nightmares too," I guessed. He didn't answer, so I pushed on. "I bet that's what David's problem is too, that's why we're all waking up. It must have to do with the explosion."

Sebastian hesitated before responding. "David and I have discussed it. We figure it's some sort of post-traumatic stress. I'm sure it'll pass with time."

"Maybe... but what if it's something else? Sebastian..." I struggled to find the right words to describe what I was feeling. There was a nagging sense of unease building within me that was difficult to explain. "Don't you find it strange that none of us can remember what happened that day in Greece? And that our memory is so patchy? It just doesn't make sense. I keep feeling like there's something that we're *meant* to remember. Something important, something dangerous…"

"No, Grace," Sebastian cut me off with a firm shake of his head. "There's nothing good in the past to remember. Just leave it alone."

For a second I was taken aback by his firm, disapproving tone and the sharpness to his voice and eyes. He had rarely spoken to me like this before and I definitely didn't like it.

"No, I won't just 'leave it alone'. Why would you even say that?" I answered firmly, responding to the fire in his eyes with a sudden blaze of my own strength.

His expression immediately softened. I could tell he hadn't meant to start an argument. He raked his hands through his messy, wavy black hair that was now long enough it curled around his ears.

"I'm sorry, Grace. I'm just tired, that's all. I've given up on trying to remember; I just want to move forward now, to leave the past and whatever mysteries it might hold behind us."

"I don't know… it just seems so strange. Doesn't it bother you that you can't remember?"

"No," he answered with a shrug, and I could see that he spoke the truth. "I don't have the slightest desire to remember those forgotten events and neither does David. We both agree that there must be something that our subconscious minds are trying to protect us from, so why fight that?"

I didn't answer. I could remember feeling the exact same way right after the accident. As the days passed, it had bothered me less and less that I'd suffered such significant memory loss. By the time we left the hospital in Athens and returned to Canada, it bothered me so little that I had almost stopped thinking about it entirely. But something had changed. Lately, those gaping holes in my memory seemed to be constantly on my mind and it upset me that Sebastian didn't feel the same way.

"There's more than just the memory loss Sebastian," I began, cautiously. He frowned, waiting for me to continue. "There were fourteen other survivors of the explosion, none injured anywhere near as badly as us but we all suffered almost identical memory loss. I've been doing some research and it turns out that there were some other strange similarities about the members of our group that I think might be important."

"What do you mean?"

"Well, almost everyone appeared to be in their twenties…"

"Appeared?"

I nodded. "Not a single person had any identification on them."

"That is a little strange, I'm sure there's an explanation though."

"But there's more. We weren't supposed to be so deep within the ruins of the Necromanteion, no one's allowed in there. We weren't with any registered tour group, they don't even know how we got in there. And they never found any cause for the explosion—nothing. The fourteen other survivors never had anyone come claim them at the hospital either, no family, no friends, no one. There was no record of them anywhere, like they didn't even exist. Just like David." I finished. Sebastian looked puzzled as he contemplated my words. He eventually gave his head a little shake.

"Grace, I think you're making a mountain out of a molehill here. If it doesn't bother the authorities or anyone else, why should it bother you? I'm sure there's an explanation but you don't need to be the one to find it. I don't like you researching the explosion, I don't like to even think about it. I almost lost you that day. I only want to look ahead, to our future. We survived a near-death experience, we're together, we're getting married," he reminded me with a gentle smile, "I have everything I need. Why would I want anything else?"

He pulled me back into his arms and I tried to relax against his chest. There was something about what he'd just said that wasn't sitting right but I couldn't quite place what it was. Maybe he was right, maybe it was best to just forget. Perhaps I should just "leave it alone". I tried to shake the feeling and focus on his warm body against mine, his strong, firm embrace, his delicious, clean scent…

"Are you ready to go inside?" he whispered in my ear. Another shiver slid down my spine but this one was warm and pleasant. I smiled.

"No, we're not finished just yet," I told him firmly. I looked up to see a slightly worried expression on his face. I let my hand slide up the side of his neck, gently and playfully twisting my fingers into his thick, dark hair. "You haven't made me forget my nightmare," I reminded him.

I expected him to smile back at me but he didn't, he looked quite serious as he gazed deeply into my eyes.

"I love you," he said quietly, his eyes steady on mine, his warm hands cupping my face. My heart skipped a beat as he slowly began to kiss me. His lips met mine gently at first, slowly and tenderly kissing me, softly brushing against mine. As always, with just the slightest touch, he had ignited a fire within me. I pulled him closer, kissed him harder, parted my lips eagerly, intoxicated by the taste of him and the heady passion that overwhelmed me. As his hand slid under the thick coat I wore, I easily shrugged out of it, completely unaware of the night's chill.

With Sebastian and David sharing a room, and the surprising vigilance of the Jensons, Sebastian and I were rarely left alone. I was ecstatic for the opportunity and decided to take full advantage of it, pulling Sebastian down with me onto David's coat that only partially protected us from the chilly, damp grass. I shivered but Sebastian was immediately beside me, warming me in his arms. His hands gently slid over my cool skin, leaving a trail of heat and desire wherever he touched. I arched my back in pleasure, shifting closer against him, slipping my hands beneath his shirt and pulling him to me.

"We should go inside," he whispered, his breath tickling my ear and making me bite my lip.

"I don't think so." My kisses moved up the side of his neck, reaching his mouth with a passionate hunger that could not be denied. My head spun, the world began to slip away as I became lost in a hazy dream of passion and pleasure, with Sebastian and myself at its center.

"Why do you have to make this so hard?" he groaned softly, his hand squeezing my hip as he gently rolled me away. As he sat up I could see where the dew had soaked into his shirt, causing it to cling to the lean form of his body. His eyes lingered on me, enjoying the dew's same effect on my thin pajamas. I reluctantly sat up beside him.

"Why do you have to be so old-fashioned?" I shot back playfully. He grinned back at me.

"Actually, I seem to remember this whole 'let's wait until we're married' thing to be your idea," he reminded me. I rolled my eyes.

"I thought you would have talked me out of it by now." We both laughed. "But seriously… why are we waiting? I can't quite remember anymore."

Sebastian smiled at me, his eyes full of amusement and mirth as he helped me to my feet and wrapped me back up in David's warm jacket.

"I feel like I've been waiting for you forever, Grace. And now that I've found you… I just don't want to rush a thing. We've got the rest of our lives to be together, let's just take it slow and savor every moment."

"Does that mean you're still refusing to set a wedding date?"

"Yes," he laughed. I threw him a grumpy look, only half-teasing. "And I'm not refusing, just delaying—for now at least. It makes sense to wait and see how your first year at university goes."

"I don't even know if I want to go to school anymore," I announced.

"Now you're being ridiculous."

"No, I'm serious. I know I'm registered to start at the University of Victoria after Christmas but I'm really enjoying assisting the curator at the art gallery and lately I've just been feeling like, well… like there's something more out there for me—for us. Maybe I'm not meant to just go to school, get married, have a career, start a family…" Sebastian smiled at the idea.

"What else is there?"

"I don't know." I shrugged. "Maybe if I could remember—"

"Not this again," Sebastian groaned, but he was still smiling. "Come on, you need to get some sleep. You're making even less sense than I usually do."

"Am I really that bad?"

"It's awful," he laughed.

"Maybe I should just stop talking then."

"I couldn't agree more." And with that, he pressed his lips against mine, effectively silencing me with a kiss. But in the back of my mind, on the very edge of my conscious thoughts, the shadows of doubt began to stir...

Chapter Two - Familiar

IDIDN'T GO BACK TO SLEEP THAT night, I couldn't. Every time I closed my eyes, images from my nightmare flashed through my mind. I didn't want to be alone either so I stayed with Sebastian in his room and watched him and David play chess until dawn. Only once the sun had risen above the horizon and the house started to brighten, did I feel safe returning to my room. The strange shadows and sense of unease that had plagued me in the night had been banished with the dark.

After I had showered and dressed, I joined the boys downstairs for breakfast with Mr. Jenson (Mrs. Jenson was away for a few days on a work-related trip). The strong scent of freshly brewed coffee and burnt toast greeted my nose as I descended the stairs. I smiled to myself, Mr. Jenson had obviously been "cooking" again. Sebastian and David already sat around the small, round table in the center of the kitchen, the charred remains of their breakfast before them. Mr. Jenson smiled at me hopefully as I entered. He was all ready and positioned in front of the toaster.

"Good morning, Grace. Sleep well?"

"Not really," I admitted with a small shrug. "No toast for me, thanks," I added hurriedly. Mr. Jenson's shoulders fell. "But I'd love some coffee?"

"Just brewed a pot myself! Let me get that for you, dear." He smiled, so obviously pleased to take care of us in Mrs. Jenson's absence that I pressed my lips together tightly to hold back a smirk.

"Good morning," Sebastian greeted me as I took the empty seat between him and David. He reached for my hand and gave it a quick squeeze, his ready smile warm and his eyes bright. He looked a lot happier now that it was daytime, and I had to admit, I was feeling the same way. Our eyes stayed locked together for several long seconds as I marveled over how after almost exactly a year, he could still give me butterflies with just one lingering look.

"Ahem," David cleared his throat from beside me, breaking the moment between us. He was smiling as I turned to face him. "Good morning, Grace." His eyes quickly looked me up and down. "You look exceptionally beautiful today. Are you off to the gallery?"

I blushed uncomfortably at the compliment, it somehow didn't seem appropriate.

"No, they don't need me again until Sunday. I'm going to be assisting in the set-up of a new installation piece."

"Then why must you look so ravishing on a rainy Thursday morning?" David's eyes strayed once more to the top buttons I had left undone on the thin cream blouse I wore, and the necklaces layered around my throat. Paired with a tight pair of jeans and a pair of heels, it was certainly a lot more fashionable of an outfit than the more casual and comfortable clothes I typically wore at home.

"She's going to visit her mother," Sebastian explained, a knowing sparkle in his eye.

"Oh, I see," David responded. He was still watching me curiously. I turned my body away from him slightly, focusing all of my attention on Sebastian.

"I was hoping you might come with me?"

"I'd love to but I promised David I'd drop him off downtown and then I have a few errands of my own to run." I didn't bother trying to hide my disappointment. Sebastian smiled. "But we could drop you off on the way and then I can pick you up again later. We could go somewhere for lunch, if you'd like?"

I smiled appreciatively. "That sounds perfect."

"Grace, you're not afraid to face your mother alone, are you? I always thought you were so… fearless," David commented, his eyes both curious and amused.

"You obviously haven't met her mother," Mr. Jenson cut in as he placed a cup of coffee down on the table in front of me. He shared a quick, knowing look with Sebastian. "Sorry, Grace, but she really is quite an intimidating woman."

"So that's where you get it from," David commented.

"I am not afraid of my mother," I corrected firmly. I shot Sebastian a disapproving look but he didn't look the slightest bit ashamed to be caught grinning. David smiled over his cup of coffee at me.

"Of course not."

"How is your mother, Grace?" Mr. Jenson asked, politely changing the subject.

"She's doing well. She's finally found a new staff member to replace Walter since he quit: a very competent woman named Ellen who has taken over running the household." I paused. When I had said Walter's name, a memory had hovered just on the edge of my thoughts almost as if I had seen him recently but I knew that wasn't true. What was it? I gave my head a slight shake. "And my mother has her sights on a recently-divorced doctor she met at the hospital. They've been spending some time together lately, so... who knows what might happen?"

"Well that's nice," Mr. Jenson responded. He sounded like he actually meant it too, which only spoke for his kind, forgiving character considering how rude my mother had acted towards both of the Jensons in the past.

"When will you be ready to go?" I asked Sebastian.

"As soon as you are."

"Alright, let's get this over with," I said as I stood.

"I can put that coffee in a travel mug for you, Grace, hold on." Mr. Jenson swooped in, enthusiastically reaching for my cup. "Does anyone want some more breakfast?"

"No," the boys answered in unison.

"Thanks though, Don," Sebastian added.

"Oh, it was nothing really, my pleasure. Now you better get going. You don't want to make Grace late for her appointment with her mother. I know I wouldn't want to be!"

"Very funny," I responded. Mr. Jenson grinned and waved as the three of us made our way out.

Since we had returned to Victoria from Greece a month ago, we had made a few interesting discoveries. One was a mysterious bank account in Sebastian's name. He hadn't even remembered the account existed until he received a monthly statement from the bank. He wasn't sure where the savings had come from but the Jensons seemed to think that his parents (whom he couldn't remember beyond the fact that they had died a long time ago) might have left him an inheritance. There had only been a few transactions over the years, one to pay my tuition at Craigflower Academy last year when my father had cut me off, and another withdrawal when he had bought his motorbike a few years before that. The real surprise was the remaining balance. The account contained a substantial amount of money. By substantial, I meant it was clear that Sebastian could easily support both of us for the rest of our lives in a way that my mother would certainly approve of… if we wanted. Neither of us had any desire to live like that but it was reassuring to know that money would not be a concern. Sebastian had withdrawn a small portion from the account after rediscovering it, and he had bought a car (since his motorbike had been lost somewhere just outside of Quetico Park in Ontario when it broke down on our road trip last summer). He had also given David some cash to help get him back on his feet while he looked for work and a place of his own in Victoria. Sebastian had offered the Jensons some money too, at the very least to pay them rent for allowing the three of us to stay with them but of course they wouldn't hear of it. They didn't truly need it either. Despite their modest lifestyle, the Jensons were actually quite wealthy themselves.

"Shotgun!" David called out as we approached Sebastian's "new" car. It was a dark blue, two door, 1970 Dodge Challenger that the previous owner had put some real time into fixing up. The boys were constantly drooling over the curved hood scoop, chrome wheels, shiny exhaust and an engine that roared when it gunned to life. It was Sebastian's compromise since I didn't want him to get another motorcycle. This old muscle car was supposed to be "safer".

"There's no way I'm climbing into the back of that thing."

"Don't call her a 'thing', Grace, she's a car," David corrected.

"It's a she?"

"Of course," Sebastian replied, grinning like a boy with a brand new toy. "And don't worry, the front seat is permanently yours—David, you're in the back."

"But shotgun rules—"

"The driver can override the rules at anytime," I cut in.

David frowned. "You never said that before."

"I'm saying it now." The smile on my face did nothing to soften the hard look in his eyes. Obviously, someone didn't like losing. I fought the urge to stick out my tongue.

"You shouldn't have taught him the game if you didn't want to play, Grace," Sebastian teased. His soft laughter was muffled as he jumped into the driver's seat.

I reached for the passenger door and heaved it open, gallantly flipping forward the seat and gesturing for David to climb into the back of the car.

"Sorry," I offered with a shrug. "But I'm not riding in the back."

David slowly moved forward, his eyes fixed on mine. Nervous butterflies suddenly fluttered in my stomach.

"Don't apologize. I don't like to play by the rules either," he murmured in a low voice as he carefully moved around me, smoothly sliding into the backseat.

"Are you going to pout back there for the whole ride?" Sebastian teased as he turned the engine on. I quickly hopped in and closed my door, ready to get this show on the road.

"Shut up," David responded, lightly smacking Sebastian in the back of the head. Sebastian laughed.

"David *hates* not getting what he wants," he told me knowingly, which earned him another smack from David.

"Just shut up and drive, Caldwood," David instructed, though his voice sounded amused.

The boys continued to banter back and forth during the short drive from the Jensons' to my mother's. She was still living in the enormous semi-mansion in the ritzy Beach Drive neighborhood along the ocean. After my father had left her for another woman (Dahlia, his young and kind legal assistant with whom he'd been having an affair) my mother had tried to sell the house but since she couldn't get the price she wanted for it, she had settled for just buying my father out of the title and redecorating. "A fresh start," she had called it. The house still felt the same to me, cold and empty. It wasn't a home, or not mine anyway.

"I'll walk you to the door," Sebastian offered as we idled at the large, iron gates at the end of the driveway. Before Sebastian could reach for the intercom box, the gates began to smoothly slide apart, someone was always watching.

"Thanks. I'm sure my mother will want to say 'hi' to you." Surprisingly, it was true. A year ago, I could never have imagined in my wildest dreams that my mother would one day be enthusiastically greeting Sebastian Caldwood at her door and begging him to come inside. Recently though, she had somehow discovered that Sebastian had his own money, money that easily rivaled her own. Now she couldn't wait to officially make him her new son-in-law and she was all smiles and batted eyelashes whenever Sebastian was around.

"I'd like to meet your mother as well," David announced unexpectedly. I frowned, uncertain if that was a good idea.

Sebastian pulled the car up to the house, the engine rumbling loudly enough that I was certain the house windows must be shaking. We both turned in our seats so that we could see David sitting behind us.

"You've made the woman out to be quite the legend," he explained. "My curiosity simply won't be satisfied until I've met her."

Sebastian accepted this explanation easily enough with a quick shrug.

I quietly groaned. I wasn't sure exactly why, but I had a feeling that this was not a good idea. I couldn't think of a valid reason to object so I tried my best to follow Sebastian's casual lead as the three of us made our way up to the main entrance of my former home.

David hung back on the bottom step as Sebastian and I approached the double front doors and Sebastian rang the bell. There was only a brief pause before the door slowly opened, I had the feeling whoever opened it had been waiting on the other side.

"Good morning, Ms. Grace," Ellen greeted me in her clipped tones. She gave a slight nod and tight smile to Sebastian. "Your mother has been waiting for you. She'll be pleased to know you've now arrived."

Ellen stepped back and held the door open wider. She moved with a surprising grace considering her stocky frame. I had initially been surprised that my mother had hired her, Ellen appeared to be the polar opposite of my mother. But after spending more time around her I could see that there was a quiet elegance to Ellen's proud stance and a cultured dignity to her manner. She stared down her large nose at me now, her dark brows pulled down slightly as if she could read my thoughts.

"Sebastian! Grace!" my mother called out as she appeared at the top of the winding staircase. She quickly descended, gliding towards the front doors with her arms outstretched. She clasped my hands briefly, as much of an affectionate greeting as I could ever really expect from her and she even went so far as to lightly touch Sebastian's arm. "What a pleasant surprise. I didn't realize you were joining us, Sebastian. Grace you should have told me! Now come inside, there's no need to hover on the doorstep like unwanted solicitors."

My mother's fingers squeezed tightly into my wrist as she led me inside, luckily my feet were already moving or I would have been dragged.

"Sebastian's not staying, Mother, he has other business."

"Yes, sorry, Ms. Chattam." Sebastian bowed his head apologetically. I gave a silent sigh of relief that he had remembered to use her maiden name. Even though she was quite smitten with Sebastian now that she knew he had money, she had already proven how unforgiving she would be to those who referred to her as Mrs. Stevenson. That was the main reason why she had replaced all of her staff with new ones since my father had left.

"I'm sure your business can wait, Sebastian. It can't be nearly as important as spending some quality time with your bride-to-be and future mother-in-law." My mother's thin lips attempted a smile as she spoke, her whole expression looking tight and strained. There was a determined gleam to her sharp hazel eyes as she waited expectantly for Sebastian to step inside. I wanted to groan at the awkwardness of it all but instead I opened my mouth to object.

"I'm afraid Sebastian has already promised to assist me in several important matters this morning." David spoke before I had the chance. He moved forward into my mother's view, climbing to the top step. My mother's eyebrows lifted at his drawling, bored tone, her lips parting slightly in surprise. "Allow me to introduce myself since Grace has obviously forgotten to do so. I'm David, Sebastian's roommate and I'll also be his Best Man."

"David?" my mother repeated, looking unexpectedly shaken. Her eyes were wide and her face had paled. Sebastian threw me a quick puzzled look but I had no idea what was going on. "What are you doing here? Is Walter with you?"

"Walter? Who's Walter?"

For some reason, hearing Walter's name spoken in David's cool, confident voice sent icy chills down my spine. Walter's demonic, bloodthirsty face from my nightmares flashed before my eyes, causing me to visibly flinch. Only Sebastian appeared to notice, my mother's eyes were locked with David's and Ellen had discreetly disappeared.

"Your uncle," my mother replied snippily, regaining some of her usual composure. "He is your uncle, isn't he?"

There was an awkward pause, my mother's eyes looking to each of our faces expectantly.

"David is a friend of mine, recently moved here from Europe. He was in the explosion with Grace and I, in Greece. He suffers the same memory loss as we do," Sebastian slowly explained.

"He doesn't remember his family," I joined in.

"Thank you, both," David frowned at us, "but I can speak for myself. Now, tell me more of this supposed uncle."

My mother arched her eyebrow at his expectant tone, her thin lips pressing together firmly. David's jaw flexed, his teeth clenching tightly together.

"Please," he added reluctantly. Sebastian quickly turned away, hiding a smile. I was staring at my mother, just as intrigued as David to hear what she was about to say.

"Your uncle, Walter Crestwell, worked for me. He was an invaluable employee, performing chauffeur and butler duties and managing our household staff. I quite enjoyed his company until he abruptly quit my services last summer and moved away to God knows where! It wasn't long after Grace and Sebastian left for their trip that he moved on. I was completely abandoned by all those close to me—it was a terrible time." Her expression twisted sourly as she remembered.

"How do you know he's my uncle? Did he speak of me?" David pressed, his gray eyes challenging. He stepped closer, crossing the threshold, his eyes never wavering from my mother's for a second. A flush began creeping across her cheeks as she stared into David's eyes. He could be quite intimidating when he chose to be, so tall and handsome, confident and always in charge. My mother licked her lips and smoothed her short, platinum blonde hair. The gesture was completely unnecessary.

"Well, you came to visit him last Christmas, didn't you? And your uncle certainly went out of his way to make you feel welcome—not that you showed any appreciation. I couldn't believe how indulgent Walter was to you, answering your every beck and call. Why, you even came here one day and took him away from his duties because you 'needed him' for something. That was the only day of work Walter ever missed during the thirteen months he was under my employment. And I never heard you say 'thank you' to him once! Why, I tell you, if Grace were to ever treat me in—"

"Where did my uncle live? Where did he move to? Did he say anything about where I was from? Or any of our other family members?" David demanded, moving another step closer to my mother. She appeared to wilt beneath the intensity of his glare, losing some of her ferocity.

"I... I don't know. He once had an apartment in Victoria but after Grace's father moved out, Walter moved into one of the guest rooms and took up residence here—just as a friend, of course. He never told me anything else about you or your family; he avoided the topic quite astutely so I never pressed. I'm not one to pry, you see. Gossip is quite unbecoming of a lady." My mother flashed me a brief look, never missing an opportunity to either chastise or lecture me.

"Where does my uncle live now?"

"I have no idea."

"Tell me," David growled, his tone implying a threat.

"I don't know," my mother insisted, the flush to her cheeks deepening. "I woke up one morning last summer to find all of his things were gone. I tried to phone him but his number had been disconnected and I haven't seen or heard anything from him since. He just up and disappeared, completely abandoning me without the courtesy of an apology or even an explanation."

David stared at her for several long seconds then abruptly stepped back. He flashed my mother his most charming smile, the intensity that had driven him moments before abruptly forgotten.

"Thank you. I shall try to find out more about this uncle of mine and will let you know if I'm able to contact him. It was a pleasure meeting you but I'm afraid we've now made ourselves late. Sebastian?"

Sebastian was obviously distracted, staring at the floor with a troubled frown.

"Sebastian?" I echoed, gently touching his arm. When he didn't immediately respond, a flash of fear jolted through me, followed by an overwhelming and frightening sense of déjà vu. I sighed with relief when he blinked and then looked up, clouds of gray swirling in his dark eyes with just a hint of blue.

"Yes, sorry. David's right, we should get going. I apologize again, Ms. Chattam, that I can't stay today." Sebastian turned to me, smoothly stepping forward and quickly kissing my cheek. "I'll be back soon," he whispered in my ear before he pulled back.

I tried my best to smile and wave as Sebastian and David got into the Challenger and the engine rumbled to life. There was an eerie numbness spreading from inside of me, a haunting sense of danger and unease. It felt like too much of a coincidence that I had just dreamt of Walter last night and then learnt of his disappearance and his connection to David today… but what did it mean? And why was it, that as soon as my mother had said Walter had disappeared, I knew deep down in my heart with a cold and deadly certainty, that Walter was never coming back, that no one would ever see him again? Was it just from that strange dream I'd had or was there something more to it than just that?

"Come in, Grace," my mother's sharp voice commanded from behind me. "There's no need to continue staring after Sebastian like a sad puppy dog."

"I wasn't staring," I corrected her politely, holding my head high as I stepped inside and closed the door behind me. "I was just lost in thought for a moment."

"I suppose it's really for the best that Sebastian couldn't join us this morning," my mother continued on as if I hadn't spoken. She began striding away from the front door, her black heels clicking against the polished marble floor. "We have a lot of wedding plans to discuss and Sebastian would only get in the way. Have you set a date yet dear?"

I hurried after her, silently hoping that the morning would go by quickly. I was already counting the minutes until Sebastian's return.

"I don't think we need to start planning anything just yet, Mother. We were planning on having a long engagement…"

"Nonsense! I'll see you married next spring, as soon as the gardens are in full enough bloom to do some outdoor portraits. Susanna needs an exact date though before she can get much further into the plans."

"Susanna?"

"Susanna Marquesa, the wedding planner." My mother stopped and spun on her heel, scowling at me in annoyance. "Oh please, Grace. I know you've heard of her! Everyone who's anyone has had their wedding planned by Susanna Marquesa. She's waiting in the dining room for us with her assistant to go over some of the early plans. Then Cassandra will be arriving at ten thirty to do measurements and go over our different fabric and design options."

My mind slowly put it all together. I felt my jaw drop. "Cassandra Battacenia? The designer from *New York*?"

"Well, who else would we get to design your wedding dress? Oh Grace, you had better not slouch like that when I introduce you to Susanna or I shall positively die of embarrassment," my mother declared. Surprisingly, she was smiling, as if she were enjoying herself. I supposed planning a wedding for her daughter to marry a wealthy young man really was right up her alley. It was all completely un-necessary considering that Sebastian and I hadn't yet set a date and I had been hoping for something low key and informal but still... I needed the distraction. And my mother did seem genuinely excited; I didn't want to rob her of her fun. Not to mention the fact that my mother's involvement in our wedding plans might light a fire underneath Sebastian...

I smiled and stood up straighter, sweeping my loosely curled hair away from my face and tucking it behind my ear.

"Alright, let's hear what Susanna's got in mind."

I marched ahead of my mother and opened the dining room door.

The morning flew by in a blur of papers, measurements and designs. By the end of it, I was feeling quite exhausted, especially with my lack of sleep from the night before. My mother had defi-nitely enjoyed herself and it had been almost pleasant to be in her company for once—if I overlooked her vanity, pushiness, and dra-matic egocentric flair. Still, I was more than ready to leave when I heard the distinctive rumble of Sebastian's car approaching. I had been right before, the windows in the house did start to vibrate as Sebastian pulled into the driveway, along with the trembling crystal hanging from the entranceway chandelier.

My mother was still going over the fine details of the design for my wedding gown with Cassandra when Sebastian arrived, so it was Ellen who showed me to the door. I skipped up to Sebastian with a smile on my face, kissing his cheek sweetly as he held the passenger door of the big old, Dodge open for me.

"You're in a good mood," he commented as we started driving away from my mother's house and along Beach Drive.

"I am," I agreed, happily reaching for his hand on the shifter. "My mother wasn't quite as bad as I expected today."

"Good." Sebastian grinned. "I'm in a good mood too but I can't tell you why."

"Why not?"

"You'll have to wait and see." He smiled at me mysteriously, his eyes bright with excitement. Butterflies fluttered in my stomach.

"Will I have to wait long?"

"No, not at all. In fact, we'll be there in just a few minutes."

"Where are we going?"

He pressed his lips together, refusing to answer. His eyes sparkled back at me.

I felt like a child as we drove along, Sebastian's excitement and playfulness was infectious. Once I realized we were going to Beacon Hill Park, I couldn't help but smile as wisps of pleasant memories drifted back to me: autumn leaves swirling, walking together hand-in-hand through the snow, the sparkling ice on the frozen duck ponds.

"We're having a picnic?" I guessed as we pulled into the parking lot.

"Yes," Sebastian agreed, not giving away anything else.

He walked around the car to hold open my door for me, then reached behind my seat and pulled out a bulging backpack. He quickly swung it onto his back and then took my hand.

"Come on, I want to show you something."

Another wave of déjà vu swept over me, his words echoing in one of the holes in my memory. There was a strange emotion building within me as we walked along the winding path beneath the towering trees. Something important was about to happen, I felt certain of it. Doubt flickered through my mind. Or else, something very important had happened here, at another time, on another day that I just couldn't remember. It was so frustrating that I couldn't remember.

"This way," Sebastian encouraged, leading me off the trail and into the surrounding trees. Not far from the path, we came to a stop at the base of an enormous, old oak. As I blinked up at the bright blue sky peeking through the leafy branches, memories sparked in my mind: the texture of the rough, brittle bark, the quiet strength of the sturdy boughs, the gentle sway of the branches up high.

"We climbed this tree," I said quietly as I remembered, my voice touched with surprise. Sebastian nodded, his eyes still bright.

"We did. I remembered today too. I had some time to kill this morning so I decided to come to the park. I wandered for a little while but I soon found myself here—but that's not all." He slipped off his backpack at the base of the trunk and linked his hands together, offering me a boost with a challenging grin. "You've got to see this."

The way he said it, I knew it was something I couldn't miss. I only hesitated for a second, nervous about how high we might climb but if I'd done it before, I could do it again. I gave him my foot and giggled as he suddenly launched me upwards and into the tree.

With Sebastian's help, I climbed higher and higher into the air. It was surprisingly fun, joyful smiles lit up both our faces. There was more to it, though. There was something familiar, something reassuring about climbing this tree together. My soul felt at ease even while my heart beat ever more quickly in anticipation. I became more tense and excited by the second as my whole body sensed that something was about to happen even though my conscious mind had no idea what it was.

As we reached the highest fork in the tree, we both found spots to sit down. The crook in the bough formed a perfect and unexpectedly comfortable seat, cradling us high above the earth. The whole tree swayed, rocked gently by the wind that was stirring the branches and twisting through my hair. Sebastian leant forward and took my hand, my heart skipping a beat as my eyes met his.

Without saying a word, he moved my hand to the bark near my leg, pulling my fingers over its peculiar texture in a slow caress. My eyes widened, as I realized there were words carved into the tree, each letter formed in such an odd, flowing script that it almost appeared to be a part of the tree itself. The carving had obviously been done some time ago, only parts of the letters still visible as the tree had slowly healed. I could still easily read our names: "Sebastian" and "Grace nn".

"It looks like you tried to carve my middle name too," I wondered as I lightly ran my fingers over the letters. "I remember now… sort of. This is our tree."

"Our special place where we made many memories we can't remember and had conversations forgotten like they were never spoken," Sebastian murmured. His voice sounded strange, like he was both happy and sad at the same time. "I have something for you too." He reached into his pocket as he spoke, felt around and then frowned. He met my curious gaze with a sheepish smile. "I left it in the backpack. Just wait here, I'll be right back."

I laughed. "Where am I going to go?"

I couldn't watch Sebastian climb back down. It made me feel dizzy to look straight down to the ground far below and without him by my side, I felt markedly less safe. Instead, I gazed out over the treetops, admiring the beautiful view spread out before me. The warm, midday sun made the autumn leaves glow in bright tones of amber, gold, even ruby red, the stunning colours sprinkled through the surrounding trees like bright splashes of paint. I could see all the way out to the ocean from here, the water blending with the sky in a hazy mist that made the horizon appear to stretch into forever. The building tops from Victoria's bustling city streets were also visible towards the border of the park. My heart swelled with happiness at the beauty of it all. I loved my home, I loved my life. Even with my missing memories and the scars that lightly wrapped around my right arm and side, and the one that marked my throat, I truly felt lucky: like I had it all.

I quickly glanced down to see that Sebastian had now completely disappeared from sight, presumably searching through his bag at the base of the tree. A sudden gust of wind rocked the tree, making me grab onto the rough bark around me. I suddenly felt nervous to be up so high in this old oak, all alone. I shivered, chilled by the steadily increasing breeze despite the sun's warm rays. Another blast of wind made my hair fly out all around me, tangling it in my face as the tree swayed once more.

"Grayssssssssssssse."

The whispered voice in my ear made my heart nearly stop. Icy fear overwhelmed me as I struggled to look around.

The tree continued to sway as the wind incessantly gusted through the branches, howling all around me in a sudden rage. Clouds were swept across the sun, the day suddenly becoming colder and darker. I thought I heard Sebastian cry out below me but his words were whipped away by the howling wind. I clutched onto the tree, my heart beating wildly as the old oak lurched back and forth.

"Grayssssssssssssse." Clear as day, the voice hissed in my ear, riding the violent waves of wind again.

"What do you want?" I cried out in fear, my words torn away from my lips as soon as they were spoken.

The wind seemed to pause, dying down briefly as if considering its response.

"YOU!" The voice roared in my ears along with the wind as a monstrous blast slammed into me, knocking the air from my lungs and tossing me backwards out of the tree.

My terrified scream pierced the air as I started to fall, my hands grasping wildly around me for something, anything, to hold onto. Branches cracked and snapped as my body bounced off them but I continued to fall downwards. An image of Sebastian flashed through my mind and I thought sadly, I don't want to die. Then… CRACK! My head connected with something hard. A bough? The ground? It didn't matter, it was over. Peaceful blackness swept through me.

Chapter Three – A Gift

"**G**RACE?" SEBASTIAN'S VOICE PUSHED THROUGH THE DARKNESS around me. He sounded so strange, so far away. "Grace, please. Open your eyes." Why did he sound so afraid? So desperate? "Oh God, Grace. I'm sorry. I'll go for help."

I hadn't realized his arms were around me until he started to move away, his steady warmth receding. I swam through the darkness desperately, chasing the sound of his voice, terrified that he was abandoning me, that I'd be lost in this blackness forever. My eyes flew open.

"No," I gasped.

Sebastian was instantly back by my side, his beautiful eyes full of fear, his expression sad and worried.

"Grace," he whispered, relief flooding through his eyes. "Are you alright? Try not to move."

I winced, a sharp pain throbbing just above my left ear. I reached up and gingerly felt my skull, my fingers carefully probing through my hair. A large, painful goose egg was already forming just behind my ear but at least there was no blood. I groaned, struggling to sit up. Sebastian realized my intention and slid his arm beneath my shoulders and helped me to sit, his eyes never leaving my face.

"I'm ok, really," I tried to reassure him, wincing again as I spoke.

"Grace, you just fell out of the top of a tree and hit nearly every branch on the way down. You're not ok, you need to see a doctor," Sebastian responded. "You have no idea how much you just scared me. If I hadn't caught you…"

"You caught me?" I looked up at him, his eyes were steady and intense on mine, a shadow of fear still lurking within them.

"Yes." He glanced up quickly at the branches directly above us, his face pale and serious as he squeezed his eyes tightly shut. "The memory of you falling is going to haunt me for the rest of my life. I don't think I've ever been so afraid," he whispered.

I reached out and gently stroked his face. "It's ok. I'm ok, a little bruised and banged up, and I might have given myself a concussion but nothing's broken, I think."

Sebastian opened his eyes, studying me seriously for several long seconds.

"That wind came out of nowhere. I never would have left you if I—"

I let my fingers slide over to rest lightly on his lips, silencing him. "I know."

He reached up to take my hand, gently kissing my fingertips before entwining his fingers with mine. The wind began to rise again beneath the trees, stirring my hair and sending shivers down my spine. A single leaf became caught in the breeze, twisting and tumbling in the wind, down, down, down. I shuddered.

"Sebastian... it wasn't just the wind that made me fall," I announced quietly. He frowned back at me, obviously confused by my hushed and serious tone. "Something strange happened. The wind... it wasn't normal; it felt supernatural. I know this is going to sound crazy but right before I fell, I swear the wind was whispering my name. And when I did fall, well, it felt like I was pushed out of the tree. I'm scared, Sebastian," I confessed. Sebastian's eyes were wide. He looked shocked.

"Don't be scared," he murmured as he carefully took me in his arms. "Grace, you've been through so much lately. I don't think you've given yourself time to process it all. Even if your conscious mind can't remember the trauma we went through in Greece, your subconscious obviously does—with the nightmares, and now hearing voices... Grace, I really think you should talk to someone about this."

I pulled back from him, confused. "I am. I'm talking to you."

"I mean a professional, Grace."

"You don't believe me," I whispered, the sudden hurt choking my throat. "You think I'm crazy."

Sebastian slowly smiled back at me. "That would certainly be the pot calling the kettle black."

I tried to smile at him but I couldn't. He sighed.

"Grace, post-traumatic stress is a common disorder with some very real and serious symptoms. I don't think you're crazy but I am worried about you and I think it would be a good idea for you to meet with a counselor or someone, even if it's just a one time thing.

"I know just how confusing and terrifying this is for you. My nightmares have been worse lately too," he reluctantly confessed. He hesitated and then slowly continued. "In my dreams, I do these horrible things: I hurt people, Grace, I beat them, I torture them, I enjoy it. I'm myself but I'm not myself. I'm evil. And then I wake and I'm so confused. Sometimes, it's like I can't remember who I am or what's real."

I stared at him in mute shock, so glad that he was finally talking to me about his dreams but so scared by what he was saying.

He shrugged. "Maybe we both need to talk to someone," he admitted. "But first, we need to get you checked out by a doctor."

His voice was surprisingly firm, Sebastian wasn't typically this bossy with me. I knew he must really be worried. I slowly nodded my agreement, then immediately regretted the action. My head swam with pain, the large goose egg on my skull throbbing mercilessly. I squeezed my eyes tightly shut.

"Ouch," I whispered.

"Maybe I should call an ambulance…"

"No, you can drive me. Just help me up, please?"

Sebastian helped me stand and then propped me against the base of the tree while he picked up a few objects that had been strewn across the ground.

"I was looking for your gift when you decided to try your hand at flying," he explained with a dry smile as he stuffed a thin blanket back into his bag. "I was quite lucky really; I just looked up in time. I must have better reflexes than even I knew. You sure knocked the wind out of me though."

"Sorry about that."

"And you ruined our picnic," he continued, his eyes searching the ground as he spoke. His expression suddenly brightened as he quickly picked up a small object from the dirt and dropped it into his pocket. He tried to appear casual but my curiosity had been piqued.

"What was that?" I asked. I tried to hide a shiver as the wind stirred the leaves around us. The sun was still hidden behind a cloud and the day was turning cold and chilled as the afternoon wore on.

"What?"

"The thing you just picked up off the ground."

"It's nothing. We can worry about that later. We should go get you checked out, Grace. You're looking pretty pale still."

"I'm always pale," I dismissed.

"And always pretty," he added with a grin. I knew he was trying to distract me.

"What's in your pocket?"

Sebastian's eyes sparkled back at me mysteriously, his lips remained firmly pressed together.

"Don't tell me it's 'nothing'. It's the reason why we're here," I guessed.

Sebastian cocked his head to one side. "I suppose it is, or it was… This wasn't how I pictured this moment," he muttered, reluctantly pulling the object from the pocket of his jeans. "This is what I came back down to get. I know it's not your birthday until next week but I had this made for you. Since it was ready today and I wanted to… well, I just couldn't wait to give it to you." He shifted, not quite meeting my eye for some reason. I felt like he might be holding something back.

Another gust of wind made me shiver. The air all around me seemed to buzz with electric anticipation so clearly I could almost hear a ringing in my ears; but perhaps it was from the fall. My hair was standing on end. I found myself barely breathing as I waited.

Sebastian hesitated, his eyes scanning over me and his earlier concern returning.

"Promise me I can take you straight to the hospital after this. No more delays?"

"Ok," I quietly agreed. My whole body was starting to throb and ache, and going to the hospital suddenly seemed like a good idea. But I had to know what he was hiding first. The wind was steadily rising, whipping at my clothes and causing my hair to fly wildly all around me. It didn't scare me anymore, not here on the ground with Sebastian by my side. I reached out my hand expectantly, a slight tremor to my fingers.

Sebastian dropped a small, coin-like object into my palm. The wind abruptly died, an eerie silence weighed down upon us as the world held its breath.

I gasped as I realized what I was looking at, what I was holding. My eyes filled with tears as I was overwhelmed by so many emotions, my pain instantly forgotten.

It was a small, silver pendant, circular and light. It formed a complex Celtic knot, the thin silver band twisting in and around itself, looping and intertwining to form a beautiful, circular silver knot. The design framed and expanded around the small amber piece embedded in its center. The tiny, familiar, amber heart glowed and sparkled with its own magical light, pulsating warmly in my palm in perfect rhythm with the faint buzzing in my ears and the fading, throbbing pain in my head. I couldn't stop staring at it, in wonder and in awe.

"It's a Dara Knot," Sebastian explained, he sounded almost nervous. He carefully picked the pendant up from my palm and threaded a thin, leather chord through it. "*Doire* or *Dara* means "oak tree" in Gaelic. The knot is a symbol for power, wisdom and inner strength. It symbolizes the oak tree, the complex and beautiful balance of power, the way the roots mirror the strong branches, lurking just below the surface in an invisible but vital source of strength. And obviously the oak tree has special meaning for us…"

I didn't speak. I could barely breathe as he leaned forward and brushed my hair aside so that he could slip the pendant around my neck. It felt unnaturally warm against my skin and unspeakably familiar. He opened his mouth as if to say something else but when his eyes met mine, he stopped.

"When did you do this?" I finally managed to whisper, blinking back my stunned tears. "After you gave me the crushed ring in the hospital, I thought I had lost it. I never thought I'd see this piece of amber again."

"You did lose it." Sebastian gave me a crooked smile. "It somehow ended up with David's things. One of the nurses must have found it and put it back in our hospital room before we left. But then I thought, since your birthday was only a month or so away, that maybe I would have the amber stone refitted into something you could wear. Don and Shauna said there was a necklace you used to always wear, and so I thought you might like another pendant… Was I wrong?" He stared at me intently, his brows pulled down.

"No, it's beautiful." I reached up to gently stroked the pendant, my fingers brushing against the small, warm heart at its center. My own heart swelled with love for this wonderful, thoughtful, amazing man. "It's perfect. Ever since we got back from Greece, I've felt like there was something missing—other than our memories. But this makes me feel complete somehow. I guess I missed that necklace that I lost," I added with a laugh, feeling silly. Sebastian beamed back at me.

"Happy birthday."

"Thank you. I really do love it. It's the perfect gift, from the perfect boyfriend."

"Perfect fiancé," Sebastian corrected happily. "Now, you owe me a visit to the hospital. Can you walk?"

"Will you carry me if I can't?" I teased.

"I'd love to."

And before I could object, Sebastian swept my feet out from underneath me and scooped me up into his arms. I giggled, breathless but was interrupted by his sudden, urgent and passionate kiss. His lips pressed against mine hard, his kiss hungry and desperate, ending just as suddenly as it began. He pulled back just enough so that he could look into my eyes. His dark eyes smoldered beneath his long, black lashes.

"Never scare me like that again. I'd sooner die than see any harm come to you." The intensity with which he spoke scared me, I'd never seen him like this before—at least not that I could remember.

I silently nodded my agreement. His gaze softened, his mouth relaxed. "Good. I love you, Grace."

"I love you too. Thank you for catching me. And thank you for the necklace."

"Thank you for loving me," he replied simply, his tone lighter as he began to walk. "Now let's go get your head checked out."

I reluctantly allowed Sebastian to take me to the hospital. I really was feeling much better; my head had hardly hurt at all since he'd given me the necklace. It was already a great good luck charm. Of course it ended up being Dr. Mackey who examined me (the doctor who my mother had her eyes on) and diagnosed me with a mild concussion. He was amazed by my lack of injuries, especially after Sebastian told him how far I had fallen. I was sure my mother would hear the story of my tree-climbing adventures from him, despite supposed doctor-patient confidentiality. I could already guess what she would think of the news that I had been climbing trees in the park. That alone was enough to make my head ache.

DAVID WAS OUT for the rest of the day, supposedly looking for a job. I had the definite sense that he had no interest in finding work or making any change to his current living situation, despite what he sometimes claimed. I could tell it bothered him to be depending on the generosity of others, but at the same time, he seemed content enough to continue on for now.

Sebastian insisted I go to my room early and get some rest after dinner. The sun had barely set when he ushered me into my bedroom and tucked me into bed himself. As he leaned down to place a kiss on my forehead, I turned my face up, my lips meeting his in a long and lingering kiss that left me yearning for more. I could tell from the brightness in his eyes that he was feeling the same way.

"Stay with me?" I asked softly, my fingers trailing slowly down his arm. I thought I saw him shiver. He slowly and reluctantly shook his head.

"Grace… you should rest. Besides, I think it would make the Jensons and David uncomfortable if I were to stay in your room."

"Stay," I repeated. My fingers slid down to his hand and began slowly tracing a spiral into his palm. "Just for a little while."

He hesitated, his conviction wavering. "I want to, Grace, but…"

"Then stay."

I boldly pulled him down on top of me, my fingers already twisting into his black, mussed hair.

He gave in with a soft moan, his lips crushing against mine roughly. My heart pounded as he kissed me, his tongue slipping into my mouth and teasing against mine, our lips moving together with an increasing need. His body pressed against me, his hands touched my face, stroked my hair, slid down my body in a gentle caress that made my back arch as I gasped in pleasure. I could feel him everywhere; I could taste his lips and smell his skin, I could feel his body down the length of mine but it still wasn't enough. I wanted more.

But, as always, Sebastian pulled back, he slowed down, he slid over to my side, trailing sweet kisses down my neck to my shoulder. I stifled a moan.

"I can't stay," he whispered against my skin. His warm breath combined with the soft movement of his lips sent fresh shivers all over my body.

"Yes, you can," I argued.

"I can't trust myself with you," he confessed, his voice rough, his eyes hungry. "Alone, in your room, in your bed, the way you look right now… I want you so badly."

I swallowed hard as his eyes burned into mine. It wasn't often he spoke so directly. It was both intimidating and exciting.

"So what's the problem?" I couldn't believe how forward I was being but we were engaged, after all. I was almost nineteen, we'd been together for nearly a year and we'd been through so much. I knew exactly what I wanted—what we both wanted—and I could no longer understand why we should let anything stand in our way.

My heart was in my throat, my body hot and flushed all over as I waited for him to answer. The fire in his eyes didn't cool for a moment.

"December 9th will be exactly a year since we first kissed," he stated unexpectedly. His eyes were smoldering with heat and passion, at odds with his choice of words.

I blinked in confusion.

"Ok…"

"Let's make it our anniversary."

"Isn't it already?" I asked, not understanding.

"Our wedding anniversary."

My breath caught in my throat. The glowing embers in his eyes flared with joy, a beautiful smile slowly spreading across his handsome face. He laughed at my speechlessness.

"Are you busy that day? We don't have to, if you already have plans."

"No, but…" He watched me uncertainly as I paused. "But that's over two months away."

Sebastian tossed back his head and laughed.

"Don't laugh at me," I scolded but I was smiling too. My heart felt light and joyful at the prospect of becoming Sebastian's wife soon, even if it was still weeks away. "Why don't we just get married now? Tonight, or tomorrow, or even next weekend? I feel like I'm always waiting, and the longer I wait, the further away it seems to get."

Sebastian smiled. "I know. I feel like that sometimes too but December 9th really isn't that far away. And besides, your mother tells me your dress won't be ready until the end of November anyway."

"When did you speak to my mother?" I asked warily.

Sebastian smirked. "Recently. Has she shared with you her plans for our wedding?"

"Yes, she did today. I actually met the wedding planner."

"Oh, did you now? And what did you think? Are we indulging her or are we going to rebel and elope?" Sebastian asked, a mischievous sparkle to his eye.

"I was actually leaning towards indulgence," I confessed. Sebastian's eyebrows lifted in surprise. I rushed to explain myself. "I'm going to tone it down—what she's planning is currently far too extravagant—but… some of her ideas are actually quite good. And I think planning the wedding might be something we can bond over and that alone is worth it to me. But that's only if it's what you want…?"

"I just want to marry you."

"You're sure?"

"I've had some second thoughts, but I think you're pretty much the best I can get."

I giggled and tried to smack him. "I'm serious, Sebastian."

"So am I. I love you. I want you. Forever. Nothing else—besides your happiness—matters to me."

His words reached out and touched me deep inside, resonating in my heart. I was moved.

He smiled and stood up, leaving me full of excitement and longing, in no condition to fall asleep any time soon.

"Only 61 days," he whispered, and I could hear the excitement in his voice.

"So far away," I groaned.

He chuckled softly. "Good night, Grace. I love you."

"I love you too," I whispered back as he closed the door.

It wasn't as difficult to fall asleep as I had predicted. It had been a long day: wedding plans with my mother, going to the park with Sebastian, the fall, the necklace, the hospital visit with Dr. Mackey. I was exhausted. My head started to spin and my eyelids drooped. The shadows around me darkened and shifted. It might have been my imagination, but I thought I heard someone whisper my name just as I was falling asleep, their stale breath tickling my ear as my mind sank into black unconsciousness.

I awoke in the morning feeling tired and disturbed, blinking sleepily as I gazed around my room. I was certain I'd had another bad dream even though I couldn't remember specifically what it was about. A shadow of unease lurked around my mind. I squeezed my dry eyes shut, straining to remember. Something to do with being lost and someone or something was chasing me but it had been so dark and confusing… No matter how I struggled, the memory of the dream rapidly faded away. I was left feeling ill at ease, the threat and danger from my nightmare seeping over into my waking mind.

Something definitely didn't feel right. I opened my eyes, sensing that something around me was out of place. Sitting up slowly, I scanned my room, searching for the source of my unease. And that's when I saw it.

There was a blanket draped across the end of my bed that hadn't been there when I went to sleep; in fact, it hadn't even been in my room. My skin prickled all over as the feel of invisible eyes on me returned. I noticed my window was closed, and I was certain when I fell asleep last night I had left it open. And the chair at my writing desk was no longer neatly tucked in. It had been pulled out at an angle, as if someone had sat there, watching me while I slept. I shivered, my eyes growing wider, my breathing becoming shallow.

Ever so faintly, the curtains at my window stirred. My breath caught in my throat.

"Who's there?" I whispered, feeling ridiculous. My voice came out breathy and weak. I swallowed and reached for my necklace, squeezing the circular pendant tightly in my fist and immediately drawing strength and reassurance from it. My curtains stirred again, brushed gently by some unseen force. I sat up straighter, refusing to be afraid anymore.

"Who are you? What do you want from me?" I demanded, my voice growing stronger with each word that I spoke. The curtains resettled and stilled, an eerie silence hung in the air. The sense that I was not alone was still strong and overpowering.

"I want you to leave me alone. Now!"

My bedroom door suddenly flew open. My heart leaped into my throat. I flinched back in fear and then surprise as David burst into my room.

"Grace? Are you alright?" David's eyes searched my room, confusion written across his handsome face. His brows pulled down into a frown. "I heard you talking to someone; you sounded afraid."

"What were you doing outside of my room?" I demanded softly, leaving the question behind his words unanswered.

David stared back at me, his face suddenly expressionless, his eyes darkening at my tone. "I was on my way to the bathroom when I heard you yell. I thought I should check on you. Who were you talking to?"

His dark brown hair was rumpled on one side from sleep and his t-shirt and pajama bottoms looked wrinkled. It was the most unkempt I'd ever seen him and I had to admit, there was something attractive about his rumpled appearance. There was a sharpness to his eyes though that didn't appear sleepy at all, a shrewd intelligence that was making me feel increasingly uneasy. I gave my head a little shake. What was wrong with me? David was just worried about me, that was all.

"I was just singing to myself. I'm sorry, it probably sounded awful." A rosy blush warmed my cheeks, giving away my lie.

He took a step closer, his eyes full of concern. My heart started beating strangely. He was making me feel nervous, I realized but my reaction to him made no sense. I shifted uneasily.

"Grace… I'm worried about you. You've been acting strangely lately. I know you think of me as Sebastian's friend but please don't doubt that I'm your friend too." He sank down onto the bed beside me, sitting so close I could easily reach out and touch him. My heart was pounding; I wanted to run. "There's a connection between us," he murmured, his eyes steady on mine. "I like you, Grace, and not just because you're Sebastian's girlfriend. I respect you. I feel like we… understand each other."

"How do you mean?" My voice sounded unfamiliar.

"We both want what's best for Sebastian. We both know him well. And we're both seeking answers to questions that Sebastian wants to ignore."

A weighted silence hung in the air. My heart pounded deafeningly in my ears.

"You want to know what happened in Greece?"

"I won't accept that those memories are gone forever, I can't anymore," David responded. "Sebastian told me you've been researching the explosion, that you'd discovered some strange similarities between the survivors. I've been looking into it too. Did you know that on the day of the explosion, a nearby hostel in Thessaloniki mysteriously burnt to the ground? They found unidentified remains inside: a girl, estimated to be in her late teens. It was just a few hours before the explosion at the Necromanteion."

"Strange," I agreed softly, not certain what to say. I felt like I was betraying Sebastian somehow by having this discussion with David.

"Sebastian said you didn't want to look into the past. That you had both agreed it was better left alone."

David's sharp eyes narrowed slightly, as if I were accusing him of something. He answered slowly and deliberately.

"I didn't want to examine the past too closely. I thought there must be something that we were all meant to forget. But then when your mother mentioned that I had an uncle, it made me start to wonder about my family, about my friends, about what my life was like before."

It sounded reasonable enough.

"I know Sebastian doesn't want to talk about it but that's why I'm here," he continued in his low voice. He leant forward. "If you need someone to talk to, I'm here. We both have questions, we both want the same thing. Maybe we can help each other rediscover what we've lost."

He spoke softly, intimately. I automatically leant back, brushing my hair back over my shoulder and running my fingers through it nervously. David's soft, quick inhale made my eyes snap back to his face. His eyes were bright, burning with a dark fire as he stared at the necklace hanging around my neck.

"What is that?" His eyes didn't stray from my pendant as he spoke. He wasn't even blinking. My body tensed under his gaze. I suddenly became more alert, my heartbeat calming, my mind and thoughts focusing. I clenched the pendant firmly in my hand, blocking it from his view. Annoyance flickered across his face.

"It's a gift from Sebastian," I told him firmly, my tone inviting no further questions.

"Pass it to me; I'd like to take a closer look," David commanded.

"No."

His lips compressed together, his eyes narrowed. He wasn't nearly so handsome when he was annoyed.

I was suddenly overwhelmed by déjà vu. I blinked, trying to clear my cloudy thoughts but instead, an image appeared behind my eyelids, a memory from the past that mirrored this moment in time. As clear as a summer sky, I could remember Walter reaching out his hand, his face twisted in anger and irritation as I had defied him somehow. I remembered how tightly I had clutched at my necklace, the perfect teardrop shape fitting precisely into the center of my closed fist. He had been so angry that I wouldn't let him see my necklace, the memory made me shudder. I could even remember how the sky outside had seemed to darken with his increasing rage...

I blinked. The memory cut off, it was severed from continuing but I still remembered it even if I couldn't entirely understand. Walter, my mother's butler and companion was more than he had seemed, he had been dangerous somehow; of that I was now absolutely sure. But why had he wanted my necklace and why had it felt so vital to keep it from him? It made no sense.

"Grace?" David watched me uncertainly. I wasn't sure how long I'd been silent for. I thought I'd only paused for a second but it was difficult to hide my disorientation and confusion.

"Thank you for checking on me but I'm fine. I'll keep in mind that you're here to talk to if I need to. It is appreciated but now I'd like you to leave," I told him plainly.

David straightened, his face becoming expressionless once more, his eyes cold.

"I need to get dressed," I added, hoping to take some of the sting from my words. I hadn't meant to offend him, I wasn't entirely sure why I was suddenly feeling so antagonistic towards him.

"Of course," he answered politely, standing as he spoke. He hesitated beside my bed, his eyes briefly glancing back to my necklace still hidden in my hand. "I'm here for you, Grace, if you need me."

"Thank you," I murmured as he turned and walked back out my bedroom door.

I let out my breath after he disappeared, only now aware that I had been holding it. My eyes shifted nervously to the chair at the foot of my bed and the gently swaying curtains at my window. My eyes widened as I realized the window was now wide open, allowing the morning breeze to find its way into my room. Had I been dreaming still when I thought it had been closed? Had I imagined the curtains moving on their own? The sense that I was being watched began to slowly return. I wondered if I was losing my mind? I grabbed my clothes and then fled from my room, wondering if I'd be able to sleep there tonight.

I didn't tell Sebastian about my strange morning: the window, my conversation with David, the brief flash of memory I'd experienced. I didn't want to hear more about his post-traumatic stress theories and I also didn't want to worry him. I really was starting to feel like I was going crazy.

I was called in to the art gallery that day and was grateful for the distraction of work to keep my mind off things. Over the next few days I put in some long hours, volunteering to stay late and working myself to the point of near exhaustion. It was never a problem falling asleep at night. But every morning I awoke with the same, strange sense that I'd suffered through another night of tormenting, violent nightmares even though I would forget all the details as soon as my eyes opened. And there was always that haunting sensation of someone silently watching me. If I listened too hard to the silence, I would start to hear strange whispered words. If I looked too long into the shadows, I would start to think I could see a figure hiding at the edge of the darkness. And so I didn't.

I kept myself so busy with work that it was nearly a week later when I finally remembered to tell my mother that Sebastian and I had set a date for our wedding. Naïvely, I had thought she would be pleased. You would think that after nineteen years, I would know better.

"December 9th? But that's a Friday! And Elisa Mayher is marrying the Thornton boy the weekend before that. We'll want some time between the two events so that her wedding doesn't overshadow ours. It'll have to be Saturday the 17th then. It's only a week before Christmas but—"

"No, Mother," I interrupted in a gentle but firm voice. "December the 9th is the only possible date. It's an important day for Sebastian and me; I can't compromise on this."

My mother's shrewd hazel eyes narrowed at me.

"You're not being very flexible, Grace," she snipped.

"No, I'm not. Not about this."

"Fine. This is going to be a nightmare to plan for a Friday though!

How selfish of you to not consult with me before discussing dates with Sebastian. Susanna and I have been arranging all the plans around the idea of a spring wedding. Now we'll have to entirely change the concept of the wedding. I thought you were planning on a long engagement?" she accused.

"We were but then last week, Sebastian decided to surprise me with a date he had in mind. The only date," I repeated, my voice still firm. My mother's eyes narrowed.

"Last week?" she repeated. "And you're only telling me now?" Her voice became more shrill as she spoke. I winced, this was going to be bad.

I left my mother's house several hours later, feeling truly exhausted. She had been more than a little displeased about my making wedding plans without consulting her and Susanna first. The afternoon had been full of criticisms, glares and sour comments, all directed at me. And that was not to mention all the new details she was now throwing at me: demanding a guest list, compiling a short-list of venues available for the ceremony and reception on December 9th, trying to get me to decide upon a photographer and a caterer, and a decorator, and the invitation details… it felt like she was punishing me.

It was probably because of my exhaustion that I didn't look too closely at the unfamiliar car parked in the driveway, assuming that the Jensons had a friend over for dinner. I was preoccupied by my own tired thoughts as I walked up to the Jensons' front door, playing absentmindedly with my necklace as I approached the front step. I didn't notice the tall, dark shadow leaning against the doorframe until it suddenly moved. My heart leaped into my throat as he spoke in a voice that came straight from my past.

"Hi, Grace."

My eyes snapped up to his forgotten, yet familiar, face and as our gazes locked, a memory flashed through my mind, clear and bright, and as hot as the sun. In my mind's eye, he knelt before me, his face pale, unshed tears in his eyes. He was terrified because I knew the truth and he wasn't sure what I was going to do with it. I knew that he and his friends were the ones who had beaten Sebastian nearly to death. And even though he had blamed Walter for pushing them to go too far, it was still Clarke who I felt the most rage towards. It was still Clarke who I had sworn I could never forgive. That I would never forget what he had done.

I stumbled on the Jensons' bottom step, returning to the present as I only just caught my balance, nearly falling flat on my face. My mind was swirling with confusion. I had just remembered how Clarke and his friends had put Sebastian in the hospital last winter. And I had also just remembered Walter's involvement in the violent attack—but why? It made no sense. My ex-boyfriend Clarke had been jealous of Sebastian, that much I remembered, but why had Walter wanted the boys to hurt Sebastian? And why had Walter, Clarke and the other boys gotten away with it? Had my mother had something to do with it too? How could I ever have forgotten? And hadn't I dated Clarke again after that? I was dizzy with confusion. I squeezed my necklace tightly with one hand and grasped for the iron railing with the other. My head was throbbing with a piercing pain, as if the memories were trying to tear their way up from my subconscious.

"Grace, are you ok?" Clarke asked, alarmed. He hurried down the stairs to help steady me. As he touched my arm and our eyes met again, the missing memories came flying back to me in a flash of searing pain.

Chapter Four – Unexpected Guests

I STARED UP AT CLARKE, TRYING TO focus as my mind was flooded with strange and convoluted memories. My head pounded in agony as if the memories were being physically hammered back into my brain, one by one.

I could remember the last time I saw him. It was the day Sebastian and I had left for our trip across Canada, but I hadn't started the day with Sebastian. The day had begun with Clarke, I recalled. We were dating again even though it was not long after Sebastian's attack, and he had proposed to me at my mother's house with some ridiculous promise ring. He had said something… I still couldn't remember quite what it was but Clarke had said something that jolted my memory. So the explosion in Greece wasn't the first time I'd suffered memory loss. I could remember now that I had forgotten before, I had forgotten last spring. Only then, it wasn't caused by an injury or an accident, it was because of Sebastian. Sebastian had made me forget him somehow—I was certain of it. He had somehow made me forget our whole relationship even though it shouldn't have been possible. He had made me forget everything we'd been through, everything I felt for him. And so I had gotten back together with Clarke and I had almost moved to Vancouver with him until I suddenly remembered Sebastian again. But how? And why? How was it possible? What did it mean?

I strained with all my might to remember, ignoring Clarke who still clung onto my arm asking me something in an urgent, worried voice. I was so close, so close to remembering something important—something vital. I was sure of it.

I could remember confronting Sebastian that day, the day I had remembered him. I could remember my anger, my hurt, my outrage. And, oh God, I remembered how much I'd missed him. But then… my mind was blank. That was it. The memories ended as abruptly as they'd began. I knew there was more. I was certain that something had happened after that. Something important—something pinnacle to my life—but what? All I had were vague impressions and mundane still-frame flashes of memories from the next few months: camping across Canada, backpacking across Europe and then waking up in the hospital in Greece. But what had happened? How had Sebastian once made me forget? And had he done it again? Was my memory loss really just from the explosion?

"Grace!" Clarke's voice demanded an answer. I reluctantly opened my eyes.

"Yes?" I calmly replied. Even in the low, evening light I could make out the concern written across his face. His eyes were wide, his brows pulled down.

"Are you alright?"

"I'm fine," I dismissed, gently pulling my arm from his grasp. He reluctantly let go. I took a moment to quickly smooth my hair, to try to sort through the mass of confusing memories that had just struck me. "What are you doing here?"

Clarke looked down at the ground uncomfortably. He'd lost some of the confident swagger that I remembered. This hesitant, uncertain boy was a lot more difficult to be angry with than the egotistical jerk who had nearly beaten my boyfriend to death because of his stupid, childish jealousy.

"I had heard you were back in town and, well, I wanted to come and see you. I knocked but no one answered," he explained with a shrug. He looked at me, his golden eyes slowly taking me in with an almost shy smile. "You look great, Gracie. I like your hair like that."

"Um, thanks." I tried not to frown as I stared back at him. I hated to think it but he really was as handsome as ever. He'd grown a little taller and filled out a bit more since I'd last seen him. His shoulders had broadened and his physique was even more muscular. His hair was slightly longer and messier too, it suited him. Despite his good looks, I remained impervious to his charm. The memories of the wrongs he had done felt fresh. I continued impatiently. "Seriously, Clarke, what are you doing here? I haven't spoken to you since June and I've been back for over a month now. If I'd wanted to talk to you, I would have called."

"I know. I heard about the explosion you were in and how badly you were burned, and your memory loss. I wasn't even sure if you would remember me. I was so worried about you, Grace." He reached out a hand towards me but I took a quick step back.

"I remember everything about you." The way I said it made him pause. He studied me with wary eyes. I didn't want to play these games with him. I wanted to know why he was there and then I wanted to be done with him. I cut to the chase. "Have you heard that Sebastian and I are engaged?"

Annoyance flickered across his face. His strong jaw clenched, his brows pulled down slightly.

"Yes. Have you heard that I'm engaged?" he shot back.

"No, I haven't." I was honestly surprised. My mother must have known and there must have been a reason why she chose to keep it from me. "To who?" I asked curiously.

"You really haven't heard?" Clarke sounded surprised himself, and almost a little hurt. I shook my head and he sighed. For some reason, he looked embarrassed. "Tanya," he confessed.

An image of the tall, gorgeous, blue-eyed blonde flashed through my mind. She had always had her eye on Clarke and she'd always been cold and snobbish towards me, like most of the girls in Clarke's group. I wasn't surprised to hear they'd ended up together.

"I hadn't heard you were dating. Congratulations."

"We haven't been dating for long," Clarke confessed, looking down at the ground guiltily again. I couldn't understand what was going on. I glanced up at the front door, wondering how long this was going to take and if I should invite Clarke inside? What would Sebastian think if he came home to that, I wondered? Would the sight of Clarke jog some of his memories also? Maybe it wasn't such a terrible idea.

"Tanya's pregnant," Clarke blurted out. My jaw dropped. He continued on in a rush. "The day you walked out on me, I was heartbroken, Grace. Things were going so well between us—I still don't understand what happened? I thought you'd be so excited about the ring I gave you and you just ran out of the house, straight back to him. And then you both disappeared, ran off together." I could hear the hurt in his voice but I guessed that it was more injured pride than anything. I refused to feel sorry for him after all that he'd done. "I kept waiting for a call. I had no idea where you'd gone. Then your mother finally heard something: that you'd been to see your father and that Sebastian had asked him permission to marry you." He paused to take a deep breath, shooting me an accusatory look. "Tanya kept calling me. I didn't want to date her, she was never my type: more interested in my family's name and money than me. And I was hoping once you came back, you'd come back to me too." He was looking at the ground again. I tried my best to keep my expression neutral anyway, just in case he were to glance up. "It was just a casual thing between us. This was never supposed to happen. She told me she was on the pill!"

I fought the urge to roll my eyes. Of course he would see this as her fault.

"How far along is she?"

"Eight weeks," Clarke mumbled bitterly. He was definitely pouting now. "She wants to keep it, she insists. I had to tell my parents. I thought my dad was going to kill me. After he calmed down, he phoned her father and they arranged everything; we're getting married in two days. They don't want anyone to know she's already pregnant but I'm sure there will be rumors, the dates aren't going to line up once the baby's born. I haven't told anyone… I don't know why I told you."

He looked completely forlorn. His eyes begged me for sympathy. I wasn't sure if I had it in me.

"Why are you here?" I repeated, slightly more softly this time.

"I thought…" He paused, taking a deep breath and then starting again. "This is it, Grace. I'm getting married on Sunday, you're engaged… this is our last chance to be together. We could run away…"

He noticed my expression and his voice trailed off. He at least had the decency to look ashamed. It took me several seconds to reign in my anger, to calm myself and choose the right words. I kept my voice level, using every last ounce of patience I had.

"This isn't our last chance, this is our last goodbye," I told him firmly. "There is no way you could have possibly convinced yourself that I was just waiting around to run away with you. What the hell, Clarke? You're going to be a father and the first thing you do is try to find a way to run out on the mother of your child?"

"I knew it was a long shot," he admitted, squirming uncomfortably beneath my heated glare. "I was just hoping, that maybe… Shit. I'm scared, Grace. I don't know what the hell I've gotten myself into. I don't know what I'm thinking. My life is ruined."

He looked so genuinely miserable and afraid that I felt the beginnings of sympathy stir in my chest.

"Running away isn't the answer."

He nodded his agreement, looking ashamed. "I just… I didn't know who to go to, Grace. No one knows she's pregnant, I didn't even mean to tell you. I just blurted it out without thinking; but really, I could use a friend," he finished lamely. "It might be hard to believe, since I was so popular in high school but… I don't have that many good friends. Not really."

"Clarke," I sighed, suddenly feeling exhausted. My head was throbbing still and my legs were aching from standing around on the front walkway. Now that I could remember Clarke's involvement in the attack against Sebastian last year, I knew I should hate him but for some reason, I still couldn't. I wasn't sure why, but I felt like Sebastian had forgiven Clarke—in fact, I was sure of it. I could vaguely remember Sebastian surprising me by not being angry when he'd discovered Clarke was to blame. Sebastian had been upset, I recalled. He'd almost felt like he deserved it somehow, like he deserved to be punished for something he'd done to me or something he'd done… a long time ago… What was it? What had happened? Why couldn't I remember? The memory floated just out of reach. I was sure it was there, I could almost remember, almost complete my thoughts but each time I tried, I drew a blank. I wanted to remember so badly; I wanted Sebastian to remember too. I was tired of all these questions with no answers. But the harder I tried, the more my head hurt and throbbed with pain.

"Come inside," I muttered as I brushed past Clarke and began unlocking the front door to the Jensons' house. The Jensons often worked late but I was surprised Sebastian and David weren't home yet.

"Thanks, Grace." I could clearly hear the relief in Clarke's voice and it made me feel a little better. I wasn't sure exactly what I was doing but I was hoping it was the right thing. Clarke needed someone to talk to, and I needed my memories back—and answers. Perhaps we could help each other.

Since neither of us had eaten dinner I made coffee and sandwiches and we sat down in the living room in front of the unlit fireplace. Clarke did most of the talking. He told me how he wasn't ready to be a father, how nervous he was and afraid, how he didn't want the responsibility and he didn't even really like kids. He told me how he didn't love Tanya, how he barely even liked her. He complained about the overwhelming amount of pressure from his parents to "do the right thing" and to uphold their family's reputation. He whined that it was all Tanya's fault and it wasn't fair that everyone was blaming him. He pouted about the fact that he was going to have to reject the rugby scholarship he'd been offered to University of British Columbia since his father wanted him to start working now that he was going to have a wife and child to support. Of course, "work" meant running one his father's many businesses for him.

"My life is really messed up, Grace," Clarke sulked, glancing at me, his hazel eyes wide and appealing for my sympathy. I frowned back.

"Do you want to hear what I think?"

He paused to consider. Clarke had never really liked to hear what I thought unless it was in agreement with him. I continued on without waiting for his permission, deciding that whether he liked it or not, this was something he needed to hear.

"I think you need to grow up and be happy with all that you have. You're marrying a beautiful girl who idolizes you, from a family nearly as wealthy and prestigious as your own; what shame is there in that? Your father is *giving* you work and buying you and Tanya a beautiful home. And in less than nine months, you're going to have a child. A tiny, perfect combination of you and Tanya that your whole world is about to revolve around. Maybe it wasn't all planned, maybe this isn't what you thought you wanted for your future but maybe you were wrong? Why can't this be a good thing?"

Throughout my little rant, I had watched Clarke's expression shift from pouty to annoyed to his current look of hesitant consideration.

"You don't think my life is ruined?" he quietly asked, his brows pulled down low over his eyes.

"No. I think it might be saved," I replied honestly. "This baby is going to be the best thing that ever happened to you, I know it." And it was true. I could see hope for Clarke. I could picture him as a loving and doting father, a hard-working provider who cared for his family. I could imagine this changing him. I could picture him growing into a mature and dependable man. This idea suited him better than the spoiled rich boy, partying at university and taking advantage of his father's name and influence.

"I hadn't thought of it that way," Clarke mumbled. He looked up, his eyes brighter, his expression a little less troubled than when we'd first sat down. "Thanks, Gracie. I knew you'd be able to help." He leaned forward to squeeze my hand, his gratitude surprisingly genuine and appreciative. I found myself smiling and squeezing his hand back. And that was when Sebastian walked in on us.

Both our heads turned as the door swung open and Sebastian walked into the room, a ready and curious smile on his face. His mirth disappeared as his eyes fell upon us. As he took in Clarke's hand squeezing mine, resting lightly upon my thigh his eyes seemed to darken. He glared at Clarke for only a split-second, before his eyes widened, his face paled and he came to a stumbling halt. The breath rushed from his lips in a stifled gasp, his eyes scrunched up in pain as he swayed on his feet. And then his eyes flew open again and he stared at us with bewildered, unfocused eyes.

It had only lasted seconds, but there was no doubt in my mind that Sebastian had just remembered something. The sight of Clarke must have triggered some lost memories for him, just as it had for me.

His eyes refocused on Clarke's face. Before I could speak, I watched as Sebastian's expression shifted into that of a stranger's. His eyes were black with fury, his mouth grim, his fists clenched, his muscles rigid with anger. He took a menacing step forward and I felt a chill run down my spine.

"Get your hands off her," he warned Clarke, his voice a low growl. He didn't sound at all like himself.

Clarke slowly leant backwards, sliding his hands from mine. He watched Sebastian warily, his eyes wide.

"Sebastian—" I began but he ignored me, his coal black eyes burning into Clarke's.

"What are you doing here?" he demanded, his voice soft but chilling. "You had better not be trying to take what I want. Grace is mine," he warned, a dangerous edge to his words. I stared at him incredulously: what the hell was going on?

"I… I…" Clarke took a deep breath and sat up a little straighter, holding his jaw at an arrogant angle. "I came to visit Grace, we are friends, you know."

"No, I don't. Now I'm warning you, and I will only warn you once: try to come between us again and you won't live to regret it."

"Sebastian, what's wrong with you?" I couldn't understand his bizarre reaction to Clarke's presence. If he remembered what Clarke had once done, shouldn't he also remember forgiving him? Why was he so angry? And why was he acting so aggressive?

Sebastian ignored me.

"Now tell me why you're really here." He glared at Clarke expectantly.

"Because… I'm getting married," Clarke admitted, not quite able to keep the petulant tone from his voice.

Sebastian blinked in surprise, though his expression didn't change.

"And I wanted to invite Grace—and you—to the wedding," Clarke continued. "It's short notice, I'm getting married on Sunday, but it would mean a lot to me to have you there." Clarke addressed the last part to me only, his voice just a little too warm, his eyes lingering on me for just a second too long. Sebastian tensed again. Was he jealous?

"It's Grace's birthday on Sunday," Sebastian informed him stiffly. "We have plans."

"Oh." Clarke's expression fell. He shifted uncomfortably. I could see his nerves building as he thought about the wedding, I could see how he really did want me there. I sighed.

"We can change our plans." Sebastian finally acknowledged me with a glare but I ignored *him* this time. "I'll be there." I couldn't speak for Sebastian, but I could promise to be there at least.

Clarke smiled, looking relieved. "Thanks, Grace. It really does mean a lot."

"I know." I turned to Sebastian, my eyes silently asking him to understand. He muttered something indistinguishable, his jaw still clenched.

"Fine. It's your birthday, if you really want to go, I will be standing there beside you," Sebastian told me. He continued to glare at Clarke, as if challenging him to object.

"Thank you."

"Can we bring David?" Sebastian suddenly asked. His voice was still cold but his whole demeanor was slowly and reluctantly relaxing. He winced, rubbing lightly at his temple.

"Um… sure, I guess," Clarke agreed with a shrug. He gave me a quizzical look.

"David is a friend we met in Europe. He was in the explosion with us in Greece and he's moved to Canada. He's staying with the Jensons as well."

"Oh. Cool." Clarke stood. "Guess I'll meet him on Sunday then. I should get going." He took a step towards me as if he were about to hug me goodbye but one glance at Sebastian seemed to change his mind. "Thanks, Grace. For everything. I'll see you Sunday?"

"I'll be there," I repeated.

"Sebastian." Clarke gave him a nod as he walked past him, giving him a wider berth than necessary. Sebastian barely acknowledged him, his brows pulled down in confusion, his head bent low. He stumbled slightly and leant against the wall.

"Sebastian, are you ok?" I whispered, not wanting Clarke to hear for some reason.

Sebastian nodded. He reopened his eyes and met mine. I breathed a sigh of relief to see his eyes were a soft gray with just the slightest hint of mysterious blue in their depths. Those hard, black eyes of an angry and dangerous stranger had disappeared. Now he just looked tired.

"I'll be right back," I murmured. He nodded again, still appearing distracted as I followed Clarke out of the room and led him to the front door. Once he had left, I returned to the living room to find Sebastian still standing where I had left him, leaning heavily against the wall. I approached him cautiously.

"When you first saw Clarke… you remembered something too, didn't you?" I asked.

His eyes snapped open.

"Too?"

"Yes. When I first came home, the sight of Clarke's face and the surprise of seeing him here jogged my memory somehow, or at least a small part of it. I remembered—"

"Don't tell me. I don't want to know," Sebastian cut in.

"What?"

"I don't want to know. Let's leave the past alone, Grace, and focus on the future."

"But…" I was too shocked to speak. I couldn't believe that even after regaining some of our memories, Sebastian still didn't want to talk about the past. "What did you remember? Why were you acting so strangely? And why can't we talk about it?"

"I don't *want* to talk about it," he repeated stubbornly, his eyes darkening.

"Well, I do," I retorted. We stared at each other, silently fuming.

"I was jealous," Sebastian finally admitted, his eyes softening slightly. He raked his fingers quickly through his hair, massaging his skull as he did so. "He was the last person I expected to see when I opened the door. And to find you sitting together so closely, holding hands like that… it made me feel so angry, angrier than I've felt in a very long time. I was just confused for a moment."

"But you did remember something," I prompted.

"Let it go, Grace," he muttered, shaking his head as if disappointed in me somehow. "Please, just let it go. For me?"

He reached out to me as he spoke, his eyes soft and warm, his gaze imploring. I still didn't understand but there was no way I could refuse him when he was looking at me like that.

"For you," I whispered as I slipped into his awaiting arms.

I couldn't let it go, not really. I pretended to, I tried hard not to bring it up again but it was all I could think about. I couldn't just forget now, not when I'd started to remember. That quick glimpse into one of the holes in my memory was enough to ignite the spark of my curiosity into a raging inferno. I had to know. I wanted to know so badly, it hurt. I couldn't just let myself forget.

The following days were torture. I felt like I was losing my mind. Each morning I awoke exhausted, more tired and worn out from my dreams than I had been when I laid down to sleep. I could never clearly remember the dreams but I always awoke disturbed, upset and afraid by something I couldn't quite remember. The shadows in my room seemed to constantly shift around me. My paranoia continued to increase with my lack of sleep and I felt eyes watching me wherever I went. And to make it worse, I was all alone. I couldn't talk to Sebastian, and I certainly couldn't talk to my mother or the Jensons about what was going on. The only other person who might possibly understand was David. But whenever I thought about going to him, something would always come up that deterred me, almost as if the universe were trying to warn me not to confide in him.

My birthday was a welcome distraction when it finally came. I awoke that morning in a cold sweat, trembling and disoriented from my terrifying dreams. I couldn't escape the feeling of danger, of impending doom settling down around me. I showered and dressed as quickly as possible, humming to myself the whole while to block out the strange whispered words I could almost hear in the silence around me.

"Happy birthday to you!" Mr. Jenson began singing loudly as

I walked into the kitchen. Mrs. Jenson, Sebastian and even David joined in, presenting me with a stack of blueberry pancakes doused in syrup and whipped cream with a single lighted candle on top. I laughed, momentarily forgetting my troubles as I blew out the flickering flame.

"Did you make a wish?" Sebastian teased, his eyes bright.

"No, um… actually, I forgot," I confessed.

"Grace, nineteen isn't quite old enough to start forgetting things," Sebastian mock-scolded.

"What does she need to wish for anyway?" David spoke up. He met my eye levelly, his gaze intense and direct. "She can have anything she wants."

"You make it sound as if Grace is spoiled," Mrs. Jenson softly chastised. I gave her a quick, thankful smile which she returned warmly. "She might come from wealth but she's absolutely down-to-earth and genuine," she scolded David.

"Is there anything you want for your birthday? I didn't get you another gift, as you requested, but it's not too late to change your mind," Sebastian joined in. I avoided looking David's way but I could feel his eyes on me still.

"No, I just want to spend the day with you."

"Then let's finish breakfast and go for a walk," Sebastian suggested with a smile. "And then once we get back we should probably start getting ready for Clarke and Tanya's wedding… unless you've changed your mind about going?"

"No, I promised him I'd be there. You don't have to come if you don't want to…"

"I'll be wherever you are," he smoothly replied. The topic of Clarke's wedding didn't seem to be bothering him at all today, for which I was grateful. "And David too. If you still want to come?"

"I might as well," he shrugged.

"My mother was invited too. I think she might bring her new 'friend', Dr. Mackey," I commented. "Ugh, I just hope that she doesn't remember I have access to the trust fund my father set up to me now that I'm nineteen. I don't want to get into that with her again."

"Sounds fun," Mr. Jenson murmured. Mrs. Jenson gave him a disapproving look, appreciating his sarcasm just as much as I did.

"We'll make sure it's an unforgettable evening for you, Grace," David reassured me. I smiled but my heart just wasn't in it, something didn't feel right.

After breakfast, Sebastian and I took a long walk through Beacon Hill Park. I carefully avoided topics such as memories, headaches, paranoia and nightmares. I knew we would just end up arguing and I didn't want to fight with him on my birthday—I didn't want to fight with him any day. It made me sad that we couldn't see eye-to-eye on this.

So we strolled around under the trees, leaves crunching beneath our feet, and over the bridges that arched across the duck ponds, and through the wilting gardens beneath the weak, autumn sun. Instead we spoke only of idle things, laughing and joking, teasing and flirting and I found myself actually relaxing, the sensation of being followed disappearing, the shadows no longer lurking on the edges of my vision.

"I could listen to you laugh all day," Sebastian commented as we started slowly making our way back towards the Jensons' home. "Especially when you snort like that."

"I do not snort!" I denied, trying to sound indignant. The effect was ruined when I started giggling again. Sebastian grinned.

"You do but don't worry, it's adorable. It makes you sound like a happy, little pig, it's very cute."

"Are you calling me a pig?"

"A beautiful, happy, little pig," Sebastian corrected, his eyes sparkling, his mirth barely contained.

"You're such a charmer." I threw a light punch into his shoulder.

"Ah! Ouch!" Sebastian grabbed his arm, over-dramatically rubbing the spot where I'd hit him. "I'm not sure if I should marry you after all. I never pictured myself in an abusive relationship like this."

"Do you want me to really hit you?" I threatened, teasingly. He held up his hands, shaking his head and grinning.

"No ma'am! I've seen what you can do when you're really mad."

"You have?" I frowned.

"Yes. Clarke's lip actually swelled up quite noticeably after you…" His voice trailed off, his expression abruptly going blank and cold as he realized his mistake.

"After I hit him," I finished quietly. I remembered now. It was right after I'd discovered he was the one to blame for the attack on Sebastian. I had been so angry, so furious, I had punched him in the face. "You remember too."

"Grace, don't," Sebastian warned, his eyes pleading with me. "I don't want to talk about it. I don't want to remember."

"But why? I don't understand, Sebastian."

"Because…" He ran his fingers through his hair, squeezing his eyes tightly shut as if in pain. "I remember them beating me," he whispered, without opening his eyes. "I remember the pain and the fear and the hatred. And then I remember you breaking up with me, you leaving me while I was still in the hospital. The pain of that was unbearable, much worse… But I understood why you did it. I didn't deserve you." He opened his eyes and I was shocked by the anguish in them. "Please, Grace. I don't want to remember any of my past life. Don't make me."

I didn't know what to say. I numbly nodded, my lips parted but silent, speechless. I didn't understand. I felt like he might remember more than I did but maybe he was right, maybe we were better off not remembering. If it hurt him this much, how could it be a good thing? But why had I broken up with him that day? And why would he say he didn't deserve me? What could he have ever done that would make him possibly think that? A part of me still hungered for answers and knowledge but for now, I pushed it aside. I couldn't bear to see Sebastian in such misery.

"I'm sorry," I whispered. I stepped forward and pulled myself against him, relief sweeping through me as his warm arms surrounded me and held me tight. "Let's forget for now. I can do that."

"Thank you," he sighed into my hair.

Even though I had promised to try to forget, I could only half-heartedly pretend. For the rest of the day, I was haunted by the image of the pain and anguish in Sebastian's eyes as he had said he didn't deserve me. It was all I could think about as I dressed and got ready to go to Clarke's wedding. And the more I thought about it, the more convinced I became that even though the past might be difficult to face, and even though we might remember things we'd rather forget, we still needed to know what we'd been through. I needed to know, to understand how I'd gotten to where I was today. There were too many unanswered questions, too many mysteries that I couldn't leave unsolved.

When I came downstairs, ready to go to the wedding, Sebastian's eyes held no trace of the pain that had flooded them just an hour before. In fact, his eyes were wide and bright, lit with joy as he watched me descend the staircase. The fabric of my silver, sequined cocktail dress seemed to almost float as it flowed from the silver satin band at my waist and lightly brushed against my legs.

"You look stunning," he breathed. He smiled as he noticed I still wore the necklace he'd given me. I'd carefully curled and pinned my hair back from my face just to show the beautiful necklace off.

"Thank you. You don't look so bad yourself." He actually looked very handsome with his hair neatly combed, his jaw freshly shaven and a dark, buttoned vest over his gray collared shirt with the top button left undone. I smiled as I noticed how he hadn't worn a tie and though his black pants were clean and pressed, they were still held up by a studded, leather belt. His black combat boots peeked out from underneath his trouser cuffs. Our eyes met, and he gave me a heart-stopping grin; he really did look amazing.

"Be careful you don't make the bride jealous," David drawled as he came around the corner at the bottom of the stairs. I swallowed hard as I looked at him. He wore a crisp, dark suit, the cut and fabric speaking of expensive tastes without being overly ostentatious. He looked very handsome and very… dark, and dangerous. I shifted nervously, dropping my gaze to the floor.

"Don't worry. Tanya won't mind that we're there," Sebastian reassured me, reaching for my hand.

"I still want to sit at the back."

"Your desire, my heart," Sebastian murmured back. I looked back at him quizzically but I didn't have time to ask as Mrs. Jenson appeared with a camera and began taking pictures until we were out the door.

I was relieved to discover that Clarke's idea of a "small" wedding was actually around 250 guests. It was easy for us to slip into one of the back rows at the ceremony, without being noticed by the wedding party or my mother who sat just behind Clarke's parents in the second row, Dr. Mackey at her side.

The ceremony took place outdoors on one of the large, cliff top lawns outside the Simons' family home. The wispy blue sky and misty gray ocean provided a simple yet beautiful backdrop to their vows. Clarke looked handsome even though his face was a little gray and his eyes were tight. He did seem to brighten once he saw Tanya coming down the aisle. She looked flawless in her long, white lacy gown that was reminiscent of the one worn most recently at a royal wedding. Her blonde hair had grown longer than when I'd last seen her and it fell in perfect ringlets past her shoulders. Her makeup was simple and clean, allowing the natural, radiant glow of her skin to show through. And she was glowing—the center of attention—marrying Clarke Simons in front of her family and friends, I had never seen her so genuinely happy. She looked stunning.

I held Sebastian's hand through out the ceremony, finding myself surprisingly moved as Clarke and Tanya exchanged rings and vows. Nerves fluttered in my stomach as I realized that this would be us in just under two months' time. David lounged in his chair on the other side of Sebastian, seeming bored and unaffected the whole while.

I was nervous after the ceremony when we went up to congratulate the couple. Surprisingly, Clarke and Tanya were both smiling happily and were quite friendly towards Sebastian and myself. David had disappeared somewhere.

"I really appreciate you coming," Clarke told us warmly as he shook our hands. He looked a lot more relaxed now that the ceremony was over with.

"Yes, so many of our friends couldn't make it. It's nice to have you here," Tanya graciously thanked us with a quick smile. I had never thought of myself as one of Tanya's friends, even when we were part of the same popular group in high school. She had always made it clear that I was an outsider, barely tolerated. But apparently, we were now finally friends. I wasn't sure if I appreciated the comment or not.

It was true, there were very few young people present at their wedding. Apart from us, Tanya's sisters, a few of Clarke's cousins and some of their parents' friends' children it was all older family members and business associates of the Ellis and Simons families. It appeared that Clarke and Tanya didn't have many real friends.

"You make a beautiful bride, Tanya. Congratulations," Sebastian smoothly complimented as he lightly kissed Tanya's hand. She batted her eyelashes, looking a little flustered by the old-fashioned gesture. I hid my smile, politely thanking the bride and groom for having us and then steered Sebastian away.

"I'm starving. Let's find our table, and David too, I suppose."

Sebastian laughed. "Oh, I'm not sure if we'll see him soon. He disappeared with one of Tanya's sisters almost as soon as the ceremony ended."

"One of the bridesmaids? Maybe we should go look for him."

"He can handle himself, just relax. Here, let's order some champagne."

"Champagne?"

"Yes, it is your nineteenth birthday."

I blinked, surprised. With all that had been going on, I had actually almost forgotten that it was my birthday and I was now the legal drinking age.

"My mother certainly wouldn't approve. What a great idea," I grinned, glad Mr. Jenson had offered to be our chauffeur for the evening.

It was much later in the night, after dinner and several flutes of champagne when David finally reappeared at our table. A slightly disheveled and guilty-looking bridesmaid had also returned to the head table, having missed dinner, speeches and the couple's first dance. Luckily, Tanya was distracted enough being the center of attention that she barely seemed to notice.

"So you're not lost after all. Enjoying yourself, David?" Sebastian asked.

David smirked but didn't answer. Instead, he turned to me.

"Have you saved me a dance, Grace?" He held out his hand and my mouth went dry. I turned to Sebastian, my head spinning slightly.

"I don't mind sitting this one out," he offered. "But it would be wise if you remembered she's *mine*." The last comment was directed at David, and from his tone, I wasn't certain if he were joking or not. He had sounded strangely possessive. David smiled anyway.

"Of course," he murmured as he took my hand and began leading me towards the dance floor. I immediately shook loose from his grasp.

"I don't belong to anyone," I warned him. "Just one dance."

David bowed his head in acknowledgement, looking amused as I stepped forwards, stumbling slightly into his arms.

"I see you've been drinking."

His face was so close to mine, his hand sliding around my hip while his other steered me out onto the dance floor. My head was still spinning but my feet automatically fell into the steps of the dance, my classical training coming back to me effortlessly.

"A little," I admitted.

"Funny how it hasn't loosened you up at all. If anything, you seem even more uptight," David commented dryly. I looked up sharply to see that he was grinning. I didn't find it funny.

"Grace, I've been waiting all evening to ask you to dance," David confessed. My heart skipped a beat.

"I thought you were busy with your bridesmaid?" I accused.

"Yes, but I've been thinking about you."

I avoided his eye, my heart now hammering in my chest. I didn't know what to say, what to do. I could feel Sebastian watching us.

"I wanted to get you away from Sebastian, so that we could talk," David continued. "Grace, something strange is going on. Sebastian's barely been sleeping at all lately and when he does, he tosses and turns and moans like he's being tortured. He stays up most of the night brooding and he refuses to talk to me about it at all anymore. Grace… I think he's remembering—I'm sure he is. And I think he's remembered something bad, really bad, and he won't tell me what it is. It could be important; you've got to help me find out." He spoke in a low urgent voice in my ear, his head close to mine.

I caught a glimpse of Sebastian as we spun past him on the dance floor. His face was expressionless, his eyes hard and narrowed. Suddenly, he looked like a stranger to me. I felt a wave of panic swelling within me.

"I think he might be remembering too," I agreed. "He won't talk to me about it either though, it's no use."

"You've got to keep trying, Grace. I think you're right—we need to get our memories back. There's something in the past that we've all forgotten, something big, something dangerous and I'm afraid it's going to come after us again…"

His words sent chills down my spine. I thought about all the strange things that had been happening to me lately: the objects that appeared to move in my room, the inescapable feeling that I was being watched, the shadows that moved in the corner of my eye, the malicious voices that whispered to me on the wind.

"I think you're right."

"I'm worried, Grace. Not just about Sebastian but for all of us."

I nodded my agreement. The music was picking up in tempo, our feet skipping over the polished floor, our bodies spinning faster and faster.

"You've got to promise me you'll keep trying to get him to talk and I'll do the same. And if you remember anything or if you should find a way to remember, you have to promise you'll share it with me," he continued, speaking rapidly and urgently.

"Ok," I agreed, feeling dizzy and out of breath.

"Promise me."

"I promise."

"Good." David sounded relieved.

"May I cut in?" Sebastian had appeared, halting our movement and causing us to guiltily break apart.

"Of course," David agreed, smiling. "I might go hunting for another bridesmaid. Don't wait up for me."

As soon as David stepped away, Sebastian spun me tightly in his arms and swept me back out onto the dance floor. I giggled with delight and we weaved and bobbed in time with the music, spinning and stepping in an intricate pattern across the dance floor that left many couples gaping and moving back to allow us more room.

"At the fine, old age of nineteen, you can still dance Ms. Stevenson," Sebastian teased. I grinned in delight at his playful mood, instantly forgetting the tense moments with David from just minutes before.

"Do you think you can keep up?" I asked coyly, gazing up through my lashes at Sebastian. His smile deepened, his eyes becoming more intense.

"Is that how you'd like to play?"

"Who's playing?"

Our steps fell faster, our bodies moved closer, the heat between us building as our dance became ever more complex. The song fell to a close, our steps slowing as Sebastian spun me one last time and pulled me into a low and dramatic dip. Polite applause broke out around us but I ignored everyone except for Sebastian. He was all I could see, all I could think, all I could feel. And I wanted him so badly, every part of him. I slipped my hand up from the back of his neck and pulled his lips to mine, kissing him deeply and passionately, with full abandon and no thought to the watching—and now whistling—crowd. Sebastian ended our kiss all too soon, pulling away with a breathless laugh, his eyes smoky with desire.

"I think you might have had too much to drink."

I shrugged, grinning mischievously. "It is my birthday."

"I should take you home."

"Yes," I agreed, staring deeply into his eyes, "you should."

He swallowed hard. He wasn't used to me being so direct and I wasn't used to it either. I could understand why alcohol was often referred to as "liquid courage", I certainly felt fearless tonight. It should also be called "spinny-maker", I thought fuzzily, swaying enough that Sebastian reached out to steady me.

"We should definitely go home. I'm calling Don now, and no more champagne," he added.

"You're no fun," I mumbled but I didn't argue. I was starting to feel quite ill.

On the ride home, I leaned into Sebastian's warm body. I closed my eyes in hopes that the world would stop spinning about me, only to fall fast asleep. When I awoke in my bed several hours later, I was confused and disoriented, having no memory of how I got there. I could only assume that Sebastian had carried me from the back of Mr. Jenson's car. I still wore the silver dress beneath the warm quilt tucked up around my chin.

Once my eyes focused, I looked over at my alarm clock and discovered that it was exactly 3:33 am. I sighed and rolled over, wincing at the pain that flashed through my head. My mouth was dry and had a horrible taste in it, my calves ached from the heels I had worn and all the dancing we'd done, and I still felt dizzy and nauseous; though not as badly as I had when we'd left Clarke's wedding. I knew I wasn't going to be able to fall asleep again any time soon, so I slowly sat up and looked about my room.

Even in the dark, there was still enough light coming from the bright, full moon outside that I could make out most of the objects around me. Surprisingly, I didn't feel uneasy. The moonlit shadows didn't feel threatening. I knew I was alone, no mysterious eyes watched me, no voices whispered in my ear. My necklace felt warm against my chest.

I sleepily stepped out of bed, moving towards my bedroom door with little thought to where I was going. My thoughts were still sluggish from sleep and champagne. It wasn't until I was halfway down the stairs that I realized where I was going—outside, to her.

I could clearly feel her presence out there. It was no surprise when I slipped out the kitchen door and walked around the house, to see the shadowed silhouette waiting for me out on the lawn, beneath the stunning full moon. Almost in a trance, I walked across the grass barefoot, the ice cold dew numbing my toes with each step. The presence called me, summoned me to her. She stood there waiting and I knew it was time.

The night fell silent as I reached her. The twinkling of the stars paused. The moon's pale light cast an eerie glow on everything, making the moment feel surreal.

"I'm here," I spoke softly, my voice as hushed as the moon's sacred light.

"We have been waiting for you," the wind whispered back in my ears. My heart leapt into my throat, I tried to take a step back but it was too late. The dark, hooded figure turned around, her face hidden within the shadows of her cowl. "It is time for you to fulfill your destiny. It is time for you to remember, Gracelynn Stevenson," the whispery voice hissed from the shadows, the sound swirling through the wind and howling through my ears as she spoke aloud my name, my one and true full name.

Chapter Five – Inescapable

AT THE SOUND OF MY FORGOTTEN NAME, **Grace***lynn*, pain hit me from every direction; there was no escaping it, no surviving it. It pierced through my brain and consumed me. My necklace flared to red hot, a searing heat that burned through my chest. I fell to my knees screaming but I was so far gone, I couldn't even hear my own screams. I was lost within myself, within a hundred lifetimes, within a million memories that seemed to go on forever.

I remembered it all, every detail of my life and glimpses of those before it. Every moment I'd spent with Sebastian, every word spoken, every touch, every thought—it all came rushing back in a never-ending torrent. I remembered the first time we had met, two thousand years ago when I, Caoilinn, had failed to save his mother. I remembered our affair, kept hidden from the other priestesses at the temple. I remembered the last time we had been together as Caoilinn and Seamus before fate and its bloody knives tore us apart. I remembered the first time I had spoken with Sebastian in the art room at school, the walks we had taken, the memories we had made, the nights we had shared. I remembered our flight from the Others, racing across the country and across Europe. Our close-encounter with the Others in Ireland and Walter's death at my hand flashed before my eyes, striking my mind like a blast of lightning that blazed deep within my soul. I cried out as I remembered Mags and the torture she had been put through before the Others stole her life, and the torture I had been through when I thought Sebastian wanted to be with her and not me. And I remembered those last forgotten moments, deep within the underground chambers of the Necromanteion when I had been sure we were all about to die at the hands of the Others, so I had sacrificed everything in an attempt to destroy the Lost Magic and wipe away all traces of its existence from our minds. I remembered David's knife at my throat, his last attempt to stop me and to end my life before I had swept all our memories away.

Time ceased to exist as the moment stretched into infinity. I swam through the pain, struggling to find the light through the endless stream of memories that flooded through my mind. My necklace throbbed with a blistering heat, a steadily glowing beacon that eventually pulled me back to the present, back to reality. I slowly opened my eyes, knowing as I did so that I would never recover my blissful ignorance again. The peaceful innocence with which I had lived these past few months was gone. I would never see the world the same way. I sensed that I would never be able to forget again. For I now remembered everything and there was no undoing or escaping the past. There never was.

I opened my eyes to find myself staring straight up into the starry, moonlit sky. The bright points of light sparkled against the black canvas and hurt my eyes. My head felt so full, it was hard to think, impossible to focus. Guilt hit me first, hot and strong as I realized I was once again, to blame for all of this. I had caused the explosion, I had destroyed the Lost Magic and I had stolen all of our memories. I had made a mistake. I squeezed my eyes shut, breathing through the pain and collecting myself before reopening my eyes to the bright and silent night.

"Arise, child. We have not much time," the dry, whispery voice commanded.

Swallowing my fear, I obeyed. I rose on unsteady feet, regarding the dark hooded figure warily as it floated before me. My head was quickly clearing, my thoughts and memories catching up to the present.

"Who are you?" I demanded, pleased that my voice only wavered slightly.

"I am all those who came before you," the voice whispered back, its breath riding the wind. "I am indebted to you and you to I. You will remember me as Niamh."

"Niamh?" I echoed. I rapidly searched through my memory, unused to the full feeling and the lack of gaping holes. A distant memory glimmered, a sense of the truth more than the knowledge of it. "The High Priestess," I gasped. "From the Sisterhood that murdered Caoilinn."

The shadowed figure tipped its head back to gaze up at the moon, allowing the hood to fall. A ghostly figure was revealed. The apparition appeared to be a woman in her early forties. She hovered before me, her eyes dark, her cheekbones high, her expression calm and confident. Her skin was deathly pale, holding a transparent hue beneath the moon's light. She was an apparition, her image flickering before me like a candle's flame. I felt both afraid and relieved for I now knew that something *had* been haunting me these past few weeks, I wasn't losing my mind after all.

"What do you want from me?" I demanded, forcing myself to speak.

"You know what I want." The spirit of the powerful priestess who had died over two thousand years before watched me with dispassionate eyes. I looked away, seeing death in her black, bottomless gaze.

"The Lost Magic," I guessed. The spirit appeared to nod. "I destroyed it. It's been lost forever." Even as I spoke the words, I could sense that they weren't true.

"The magic cannot be destroyed, it is as old as time. It can only be lost and rediscovered. You have rediscovered it, Gracelynn, now you must embrace it."

"I don't understand," I whispered, my fear increasing with each whispered word that the spirit spoke.

"The magic cannot be destroyed," the spirit repeated, her voice stern and terrifying. "You have done a noble, yet dangerous thing. You gave up your magic along with that of the Others and trapped it within the amber stone which you tried to destroy. But it cannot be destroyed. The magic lives on within that necklace around your neck and now whomever wears it can access its power if they so choose. You must release the magic from the stone and take it back into yourself. It is too dangerous to leave as it is."

"No," I denied, shaking my head. "I don't want it—I don't want any of this. I just want to live a normal life. I gave it all up. I destroyed the magic and erased any memories of it."

"You destroyed the magic that had been given to those unnaturally," the spirit corrected. "But it still lives within those who have the natural ability to access it. It lies dormant, waiting. It is time for you to release the magic and reawaken the power within."

My lips formed a silent 'no'. I shook my head—I couldn't, I wouldn't.

"It is your destiny," she warned. "For thousands of years, no living soul has ever gained full access to the magic—until now. Your willingness in the Necromanteion to sacrifice everything, to give up your love, your life and your power, has earned you the right to access the full and true magic. You no longer need to use the amber stone to focus your abilities or the designs to contain your spells. The magic shall live inside of you and be subject to your command. It is a feat not even Caoilinn could accomplish, though she might have tried if her time on Earth weren't cut short. You have rediscovered the true power of the magic—now you must embrace it."

"But I don't want it."

"Which is why you have been given this power. The true magic is only for those who have earned the right, for those who do not seek or desire to use its strength. You vowed in the Necromanteion, on the border of the Underworld, to help the Others meet the full potential of their magic. The spirits have heard and accepted your vow; it is time to fulfill your promise."

"But I stripped the Others of their magic, they can no longer access it," I objected, feeling desperate.

Niamh watched me with her dark, impassive eyes. Her image flickered in and out of focus, the moon's rays falling right through her and leaving no shadow on the ground.

"You destroyed the magic that was granted unnaturally. A few of the Others had the natural ability within them, though most did not. There are several souls around the world who also have the potential to access the magic, and more waiting to be born; you will guide them. Once you release the magic from the stone, the magic that they have never known before will awaken. Their lives are about to change and it is your responsibility to help them, to teach them control and how to live with the magic. Not all will walk the path to the light, some will fall to temptation, to darkness. If you deem them unworthy of the magic, you must not teach them. It is your responsibility to strip those unworthy of their magic in the only way possible: by letting it bleed from their veins before they turn to the darkness and endanger the world."

"What?" I gasped. I felt the blood drain from my face. "No, I can't…"

"You have spoken a vow before the living and the dead. It is your destiny. You shall guide them, you shall teach them, you shall maintain order," Niamh repeated, her voice rustling like dead leaves in the wind.

"The power has lain dormant within them, as within yourself, for centuries. With no one powerful enough to guide them, the ability has not been realized. But you have rediscovered the magic, you shall be the one to awaken their power. They will seek you out and reveal their power to you. But you must guide them and teach them the ways of the Lost Magic."

I was speechless. I couldn't believe this was happening. I desperately wanted Sebastian to be with me then—I needed his support, his strength, his wisdom.

"Will Sebastian remember now? And David?" I shuddered at the thought. I had forgotten how dangerous David was; it seemed impossible now that I ever could have forgotten but I had. I could hardly believe we'd been living under the same roof as him for months, thinking him our friend and not remembering the deadly, ancient being that he truly was. "Will they regain their powers now too?"

"The magic shall be awoken in only those who possess the natural ability. They will come to you. You must guide them," the spirit repeated monotonously. "The spell you created to erase the memories of your companions can only be undone by the speaking of their true, full names. That decision is yours alone."

"But I don't know David's full name."

The spirit ignored me.

"It is time."

The necklace that lay against my chest began to glow, the sparkling amber light pulsating in time with its throbbing heat. Niamh watched me.

"Why?" I stalled. "Why are you here? Why have you been haunting me?"

The spirit appeared to sigh, her image flickering with what might have been irritation.

"I owed you a debt. I ended your life once, too soon. I vowed that I would right that wrong. Coming to you on the physical plane like this requires a great deal of strength. I have no physical body from which to draw strength, so the power is drained from my spirit. I know not if I shall continue to exist after this but I shall hope so. I have been watching you and waiting for the right time. I could not afford to approach you before you were ready and willing to listen lest I use all my strength and fade away," Niamh explained. Her image grew fainter as she spoke, her body blending into the night and only her pale, ghostly face remaining visible as it flickered in and out of focus before me. Guilt flashed through me at the thought of extending our conversation any longer, but there was one more thing I felt I had to know.

"Why did you push me from the tree?"

"Sebastian was holding the necklace. He was touching the stone and he sensed its power. We could not risk him drawing from it." The way Niamh spoke made it clear that would have been a very dangerous thing.

"But Sebastian wouldn't abuse the power. He was about to give it to me anyway."

"Perhaps…"

Niamh's face disappeared entirely as she spoke, leaving her words echoing in the sudden silence around me. I waited tensely for her to reappear but found myself alone under the moon's chilling glow, the amber stone in my necklace still glowing with its warm, magical light.

The cold night wind picked up, swirling the air and whispering in my ears.

"It is time," the wind whispered softly in Niamh's breathy voice. I sensed her presence though she didn't reappear.

"I don't know what to do," I whispered back desperately. Panic was rising within me. The wind gusted one more time, sending my hair flying out behind me and chills rippling up and down my spine.

"Embrace... the magic..." the wind whispered.

I nodded. What choice did I have? Niamh had risked not just her life but her eternal existence to bring me to this moment, to guide me to my destiny. I still wanted nothing to do with the Lost Magic and I certainly didn't want to be responsible for reawakening the magic in individuals across the world who had never even known it existed before. But to leave the incredible strength of the Lost Magic trapped within my necklace, where anyone who held it could access and harness its power was foolhardy and potentially disastrous, especially with people like David around. However reluctant, I knew what I had to do.

The small, flat disc of my necklace felt hot against my palm as I wrapped my fingers tightly around it. The light beamed out of the small, heart-shaped piece of amber at its center and glowed brightly between my fingers, sparkling and dazzling, impossibly beautiful to behold. I closed my eyes and pressed the necklace firmly against my chest, its heat burning into my skin.

"I'm sorry," I whispered to the night. I was apologizing to Sebastian, for not destroying the magic as I had promised him I would. I was apologizing to Niamh, as it seemed impossible that I would be able to keep the rashly spoken vows I had made in the Necromanteion. And I was saying sorry to however many people around the world, whose lives I was about to change by embracing the Lost Magic and reawakening the magic that had lain dormant within them.

A tear slid down my cheek as I mentally reached out and opened myself to the heat and power of the Lost Magic. I was sad but I wasn't afraid. I should have been; I was about to open a floodgate.

Raw, untamed power blasted through me in a wave of blinding, blistering heat and pain. Memories flashed through my mind: the pain of the Binding, the explosion in Greece, falling from the top of the oak tree; but it was all nothing compared to this. I couldn't move, I couldn't think. There was only pain and power coursing through my veins.

Abruptly, it ended. I fell to my knees, the night's frost biting into my skin. My heart was still pounding as I opened my eyes. Everything looked brighter, in vivid focus despite the moon's milky light and the murky shadows around me. My necklace was no longer glowing though it still felt warm against my skin. The night was quiet, peaceful even but I was not. I could feel the magic racing through me. It filled my blood, sank into my bones, reached out to envelop every tiny cell of my body. Its power was unbelievable. I knew I now had the power to do anything, absolutely anything that I wanted. But I wouldn't, I couldn't. How could I embrace this power when it had cost me so much? I didn't want this, I didn't want any of it. Suddenly, all I truly wanted was to forget again. But it didn't happen. A wave of fatigue swept over me.

I decided it was time to go back inside, to go to sleep, and to pray that in the morning I would awaken and this would all make sense.

My thoughts were fuzzy as I stumbled back to the house and made my way up to my room and into bed. Just as I drifted off to sleep, a thought occurred. I would have Sebastian and David to deal with in the morning. Was it possible either of them could have developed a natural ability to access the Lost Magic after years of possessing it unnaturally? And what would I do if they had or if they hadn't; if Sebastian were normal? Should I just let them live their lives in blissful ignorance? Sebastian might want that now… but how could I do this alone?

As I sank back down into a heavy sleep, I thought I heard an ancient, dry voice whisper in my ear, *"Guide them."*

The next morning, I awoke to the warm sun shining through my bedroom window. A glance at my alarm clock told me I had slept in. I stood up and stretched, feeling unexpectedly refreshed, energized and optimistic—until I remembered.

My good mood vanished and my jaw dropped open as I remembered the bizarre events from last night. It felt like a dream but I knew it was real because I *remembered*. I remembered everything I had forgotten, I remembered how I had tried to destroy the Lost Magic and I had failed. I had made a mistake. The magic couldn't be destroyed, it wouldn't leave us alone and now we were right back to where we had started—almost.

I desperately needed to see Sebastian, to talk to him. I began throwing on my clothes.

I could remember how dark and deadly the Lost Magic could be: how it had once, hundreds of years ago, corrupted Sebastian himself, along with the Others that he and Mags had created. I knew the cost of using the magic too well. Painful, haunting images flashed behind my eyes: Mags' head hanging at an unnatural angle to her body, the expression on Walter's face as I knowingly took his life, Sebastian's eyes black with hatred and fury, burning into mine. I remembered everything I had ever learned and ever experienced of the Lost Magic and even though it now filled me to the brim, even though my whole body vibrated and pulsated with its strength, I wanted nothing to do with it.

"This is not my destiny," I hissed to my empty room. "I will make my own destiny. I will choose my own path."

And before any shadows could shift or voices could whisper on the wind, I spun on my heel and marched out of my bedroom, slamming the door emphatically behind me.

I strode into the kitchen, feeling full of righteous determination but the sight of David, sitting alone at the table, made me pause.

We considered each other. David wore a strange half-smile on his face, his head cocked to one side as he studied me. Anger and bitter hatred flashed through me as I recalled all the misery he had caused. Magic seethed within me, begging to be used, desperate for release yet even still, I refused it. It was both nauseating and infuriating to think how close David and Sebastian had become, how we had all trusted him and let him into our lives these past months. That was all about to change.

"Something's different about you," David stated, eyeing me curiously.

"Yes." I couldn't help but glare at him, my whole body tensed with emotion.

"Are you angry with me?"

"Furious," I murmured between clenched teeth.

"And what could I have possibly done to arouse such a passionate response?" he smirked.

"I remembered."

David's lips parted in surprise, his condescending mirth instantly disappeared. He leaned across the table towards me in earnest, his eyes intense, his face pale.

"Everything?" he asked with a quiet hope that caught me off guard.

"No," I lied, "but enough."

His eyes flickered across my face, taking in my expression with a frown.

"It must be bad then, isn't it?"

I didn't respond. My anger was slowly cooling as I watched him. As I saw the apprehension and frustration in his eyes, it was clear that he didn't remember any more of his life today than he had yesterday. And why should he? I certainly didn't want him to remember and I wasn't about to speak his full name, even if I knew it. But still… something didn't feel right.

"The explosion… it was my fault, wasn't it?" he asked quietly. He dropped his eyes to the table in shame. I blinked in surprise, my anger evaporating.

"Why would you ask me that?"

He shrugged. "I've been feeling strangely lately—guilty I suppose, though 'guilt' doesn't even come close to describing it. It's as if a part of me knows that I've made some awful mistakes in the past and even if I can't remember them, I know that they are there. The… guilt… it's been so bad lately, I hardly sleep. I fear it could destroy me if I let it. Sebastian sees things differently. He thinks this is my chance to make retribution, like I was meant to forget the past so that I could start over again."

I searched his eyes but they were clear and honest. I found myself wanting to believe him.

"Do you want me to tell you the truth?"

I watched him silently consider, his eyes bright with intellect and his face drawn with a sadness that I had never glimpsed before.

"No," he finally answered, "not yet. Maybe one day I will be ready to hear it but not today. Maybe I'll even remember on my own, soon enough."

"Maybe." I eyed David uneasily. It would be extremely dangerous for him to remember his past—dangerous for all of us. Especially if he had any natural inclination towards the Lost Magic… but he didn't seem any different than he had yesterday, did he? Goosebumps prickled on the back of my neck. I still couldn't feel comfortable being in the same room with him, especially with no one else around. Not now, not after all I had remembered. "Where's Sebastian?"

"I don't know. He woke early—at dawn, and he left immediately. He was acting strangely," David added with a scowl. Hope sparked within me.

"How do you mean? What was he doing?"

"He was muttering to himself as he got dressed; he was quite distracted. When I asked him where he was going he barely acknowledged me. He just mumbled something about going for a walk."

"And you let him? That was hours ago and he still hasn't come back? Didn't you think you should have mentioned this to me or the Jensons sooner?"

David shrugged. "Sebastian can be strange at times but he's more than capable of taking care of himself."

"Some friend you are," I muttered as I stalked out of the room. I couldn't believe how uncaring and nonchalant David was behaving when Sebastian had just abruptly taken off at dawn and was missing hours later. This was definitely not normal behavior for him. I was worried but I was also secretly optimistic. Perhaps he had remembered too, perhaps he did have some natural ability in the Lost Magic and its awakening last night was now disturbing him. Perhaps.

On my way out the door, I picked up my cell phone and tried to both call and text Sebastian. I wasn't surprised when he didn't respond to either; Sebastian disliked using cell phones and rarely checked his messages. There were several missed phone calls and a text message from Clarke but I didn't bother opening these—I had more important things on my mind. Glancing back over my shoulder, I could see David through the glass panes in the door, still sitting at the kitchen table. He was staring into his coffee cup, apparently lost in thought. The ghost of a smile hovered on his lips, filling me with sudden unease. The Lost Magic rose and swelled within me, and this time I did not deny it, this one time, I decided it was necessary to make an exception.

"I don't want you to remember," I whispered. The wind picked up as I spoke, swirling my words around me in an icy gust. Magic poured from my heart, coating each whispered word with a finality that hung heavily in the air. And just as quickly, it was done. David sat, staring into his cup still. Was it my imagination, or had his smile disappeared? What did it truly matter? I shook myself, turning away from the door and striding towards my car. I had to focus on the important task at hand of finding Sebastian. I needed him and I had a niggling feeling that he needed me too.

I spent the next several hours driving around Victoria, searching all of Sebastian's favorite places—Beacon Hill Park, the old bookstore downtown, the inner harbor, the windy, wave-tossed beaches and quiet forested trails around the city—but he was nowhere to be found. I was quite concerned when I returned to the Jensons' home shortly after noon and there was still no sign of him. David had gone now so I could only hope that Sebastian had returned home and they were now out somewhere together. The thought didn't offer me much comfort. Wouldn't Sebastian have called?

I forced myself to sit down with some tea and toast for lunch. I nibbled away nervously as I checked my phone's messages, hoping to find something new. There was nothing from Sebastian but the unopened message from Clarke was still there, along with several others. Absentmindedly, I opened the first text from Clarke which had been sent early that morning.

Call me. It's important.

Which was followed by:

> I really need to talk to you, Grace. Call me as soon as you get this.

The third message had been sent just ten minutes ago:

> I can't wait any longer. I'm on my way over.

Just as I finished reading the message there was a knock at the kitchen door. Before I could even stand to answer it, the door opened and Clarke let himself in. My brows pulled down into a puzzled frown as I tried to make sense of his bizarre appearance.

He looked awful. He was still wearing his wedding tux, or at least, he was wearing the pants and the half-unbuttoned dress shirt, the vest and jacket were missing. His face was pale and sweaty, his dark brown hair uncharacteristically messy and out-of-place. There were bags under his eyes, eyes which looked slightly puffy—had he been crying?

"Grace, I'm so glad you're here." He stepped forward as he spoke, pulling me into his arms and hugging me tightly, desperately. I wrinkled my nose at the sour scent of booze and cigarette smoke that clung to his clothes. "I really need your help, Grace."

"Um, ok." I politely wriggled out of his embrace, taking a firm step back. "What's going on? Aren't you supposed to be on your honeymoon?"

Clarke flushed.

"Yeah, we're supposed to be leaving in a couple of hours for Jamaica but… well, Tanya and I got in a fight this morning and now she's saying she wants to get the marriage annulled!"

To my surprise, Clarke didn't just look ashamed, he actually sounded upset. It was distracting enough for me to forget my own problems, for the time being.

"Tell me what happened," I offered, gesturing to an empty chair at the table. He gratefully dropped into it.

"I drank a lot last night—too much," he admitted. "I was really hung over this morning and I guess I just wasn't thinking straight.

Tanya asked me if I enjoyed the wedding and I said, 'Yeah. It wasn't as bad as I thought it would be. I'm really glad Grace was able to make it.' Then Tanya started acting weird, and she said something like, she couldn't believe it when she saw you and I agreed and said you looked amazing."

"Clarke," I groaned.

"I know—it was stupid to say, even if it was true. Tanya was pissed. She started yelling at me and throwing things, and I was tired and had a headache and I started yelling back. We both said some stuff... Man, she was mad! But... I don't want to get our marriage annulled. I'm actually kinda glad we got married. We're going to have a baby and I've decided I want to be a good dad, I want to be around. But we've only been a family for less than twenty-four hours and I've already screwed it up. She said she's going to raise the baby on her own, that she wants me to stay away from both of them." He buried his face in his hands.

"What am I going to do, Grace?" He looked up at me, his blood-shot eyes filled with desperation and tears. No matter how stupid Clarke could sometimes be, no matter how egotistical and self-centered and vain, right now he really did need a friend and whether I liked it or not, I might be the only real friend he had.

"It's going to be ok," I began, speaking in a soft, calming voice. He nodded eagerly, wanting to believe my words. "You need to go talk to her, Clarke. You shouldn't be telling me these things, go tell her. Look, you've got just enough time to convince her to take you back, to go to Jamaica still. Go! Tell her you're an idiot and you didn't mean whatever you said, tell her you want to be a family, tell her you're sorry and you love her."

"But... I don't know if I can say that."

"Why not?" I asked, completely exasperated.

"Because... I don't know if I love her yet, or what I mean is, I think I'll grow to love her—"

"Don't tell her that," I muttered. He pretended not to hear.

"But I can't say I didn't mean the things I said because I did mean them. I do mean them, with all my heart," he continued in a softer voice. He looked up, his eyes burning into mine. "I'm still in love with you, Grace. I'm still hoping, even now, that there might be a chance…"

"No," I cut in. "Clarke, we've been over this. You and I are only friends, that's all we'll ever be but I don't know if we can even be that if you keep declaring your love for me," I stated bluntly. "I don't think you even really love me—you're just afraid and you're looking for something familiar. I'm not the same girl you knew in high school, Clarke. You need to focus on you and Tanya now. Maybe one day we can be friends again but I can see it's just not going to work now. If you want to save your marriage, you need to go. Now. Go talk to her, go apologize. Tell her that I'm permanently out of your life. Tell her that our friendship, at least for the time being, is over."

"But—"

"You need to leave." I looked pointedly at the door. His eyes drooped, his mouth pulled down at the corners. I could tell I'd hurt him but what choice did I have? I couldn't be much clearer and he just didn't seem to be getting the message.

"You're right. I should go." He stood, not meeting my eye and slowly moving towards the door. Out of habit, I rose, ready to escort him out. When he suddenly spun around and clasped my shoulders, it caught me completely off guard.

"Goodbye, Grace," he whispered, his voice husky. And before I could stop him, he was pulling me against him, his lips pressing firmly against mine in a one-sided passionate kiss.

I was too startled to immediately react. It took me a second before I managed to wriggle my arms free and pull away, firmly and angrily shoving him backwards.

"Clarke! Seriously, what's wrong with—" I began but my throat constricted, choking off my words as I saw who stood behind him in the doorway.

Clarke, looking completely unapologetic, turned lazily. He glanced over his shoulder, following my gaze to the open door, then he froze.

David stood in the doorway, an unreadable expression on his face. He looked tired, and perhaps wary. Behind him stood Sebastian. My first reaction was one of instant relief: Sebastian was home, he was safe. This immediately changed to panic as I took in Sebastian's expression. This was not good, not good at all.

Sebastian was glaring at Clarke, his expression more fierce and terrifying than I had ever seen before. His eyes burned with pure hatred. They had become so dark that they appeared to be black. His skin was even paler than normal, making him look to be some kind of dark demon. His eyes were narrowed, his jaw clenched, his lip curled up slightly in an unfamiliar expression. I'd never seen him so furious, it was truly terrifying.

He pushed past David, stepping into the kitchen with death in his eyes. His gaze never left Clarke's face for a second.

"I warned you," he muttered darkly, "she's mine." His voice was low and possessive, completely opposite to his usual light and lyrical way of speaking. I watched in mute horror as he reached into his jacket and pulled out a silver handle. With a quick flick of his wrist, a dangerous-looking blade was revealed. Confusion briefly registered in my mind; where had he gotten that knife? I didn't even know he carried one. And what was he doing threatening Clarke with it? I couldn't understand what was happening. And then everything happened at once.

Sebastian charged Clarke, his movements lithe and deadly. I heard myself scream, frozen in panic and horror. Clarke's eyes were wide with fear as he tried to step backwards. David reached for Sebastian as if to stop him but he was too late. To my horror and total disbelief, Sebastian thrust the knife deep into Clarke's gut. Dark red blood was already soaking into Clarke's rumpled white shirt as Sebastian's momentum carried them both to the ground. The look on Clarke's face as he fell, I would never, ever forget, along with the piercing sound of my own scream.

Chapter Six – Unveiled Threats

I SCRUNCHED MY EYES TIGHTLY CLOSED, COVERING my face with my hands. I panted into my palms, desperately chanting, "That didn't happen. It's not real. That didn't happen."

"Grace!" David yelled, his voice tense and impatient.

My hands fell from my face and I opened my eyes. David had managed to pull Sebastian off Clarke and Sebastian had lost his knife somewhere. David was barely able to hold onto him. Sebastian thrashed wildly, struggling with an inhuman rage to reach Clarke. I was still too stunned to do anything but watch this nightmare play out in front of my eyes.

"Let go, David," Sebastian growled.

"I'm trying to help you. You don't really want this," David responded, speaking through clenched teeth as he strained to hold onto Sebastian.

"Don't tell me what I want." Sebastian's voice was low and deadly calm; it sent chills down my spine. It was the voice of a stranger, the voice of a monster. His thrashing stopped, his breathing slowed. He turned to David with his deadly, black eyes. "Let go," he commanded. David didn't move, didn't flinch. Sebastian's jaw tensed and then suddenly he struck, his body spinning and twisting so fast that he was out of David's grip in almost the exact same instant as he was slamming his hands into him, throwing him halfway across the room against the far wall.

David cried out as the air was driven from his lungs and he fell onto the floor. He scrambled back to his feet, his eyes full of barely concealed fury. "Have it your way," he spat at Sebastian, panting slightly. He stormed out of the house without looking back.

Sebastian slowly turned back towards Clarke, a crumpled, motionless heap on the floor behind him. His eyes gleamed with cruel anticipation.

"Stop." I spoke softly but my words sliced through the air, immediately halting Sebastian's steps. He looked at me for the first time and for a second his conviction seemed to waver. His eyes softened, his brow creased, his stance started to relax but suddenly he tensed, shifting back to the strange, aggressive, dangerous Sebastian.

I knew I had no choice. I gathered the magic within me, directing it easily and effortlessly at Sebastian and Clarke. It poured from me, an invisible flood of light and power that swelled to fill the room. The air vibrated with power, my power. I took a slow, steady breath and then closed my eyes, focusing on what I so desperately wanted. I didn't want this to be real; I didn't want this to be happening. I didn't want Clarke to be hurt, I didn't want Sebastian to be capable of this kind of horrible, terrifying violence. I didn't want any of this.

"Please, stop," I whispered, my voice breaking with pain and desperation. I slowly opened my eyes to find myself looking directly into Sebastian's.

We stood just a few feet apart. I could already sense the change in him, the anger abruptly snuffed out but it had been replaced by something else, something almost worse. He stared at me with his large, gray-blue eyes, traces of black still shadowing his irises. He looked horrified.

"It's too late," he whispered back in a hollow voice. Then he turned and ran out.

I fought the strong urge to follow him. I wanted to make sure he was ok, I wanted to understand what was going on. But right now, I had to attend to Clarke. I hesitantly approached him, holding my breath as I nudged his leg with my foot. There was no response. He had to be ok, I wanted him to be ok. I tried to believe that he was.

"Open your eyes," I quietly commanded. The instant the words escaped my lips he began to stir. A low moan rose up from him as he slowly rolled onto his back. My eyes quickly searched his chest for the knife wound, for blood or any sign of the serious injury I had seen him sustain but there was nothing there but a couple miss-ing buttons and a small tear in his shirt. Relief swept through me.

"Ugh… where's Sebastian?" Clarke groaned, wincing as he sat up.

"He left."

"What happened? Did he knock me out?"

"Yes." It was the easiest answer.

"Shit. I thought he was going to kill me for a second." Clarke shook his head, mumbling a few other choice swear words. "I could have taken him, you know. He just caught me before I was ready, knocked the wind out of me and must have gotten a good shot in to my head."

I glared back at him. "I'm glad you're ok—I really am—but you need to leave, now."

"Don't worry, I'm not going to go after him," Clarke muttered, stumbling to his feet unsteadily. "I probably should though, little punk."

"Just go! Get out of here. Go talk to Tanya."

"Oh… Tanya. Right. Ok… well…"

"Go," I repeated. "And please don't come back here. Don't call, don't text—just go, forget about all this, forget about me."

Clarke stiffened slightly. "Fine, if that's what you want."

"It is. Go."

Clarke's eyes lingered on me a moment longer. His lips parted as if he were about to say something else but I shook my head, silenc-ing him.

"Goodbye, Clarke."

The instant he was gone I collapsed at the table. I couldn't believe what had just happened—it had happened, hadn't it? It didn't seem real. I could barely believe that it was real. Clarke obviously didn't remember being stabbed and there was no sign of the knife or a trace of blood any where. I couldn't believe Sebastian was possible of such violence. How could he be? But he had stabbed Clarke, hadn't he? Where was he? What was going on?

As I tried to make sense of everything in my head, I made my way outside. I immediately noticed the faint scent of cigarette smoke that trailed through the air.

It didn't take me long to find him. He was down at the back of the Jensons' garden, sitting on the edge of the pond, the large koi fish slowly circling before him. His back was to me and he didn't turn as I approached. His shoulders were hunched and he appeared to shudder between taking deep drags off his cigarette. I paused a few feet back from him, staring at this stranger before me. How could he have attacked Clarke like that? He had tried to kill him. What the hell was going on? I felt like my whole world had turned upside down, like I didn't even know Sebastian anymore. It was both heartbreaking and frightening. I felt so lost.

I didn't know what to do or say. Already, my mind was trying to make excuses for Sebastian's behavior. Perhaps I had inadvertently wanted him to react that way? Maybe I had less control over my powers than I thought. Or maybe someone else had wanted him to hurt Clarke, someone whose ability had recently been awoken… David? Was it possible? I didn't know what to think. Would Sebastian remember stabbing Clarke? It had happened so quickly and then been so quickly undone… had it even happened? Was I losing my mind?

The sounds of Sebastian's rough breathing broke me from my bleak, entangled thoughts. He trembled slightly, his free hand roughly wiping his eyes. My heart broke at the sight of his tears. My decision was made in an instant.

"Sebastian," I said quietly as I stepped up beside him. He immediately tensed, his whole body motionless except for the cigarette smoke that slowly coiled up into the cold air. He resolutely stared straight ahead.

I lowered myself down to sit beside him. Without hesitation, I leant against his warm side, closing my eyes and holding in my own pain. His body was rigid, he still didn't move.

"That cigarette stinks," I commented, not knowing what else to say.

My voice seemed to finally reach him. His muscles shifted from steel to stone as he moved, butting the cigarette out amongst the small pebbles where we sat. He cleared his throat.

"Sorry."

Just one word but it conveyed so much. I turned to face him. There was so much pain in his eyes, anguish and regret weighing down each feature of his face. He looked years older. He looked tormented and confused and yet his wide eyes seemed to also be pleading with me, silently asking me for… something.

"What happened?" They were my only words when I wanted to ask him so much more.

He shook his head, lowering his eyes.

"I don't know." He paused, his brows pulled down, sparkling tears still clinging to his long, thick lashes. He brushed at them in irritation. "I lost control," he confessed, in a soft and angry voice. I knew he wasn't angry at me, he was furious with himself. "I've been having a rough time lately. I'm so confused, Grace. The nightmares and… I don't know. I just don't understand what's happening to me." He paused again to take a deep breath, and then his words came faster. Flying from him as if he'd been holding them in so long, they were bursting to come out. I didn't dare interrupt him. "When David found me today, I was pretty worked up. He talked me down from it, convinced me to come home—to you. I wanted you. I needed to see you, to talk to you, to be with you so badly. It's better when I'm with you—I'm better. But then when I walked in and saw you with Clarke, in his arms, his lips on yours… For a second I was devastated, I thought you'd finally realized that I'm not… that I can't… I thought you'd chosen him. Then I saw you push him away, I saw how angry you were and as soon as I realized he'd kissed you without your permission…" His whole body trembled, his voice thickened with fury. "I wanted to kill him. I wanted to kill him like I've never wanted anything before in my life. I couldn't think, I couldn't stop. Even now, it's hard to remember that it's wrong. That I shouldn't want that…"

Fear prickled at my skin. Not fear of Sebastian, that was ridiculous, but fear for Clarke. I suddenly felt the urge to not only protect Clarke from Sebastian, but also to protect Sebastian from himself, and there was only one way I knew how. I silently hated myself for using the magic again—especially for using it against the man I loved. It was probably an unnecessary precaution really but...

"Sebastian, I would never want you to kill Clarke. Ever." I spoke quietly but the magical strength behind my words reverberated through the air. The koi fish scattered before us.

"I know." He spat the words back at me, his voice angry and bitter still. I recoiled from him, stung by his tone.

"What's going on? Why are you acting this way?" The pain and fear I was struggling to contain somehow threaded its way through my words. Sebastian looked at me in concern. The angry, frightening, dangerous Sebastian had disappeared and the boy I knew and loved had returned.

"I'm sorry, Grace. Please don't worry. It'll be ok, I promise. I'm just... having a hard time."

"You said that but I still don't know what it means."

He sighed. "It means... I've just been really confused lately. The nightmares are getting worse. I barely sleep anymore and I'm so exhausted all the time that I feel like I'm losing my grip on reality sometimes. The headaches, the insomnia, the disorientation—at times it overwhelms me and I feel like I can't remember who I am, or who I was... I don't know."

My heart broke to hear him speak like this but at least I had a ray of hope to offer him. I knew I had to proceed cautiously.

"Sebastian, I can help you. I think I've found a way that you can remember, a way to get back your lost memories—"

"No," he cut in firmly. He grabbed my hands, clasping them tightly in his. His eyes were wide and staring intensely, almost desperately into mine. "Don't. Promise me you won't try."

"What? I don't understand?"

"There's nothing good in the past, Grace. Please. I don't want to remember anymore, I don't want anything to do with it."

I stared at him, bewildered by his sudden intensity that bordered almost on panic.

"You're wrong. I know that there are a lot of good things in our past, Sebastian. There are thousands of beautiful memories waiting—important memories. I think we have to remember, in order to move forward—"

"No, don't. Promise me you won't. Don't try and remember, promise me. I can't bear to lose you," he begged, his hands squeezing mine so tightly it was beginning to hurt.

I looked back into his wide and frightened eyes. I couldn't understand the fear in them but as always, I was powerless to deny him anything he wanted.

"I promise," I lied, realizing that I could never reveal to him the truth. That I already remembered, that the Lost Magic was back, that he no longer could use it.

"Thank you," he breathed, his whole body sagging with relief. He pulled me into his arms, holding me tightly against his chest. "It's going to be ok, Grace. I'll get better, as long as I have you."

I didn't answer. I was afraid to speak, afraid he might hear the shame in my voice. Because I knew now that I was the one who had done this to him, I was the one who had stolen his memories and left him this way. I was the cause of his nightmares, the reason for his confusion and pain. If I had never tried to destroy the Lost Magic and erased his memories of the past, he would be happy still, life would still make sense. And even though I knew how to cure it, how to clarify his confusion, I had promised not to. I could make him remember but I wouldn't as long as he didn't want to. I'd just have to find a way to convince him that he did.

My heart was heavy with sadness as I realized the truth. He didn't have any natural ability to use The Lost Magic, he couldn't. He was running from it even when he couldn't remember it. And if he did remember, would he run from me too?

"I love you," he whispered into my hair.

I pulled myself even tighter against him.

"I love you too. Don't run away from me again, please."

He didn't answer, he just sighed into my hair.

I knew I could never tell Sebastian the truth. He didn't want to believe it but more importantly, he didn't want to hear it. I was miserable. It seemed so unfair that this destiny had been thrown upon me with all these unwanted powers and responsibilities. How could I have a destiny that didn't include Sebastian? It didn't make sense and so I stubbornly refused to accept it. I would ignore the Lost

Magic, I would push it away and refuse to allow it to be a part of my life so long as it was not a part of Sebastian's.

In the following days, Sebastian and I spent a great deal of time pretending that nothing was wrong. We made wedding plans, went on dates, I even called in sick to work so that we could spend all day together. It should have been fun and at times, I almost enjoyed myself but in the back of my mind, I couldn't forget the expression on Sebastian's face when he had stabbed Clarke in front of me. It was like a nightmare that was on continuous replay in my mind. It haunted my every waking thought.

As the days turned into weeks, it was obvious that Sebastian and David didn't remember the truth of what had happened with Clarke and I could safely assume that Clarke himself didn't remember. I didn't hear from Clarke at all, as I had requested, but I did hear through my mother that he and Tanya were enjoying Jamaica. Clarke's mother had spoken with him on the phone shortly after they arrived at their destination and since she and my mother were still friends, my mother kept me up-to-date. I was happy for him.

I tried not to think about the Lost Magic. I ignored the tingling that continuously raced through my veins. I pushed aside the knowledge that I could attain anything that I truly wanted, that any and all my struggles were truly unnecessary. All I really wanted was for things to feel normal again, for Sebastian to be happy and for us to get married and go live somewhere else, somewhere far away from here where we could leave David, the magic, and all our troubles far behind us. I couldn't do it though. I refused to use the magic; I refused to manipulate my future that way. I tried my best to pretend everything was normal and for a while, I was almost convinced that I could live this way.

"Are you happy?" I asked Sebastian one day. We were sitting on a bench along the waterfront—not far from my mother's house—sipping steaming coffees and gazing out over the gray ocean. Sebastian frowned at my question.

"Of course I am. I'm with you."

"Are you still having nightmares?"

"I don't want to talk about it," he responded firmly, confirming my suspicions. Worry gnawed at my gut.

"You need to talk to someone about it, Sebastian."

"I am. I've been talking to David and Mr. Jenson."

I looked at him in surprise.

"I didn't realize you and David were speaking again," I stated. There had been an obvious rift in their friendship since the day David had attempted to intervene between Sebastian and Clarke.

"He apologized a few days ago," Sebastian announced, surprising me even more. I couldn't imagine David apologizing, especially when he really hadn't done anything wrong. Still… I supposed it was good that he was talking to someone about his troubles, even if it were David and not me.

"I'm glad you've been talking to Mr. Jenson too. Has he had any useful advice?"

"I don't want to talk about it, Grace," Sebastian repeated, gently but firmly. His comment stung.

"You'll talk to them but not me?"

"Yes. Sorry," he added when he noticed my expression. He forced a smile and reached out to lightly stroke my cheek. "I don't want you to worry." He quickly kissed my lips, breaking away before I could object and returning to his silent brooding. I wasn't worried; I was beyond worried. I was afraid and concerned and confused. With no one to confide in about the return of my memories and the Lost Magic, and no idea what to do, I felt so lost and alone. I just wanted someone to talk to, someone who would understand and could offer me some advice. My prayers were answered when she came to me in my dreams that night.

I had fallen asleep, tossing and turning, worrying about Sebastian and our future together. My dreams were full of fragmented images and emotions, blurring and wrapping around one another in a distorted, entangled mess. I must have finally relaxed enough to fall into a deeper sleep because suddenly, my dreams took on a different tone. Calming gray fog rolled through my mind, surrounding me in a fuzzy, soft haze of light as if I were floating in the center of a cloud. It was the strangest dream I had ever experienced as I was both aware and unaware that I was sleeping. A voice drifted through the dense fog towards me.

"Caoilinn, what are you doing?" She sounded irritated, her low voice a near growl. I spun around in the dream cloud, searching for the source of the familiar, forgotten voice.

"My name is Gracelynn," I corrected. My words seemed to be stifled by the cloud, thrown back into my own ears.

"Well, at least you know your present name even if you have forgotten who you are."

I turned in the direction of the scornful sound but saw nothing.

"I know who I am," I retorted, feeling slightly ridiculous arguing with this bizarre dream-cloud before me. I suddenly realized how strange it was to recognize this as a dream, to know that it wasn't real even as I stood there and participated. "Who are you?" I demanded.

"I've been watching you, Gracelynn. I've been watching you and Sebastian. I see what's happening. It's not too late to stop it but you need to accept your destiny, you need to harness the powers that you have been given. There is still hope." The voice came from every direction, it filled the cloud of light around me. Her voice was so familiar but my mind wouldn't let me place the familiarity within my muddled memories.

"Guide those who seek you out. Embrace your destiny. You must find a way to save Sebastian." The voice was fading, the fog was thinning. I began to feel panicked.

"Save him from what? What do you mean? How can I help him?"

Silence answered me. I wanted to scream.

"I don't know what to do! Please, help me! I can't do this alone," I cried, realizing my fears and admitting my weaknesses aloud. And just as the last wisp of fog unraveled and began to fade away, I heard a voice as thin and airy as the wind breathe into my ear, "David. He is the key."

"David? I don't understand."

But there was no response. I was alone. The light, the cloud, the fog: it was all gone. The dream was over. My eyes flew open.

It was still dark out but a quick glance at my alarm clock told me it was 6am. I flicked on my bedside lamp and rubbed my eyes, a weary ache already building behind them.

David is the key. The words echoed in my mind. What did it mean? And who was it that had invaded my dreams: another of the dead priestesses? Or a different spirit? Could she be trusted?

I slowly sat up, feeling exhausted even after a full night's rest. And that was when I noticed it.

The chair from my writing desk had been pulled out and positioned at the foot of my bed. Someone had sat, watching me again as I slept. Goosebumps prickled all over my skin. I was about to run from the room when I noticed a small object left directly in the center of the chair's seat. I hesitated, then moved towards it.

As I got closer, I recognized it as a tiny charm from a bracelet my father had given me on my tenth birthday. The bracelet had been tucked away in my jewelry box; I hadn't worn it for many years but I had saved it. My hands trembled as I reached for it now.

The charm that had been taken off my old bracelet and left for me on the center of the chair was a small, silver key.

The message was clear. The spirits were watching me still. They had given me the key, now it was time for me to use it. I picked it up with trembling hands and hurriedly put it away back in my jewelry box, out of sight but not out of mind. I knew I had no choice about what to do next. I needed to speak with David.

I knocked on his bedroom door expectantly, with no concern over the early hour. Sebastian had been going running in the mornings lately and though David never went with him, I knew he would be up.

"Sebastian's not here," David called, his voice muffled from inside the room.

I pushed the door open, letting myself in. David looked up in surprise. He was sitting cross-legged on his bed, fully dressed, his hair damp still from the shower.

"I know he's not here. I came to speak with you." I closed the door behind me and sat down across from him on Sebastian's neatly made bed. David eyed me warily.

"Oh? I was under the impression that you did not wish to speak to me. Haven't you been avoiding me lately?" He watched me coolly, his eyes hard, his face expressionless. I refused to be intimidated.

"Yes. But now I'm ready to talk—I need to talk."

"I'm listening."

"It's about Sebastian…" I began.

"Isn't it always?"

I ignored David's interruption and continued.

"I'm worried about him. He's been acting so strangely: always brooding and disappearing on his own. I know he barely sleeps and his headaches are obviously getting worse. He seems so confused and so angry all the time but he won't talk to me about it."

"Grace, I won't betray Sebastian's trust," David warned.

"I'm not asking you to. I just want you to tell me how I can help him." I struggled to speak normally, to resist the nearly overpowering desire to twist a thread of magic through my words, to force him to give me the answer.

"I'm sorry but I don't know. Just give him some time."

I searched David's face, desperately wanting more answers, wanting to unlock the secrets hidden within his mind but I couldn't. I had promised myself I wouldn't. I sighed, disappointed but also irritated. Some "key" he was.

"What's wrong?" David's bright eyes studied me intently. He slid to the edge of his bed, his knees just inches from mine. "I can see there's something else bothering you; it's not just Sebastian. You can trust me, you know."

"I don't know if I can."

He watched me steadily with eyes that were just a little too knowing and definitely too intense. I was starting to feel uncomfortably aware of how close we sat.

"Do you trust yourself?" he asked quietly, his eyes smoldering.

My traitorous heart skipped a beat. Words eluded me as he caught me completely off guard. What did he mean?

A knock at the door made us both turn.

"David, are you up?" Mrs. Jenson called softly from the other side.

He quickly stood and opened the door. Mrs. Jenson stood in the hall, dressed and ready for work, her car keys and purse in hand.

"I'm up," he answered, politely.

"Oh good. There are two young men at the door, asking for you. I would have sent them away but since they insisted they're friends of yours, and we all know you're an early riser… Grace? What are you doing in here?" Mrs. Jenson blurted out in surprise.

I flushed, refusing to acknowledge why I felt guilty. No wonder Mrs. Jenson looked so scandalized. It was just after 6am and I was in my pajamas in David's room.

"I wanted to speak with David privately about something, while Sebastian was out on his run," I explained as honestly as I could.

"Oh… of course," Mrs. Jenson blushed also. She flashed me a quick, apologetic smile.

"I'll go down and see them now," David interrupted. There was an edge of excitement to his words that caught my attention.

"Did David's friends tell you their names?" I asked Mrs. Jenson curiously as he strode off down the hall.

"Yes, Nate and Jay or something like that. Now, I must get going to work. Have a good day, Grace and please…" she hesitated, blushing again. "I don't think you should be in the boys' room with the door closed like that. What would Sebastian have thought?"

"No, you're right. Sorry," I muttered, distracted. Propriety was the least of my worries right now. There was something about those names that just wasn't sitting right. "Wait!" I gasped. Icy cold fear slid down my spine. Mrs. Jenson spun back around. "Were their names Nathaniel and Jai?"

My heart pounded in my ears as I waited for Mrs. Jenson to respond.

"Yes, that sounds about right. Do you know them?" she asked, looking puzzled.

"Which door?"

"Um… the kitchen door but why…"

I took off running before she had finished, sprinting down the stairs. Two of the Others were here, asking for David (their former leader) when they shouldn't even be able to remember his name. Which could mean only one thing: they had their memories back and they might be able to restore David's.

I couldn't let that happen.

Chapter Seven – Stirring Shadows

As I raced through the Jensons' house, I gathered the ancient magic that trembled through out my body and focused it to a small point through the tiny amber heart in my necklace. Niamh's spirit had said that the amber stone wasn't necessary for me to focus my powers anymore but old habits die hard. The pendant throbbed and burned with power, a dagger poised for the kill. As I burst into the kitchen, I was ready for anything.

I skidded around the corner and then froze.

"Grace?" David cocked his head to one side. He was in the process of filling the kettle. Nathaniel and Jai sat at the kitchen table, empty tea cups before them. They both stared at me curiously. Jai smiled, a little too warmly, his large, almond eyes were bright.

"Do you remember me?" I demanded, my voice hard and unfriendly. Nathaniel opened his mouth to speak but I cut him off. "Tell me the truth." My words pierced the air, laced with magic and demanding to be obeyed. Nathaniel paled and dropped his eyes, his messy brown hair falling into his face.

"Not exactly," Jai hedged in his smooth, English accent. He sounded a lot calmer than he looked.

"Manners, Grace," David chastised as he flipped the switch on the kettle. "This is Grace. She and her fiancé, Sebastian, also survived the explosion. We all live together here," he explained to them. He turned back to me. "Jai and Nathaniel have traveled all the way here from Italy. They are also survivors of the explosion at the Necromanteion, though I expect you already knew that. Nathaniel was just telling me how they came across my name and whereabouts before you so rudely interrupted. Tea?"

My eyes were still locked with Jai's. I imagined many secrets were hidden behind them. As it was, the two obviously posed no immediate threat and it wasn't like I couldn't deal with them... if I used the Lost Magic. Despite my readiness to throw all forms of ancient magic and spells at them, I had no desire to do so unless absolutely necessary. I was still trying, perhaps in vain, not to use the magic, not to let it become a part of my life.

"Sure, tea would be good," I murmured, moving slowly to lean against the counter. It felt absurd to be planning on sipping tea while in a room with three of the most dangerous men I could imagine, or they had once been anyway. But I needed answers and I was sure these two had some.

Jai nodded to Nathaniel.

"Well, actually, we only came looking for you, David, to see if you knew the whereabouts of a girl who was also in the explosion. A girl with an amber necklace," Nathaniel spoke quietly, his hair still in his face. I felt all of their eyes go to me, to my hand resting upon the pendant that hung about my neck. Silence settled over the room, the only sound that of the kettle's water slowly bubbling and boiling, steam pouring from its spout. The kettle's sudden shrill whistling broke the tense moment.

"Why were you looking for Grace?" David asked as he moved the kettle off the stove. I hurried to speak before either Jai or Nathaniel could answer.

"How did you find out about David? Didn't you suffer memory loss from the explosion?" I quizzed.

"Yes, we did—we do," Jai quickly corrected. "After the explosion, we were kept in the same room at the hospital, both under observation for several days. We became friends, though we are both fairly certain we were friends before all of this. We left the hospital together and had not only the exact same symptoms—headaches, memory loss, strange dreams—but we also had the same questions."

"I began doing some research," Nathaniel joined in shyly. "We couldn't find any information about the other survivors, except for their ages, genders and injuries. But then I found out someone else had been researching, someone else was asking the same questions that I was: a young man, from Victoria, BC, named David. And so we came to talk to you."

"To see if I could lead you to her?" David nodded his head in my direction as his hands were full carrying the tea and cups to the table.

"We wanted to speak with you, to see if you had any more information than we did. But our prime reason was to find her," Jai finished, his eyes resting on me.

"Why?" David demanded and before I could stop him, Nathaniel spoke.

"Because we both dreamt of her, the same dream. A young woman stood before us in the depths of the Necromanteion, her face hidden in shadows but the torchlight flaring brightly behind her and her amber necklace glowing. And she spoke a vow that echoed in both our minds with the tones of prophecy. She promised to guide us, to give us all the answers we seek, to reveal all the secrets that have been hidden. Then a few nights ago—"

"Stop," I interrupted, my voice firm but without any magical aid. Nathaniel didn't seem to hear me.

"A few nights ago, we both awoke just after midnight and we both felt… different. Strange things have been happening ever since—"

"Stop," I repeated. David's eyes were wide. "You need to leave," I announced, quickly crossing the kitchen and holding open the door. "Now."

"Grace!" David objected but I threw him a glare and surprisingly, he backed down.

"It's you, Grace, we know it's you," Jai declared. "You have the answers we're seeking."

I shook my head.

"I can't help you. You need to leave. Now."

"Please," Nathaniel joined in, his voice soft but pleading. "Grace, we don't understand what's happening but it's all led us to here, to you. Please, help us—guide us."

And it was that one word that pushed me over the edge.

"No! Get out! I didn't ask you to come here. I don't want you here. Go! Just leave me alone," I yelled. Tears of fury shimmered in my eyes as I could feel my life falling apart. Between work, planning a wedding, Sebastian acting so strangely, and all these ghosts and spirits and magic… I just couldn't handle it all. I didn't want any of this!

They were all staring at me; David's face was blank, Jai looked shocked, Nathaniel looked disappointed. I refused to feel ashamed.

"Get out," I repeated in a calmer voice. "Sebastian will be here any minute. You need to be gone before he gets here. I'm not sure what would happen if he saw you but I can almost guarantee it wouldn't be good."

My words brought David back into action.

"She's right. He doesn't want anything to do with the past. Seeing you here might trigger some of his memories, it could send him over the edge. You need to go, now." David stepped forward, shoulders back and dark eyes glaring. Even without magic, he was intimidating and commanding. I was relieved that he was presently on my side.

"Please," Nathaniel whispered, hesitating as he passed me. I just shook my head.

"I can't help you."

"I think we'll stay in Victoria for a while," Jai suddenly announced from just outside the kitchen door. "We'll be waiting, Gracelynn."

And with that, they both walked off. David closed the door behind them and then spun around to face me.

"You remember everything, don't you?" he demanded with a quiet intensity that made my mouth go dry. I didn't see the point in lying anymore.

"Yes."

"Can you restore my memories?"

"I could try, if I wanted to."

"But you don't?" he guessed.

"No, not yet."

"Will you tell me what's going on at least?"

I hesitated. Maybe it was a mistake, but I had no one else to talk to. Sebastian didn't want to hear it but I needed someone to confide in. I wasn't sure if I could do this alone.

"Some of it. I can't trust you with it all."

"I see," he answered haughtily, his eyes and voice growing cold. "And why is it that you get to decide what exactly I should and shouldn't know? Why should you have so much power over what I can and can't remember? Who are you, Grace?"

His eyes burned into mine, molten steel clashing with sapphire ice. I found myself speechless, lost in the fury in his eyes.

The kitchen door opened.

"What's going on?" Sebastian demanded. Sweat clung to his brow and darkened the neck of his shirt. He was still breathing heavily from his run, his eyes alert with adrenaline, darting back and forth between us.

"Nothing," we answered simultaneously, both stepping back.

His eyes moved to the steaming pot of tea and the four cups that were set upon the table.

"Expecting company?"

"We were going to make breakfast," David answered smoothly. "Just waiting for you to get back. I didn't realize you were such a slow runner. Grace, you've put an extra cup out."

It was a frightening reminder how quickly and convincingly he could come up with a lie.

"Oops," I smiled, shrugging it off as I returned the fourth cup to the cupboard. I could feel Sebastian's eyes on me as I moved.

"I'm going to have a shower," Sebastian announced. It felt like he had changed what he was going to say. "Maybe you want to get dressed before breakfast too? I'm sure David can handle the cooking on his own." Sebastian's eyes twinkled with amusement. I assumed he was making reference to my complete ineptness in the kitchen or perhaps he was laughing at me—I'd forgotten I was still in my pajamas. Either way, at least he seemed to be in a good mood.

"Maybe I'll join you in the shower," I teased boldly, hoping to distract him.

David rolled his eyes and turned his back on us but Sebastian smiled back at me wickedly.

"That's a hard offer to turn down, but you aren't Mrs. Caldwood yet," he reminded me as he pulled me close. I leant against his chest, breathing in deeply and filling my lungs with the light, clean scent that always clung to him, despite his run. "And I know you're hiding something, you're an awful liar," he murmured softly into my hair. His voice was a low, seductive purr. "Do I even want to know the truth? I could easily make you talk, if I wanted to."

"Probably not," I whispered back into his ear, aware of David's still silence behind us. "But I'll tell you if you want me to."

He sighed. I shifted back from him to see that his brows had pulled down, a crease appearing between them. Up close I could see the light purple marks shadowing his eyes and the hint of tension to his gaze, as if he were somehow in pain.

"You can have the first shower," he offered as he let me slip from his embrace. "I want to speak with David privately anyway."

I stiffened, my feelings instantly hurt but I tried not to let it show. I had known he wouldn't take me up on my offer, he didn't want to know anything that might have to do with the past. But I was hurt that he wanted to speak privately with David and not with me. Maybe I deserved that. I had, after all, just been caught trying to deceive him and yet still couldn't show any remorse for it. He forced me to keep secrets until he was ready to hear the truth.

"Thanks. I actually shouldn't stay for breakfast, I need to be at the gallery before eight thirty today."

Sebastian nodded, barely acknowledging my words as he poured himself a cup of tea, a frown still on his face. I left the kitchen with a new sadness weighing upon my heart and a sliver of fear piercing my soul. Jai and Nathaniel could both obviously access the Lost Magic, it wouldn't be long before their memories returned. I knew there would be others coming to seek out my guidance too—how could I continue to turn them away? What would happen if I did? Niamh had warned me that some of those who possessed the Lost Magic might be dangerous yet they would still seek me out. How could I put the people I loved, my family, my friends, the Jensons and Sebastian in that kind of danger? Could I hide it all from Sebastian? Could I do this without him? And what was wrong with him? Why did it feel like I was losing him, like he was pulling away from me somehow? What was I supposed to save him from and how?

As I reached my bedroom door, I saw something shiny dangling from the knob. It was the charm bracelet my father had given me. The whole thing hung from my doorknob, its one and only charm—the single, silver key—returned to its place.

I wanted to take it and throw it, to scream at the top of my lungs. But instead, I calmly removed it and dropped it back into my jewelry box in my room. I moved slowly and deliberately, my skin crawling with the sensation of invisible eyes on me.

Once I'd gathered my things for the shower, I paused in my bedroom doorway.

"Don't push me," I hissed back into the empty room, "or I'll push back." And with that, I slammed the door shut, vowing to myself that I would forget about it all. I would not allow the Lost Magic to push its way back into my life. I would not allow it to come between me and Sebastian. I was getting married in just six more weeks and I was certain that if I could just push through, if I could just make it to that day, once Sebastian and I were married, everything would be ok, everything would make sense again. Perhaps it was a childish belief but I clung to it with all my heart.

I was worried Nathaniel and Jai might show up at my work but they never came by the art gallery, even though I would sometimes think I caught a glimpse of them in the busy Victoria streets outside. The demands placed on me by the gallery's curator continued to increase but I enjoyed the added pressure and workload; it kept me busy and my mind off my troubles. It also gave me a good excuse to avoid David, and Sebastian too, since they were usually together. Sebastian said he understood the long hours I was putting in at work, and I had to admit, all the time he was spending with David did seem to be doing him some good. He had apparently started to sleep better, and he was starting to smile more even if it was in a bitter, wry sort of way.

No one else came looking for me over the next two weeks; magical spirits and humans alike left me alone. Sometimes I could tell I was being watched, and once or twice I thought I heard my name whispered on the wind but I was able to push it all away. I didn't want to let the Lost Magic into my life and so I broke my own rule and used the magic to keep it all away. I was starting to think that my bizarre plan might actually work, that I was going to be able to make it to my wedding day without any further setbacks. That Sebastian and I would be together, forever, in the way that we had always dreamt.

There was only a month left before the wedding when my mother called an emergency meeting with Sebastian and I. I was actually grateful for the opportunity, it was the longest we'd been alone together in a few weeks and the perfect excuse to ditch David. Things felt strained between us as we drove in silence over to my mother's house.

"Are you ok?" I asked Sebastian as we turned onto Beach Drive.

"I'm fine," he responded politely, his eyes never straying from the road ahead.

The sky outside was gray and overcast. A winter chill had settled into the air and seemed to invade the space between us. I tried to push my anxiety aside.

"You're not saying much," I commented.

"Just trying to concentrate on driving."

"Oh. Ok." I shifted uncomfortably in my seat. Something was definitely wrong but I didn't know what to say or how to approach the subject. Ever since the day Sebastian had attacked Clarke, I wasn't entirely certain of how to tread around him. He had acted so differently that day, sometimes I felt like he was a stranger to me which was bizarre and untrue but still… "I'm worried, Sebastian. I know we haven't been spending as much time together lately but—"

"I'm sorry," he apologized. He slipped one hand off the wheel and linked his fingers through mine. I relaxed slightly. "We've both just been really busy, that's all. We're good," he reassured me.

"But I don't even know what you've been busy doing." I wished I didn't sound so petulant.

"Oh, the usual: helping David look for work, finding a place for us to live after the wedding, arranging our honeymoon," he added with a grin. The idea immediately brightened my mood. I could tell the thought of our honeymoon had the same effect on him. He squeezed my hand gently, his thumb slowly massaging the back of my hand.

"I didn't realize you were arranging our honeymoon."

"I know, it's supposed to be a surprise. You didn't think I'd let your mother plan that too, did you?"

We both laughed. It felt so good to laugh together.

"I suppose not," I admitted, still smiling. As we settled back into a more comfortable silence, our smiles both slowly faded. "What about you though?" I continued more seriously. "How are you doing? I know you don't like to talk about… what you're going through but is it getting any better?"

Sebastian immediately frowned. He released my hand to make the turn into my mother's driveway, the gates sliding apart as soon as we approached.

"I'll be fine," he dismissed. He had pulled away from me again, his eyes distant, his demeanor cold.

"Are you still getting headaches? And the nightmares, are those getting any better? And the… confusion?" I didn't mention his strange mood swings, I didn't need to. We both knew what I was getting at.

"Don't worry about me. I'm dealing with it, it's getting easier. That's all you need to know—that's all I want you to know," he told me gently but firmly. His eyes looked tired again.

"Ok," I answered quietly. He turned the engine off and got out the car, coming around to open my door for me.

"Come on, your mother's waiting. Let's go face this wedding crisis." He offered me his hand with a smile. I knew he was trying but his eyes weren't sparkling today, they looked as dark and shadowed as a moonless night.

"Ok, let's go," I agreed and I tried to smile back. In the back of my mind, I began to wonder: when did I start having to "try" around Sebastian?

My mother was thrilled to see us, and by thrilled I mean she smiled and was polite towards Sebastian and only criticized my outfit once. The wedding emergency that she had called us over for was all to do with the seating. She had received most of the RSVP's from the three hundred invites she'd sent out. But now she was trying to arrange the seating so that the most important guests sat near the front and all the right people sat together, and divorced couples (like herself and my father) and other enemies were kept apart. It actually was quite complicated.

"Now, Clarke and his wife, Tanya, were supposed to sit with their parents at table six," my mother explained, gesturing to the large seating chart that had been spread out over her long dining room table.

"You invited Clarke?" I glanced at Sebastian nervously but his expression was relaxed and completely impassive.

"Of course I did. The Simons are practically family! Miranda and I have become so close over the past year. And we were all invited to Clarke's wedding," she reminded me. "Besides, you said you had checked the guest list weeks ago before the invitations were even sent out. If you didn't want me to invite him, why didn't you bring it up then?"

I bit my tongue. I couldn't exactly tell her that the guest list sat as an unopened email attachment in my inbox even as we spoke. Instead, I studiously avoided her eye and gazed at the massive seating chart before us. Hundreds of names were spread out before me, patterned around circles that represented the tables and color coded by importance, or menu preference or relation… I wasn't entirely sure and I didn't honestly care. My head swam and the lines and letters blurred before my eyes. Two-thirds of the names I didn't even recognize, my heart began to sink. Was this really what I wanted? At the head of the chart were mine and Sebastian's names, seated at our very own table accompanied by David, Sebastian's Best Man, and…

"Bridgette?" I spoke aloud, interrupting something my mother had been saying. I tapped the name written in flowing cursive, silver ink beside mine. "Bridgette Kaiser?"

My mother glared at me.

"Yes, she's your Maid of Honor. Grace Lynn Stevenson have you looked over a single thing that I've sent you?" My mother spoke softly and sharply, her lips tightening to show the thin lines around her mouth.

"I have but…" I rapidly searched my mind for a believable semi-truth. "There's just been so much going on lately and I'm still having headaches. My memory's just not what it used to be. I just… my Maid of Honor? I haven't seen her since I was sixteen, Mother."

Her expression barely softened. I glanced to Sebastian for help but he was looking down at the chart, his brows pulled down and his lips muttering silently. My mother's gaze burned into me for a moment longer before she finally spoke.

"Sebastian has a Best Man, you must have a Maid of Honor to balance the wedding party; it simply won't look right otherwise. You've said it yourself, Bridgette was like a little sister to you while you stayed with the Kaisers in Berlin. And you've kept in touch over the years."

"Yes, through Christmas cards and the occasional email. I haven't heard from her in months." Actually, that wasn't true. Bridgette had sent me a birthday card and had emailed me several times over the past few months. I'd been so preoccupied with everything going on, I hadn't yet answered her. I shifted uncomfortably.

"Well, sadly she's the closest thing to a friend that you have, Grace. She was thrilled when I told her she was to be your Maid of Honor. Her parents have even been discussing flying her out here a few days early so that she might help you prepare. The girl completely adores you, Grace. And she'll compliment you perfectly at the altar: she's much shorter and plainer than you," my mother added matter-of-factly.

We were interrupted by Ellen's sudden entrance. I couldn't help but appreciate her timing.

"There are two young people here for Ms. Grace," Ellen announced, her eyes glaring down her hooked nose disapprovingly at me.

All eyes shifted to me. Even Sebastian looked up, his eyes suddenly bright and focused. Unease crept down my spine.

"Why are your friends suddenly calling upon you at my house?" my mother demanded, obviously annoyed. "I have better things to do than take phone messages for you all day. This is getting ridiculous! Send them away."

"You've been getting calls? From who?"

"I don't know, they never leave their names," she dismissed. "Go answer the door and come back quickly—we're not finished here."

Sebastian and I locked gazes.

"Do you want me to come with you?" he asked, his voice low, his expression, dangerous. Did he know something?

"No," I answered, a little too quickly. "I'll be right back."

I followed Ellen to the front door, my nerves increasing by the second. I knew this couldn't be good. Two people stood in the entranceway, one I instantly recognized, the other was unfamiliar to me. The Lost Magic prickled all over my skin. I was instantly focused and alert.

"Thank you, Ellen. That will be all," I dismissed, my eyes never leaving the couple for an instant. I waited until she was out of sight before speaking again. "Hello, Lily. Who's your friend?"

Lily's large, brown eyes widened, her full lips parting slightly. I remembered the last time I had seen her, in the chilling depths of the Necromanteion, flickering torchlight throwing shadows across her face as she coldly pronounced my death.

"How do you know my name?" she asked quietly in a soft, full voice.

I had forgotten she wouldn't remember me.

"Why are you here?" My voice was cold and unfriendly, it echoed around the room though I had barely spoken louder than a whisper.

The man beside her cleared his throat. He was older, in his early to mid-thirties if I had to guess. He had dirty blonde hair and sported a shaggy goatee. His clothes fit loosely on his thin frame and he was dressed as if he were twenty years older. He looked distinctly out of place in my mother's grand entranceway, standing on the shiny marble beside Lily, the exotic Hawaiian beauty.

"My name is Jeremy," he began in a surprisingly clear voice. His eyes were sharp, his tones crisp. I immediately found myself re-evaluating him. "We've traveled a long way to meet you, Grace and please, don't try to deny that's who you are. The power is practically radiating from you."

The crystal in the chandelier overhead trembled as if for effect.

"I don't know what you're talking about," I lied.

"There are others, Grace, from all over the world. We're gathering here, in the city. We are drawn to you as the sun's heat and warmth directs the seedling's path to the sky. Guide us," he whispered, his words too intense, his eyes manic.

I flinched at his choice of words. I started to panic.

"You're wrong."

"No," Lily argued, recovering her voice. She spoke softly, her words hushed, almost awed. "You haunt our dreams—*all* of us. Each day it becomes clearer, each passing moment… The closer we are to you… I think I remember—"

"Stop," I interrupted. They both froze, barely breathing. "You've made a mistake. I'm not the one you're looking for—I can't be. Go back to wherever you came from. Tell the others you were wrong."

Lily's long, black lashes fluttered rapidly, disbelievingly. Jeremy shook his head.

"No. We need you, you're the only one who can help us. Please?" he begged, his eyes still wild.

I hesitated. Part of me wanted to help them, wanted to be the person they thought I was. But how could I without Sebastian? How could I go to them when it might mean losing him? Jeremy made me wary, I could sense that he wasn't quite stable and I knew I shouldn't send him away. But if I refused to guide them, if I refused to teach them how to use the Lost Magic then they would never learn more than what they stumbled upon on their own. Their magic would be useless, wouldn't it? The others could only pose a threat if I let them, if I taught them. So perhaps the solution really was to do nothing, to turn them all away and let the magic be forgotten once more.

"I can't. I'm getting married in three weeks and I… I can't help you."

Lily's face fell, Jeremy's tightened. His fists clenched, his eyes narrowed, his whole posture changed. Alarm bells went off in my head as I desperately tried to placate him.

"Perhaps after the wedding, things might be different. In a month, I'll find you—"

"You selfish, spoiled little bitch," Jeremy spat. "You're too busy to help us, to fulfill your destiny because you want to play bride first?"

"You seem remarkably well-informed," I commented, sounding much calmer than I felt. I noticed Lily looked confused. "What do you know about my destiny?"

"Wouldn't you like to know?" he sneered. "You'll live to regret this, Grace. Or perhaps... you won't." A smile twisted his lips that was truly terrifying. The Lost Magic tingled under my skin, my whole body buzzing with energy that was begging to be released.

"If you ever threaten her again, I will kill you," Sebastian announced, suddenly appearing behind me. I jumped at the harsh sound of his voice. "Slowly," he promised, the cruelty in his eyes flooding them with darkness and obscuring any light. Lily and I gasped almost simultaneously.

Jeremy took a small step back, his eyes locked with Sebastian. Something seemed to pass between them, a silent communication. Jeremy paled and gave a small, curt nod.

"Let's go," he instructed Lily.

Lily risked one last, fleeting glance at me before slipping out the door. Jeremy hesitated, his too-bright eyes meeting mine.

"This isn't over," he murmured.

"Out!" Sebastian thundered, his voice echoing about the entranceway so loud I wanted to cover my ears. The click of the door closing sounded loud in the silence that followed. I could feel his eyes on me.

"How much did you..." I began to ask.

"That man is dangerous. I want you to stay away from him," he cut in coldly. His eyes were as hard and unyielding as ice. I bristled at his tone.

"I don't plan on going anywhere near him. Or her," I added.

"Good." He turned and started walking back towards the dining room. I found myself hurrying after him.

"Aren't you going to ask me who they were?"

He didn't even turn to answer me.

"No."

"Sebastian…" I grabbed his hand, forcing him to turn and face me. "How much did you hear?"

"Not much. Your mother asked me to check that you were sending your guests away. As I walked in, I heard that man say, "you'll live to regret this". I saw the way he was looking at you… it was difficult to control my temper for a moment. I'm sorry." The crease between his brows reappeared, a warm shade of blue began to glow within the blackness of his eyes. He sighed. "Were they friends of yours?"

I could tell he didn't really want to know how I knew them, but he knew I wanted him to ask. I needed to explain, as much as I could, anyway.

"She was an old acquaintance. I'm not sure about the older guy, Jeremy. They needed help but it's not the kind of help I can give them, at least not now… Or maybe I should have…"

"No," he answered firmly but softly. "Friends don't show up on your doorstep demanding help and then threatening you when you say you can't. They're trouble, Grace. Please, stay away from them— I mean it. I don't need to know who they are or what they wanted, but I can tell you that much. Whatever they need they can get it from somewhere else."

I nodded my silent agreement. Guilt was still gnawing at my stomach.

"Come on, your mother's waiting," he reminded me gently. He linked his fingers through mine, leading me down the hall. I knew I was a selfish coward but it was so easy to follow him. He was my future; I had to leave everything else behind me.

It took hours to figure out the seating chart with my mother and she refused to let us leave until it was all completed to her satisfaction. I was certain it was punishment for not having read all of the wedding related emails she sent me. I supposed overlooking the guest list was a pretty big slip-up.

"So what's this Bridgette like?" Sebastian asked as we drove back home.

"Young," I answered without thinking. He raised an eyebrow. "She was thirteen when I lived with them," I explained. "She really was like a little sister, I suppose, trapped within a very similar life: wealthy parents trying to climb the social ladder, high expectations and sheltered lifestyle."

"Sheltered within a mansion?" A smile pulled at Sebastian's lips.

"Something like that," I admitted. "My only communication with her over the years has been through largely superficial emails. She tells me about her friends, the parties she goes to, the people she knows, and spends a lot of time complaining about her parents; typical teenaged stuff."

"Typical mega-rich, high society teenaged stuff," Sebastian corrected.

"That's getting old."

He grinned back at me.

We were at the Jensons' house now, it was after eleven and all the lights were off, the house encased in the pitch black of an icy, moonless night. We didn't bother switching on any lights as we were both headed straight upstairs to bed. Sebastian reached to help me out of my thick, winter coat, his fingers brushing against the nape of my neck and sending an electric charge through me. I gasped and he paused. I could sense him so clearly in the darkness, his steady breathing, the smell of his clothes, the warmth that constantly radiated out from him. The night-blindness had made me hyper-aware.

Slowly and purposely, he placed a hand to each side of my face. It was too dark to even see him this close but I could feel his eyes on me and I recognized the burning hunger in them. Something within me responded and I slipped my arms around his waist, pulling myself against him. I suddenly felt too warm, heat erupting all over my body. His warm, gentle exhale tickled against my ear. My hands tightened in response as I pressed myself even closer to him, my heart pounding loud in my ears.

His hands slid down either side of my neck, his fingertips lingering on my collarbone. His fingers spread and he gently slipped my coat from my shoulders. The cool air was a relief but it wasn't enough, I was burning up from the inside out. I rose on my tiptoes, my lips seeking his. With a quick inhale of his breath, my lips parted and our mouths pressed together.

I closed my eyes though it made no difference, I could see nothing in this darkness. Nothing else seemed to exist. All there was in the world was his body and mine and the overwhelming desire that raged within me.

"Come up to my room," I whispered though my voice sounded much too loud and breathy. I needed him so badly right then I couldn't think straight. My heart beat even more quickly.

"Ok." His agreement caught me by surprise even though it was the answer I had been hoping for. Before I could think it over his lips crushed against mine again and I was burning up with desire, all rational thought and reason chased from my mind.

He carried me upstairs as if I were already his bride. My heart raced. I was almost his wife and right now, almost felt perfectly good enough.

Chapter Eight – Lost

THE BED SHEETS FELT COOL UNDER MY unnaturally hot skin but it was only a moment's relief as he lay down right alongside me, his body throbbing with heat. I slid my hands beneath his shirt, enjoying every inch of smooth, warm skin as I pulled his shirt up and over his head. Mine quickly followed, tossed aside without thought or embarrassment. I was thrilled by the sensation of his skin against mine. He kissed my neck almost roughly but I still couldn't get enough. I twisted my fingers tightly into his hair, pulling him even closer. I gasped as I felt his hands on me, so strong and steady, gently massaging, teasing, making me arch my back and writhe in pleasure beneath his touch.

Everything was going too fast but I couldn't stop. Being with him like this, it was exhilarating and intoxicating… I couldn't think straight.

His hands slid back up to my face. He kissed me slowly and deeply, leaving me gasping for more. I arched my hips up to meet him as he began unbuttoning my jeans. My whole body burned and trembled in anticipation but for some reason, I started to question what we were about to do. The heat began to cool.

"I'm an idiot," I mumbled into the darkness.

"No, you're not," he whispered. He bent his head and kissed his way down my torso, his lips slowly trailing across my waist, making his way from one hip to the other as he began gently tugging my pants down.

I moaned softly, half in pleasure, half at my own stupid self, as I gently placed my hands over his, stilling his movements.

"We should stop," I whispered, hating myself for every word I spoke.

"No, we shouldn't."

I blinked into the darkness in surprise. He began kissing his way back up my stomach, all the way up to the side of my neck, one hand slowly trailing behind his lips. It was very hard to focus, very hard to think straight, especially when he was the one usually reminding me that we had to slow things down. I wasn't used to this role.

He began kissing me again, very convincingly.

"Sebastian," I moaned. His lips broke free from mine and began teasing at the edge of my jaw, his tongue flicking. "Why are you making this so hard?"

He laughed softly against my skin and I shivered.

"Because I don't want to stop."

"I don't either," I sighed but then I refocused. "But we should. Just three more weeks…"

"Too long," he murmured. His lips found mine again, silencing me for several more minutes. The passion building between us was so intense, it was starting to scare me. His kisses grew more urgent, my heart beat even faster. His hand slid back down over my waist, gently tugging my jeans even lower on my hips.

"Stop," I breathed.

"No." He didn't even pause.

"Sebastian," I warned gently, no longer amused by this game. His hands squeezed my hips tightly, almost painfully.

"I want you." His voice was husky in the darkness, the hunger in it clear. "I need you. You know you want this too."

"I do, but not now, not tonight. Sebastian, stop." I pushed his hands off me, my passion shifting from desire to frustration.

"No."

I couldn't believe my ears. He shifted from my side to overtop of me so that his whole body was pressing down against mine, pinning me to the bed. He started kissing my neck again as his hand slid down over the curve of my waist but this time I was having none of it.

"I said, stop!"

I shoved him as hard as I could, flipping him not only off me but right off the bed and onto the floor. He hit the ground with a thud. Flicking on my bedside lamp I turned to glare at him, and my breath immediately caught in my throat.

"Damn it, Grace!" he growled, kneeling on the floor beside my bed. He was shirtless, his muscles tight and flexed and perfect in every way. His hair was mussed, his eyes were smoldering, glaring at me with an indescribable heat. And even then, when I was so angry with him, I was also nearly breathless with desire.

Without breaking eye contact, he pushed himself up onto the bed and crawled forward, his movements slow and precise, predatory. His eyes were black coals, burning into mine, reigniting the fire within me. He paused, half-leaning over me and suddenly I desperately wanted him to kiss me again and at the same time, I was terrified he would because I knew that this time, neither of us would be able to stop. He looked so angry and fierce, so passionate and wild. I had never seen this side to him before and it was both incredibly sexy and intimidating. I wasn't sure what was right or wrong anymore or what I truly needed or wanted, all I knew was one thing.

"I love you," I whispered, surrendering myself to his will. I could no longer deny him.

He blinked. The fire in his eyes cooled, a deep and gentle blue flooded their black depths. He pulled back. Relief and disappointment mingled together in my stomach.

He swore loudly, turning away from me. He jumped up off the bed and punched one of the thick, canopy posts so hard the whole room seemed to shake. "What's wrong with me?" he muttered. His hands trembled, the fist he had just driven into the post was already bright red across his knuckles.

"Sebastian, calm down."

He shook his head and swore again, running his fingers through his messy hair. "You can't do that to me, Grace." He turned to me with eyes full of pain that I couldn't understand. "I almost lost control. I don't think you understand."

"No, I do. When I'm with you like that, it's hard for me to think straight too."

"It wasn't hard to think straight, that's just it! I knew exactly what

I was doing. You don't understand, Grace. If you only knew…" his words trailed off and he turned his back, hiding his face from me. I slid to the side of the bed, reaching for his hand.

"Tell me then. I want to understand what's going on with you," I implored.

"No," he whispered without turning back. "I'm sorry, I can't." He let my hand drop. "I'm going for a walk."

"What? Now? It's nearly midnight."

He shrugged.

"It's not like I was going to sleep anyway. The nightmares will have to wait for now."

He sounded so bitter, so strange.

"Sebastian, I'm really worried about you. Look, we need to talk—both of us. There are things we've been keeping from one another and I think it's past time we both just sat and listened." The words felt right as I spoke them, I knew it was time. Time to come clean, time for him to remember, time to confide in one another as we should have been doing all along. But he shook his head, he moved towards the door.

"I'm sorry, Gracelynn. I can't."

"Sebastian, come back!" I called but it was too late, he'd already gone.

I lay awake for a long time, waiting and listening for the sounds of Sebastian returning home but I never heard them. Eventually, I fell asleep but my dreams offered me no rest. I was worried about Sebastian and terrified of how things felt like they were changing between us. And I couldn't forget Jeremy either, and his anger when I had turned him away.

I awoke in the morning with a word already on my lips.

"Gracelynn," I whispered to myself. *Gracelynn, Gracelynn, Gracelynn.* The room whispered it back to me. The soft, dry voices that spoke in my ear real or imagined, I didn't know nor did I care. "He called me Gracelynn," I realized aloud. Sebastian had called me Gracelynn, a name he hadn't used since before the explosion, before his memories were erased.

What did it mean?

Had he remembered? Had Sebastian recovered some of his memories after all? And if he had remembered, then what was the problem? Was there any way that he could, perhaps, have a natural ability to use the Lost Magic? Had there been something, some sign that perhaps I'd missed? My heart said no, but I wanted to believe so badly, I needed to give myself some hope. I knew I had to talk to him but when I went to his room, he wasn't there.

I hurried downstairs to find David and both of the Jensons in the kitchen.

"Where's Sebastian?" I demanded.

David rolled his eyes.

"Morning run, I would expect," he drawled lazily.

"He must have been up early this morning," Mr. Jenson commented. "I've been up since 5am and haven't seen him."

"I don't think he slept very well last night," David replied, glancing quickly at me. Relief settled over me—good, he had come back from his walk at some point.

"Would you like breakfast, Grace?" Mrs. Jenson offered. She was flipping French toast in a frying pan and the kitchen smelled of cinnamon and browned butter. I glanced at the clock.

"I have to be at the gallery in less than an hour. I'm not sure I have time."

"Sit down and eat, dear," Mrs. Jenson encouraged. "It'll only take you a few minutes and I'll put some coffee in a to-go cup for you."

"Thank you."

The Jensons smiled at me, their calm, gentle ways so reassuring. I couldn't relax. I just couldn't shake the feeling that something was wrong.

Sebastian didn't make it back before I had to leave for work. I wanted to ask David to get him to call me when he came in but he had disappeared somewhere while I was in the shower. I settled for sending a quick text message to the phone that Sebastian never seemed to check.

I love you. Missed you this morning. We need to talk tonight.

I hit send and then dropped my phone in my purse. I was running late.

I didn't have time to check my phone again until after lunch. There was one new message which I opened eagerly—only to discover that it was the text I had sent Sebastian, returned to my phone with "unable to send" attached to it. I tried to resend it and once again it didn't go through. With a growing sense of unease, I tried to call his cell. I was immediately greeted by the recorded voice of the operator, informing me that "this number is no longer in service". Something was definitely wrong.

I couldn't leave work but I knew I wouldn't be able to focus if I didn't do something, so reluctantly, I dialed David's number. He also didn't answer but I left him a voicemail, asking that he call me back and have Sebastian call me immediately if he saw him. It was all I could do for now.

I was the last one left in the gallery that evening but was proud to have been entrusted with the important task of locking everything up myself. It was dark when I stepped outside and ice had already formed a slick surface, transforming the parking lot into a sparkling rink. A frigid breeze gusted past me, nearly knocking me off my feet and tiny, delicate snowflakes swirled through out the air as they started lightly falling from the sky. I stepped slowly and cautiously, irritated that when I was in such a rush to get home I would be forced to drive slowly.

When I finally pulled into the Jensons' driveway I was relieved to see Sebastian's car parked ahead of me. The snow was starting to stick now and it was good to know that he wasn't out driving in it. But then I noticed the driveway beneath his car was bare, he obviously hadn't left since it started snowing. Had he not left the house today? What was going on?

My nervousness increased as the front door opened just before I reached it. Mrs. Jenson stood there, looking uncomfortable.

"Hello, Grace. Um… I thought I should warn you, dear. Your mother's here," she announced unexpectedly. The news completely distracted me.

"What? Why? What's going on?"

"She's brought a guest with her. Someone who just couldn't wait to see you and meet Sebastian… where is Sebastian?" She searched the empty driveway behind me in confusion. My heart dropped.

"He's not here?"

"No, we thought he was with you."

"I was working late. I haven't seen him since last night."

My voice trembled slightly. Mrs. Jenson smiled at me, patting my hand reassuringly as she led me inside, though she too looked worried.

"I'm sure he's fine, dear, just busy. David's been gone all day too: they must be out together, causing trouble as boys do."

I tried to smile but it was a weak effort.

"Don't worry," she repeated just as my mother walked around the corner.

"Don't worry about what?" my mother demanded, her small eyes immediately narrowing. Mrs. Jenson waited for me to answer.

"I haven't seen Sebastian all day and I can't get through on his cell phone; it says the number has been disconnected."

"Oh, Grace, you can go a day without seeing him, really! In just a few weeks, you'll be seeing him every day for the rest of your life. You might as well enjoy this time apart while you have it," my mother dismissed. She smoothed back her short, blonde hair with one hand, drawing attention to the sparkling diamond earrings at her lobes and throat. She had never come to the Jensons' house before and in all her snobbish finery she looked completely out-of-place. In fact, she seemed even more done-up than usual. I wondered what the occasion was?

"Sebastian often forgets he owns a cell phone, Grace," Mrs. Jenson gently reminded me. "I wouldn't be surprised if he forgot to pay the bill. He's been quite distracted lately. Don't worry, I'm sure the boys will be home soon."

"Come, come," my mother instructed, speaking over Mrs. Jenson. She eyed me critically, brushing snowflakes from my hair and inspecting my outfit. "There's someone waiting to see you in the living room."

"It's not Clarke, is it?"

"Why on earth would you ask that? Clarke and Tanya are actually still in Jamaica. They've been having so much fun, Miranda's barely heard from them! Except for an email announcing that they've decided to extend their honeymoon for several more weeks. I already told you all this, Grace, don't you ever listen anymore?"

There was no safe way to answer that so I chose not to respond.

"Come, say hello," my mother instructed, practically dragging me around the corner and into the Jensons' cozy living room.

"Grace?"

A young woman was sitting near the lit fireplace. She rose as I entered, her slim brows arched, her brown eyes large and round. It took me a minute to recognize her; there was nothing short or plain about the girl who stood before me. She was tall and slim, and beautiful in a very distinct way. Her makeup was simple but flawless, emphasizing her green eyes that looked a little too large for her small face and distracting from her slightly snub nose and overly full lips. Her long, brown hair was loose and fell in waves so perfectly and precisely formed there was no way it had occurred naturally. Her clothes were stylish and obviously expensive; I recognized the black and white sweater she wore from a fashionable boutique my mother had dragged me into recently. She held a gold, patterned clutch in her hands, a Louis Vuitton symbol peeking out from under her shiny, manicured nails.

Everyone was staring at me expectantly, waiting for my reaction. Mr. Jenson smiled encouragingly. I remembered this young woman as a shy, intelligent, pretty little girl. The only similarities between the beautiful teenager who stood before me and the girl of my memories was the hesitant smile she offered me now.

"Bridgette. Wow. I can't believe you're here!" I forced myself to smile, trying to forget about Sebastian. We shared a quick embrace. "What are you doing here? The wedding's not for three more weeks!"

"I know, but I couldn't wait! Since your mother asked permission for me to come and be your Maid of Honor, I've hardly been able to stop thinking about you. I had to come. And since I'm doing that distance education thing, I convinced my father that it would be alright to come early and bring my school work with me. I'm staying at The Queens Hotel; my father has booked me a gorgeous suite for the next few weeks." She spoke confidently, holding her head high and tossing her long hair over her shoulder. Bridgette had attended a bilingual high school and she spoke English perfectly with just the faintest trace of her German accent.

"You're doing a distance education thing? Is that like home school?"

"Sort of… didn't you read my last email?" She looked hurt for a second, her eyes widened, her pout deepened.

"I did," I lied, "but I've been so busy lately with work and the wedding and everything else that's going on, I must have forgotten." It was my usual excuse but one people seemed to accept. Bridgette didn't look entirely convinced.

"Oh, yes, of course. I hardly have any free time either," she added, her mood quickly changing to dismissive. She tossed her glossy hair again, rings sparkling on her fingers and a Cartier watch decorating her wrist. "We have so much catching up to do. You'll have to come and meet Lena, my chaperone and tutor. And I can't wait to tell you about all the adventures I've been having: shopping in Paris, meeting royalty, and my new boyfriend." Her green eyes sparkled, I tried to share her happiness.

"Why don't we all have lunch at my house tomorrow? Grace, you can bring Sebastian. Then afterwards, you can take Bridgette to her dress fitting and catch up," my mother suggested.

"That would be nice," I agreed but I was barely listening. I was distracted by the sound of the front door opening. My heart leapt into my throat. I craned my neck, trying to peer down the hallway to see who it was. I was disappointed to see only David.

"Hello," David greeted politely as he walked into the room. His eyes immediately went to Bridgette, taking her in from head to toe and lingering just a little too long.

"This is my friend, Bridgette," I informed him, suddenly feeling protective. It was true, I had once thought of Bridgette as a little sister and no matter how much she had changed, I still felt the instinct to look out for her. "She'll be staying here in Victoria until the wedding—she's my Maid of Honor. And she's sixteen."

The gleam in David's eye faded. He smiled, almost apologetically.

"How nice to meet you, Bridgette."

"Yes, you too." She held out her hand expectantly and David smoothly leant over to kiss it. I threw Bridgette a withering look but she wasn't looking at me, she only had eyes for David. Mrs. Jenson and my mother shared knowing, amused smiles.

"Where's Sebastian?" I demanded. I felt like I had been asking the same question all day.

"How should I know?"

The Jensons were both frowning now. Worry ate away at my stomach. I completely ignored Bridgette and focused all of my attention on David.

"You weren't with him? Didn't you get my message? He's been missing all day. I haven't seen or heard from him since late last night—after we got back from my mother's."

Now David was frowning too.

"Didn't you see him this morning?" he demanded.

"No, you said *you* saw him this morning. You said he went for a run," I reminded him. I had a really bad feeling and was starting to feel sick.

David's eyes flicked between myself, my mother and the Jensons. He looked distinctly uncomfortable, an unfamiliar look for him when he was typically so cool and self assured.

"What's going on, David?" Mr. Jenson joined in. His features were still pulled down in concern. "Have you seen Sebastian today or not? Do you know where he is?"

"No. I… I didn't actually see him this morning," he admitted. My stomach dropped, icy fear filling the empty space within me. "I, uh, I heard him and Grace talking in her room last night. There were some unusual noises coming through the wall, I assumed he spent the night with her. I was just trying to cover for you this morning," he added, turning to me apologetically.

My face burned red hot. By 'unusual noises' he obviously meant the bumps and thuds of me throwing Sebastian off the bed and Sebastian punching the bed post. I couldn't exactly explain that, not that it was my biggest concern anyway.

"Grace Lynn Stevenson!" my mother cried, sounding scandalized.

"He didn't spend the night in my room. We were just talking and we got into an argument. He was upset and he left around midnight, he said he was going for a walk... Oh no." My voice was rapidly losing strength, my words barely louder than a whisper as I finished. Everyone seemed to hear me. The silence that followed rang in my ears. I wanted to throw up.

"I'm calling the police," Mrs. Jenson announced, abruptly leaving the room.

"Grace, stay here—keep trying his phone and call anywhere that you think he might have gone today," Mr. Jenson instructed, quickly taking charge. "David, come with me. We'll take the Audi, it has all wheel drive and should be good in the snow. We'll check his usual spots."

"I want to come with you," I objected.

"No, you should stay here, Grace. If we find him... he might be in rough shape," David told me quietly and seriously. Mr. Jenson shot him a warning look.

"What do you mean?" My heart was beating too quickly, my breathing shallow. I wondered if I were about to faint.

"She should know," David said to Mr. Jenson, who slowly nodded his agreement.

"Grace," Mr. Jenson began, his eyes large and kind. He gently took my hands. "Sebastian has been going through a lot since you came back from Greece, as I'm sure you've noticed. He's fighting a very serious depression. He didn't want you to know, only because he didn't want to worry you and he was so sure that he could get a handle on it but... it's very serious Grace. He's been having some suicidal thoughts."

My mouth dropped open.

"No," I gasped, shaking my head. I couldn't believe my ears. "He wouldn't... he would never..." But the truth was, I didn't really know what Sebastian would and wouldn't do anymore.

I began shaking all over, my whole body violently trembling.

"Calm down, Grace, it's going to be ok." I was surprised to find my mother comforting me. Bridgette sat silently, wide-eyed in the corner. I didn't need my mother's stiff words and awkward touch, I wasn't upset—I was furious. How dare he go through something like this without ever telling me? How dare he confide in others? Confide in David and not me! And how could he ever even remotely consider the possibility of harming himself or taking his own life! No, there was no way. I wouldn't allow it. There was no way I would lose him just like that.

"Sit down, Grace. You're shaking all over," my mother instructed. She tried to push me into a chair but I shook off her hands.

My whole body vibrated with anger, pain, fear, and pure, raw ancient power. I clasped my necklace tightly in one fist, its smooth, round shape fitting perfectly in the palm of my hand. The small piece of amber at its center burned red hot.

"No." Everyone turned to stare at me. "No!" I repeated louder and ran out of the room. I rushed out the front door, breathing heavily, my head spinning. "This is not happening. I will not allow you to hurt yourself. This is enough!" I yelled to the darkness, my voice tormented with pain. I harnessed the indescribable power within me and focused it through my necklace, directing it to flood out into the night as I screamed desperately, "I want you to come home! I want you to be fine and I want you to come home!"

The torrent of invisible magic poured from me and filled the air. It sliced through the quiet night as a boom of thunder, reverberating all around me. The electric charge of it remained in the silence that followed, causing all of my hair to stand on end.

My shaking had stopped, my voice was raw from screaming and my knees weak from the huge amount of power I had just embraced. I tried to take a step forward but my knees buckled, and I collapsed to the ground like a puppet whose strings had been cut. I hated using the Lost Magic when I had promised myself I wouldn't but in this situation, I had no regrets. It was worth it to save Sebastian, anything was worth it to keep him safe.

"I'll do whatever you ask of me," I whispered to the spinning sky. I knew somewhere, the spirits were listening. I could sense them in the shadows at the edge of my thoughts. "Just bring him back to me." And with those last words, I tumbled into the waiting darkness.

Chapter Nine – Allies

EVEN IN UNCONSCIOUSNESS, THERE WAS NO ESCAPE for me, there was no respite. The fog rolled in, thick and icy, soft and warm. It surrounded me.

"Caoilinn," she called, her voice echoing all around.

"Leave me alone," I growled.

"Caoilinn, I don't have long. I'm here to help, if you can swallow your damned pride long enough to let me!"

That caught my attention. I glared into the misty cloud.

"My name is Gracelynn. And I don't have time for your games, spirit. Leave me alone."

I spoke loudly and clearly but once again, my voice seemed to bounce back off the cloud as if I were speaking directly into my own ear. There was a long pause, for a minute I thought she might have actually listened to me.

"This is no game. You can still save Sebastian but you're going to have to fight for him and you will need to accept the aid offered by others."

"He should be home when I open my eyes. I summoned him with my magic. I don't need your help," I denied.

"It won't work, he's too far gone." Her voice echoed all around me, sending shivers down my spine.

"You're wrong!" I yelled, my voice sharp with anger, my stomach twisted with fear. "Where is he? What do you know? What have you done to him?"

"He has been taken from you but not by any of the spirit world. He is in grave danger; you should not fear for his life, you should fear for his very soul! He has been taken where even I can't reach him but you might be able to. If you'll accept the others who wait for you, if you will guide them."

"Is that what this is about? You've taken Sebastian somewhere to try to manipulate me into fulfilling my promise? I already said I'd do it. I'll do whatever you need me to but I swear, if you don't leave him out of this you will all regret this. Living or dead, I will hold you accountable."

"You don't know what you're saying, you idiot. Be careful!" she snapped, her voice cracking through the air all around me. The fog swirled in irritation. "The blame does not lie with the dead, Grace-lynn; we're only trying to help you. But you can't do this alone and your magic won't be strong enough without assistance. You don't know what you're up against."

I hated her, whoever she was. I didn't want to believe her but I sensed that she spoke the truth. And it made me even angrier.

"How can I find him?" I asked quietly, bitterly.

"David, he is the key," the voice echoed around me. I could feel the spirit's presence pulling away.

"What does that even mean?" I cried out in frustration.

"Ask him. Ask David Turner to help you. Guide them."

My jaw dropped.

"David Turner? Is that David's full name? Does that mean… does he have the ability to use the Lost Magic? Has he been hiding it from me?"

"David… he is the key…"

The voice faded away and the fog thinned around me, the tendrils slowly unfurled and drifted apart in wispy waves. I could feel my physical body stirring, my mind struggling to awaken.

"I'll find him," I promised the fading light as darkness crept in around me. "I will save Sebastian. And I will take revenge against those who have taken him from me."

I opened my eyes to find myself upstairs in my bed. My skin crawled as I realized someone must have carried me there, and that David was the only one likely to be strong enough to do so. I had been left in the dark but the faint glow of light was coming in from under my door, I moved towards it. Slowly and quietly, I crept out of my room and over to the top of the stairs. The Jensons were still awake and were talking downstairs, just beyond my sight. Their hushed voices floated up to my ears.

"We looked through everything in his room and Grace's. There's no sign of a note or any indication that he was planning on harming himself or running away," Mr. Jenson murmured.

"The police won't do anything until he's been missing for over 72 hours and even then, he's considered an adult now... Oh, Don, I'm so afraid." Mrs. Jenson's voice was strangled as if she were fighting tears.

"It'll be ok, Shauna. We need to be strong—for Grace. Just imagine what she's going through. She didn't even know how bad he'd gotten. Perhaps we should have told her sooner, despite his wishes."

Yes, you should have, I thought bitterly, but my anger was only half-hearted. I couldn't blame the Jensons. I knew they loved Sebastian as if he were their own son. They had only done what they thought was right. They had only done what he asked. And in truth, I had realized for some time that something was seriously wrong with Sebastian. I had just been trying to ignore it, trying to pretend everything was going to be fine. I think Sebastian and I had both wanted to believe it, even if we never truly had. Fear chilled my heart as I recalled the spirit's warning, that I should fear not just for his life but for his very soul. The situation was much more dire than any of us had realized. How would I find him? How would I save him?

"Hear anything interesting?" David remarked from behind me. He spoke in a low, soft voice but even so, I scowled, holding a finger over my lips. The voices below us had fallen silent. "Come," he whispered, gesturing for me to follow. Warily, I tiptoed after him down the hall to the room he shared with Sebastian.

He sat down on his bed, I sat on Sebastian's. We stared at each other in silence, both expressionless, both waiting for the other to speak. Finally, I could take it no more.

"I'm tired of playing these bullshit games, David. I need the truth. I want you to tell me the truth." I released a thread of magic, weaving it around my words to ensure that he could not disobey them. It made me angry that I had to resort to using magic but my choices were limited, my hands bound. I would do anything and everything to get Sebastian back.

David's expression didn't change for a second.

"The truth for the truth," he finally offered. I nodded my agreement.

"Do you know where Sebastian is?"

"No. The Jensons are worried that he might have harmed himself or run away but, I don't think he did."

"He didn't," I stated flatly. David tilted his head to one side curiously but I didn't pause. "How much of the past do you remember?"

He opened his mouth as if to speak and then closed it again. He shrugged.

"Not much."

"How much? Tell me exactly what you remember."

His eyes narrowed, his gaze hardened. He began speaking slowly, as if I were somehow dragging the words from him.

"It didn't take me long to realize that the nightmares we've been experiencing since the explosion contain elements of truth. There are memories tied into them. It was just separating fact from fiction that was the problem."

"But you have?"

"I've made educated guesses," he conceded. "Then a few weeks ago, something changed. I know there's darkness in my past, I think we all have secrets that might be better to remain hidden, but I no longer fear the truth. With acceptance comes power. Once I really and truly wanted to remember… I did."

That was when the realization struck me; he could use the Lost Magic again. I had awoken the ability within him, he was one of those that I was supposed to guide, despite the fact that he hadn't really sought me out. David could use the Lost Magic, of that, there was no longer any doubt.

"How much do you remember?" I repeated. I was gathering the magic within me as I spoke, ready to defend myself if need be, ready for anything.

He leant forward on his bed, his eyes burning intensely into mine. Despite myself, I couldn't help but be aware of how attractive he was, his angular features, his solemn eyes, his tall, muscled frame. An electric energy filled the air, flowing freely between us. I tried to calm my heart but it seemed determined to steadily rise to a wild and nervous pounding.

"I remember too many things; too much for just twenty years or however long I'm supposed to have lived. I can't remember my family but I do remember my friends, Sebastian and several others. The two who came looking for you, Nathaniel and Jai: I'm sure I knew them once before." He paused to study my expression but I kept it neutral, careful to give nothing away—for now. I was secretly relieved to hear that he hadn't remembered everything yet, but what he had remembered might still be too much.

"I remember being powerful. I can remember feeling invincible, immortal almost. There was a time when I was an unstoppable force. I remember some of the horrible things that I have done and experienced, and it makes me wonder why I only now feel guilt? I'm certain that I've never felt it before but I should have. I should have lived every day in horror at what I had done, my every move shadowed with remorse and regret. It makes me afraid to remember who I once was that I should feel no shame, no sorrow at my actions. Some of the things I've remembered..." His voice trailed off. He squeezed his eyes tightly shut as if blinding himself to the horrific memories. Slowly, he reopened them. His face was pale, his expression solemn.

"I can remember loving Sebastian as my closest ally and brother—both in the past and now. And I remember hating him as my most bitter enemy once, as well. I can also remember hating you with such angry, bitter passion it terrifies me... but I don't know why I should have hated any of you?" His voice was cool and detached, a cold curiosity for the truth and nothing more. I wasn't sure how to respond.

"Now will you answer my questions?" he asked.

"Some."

His lips tightened but he didn't object. Surely he had expected no less.

"I remembered a girl," he began slowly, his eyes studying my face. His cold curiosity was gone and had been replaced by a soft and reverent passion. "I don't know who she is. I can't remember her name or her face, just that I loved her. I *worshipped* her. But I wronged her, I know it. Who was she? Tell me her name."

I blinked rapidly. It was the last thing I had expected him to say.

"I don't know. I never knew there was a girl you loved… Sebastian might know but he knew you so much longer than I did. We only ever met twice: once in Ireland and once in Greece, in Thessaloniki and at the Necromanteion, on the day of the explosion."

He scrutinized me through narrowed eyes and then finally he nodded.

"I don't remember traveling to Ireland at all or ever having met you before Sebastian introduced us in the hospital in Athens. Why can't I remember much of what happened before the explosion? I know that you know."

"Because I erased all of our memories," I answered without hesitation. Surprisingly, David took this in stride as if I were just confirming what he already knew or at least had suspected.

"How?"

This time I paused.

"With magic," I finally answered.

"And I used to be able to use this magic as well?"

"Yes. We all did. But you and your friends were dangerous. Sebastian and I were trying to stop you and we took away your powers—all of our powers," I corrected.

David considered this.

"How long have I been alive for?"

"I don't know exactly. Once again, Sebastian would be able to tell you more."

"If you had to guess."

Again I paused, unsure of how he would react.

"At least several hundred years. Maybe a thousand, maybe more."

He stared at me, silent but unfazed.

"You still have powers," he stated. "I can feel it. You have bound me to speak the truth and I can't make a single false word cross my lips. How did you do that?"

"It's complicated. But enough of this. Do you want your memories back?"

"The ones you stole from me? Yes."

I briefly winced at his choice of words.

"I will restore your memories but I will need you to make me some promises first. I will bind you to your words with magic; you will not be able to break these promises," I warned. I felt uncomfortable doing this: I knew it was wrong to control someone else this way but how else could I trust him?

"What do you want from me?" he asked suspiciously.

"I will restore your memories and with them, I think you will be able to control your own magic again. But I will only do this if you promise you will help me to find Sebastian and if you promise you will not harm me or Sebastian or anyone else."

"No," he answered immediately. "What if I need to protect myself?"

"Fine. Promise you won't harm me or Sebastian or anyone I say is a friend."

"No." David's eyes gleamed. "I won't harm you or Sebastian or anyone who *Sebastian* tells me is a friend. Even though I remember hating him once, I also remember loving him as my brother. Sebastian I know, Sebastian I trust. You, I no longer can."

I glared back at him. It was almost a relief not to have to pretend to be friendly anymore.

"Not good enough. It might take us some time to find Sebastian and I won't have you hurting whoever you want along the way. Promise you will only harm another person if you must do so in defense of your own life. Say it out loud and I will bind you to your words. I want to be able to trust you. I want you to keep your promises." The magic flowed through me as I spoke, my words echoing slightly about the small bedroom. David lifted his eyebrows but he didn't further comment.

"I swear I will help you to find Sebastian. I swear I will not harm you or Sebastian. I swear I will not harm any person unless I must do so to defend my own life. Satisfied?"

"For now."

"Now give me my memories back."

"I will but I can't give them all back to you."

His eyes flashed with anger. He jumped to his feet, leaning towards me menacingly. Suddenly, I remembered how he had nearly slit my throat in the Necromanteion, and despite the vows he had just spoken not to harm me, I still felt a sliver of fear pierce my heart. A soft gasp escaped my lips before I could stop it.

"Don't break your word to me, Grace, or I might find cause to break mine."

"You can't break your word but that's beside the point. I can't give you all of your memories back at once because it would kill you," I explained. He slowly sat back down, his eyes throwing daggers. "I did it to Sebastian once by mistake. I didn't realize what I was doing and I thought I was helping him by making him remember everything but it only made things worse—more nightmares, spells of confusion, headaches that would make him bleed from his nose and ears—it was slowly killing him. I can't make you remember absolutely everything but I will give you back your clearest memories, the ones that would have meant the most to you. The rest will be there too but they will be fuzzier, less focused and harder to dredge up from your subconscious. It's the best I can do."

"Fine. Do it."

"It will probably hurt," I warned him. "And once you remember… you're probably going to be angry. You're going to hate me, and most likely Sebastian too. You're going to be a very different person."

"I doubt that," he dismissed. "I'm already very angry with you, Grace, and as I said, I don't trust you. But I can't imagine hating you again, not now after all the time we've spent together. And Sebastian is… he's like family to me. He's all I have. I couldn't hate him, no matter what. And besides, what do you have to fear? I made you those promises, as you asked."

"Yes but…" How could I explain to him just how evil, how dangerous he once was? I supposed it didn't really matter. He'd remember himself in just a few minutes. "Are you sure you're ready for this?"

"Yes."

"You definitely want, more than anything else, to remember your past?"

"Yes," he answered impatiently, not understanding that his own desire was an important part of the spell.

I grabbed my necklace, squeezing it tightly for strength and courage while allowing the wild torrent of magic to flow through me and flood into David's mind.

"Then remember, David Turner," I whispered.

David's eyes flew wide open as my words and magic reached him. For a moment he just looked shocked and then his face crumpled, his whole body curled up and slid to the floor, writhing in silent pain. For that I was grateful, his screams would surely have brought the Jensons upstairs to investigate. It only lasted for a minute and he only made one noise, a quiet, strangled moan as a single drop of blood trickled from his nose.

It felt strange just to sit back and watch but I knew that there was nothing I could do. I anxiously waited for his body to still, for his eyelids to flutter, then open. His gray eyes stared straight up into mine.

"You," he fumed. His eyes were bright with anger and recognition.

I swallowed nervously, trying to hide my fear. There was no doubt that he had remembered, that the spirits had given me his true name after all.

"Hello, David Turner," I answered calmly.

"*Never* call me that again," he warned. He slowly sat up, dabbing the blood at his nose. He looked furious.

"I take it you remember me now?"

"You've gone too far this time, Caoilinn." He rose threateningly as he spoke.

"Sit down. You can't hurt me," I reminded him.

"Can't I? But I want to so badly," he purred, showing me a terrifying smile.

And that was when I felt it, his magic pushing against mine, his will trying to manipulate me. He was desperately trying to take back the vows he had spoken just minutes before. He was trying with all his will and all the magic at his disposal to break the bonds that tied him to me. I knew he wouldn't be able to find a way out of it but I was still shocked and a little afraid. It was confirmation of what I had feared. Not only did he have a natural ability to use the Lost Magic but now that his memories had been returned, he could control his magic just as easily as he ever had. David would need little guidance, little training; he was almost as powerful as me.

"Stop trying to use magic against me—it won't work."

"What are you talking about?" David snapped. His efforts abruptly stopped. I knew it had been him, there was no doubt in my mind, but either he was trying to cover it up or he had been unaware of what he was doing. Either way meant trouble. David was definitely back and he was just as dangerous as ever.

"You can use the Lost Magic again. That's why I restored your memories and that's why I need you to help me. I think someone else who controls the Lost Magic has taken Sebastian."

"I thought you took the magic away from everyone and then destroyed it?"

"Yes, well, it didn't work out exactly as I had planned. I'll explain it all later but right now—"

"You will explain it now," David interrupted, his voice icy cold. "I realize that I am bound by your deceitful magic to help you, but how will I be of any use if I do not understand exactly what it is that I am up against?"

He had a point.

I fidgeted impatiently. I was eager to start looking for Sebastian but he was right, he needed to know.

I explained to David as quickly and simply as possible about how my attempt to destroy the Lost Magic had failed, how I had awakened the natural, dormant ability within people around the world and how they were now all my responsibility because of the hasty promises I had made before the spirits in the Necromanteion.

"Then where are all the others who should have come flocking to you? Was it just Nathaniel and Jai you sent away, or were there more?" He smirked when I didn't immediately answer. "Let me guess. Selfish Caoilinn, always thinking of yourself—you don't want to help them, do you? They're inconveniencing you and complicating your relationship with Sebastian, so you thought you'd just leave a group of extremely powerful near-immortals with no control or understanding of their abilities to their own devices? Bloody brilliant," he spat at me, reminding me for a split second of Mags. I gave my head a quick shake.

"I just needed some time. It wasn't like that."

"It was exactly like that."

Our eyes locked together.

"You do realize, *I* never promised not to hurt you," I pointed out.

"Careful, Caoilinn. Remember who it is that you're playing games with."

"My name is Gracelynn," I snapped back. "Try to remember my name, David Turner, and I will try to forget yours."

He glared back at me but for once, he didn't speak.

"There was a man who came to my mother's house the other night, he was with another old acquaintance of yours, Lily. He became angry when I said I wouldn't help them, he threatened me. I think he might have something to do with Sebastian's disappearance, it's a starting point at least. Whoever took him, there must be others helping him because they're blocking my magic somehow. If I'm to stand a chance of getting Sebastian back and stopping the people who took him, I'm going to need numbers on my side— starting with you. Will you help me?"

"Don't act like I have a choice. But yes, I will. Despite how I feel about you, Sebastian might still be worth saving. It's midnight— we'll start in the morning. Until then, get the hell out of my room."

And with that, he rolled onto his back and shut his eyes. I had been dismissed.

"I'll see you at dawn," I murmured as I left. I might as well have been talking to myself for all the acknowledgement I received.

I didn't sleep that night, I couldn't. I was vibrating with magic and restless energy, battling guilt and fear, working my way through my shame and regret. There was nowhere to go but forward. I would save Sebastian and I would make everything right. I had to focus on the future and stay positive. The alternative was too bleak to consider.

I realized I needed to let my mother know that I would be leaving town for a few days. We were going to have to postpone the wedding indefinitely. Since it was around three am when I made this decision, I sent her an email making up a ridiculous story about needing a last minute retreat to a remote spa to escape all this stress while we waited for Sebastian to return. It was frivolous and vain: my mother was sure to understand. I also emailed the head curator at the art gallery and told her a story as close to the truth as I could allow: that my fiancé was struggling with depression and had gone missing. I explained that Sebastian's good friend and I had an idea of where he might be and we were going to try to find him and bring him back home. I told her I didn't know how long I'd be gone for or when I'd be ready to return to work. I hoped she wasn't too angry but honestly, I didn't really care. All that mattered now was finding Sebastian and bringing him back home safely.

In the last few hours before dawn, I tried to formulate a plan. What would I say to the others I had turned away? What would I do if they wouldn't help us? And where might Jeremy have taken Sebastian? And what if he hadn't taken him after all, what if I was wrong? Who else might have kidnapped Sebastian? What could they possibly want with him? Or what if Sebastian had run away? And could I really trust David, even with the vows he had spoken?

Eventually I came to one miserable conclusion, that this was all my fault. I had ignored the tasks laid out for me by a powerful priestess, dead for two thousands years and now I was being punished. I had made the worst mistake of my life and now I was having to pay for it. And worst of all, not only was I suffering for my foolish pride but Sebastian was too. The spirit in my dream had said he had been taken somewhere so far away, that even she couldn't reach him. She had warned me that I didn't know what I was up against… And I was afraid I wouldn't be strong enough. I was afraid I might never find him and even if I could find him, what if I couldn't save him? Tears shimmered in my eyes, blurring my vision.

I walked over to my window and let my gaze wander, my eyes reaching out to the horizon. The sky was shifting from night's inky black to the bright and clear blue of winter's cold dawn. The rift between sky and earth was filling with pure, golden light. As the sun's rays cracked above the horizon, blazing through the gathering clouds and washing the sapphire sky with light, I felt emboldened, I felt inspired. I brushed my tears away. I would fight, I promised myself, and I would win.

The sun slowly rose above the horizon, a blazing ball of golden fire and light. The day had begun. It was time to go.

The Jensons were already awake. I could hear Mrs. Jenson's soft steps in the kitchen, a spoon clinking against a mug as she stirred her coffee. Mr. Jenson was on the phone already, his words indistinguishable but the steady, low hum of his voice carrying to the small entranceway. I wondered if they'd slept at all either. They must be almost as worried about Sebastian as I was.

I quietly gathered my things and made my way down the stairs, careful to avoid any creaky steps. David stood by the front door, waiting for me.

He met my eyes with a cold, flat stare. He looked more like his old self than he had in months: clean-shaven, slicked back hair and dressed all in black. Somewhere, he had gotten his hands on a crisp, black, button-up shirt and a pair of pressed black pants. He wore a pair of biker boots and a leather jacket that looked suspiciously like Sebastian's. In fact, the jacket was Sebastian's—I was sure of it.

David smirked as he followed my eyes.

"Don't worry about it, *Gracelynn*. Sebastian won't mind," he murmured in a soft, low voice.

I glared back at him but didn't speak as I pushed past him and out the front door. I was almost too angry to respond anyway. David slipped out behind me, closing the door as quietly as possible, so as not to alert the Jensons. I had left a note for them up in my room explaining that we were going to look for Sebastian and we wouldn't be back until we found him, however long that took. My mind was set, but I still didn't want to give them the opportunity to try to change it. I had begged them not to tell my mother or father that I had gone looking for Sebastian, worried that they might come looking for me. Instead, I'd suggested they stick with my story that I had gone out of town on a retreat, to escape the stressful situation I'd found myself in and to try to relax while they continued searching and waiting for Sebastian.

Outside, we hopped into my Austin Mini and without giving the engine time to warm up, I quickly backed down the Jenson's driveway and pulled out onto the street.

"I assume you have some kind of plan?" David asked after several minutes of silence.

I drove slowly and carefully, aware of the slick roads and the silver frost that had crystallized over everything overnight. My eyes remained fixed on the road as I responded in a quiet and level voice.

"I'm hoping some of the others that I'm supposed to 'guide' are still in the city; if they weren't involved in Sebastian's abduction, of course. I've glimpsed Jai and Nathaniel a few times and they were often accompanied by others, strangers I didn't recognize. We need to find them first and get their help to find Sebastian…"

"And?"

"And to make sure whoever took him pays." My voice was soft and chilling. I could feel David staring at me but I didn't look away from the road. "I've seen Nathaniel and Jai twice near the waterfront: once by the museum and again near Bastion Square. If they're still in the city, that's where we'll find them."

"That's your master plan? What makes you think that Jai and Nathaniel will just be wandering around near the waterfront at seven thirty in the morning?" David drawled.

"They'll be there because I want them to be there. If you want to be useful, you could try doing the same."

"You're as charming as always this morning, Caoilinn."

I gritted my teeth and didn't comment. Instead, I attempted to focus on the task at hand. I was so worried about Sebastian I could barely think straight. It would be extremely foolish to relax around David now or to let my guard down around anyone. And I was so exhausted both emotionally and physically, I wasn't sure how I could possibly get through today, let alone the possibility of more days to come without Sebastian. I was living a nightmare, a nightmare I had created. Perhaps that was the worst part, knowing that this was all my fault. The guilt would easily consume me if I let it.

I parked my car in a small parking lot down near the inner harbor. The air was still bitingly cold, even though the sun was now attempting to weakly break through the gray clouds. I wrapped a knitted gray scarf twice around my neck and stuffed my hands into my jacket pockets, shivering already from the brisk morning air. Wherever Sebastian was, I hoped he was inside, and warm, and safe.

"Lead the way," David gestured politely.

"We'll find them at the square," I announced confidently, marching on ahead. David followed in silence, matching his pace to mine.

Seagulls called out overhead as we made our way alongside the inner harbor. I breathed in deeply, loving the mixed scents of the salty ocean and the bustling little city. Over the past year, Victoria had really started to feel like home to me. I might have even enjoyed this morning stroll if it weren't for the dangerous person walking just a few feet behind me, and the reason for why we were there in the first place. I tried to push the thoughts aside. We were almost at Bastion Square now and I needed to concentrate. I focused on the noise and rhythm of the traffic that passed us by, waiting for the right moment to slip out and dash across the street between cars. When I found the perfect moment, I abruptly hopped down onto the street and quickly jogged across the road. David cursed, and then ran after me.

"There's a crosswalk just down the street," he remarked, glaring at me disapprovingly. I shrugged.

"We're in a hurry. Try to keep up." And with that I made a quick turn and attempted to skip up the stairway that ran alongside the sidewalk and up to Bastion Square. I should have grabbed onto the railing but the metal was sure to be freezing cold and my hands were warm in my pockets. Just as I reached the top step, and noticed with disappointment that the square was empty, my foot flew out from underneath me. My stomach dropped as I fell backwards and

I found myself staring straight up at the cloudy, overcast sky with nothing but air underneath me. There was no time to pull my hands from my pockets. I fell, helplessly, backwards, wincing as I waited for the moment when my head made contact with the steps.

The air rushed from my lungs as I fell against something hard. It wasn't hard enough or cold enough to be the concrete steps. In fact, my head wasn't touching the ground at all. I opened my eyes in wonder, my head spinning and adrenaline coursing through me.

Sebastian's arms held me tightly against his chest, cradling me protectively. He smelled just like I remembered, of ice and oak trees and magic. My heart swelled as I tipped back my head, leaning against his leather jacket and gazing up at his face in wonder, not understanding how this was possible.

My breath caught in my throat.

It was David's face only inches from mine, his eyes wide with surprise and another emotion that I couldn't identify. I had always thought of his eyes as black, but this close I could see that they were really a warm and soft shade of gray, like pools of molten silver. There was a depth to his eyes that I had never noticed before, a warmth that glowed steadily from within him, hypnotically pulling me in. We stared at each other like we'd never truly seen the other person before, and perhaps we hadn't. Confusion was bubbling up within me. I wasn't sure what was happening or why I was feeling this way. What had just happened?

"What are you doing?" I questioned, it was difficult to catch my breath enough to speak.

"I'm here to help, aren't I?" Was it my imagination or did he sound out of breath too? "Why are you staring at me like that?"

"I... I thought you were Sebastian, for a second," I tried to explain, my brain unexpectedly fuzzy. "Why are you still holding me?"

"I don't know." He broke his gaze from mine, only for a second, but it was long enough for us both to regain our equilibrium. He looked back down, his grip on me slowly relaxing. "It looks like things just got more interesting," he smirked as he gently placed me back on my feet.

"What do you..." My eyes followed his across the square.

Nathaniel and Jai were walking towards us, marching confidently across the cobbled stones. I wasn't truly surprised to see them, I had summoned them to me after all. But it was the third figure who skipped along beside Nathaniel, her arm looped through his as she strutted across the stones in ridiculously expensive and dangerously high heeled shoes. Her long brown hair flared out behind her in the icy morning breeze, her pale cheeks unusually rosy from the frigid air. She waved as she saw me, her delight and excitement obvious. I felt my jaw drop.

What was Bridgette doing here?

Chapter Ten - New Lessons

"**G**RACE!" BRIDGETTE EXCLAIMED, BEAMING WITH PLEASURE. I couldn't stop staring. "How strange to see you here! We were just talking about you. Oh, my goodness, you look awful! Are you alright?"

Nathaniel and Jai greeted me with subtle nods, waiting patiently for me to speak. They barely acknowledged David which was probably for the best, I could feel him fuming with silent anger beside me despite the fact that I had warned him we were here to meet with them. Their presence had definitely set him on edge. Luckily, Bridgette seemed oblivious to all the tension going on around her.

"No, I'm not all right," I answered in carefully modulated tones. I fought the unexpected, violent urge to slap her. "Sebastian is still missing. I haven't slept all night and I'm worried sick. I have more important things to worry about than how I look, not that you'd understand." My words wiped the smile off Bridgette's face as quickly as a slap. She looked stunned, her eyes wide and her neatly arched brows lifted. I only felt the slightest glimmer of guilt. "What are you doing with these two anyway? Where's your chaperone... Lena?"

"She's back at the hotel," Bridgette sniffed. She straightened her shoulders and looked haughtily down her nose at me. "I'm not a child, Grace, I know how to take care of myself. Besides, I have my friends here to look out for me. This is Nathaniel and this is Jai; they're guests at The Queen's also. We met in the restaurant this morning and ended up having breakfast together. The boys were just about to escort me on a stroll around the inner harbor." Bridgette smiled sweetly, batting her eyelashes up at Nathaniel, her arm still looped through his.

"Bridgette told us she was here for your wedding, to act as your Maid of Honor," Jai commented, his brown eyes apologetic. "Naturally, we were curious."

"Wait, do you know each other?" Bridgette asked sharply. Her eyebrows drew together, her eyes flashing back and forth between us.

"We've met Grace before, yes," Nathaniel admitted softly. "And her friend, David."

"I am *not* her friend," David immediately corrected. His sharp words caught all of our attention. "I am only helping her hunt for Sebastian since she has deceived and manipulated me with her magic so that I no longer have any choice."

"Her magic?" Bridgette echoed curiously. Her eyes had lit up with excitement.

"David, shut up," I warned, glaring at him. He laughed, a harsh, chilling sound.

"What's wrong, Caoilinn? Don't like how the truth sounds?"

"Stop it—now. I'm warning you."

"Or you'll what? Don't think I haven't noticed your reluctance to actually use the Lost Magic. Only if you deem it truly necessary, if there's no other way—is that how it works? You're a fool and a coward."

"This isn't a game, David," I growled. I felt like I was rapidly losing control of the situation. Nathaniel and Jai were watching me silently, waiting to see how I would react. Bridgette was looking back and forth between David and I, her eyes wide with confusion.

"What's going on?" she demanded. She turned to glare at David, I was surprised by the fiery spark in her eye. "And you should *not* be talking to her like that!" she scolded, looking and sounding indignant.

"Grace isn't who you think she is," David announced, turning to Bridgette with gleaming eyes. "And neither are these two *boys*. Isn't that right, Nathaniel Gregory Lewis and Jai Ashok Tagore? Remember me now?"

"David—no!" I yelled but I was too late.

Nathaniel's eyes rolled back in his head and he crumpled to the ground. Bridgette's arm was still linked through his and she desperately tried to support his weight, preventing him from hitting the cobblestones too hard. Jai collapsed a split second later but there was no one close enough to slow his fall. His head bounced off the stones with a sickening cracking sound. I stared in horror at the two young men, one thrashing against the ground and moaning, the other lying motionless and mute.

"Grace, help me," Bridgette called. She had left Nathaniel's side and was leaning over Jai, her fingers pressed against his throat, searching for a pulse. Surprisingly, she appeared calm and in control, all traces of the vain, spoilt teenager from moments before had vanished. "He's bleeding," she announced as blood began to slowly trickle from Jai's nose and ears. I made no move forward to help her, I could do more help from where I stood. I turned to David, my whole body trembling with rage.

"You're making them remember *everything*," I hissed. "I warned you what would happen. Their minds can't handle it!"

He shrugged. "Oops."

"Grace—help me!" Bridgette demanded, this time with real fire in her voice. My attention snapped back to her.

"Does he still have a pulse?"

"Yes, but it's faint," Bridgette immediately answered. Despite her cool exterior, I could see that she was alarmed, the panic rising in her eyes. "He needs help, and now. Help! Someone help us!" she began yelling, her eyes desperately searching the square.

"No, I don't want anyone else involved in this." My voice was hard and thickly coated with magic, refusing to be disobeyed. Bridgette gaped at me, her voice immediately silenced by both magic and her own surprise. I turned from her without a second thought. "Nathaniel Gregory Lewis and Jai Ashok Tagore, you will recover only the memories that I took from you in the Necromanteion, nothing more. You will awaken and you will be peaceful. You will help us and you will harm no one other than to defend your own lives. You will follow where I guide you. Heal. Live."

The instant I pronounced the last word, Jai sucked in a deep, rattling breath that almost immediately turned into a hacking cough.

With that same surprising calm, Bridgette helped Jai to sit up, I noticed her hands were trembling.

"Thank you, Grace." Nathaniel's voice came from behind me. He was wiping the thin trails of blood from his upper lip and glaring at David. "I should kill you for that, you bastard."

"Look who finally grew a backbone after seven hundred years. You actually think that *you* could kill *me*? Please, I would love to see you try," David taunted.

"Stop. He's bound by the same rules as both of you. He can't hurt either of you unless he feels you're a threat to his own safety," I warned.

"Can't hurt us?" Jai wheezed disbelievingly. He was standing now, thanks to Bridgette's help, and was running a hand through his hair, no doubt searching for the crack that had been in his skull moments before.

"My intention was not to hurt either of you," David answered. "My only goal was for you to remember what you need in order to be of any use to us. And to motivate *Gracelynn* to embrace the powers she continues to deny. This whole tiresome ordeal will go a lot more smoothly if Ms. Righteous here gets over her incomprehensible reluctance to actually utilize the Lost Magic."

All eyes turned to me. I didn't know what to say; I couldn't deny the truth to David's words but how could I explain that I was still wary to let the Lost Magic back into my life? I was afraid each time that I used it that there would be a price to pay. That each time I changed fate, there would be a repercussion. I feared that every time I used my powers to get what I wanted, I was somehow putting my wants and my will above all others and I knew that couldn't be right. I was afraid I would lose myself to the magic. And even worse, I was afraid I would eventually lose Sebastian as my magic would somehow drive us apart. In many ways, it already had.

"Someone has got to fill me in," Bridgette announced, her breathless voice cutting sharply through my thoughts. I had almost forgotten about her. I sighed as I realized I was about to have to use the magic again to manipulate another person's memories and desires. I steeled myself against her large, imploring eyes.

"Let's all go back to your hotel," David interrupted. "We can talk as we walk, get you all caught up. Come."

To my annoyance, everyone fell into place behind him as he began marching across the square. At least Nathaniel had the courtesy to look ashamed as he allowed Bridgette to slide her arm back through his, but only for a moment before he was distracted by that pair of beautiful emerald eyes gazing up at him adoringly. Their heads bent close together as they whispered quietly back and forth, Nathaniel revealing far too much about the Lost Magic and all of us to Bridgette, for some reason. Not that it really mattered, I would erase her memory as soon as we returned to the hotel.

At the edge of the large, open square, David paused.

"I don't know where we're going," he admitted without the slightest bit of shame.

I marched ahead and allowed David to fall in behind me. "Follow me."

"Don't I always?" he murmured with an arched brow.

"Are the others staying at The Queens also?" I asked Jai, speaking over my shoulder to him. It wasn't necessary to clarify who I meant.

"We *were* all there," he confirmed, his voice still carrying a rough edge. "We were all drawn together as soon as we entered the city. There were seventeen of us but our group quickly became divided. Nathaniel and I, and three others, wanted to stay and wait for you to come to us. There was one man who led the group in opposition to ours; he was advocating for immediate action… against you."

"Jeremy," I stated, ice forming around my heart.

"Yes," Jai agreed. "He disappeared two nights ago, five others went with him. He had said he was going to do something to get your attention, something you wouldn't be able to ignore."

Fiery rage ignited my heart. "And you never thought to warn me?"

"We didn't realize they'd left until the following morning and by then it was too late." It was Nathaniel who spoke this time, in his gentle, hesitant voice. "Besides, we needed to get your attention too."

I spun around, halting our whole party. Without thinking, my hand went out to Nathaniel's throat, my fingertips squeezing delicately against his windpipe. I was so furious, I didn't even have to speak the words. I wanted for him to remain motionless, for him to be under my full and total control—and he was. He stared at me helplessly, a faint gurgling sound bubbling in his throat.

"You have my full attention. Was it worth dying for?"

"Grace!" Bridgette gasped, her shocked voice bringing me back to reality. My anger evaporated as quickly as it had overcome me, my head instantly clearing. "What are you doing? Let go of him!" she cried. I let my hand drop down to my side.

"His friends took Sebastian; they could hurt him, they might even kill him. And he could have stopped them." My fury had faded to a quiet, simmering anger that made my voice crack.

"But… Nathaniel just told me that he came to you for help and you turned him away. Despite what the people he was staying with may have done, if you wouldn't help him then why should you expect his help in return?" Bridgette asked. I stared back at her wide, innocent eyes. David barked out a laugh beside me.

"You don't know what you're talking about, Bridgette. It's much more complicated than that," I stated stubbornly.

"Is it?" David smirked.

"This is how we stand. Jeremy and the other 'rogues' have taken Sebastian, whether just to get my attention or to actually cause him harm is unclear. Either way, I'm not waiting to find out. I need your help to rescue him and in return, I will teach you how to control your abilities and discover the full potential of the Lost Magic. I will guide you."

Nathaniel, Jai and Bridgette all stared at me wide-eyed. David scoffed quietly. I allowed a few seconds to pass, to let my words sink in and then I turned, continuing onwards through the awakening city streets and towards the massive Queens Hotel that overlooked the waterfront.

"What kind of offer is that?" David demanded. It pleased me to hear he was slightly out of breath, I was setting a quick pace and any discomfort I could cause him, no matter how small, was worth it. "We all remember how to use the magic now that we have our memories back. You offer us nothing."

"You remember how you used the abilities given to you unnaturally; this is different. The Lost Magic no longer bends to your whims to make what you want come to be. The magic that has lain dormant in your souls for centuries has now been awakened. It runs wild through your body and can only be used to fulfill the strongest desires with the most unwavering focus."

"What do you mean?" Nathaniel asked from behind me. "Didn't David just use the Lost Magic to reawaken our memories?"

"Yes, but only because he was so angry. He's furious at me and perhaps at you as well. Because of his previous experience with the Lost Magic, he still has a measure of control. It should come more easily to you and Jai as well. I've learnt how to control the Lost Magic in a way that you've never had to experience. I know how to focus my ability because my powers have always existed this way. When you are angry or when you feel the most passionate, the magic will come more easily to you but you need to be able to control it with a calm mind, with clear intentions. For example, if you were hungry right now and tried to want food to come your way, it will not happen. If you were starving and you wanted food more than anything else, if you truly believed that's what you needed most in the world at this moment, if you could summon enough strength within yourself and focused your magic to get what you desired… you would find food."

"If you're so powerful, why can't you just get Sebastian back on your own?" Bridgette suddenly asked. She was catching on fast, her question surprisingly intuitive. I realized I may have misjudged her but it didn't make a difference, she was going to have to forget all of this soon enough.

"I would assume that Jeremy and the ones with him are very angry with me. They must be using their anger to gain some control over their powers as well. No matter how powerful I am or how much control I might have, they still outnumber me."

"Does Sebastian not have any magic to fight them with then?"

Bridgette's sweet, curious voice sent a flash of pain through my heart.

"I can only assume, no, since he was not able to stop them from taking him. He might have been outnumbered but… no, I don't think he does," I answered quietly.

We rounded a last corner and reached the Queens Hotel. The old, gray building towered above us, reminiscent of a castle with its gargoyles, arched windows and steepled roofs. Thick, dark green vines covered much of the front of the building as it looked out towards the still and placid harbor. I marched towards its entrance, turning to face the rest of my group just before the arched entranceway and the massive glass doors.

"Time's up. Are you with us or not?" I demanded, cutting to the chase. "I won't force you to join us, I would like the decision to be yours. But I would ask you for your help."

Jai and Nathaniel exchanged a quick glance. To my extreme irritation, they both looked to David briefly as well before meeting my eye.

"We've been waiting for you to guide us. We will follow where you lead," Jai pronounced prophetically.

"The others are sure to come now too," Nathaniel joined in, sounding confident.

"Good. Go inside, gather your things and let the ones who have remained know that I am ready. It's time to go."

Nathaniel nodded again and turned to follow Jai inside. Bridgette moved as if to join them.

"Not you, Bridgette," I gently called. She turned back to me warily.

"I thought you needed our help to rescue Sebastian," she stated with a frown. "What kind of Maid of Honour would I be if I bailed on you now? That's why I'm here, Grace, to help you. I'm coming too."

"No. Absolutely not. I can't be responsible for you, Bridgette. This is going to be dangerous—extremely dangerous. Rescuing the groom from a group of angry people with an ancient and powerful magic at their disposal does not fall under the list of duties or expectations for a Maid of Honor. You don't know what you're getting into," I added, speaking more softly.

Bridgette's full lower lip pulled down in a pout.

"Well, then explain it to me. I'm not a kid anymore, Grace. I want to come, I want to help. I'm so bored here already. I'm not about to let you run off and have an adventure without me," she declared. Her eyes were bright with excitement. I stifled an impatient sigh.

"I'm sorry, Bridgette. I don't have time for this. I'm going to have to make you forget now."

Bridgette gasped and then surprised me by taking an angry step forward, her full lips pressed into a tight line, her round, pretty eyes narrowed.

"You will not! You wouldn't dare!" Her German accent was much clearer as she spoke, revealing just how angry she was.

"You can't erase her memories, Grace," David drawled. He looked almost bored.

"Why not?"

"Do I really have to explain it to you? Can't you see why she's here?"

"I don't know what you're talking about," I denied, slowly shaking my head. I felt like I already knew the truth but I just couldn't admit it. It couldn't be.

"Focus, Grace," David snapped in irritation. "I know you can feel it too. It's faint but it's definitely there."

"What? What's there? What are you talking about?" Bridgette demanded.

I closed my eyes, shutting them all out. I slipped my hand under my scarf, reaching for the comforting warmth of my necklace, the beautiful Dara knot necklace that Sebastian had given me. Taking a slow breath, I tuned out all the noise around me: Bridgette, David, the traffic passing by the hotel, the distant cries of the seagulls, the chilly gusts of wind. I focused on the ancient magic vibrating and pulsating within me, letting it fill my mind and dominate above all else. And as I focused, I became aware of a quiet echo, a glimmer of power pulsating before me in perfect time to the rhythm of the Lost Magic within me. It was Bridgette.

I opened my eyes with a softly muttered curse.

"What? What is it?" Bridgette demanded, her eyes going back and forth between David and myself.

"There is a small amount of the magic in you. However weak, it was still powerful enough to bring you to me for guidance. You're coming with us," I sighed.

"Really?" Bridgette looked thrilled.

"Yes. Now go get your things. Tell Lena we're going to a spa for a few days and that that you're joining me on my 'retreat'. That's where my mother thinks I am."

She clapped her hands together excitedly.

"Ok, I'll be really quick. Oh, I have so many questions. There's just so much I want to know. Wow. This is so exciting! Thank you, Grace," she gushed, skipping around happily and dancing into the hotel.

"You knew all along," I accused David as soon as she left.

"I suspected. I had hoped I was wrong. Her personality grates on me even more than yours."

"Well at least that's one reason I can be grateful she's coming along."

David took several steps away from me and then lit a cigarette. The familiar fragrance of cigarette smoke on a cold winter's breeze tugged at my heartstrings. I moved even further away.

He had just finished his smoke when I saw Jai and Nathaniel walking across the hotel's grand lobby towards the front doors. Bridgette followed closely behind them (wheeling a small suitcase behind her, of all things) and three others walked in her wake, a man in a suit who looked to be about forty with bright red hair and piercing blue eyes, a woman in her late twenties with short, bleached hair, ripped jeans and a nose ring and a tall, slim woman who looked to be in her early twenties, with shoulder-length black hair and brown skin. They all came out the hotel's front doors and walked straight towards us.

"Is Lily with Jeremy then?" I asked, immediately disappointed. Her previous experience with the Lost Magic would have been a benefit to us, once I returned her memories.

"No. She was one of those who remained undecided. She left

last night, going her own way," Jai answered. He turned to the man in the suit who had walked up beside him. "Gracelynn, this is Red." The tall, red-haired man grinned at me, his eyes crinkling at the edges and his blue eyes sparkling.

"How do ya do?" Red greeted me, his Australian accent only adding to his charm. I found myself smiling back at him.

"Nice to meet you," I responded politely as I shook his hand.

"And this is Ella." Jai indicated the punk-looking girl with the nose ring who surprised me by having a full and sweet smile that lit up and transformed her whole face.

"Hi, Gracelynn," she murmured, almost shyly.

"Hello."

"And I'm Sylvia," the tall, dark-haired woman announced, a faint accent that I couldn't place coloring her voice. "I am glad you have decided to lead us."

"And I'm David and I am warning all of you now, to stay out of my way. So where, exactly, is it that you are 'leading' us to?" David stared down his nose at me, the heat in his gaze intimidating. I let my eyes burn back into his, refusing to submit. I clasped my necklace tightly.

"To the park, to teach you all your first lesson."

He snorted.

"Which is?"

"We need to know where Jeremy and the others took Sebastian, and we need to know exactly who they are and what it is we're up against. We are going to perform a group ceremony to contact the spirits and ask for their help."

I thought I heard Bridgette gasp.

"Can't you just want to know and you'll find out?" Bridgette asked quietly. "Nathaniel made it seem like that's how it worked…"

"I do want to know and my gut tells me this is how I will find out. We don't have time to wait for the information to come to us. We will summon the spirits and we will do it now."

"Why at the park?" Red asked curiously.

"Because that is where I feel the strongest connection to Sebastian and the spirits have come to me there before. Now if you are going to question everything I do and say, we will never get anywhere. I'm sorry but you're just going to have to trust me. No more questions, for now."

"How about a suggestion?" Sylvia interrupted softly. She held up a set of keys and jingled them in front of me. "Why don't we take my van?"

A couple people laughed, breaking the group tension. I slowly allowed myself to smile.

"Sure."

She grinned back at me but her smile vanished when David snatched the keys from her hand.

"I'll drive." His eyes challenged her to argue but she just shrugged, looking away. I didn't like the way they all seemed so wary of him. I realized it was going to be difficult to lead this group if they were all more afraid of him than me but did I really want to be their leader? Either way, the idea of being squished into a van with seven others all asking questions and making demands on me didn't appeal at all. Until we found Sebastian, I just wanted to be alone.

"I think I'll take my car," I announced as I began searching through my pockets for my keys. David immediately shook his head. He stepped in close, lowering his voice.

"Bad leadership move," he murmured in my ear. I fought the strange conflicting desires to lean in close and smell the skin at his neck while at the same time being repulsed by his proximity and wanting to pull away. "You're going to be depending on their help— you should spend as much time with them as possible."

"Fine," I grumbled.

"Don't pout, Grace," David scolded in a louder voice. He smirked down at me. "If you're nice, maybe we'll let you sit shotgun."

A few of the others chuckled. I glared them into silence.

"Let's go."

I didn't have to answer any more questions in the van; the others seemed to sense that I was not in the mood so they kept any curiosity they had under wraps. I listened to their quiet conversations as David navigated the large van through the city streets. Bridgette flirted with Nathaniel and Jai, giggling and causing me to roll my eyes. Sylvia and Red were talking about a restaurant they had eaten at the night before. Ella plugged a pair of headphones into her ears as soon as we got in the van and closed her eyes, leaning against the window as if she were going to fall asleep. David and I were silent.

The oak tree was near the center of Beacon Hill Park. We parked as close to it as we could get and then all got out to walk the rest of the way through the sparse winter gardens, over the duck pond bridges and under the tall trees. As our group approached the towering, ancient oak, all conversations died.

I tipped my head back and gazed up at the tree, its powerful branches twisting upwards, reaching for the misty sky. For a brief moment, I closed my eyes and all I wanted in the world was to be with Sebastian, for him to be safe, for this to be over with. But nothing happened, nothing changed.

Slowly, I turned to face the group who stood in a loose half-circle before me.

"I'm not sure how much you know or how much you've been able to figure out, but let me begin by telling you the truth. You, and a few others around the world, are able to access a powerful and ancient magic that lives inside of you. It is known as the Lost Magic and it is as old as time itself." All eyes were on me, their attention so intense some of them barely blinked or breathed. Even David looked on with interest.

I continued on, explaining what I had learned of the Lost Magic from my life as Caoilinn and the pieces of information the spirits had shared with me.

"A long, long time ago, before the magic was "lost", it was a very present and important part of everyday life. Not everyone could access it but everyone knew of it. Slowly the ability disappeared, it stayed with the souls who possessed it but it lay dormant within them, so that they had no knowledge or awareness of the magic in their next lives. Two thousand years ago, when I lived as the Celtic priestess, Caoilinn, I was one of the last living people to possess the magic naturally."

"Excuse me, but what did you just say?" Red interrupted. He wasn't the only one who looked confused. "What do you mean, you lived two thousand years ago?"

I realized my mistake, continuing on patiently.

"The truth is, though our bodies die, our souls never do. We are born and live again as our souls continue their journey through different incarnations. It is the same for every single living person on this planet; we have all lived before and we will all live again." Jai and Nathaniel nodded knowingly but the others just looked stunned. David appeared indifferent.

"It may be difficult to accept at first but you will know in your hearts that it's true. Many of you may have known each other in different lives and we are naturally drawn to others who have the Lost Magic within them. Though not always," I added, thinking of Sebastian and then quickly pushing his image and all the emotions that came with it away. I took a deep breath and continued.

"There are spirits who exist in a place between life and death, a place sometimes accessible by those who possess the Lost Magic or who have a natural ability to access it. These spirits once lived but then their souls were not reborn in the usual way or perhaps their souls are just waiting for the right body, the right life to choose. Either way, they exist in limbo in this otherworldy place that both touches the Earth and doesn't. These spirits have great power and great knowledge, they are watching and listening, even now."

As I spoke, the wind picked up, rattling the branches above us and causing several among us to shiver and shift uncomfortably.

"A month ago, under the last full moon, the spirits came to me and instructed me to awaken the Lost Magic. They said the ones who were able to control its power would be drawn to me, would come seeking me out." I hesitated, unsure of how much to reveal. "They warned me that not all would have good intentions, that some would be tempted by darkness and would pose a great threat not only to us but to the world. They told me to judge who was worthy to control the magic, who was ready to learn its secrets and master its powers. I have also been instructed to deal with those who are deemed unworthy."

"What do you mean 'unworthy'?" Ella asked softly. She blushed as all eyes turned to her.

"The magic should not be used for your own gain, for manipulating others or causing others harm," I replied. "The ones who took Sebastian, are obviously unworthy. I am sure they have turned to darkness though I'm not sure how they have learned to use their abilities without my guidance. It would be too dangerous to leave them with the ability to use the Lost Magic."

"So you're going to take their powers?" Jai frowned.

"Yes." I held his gaze, refusing to let the shame and fear that I felt show. I could not destroy the Lost Magic and the only way I could strip another of their powers was by taking their life, as the spirits had instructed me. Soon enough the others would realize that, but I was not about to share this information now.

"I will teach you how to use your powers, I will share with you all that I know of the Lost Magic: what I have learned in this life and what I remember from my past life. But if you do anything to make me think that you are unworthy of the magic, you will also be stripped of your powers," I warned.

"Do you see yourself as above these laws then, Caoilinn?" David tilted his head at me, his eyes narrowed. "Have you not already used the magic to manipulate and to serve your own best interests?"

"I want to rescue Sebastian for myself but the spirits have also charged me to hunt down and deal with those who are unworthy, which his captors most certainly are. They have instructed me to save him and so I am justified to use the magic to complete these tasks."

"You said we were going to contact these spirits?" Bridgette asked. She held her head high and spoke confidently as the attention was redirected to her.

"Yes, we are going to now. I am going to teach you how to combine your magic. Most of you will not be able to use your magic for some time unless you are feeling a particularly strong emotion. I am going to be directing your magic through you, so that you can feel what it's like, so that you can experience the strength and the sensations of using the Lost Magic while I actually manipulate it. It will better help you connect with your own abilities and it will give me more than enough strength to contact the spirits. I will focus all of our magic together. You should all be able to see and hear everything that the spirits have to say, though I would ask that you do not address them directly, just observe."

I examined the faces before me. David looked skeptical. Bridgette giggled nervously while Red looked excited. Ella, Sylvia, Nathaniel and Jai were giving little away, their eyes were bright and focused. No one else spoke.

"Let's begin. Join hands in a circle around the tree," I instructed.

The group moved quickly. Bridgette skipped forward and took one of my hands, David slid his hand around my other. His fingers were long, his skin smooth, his grip firm and strong. I was surprised by the comforting feel of his hand in mine.

"What if someone sees us?" Bridgette suddenly asked, her eyes darting back towards the trail. "We look ridiculous."

A few others rolled their eyes. Red snorted softly.

"I don't want anyone to pay attention to us, so they won't," I informed her curtly.

"Oh… right. Well, good." She giggled and tossed her head, sharing a quick smile with Nathaniel who held her other hand. I cleared my throat.

"Close your eyes and follow my instructions. Become aware of your own breath, your own heart beating. Relax and slow down your breathing, slow down your pulse. Good…" I followed my own instructions as I spoke, slowing and deepening my breaths. "Now reach out slowly with your mind and focus on the breathing of the people to either side of you. Connect your breath with theirs, fall into the same rhythm, feel their pulse matching yours through your hands."

My necklace was slowly growing warmer, its gentle pulsating throb matching the rhythm of my own heart, the rhythm of the group. I continued speaking, my voice soft and hypnotic.

"Let yourself become aware of the energy vibrating within you, pulsating with its own rhythm so closely entwined with your heart. Feel that power, that quiet strength just below the surface that is waiting to be used. Let it spread, let it fill you, let it become you. Feel the magic in every fiber of your being, in every heartbeat, in every breath. Feel it inside you and feel it all around you. Let the magic flow through the circle, through all of us. Let it travel through your left hand and out your right in a never-ending cycle. Let it travel through your body, your heart and your mind with each heartbeat, each breath."

The magic swelled within me, rushing through me in an amazing current. My senses were all heightened, making me hyper-aware of the birds far overhead, the distant splashes and calls of ducks, the hum of the city's traffic, the icy bite of the breeze against my cheeks. It was amazing. It was a rush.

"Wow," I heard Bridgette whisper beside me. I smiled.

"Good. Now I'm going to direct the flow and use it to contact the spirits. Feel my focus, feel the control, feel the way the magic is shaped around my desire." I paused, ensuring they were all focusing. "Hear me. I need your aid," I called to the spirits. My words echoed eerily around the woods, my voice bouncing back off the trees. The day suddenly grew darker, the clouds shifting to obscure even more of the sun. I opened my eyes and watched as tendrils of mist began unraveling all around us. They appeared from the thin air but quickly formed a solid gray wall around our group, blocking out the rest of the forest and swirling around the ancient oak in the center of the circle. I knew it was both real and unreal; a blurring of boundaries, a blending of worlds. "Open your eyes," I whispered to the others. "And focus."

The damp mist continued to roll in around us and with it came a definite sense that we were no longer alone. A powerful presence had entered our circle, invisible to our eyes but I could tell the others had all sensed it too. Only Red, Ella and Sylvia looked afraid, the rest of us appeared calm.

"Gracelynn," the wind whispered. I watched as the others' eyes all widened, realizing they heard the voice too. "Why do you summon us?"

The mist rolled and tumbled around the tree at the center of our circle, the dry, ancient voice seeming to speak from the oak tree itself as the wind around us steadily rose.

"Sebastian has been taken by some of those who can control the

Lost Magic. We need to find him, to rescue him and to stop the others but we don't know where they went, where to start," I explained, my voice clear and crisp but my words still muffled and muted by the thickening fog.

"Those you have turned away, the angry ones, they have turned to a darker source as you were warned. They are dangerous. The evil that they are capable of, the horrors that will unfold at their hands if you let them continue down this dark path. They must be stopped. You must destroy the darkness that guides them," the voice hissed on the wind, whipping through my hair and into my ears almost painfully.

"The one you seek is with them, he still lives but he hurts… The pain… The darkness… It is almost too late." The wind carried the words to my ears, sending waves of shock and fear through my heart, almost causing me to lose focus. The mist began to break apart with my loss of control.

"Where are they? How can we find them? How can we save Sebastian?" I demanded, an edge of desperation to my voice as I called out into the steadily rising wind.

"They have been led from the light and into the darkness, tempted by the darker side of the magic. They must be stopped. Destroy the darkness that guides them and save the ones you seek. They set a trap but you must go, you must lead the others… you must stop them…" The wind blasted each word into my face, so strong now it nearly knocked me down. I planted my feet determinedly, squinting into the wind, watching the mist swirling up and around the old oak tree. David squeezed my hand tightly in encouragement.

"I will go. I will lead them—just show me where. Show me how," I begged.

The wind swirled faster, creating a spiraling cyclone with the oak tree at its center. The remaining tendrils of mist were sucked into the vortex, creating a thick, gray cloud around the tree, blurred in places by the violent wind.

"The dark ones must be stopped." The words came from all around me, the voice splitting and turning into a hundred whispered words upon the wind. "See," the wind whispered over and over.

"See."

The gray cloud around the tree thickened and seemed to solidify, an image forming faintly at its center. I strained to make it out.

I saw a gray ocean, tossing and turning, waves crashing steadily against a long, sandy beach. A motorboat rode the waves, its name painted near the back of the ship, *The Sea Spite*. A few dark figures were visible, huddling into their coats as they were battered by the wind and the rain. I thought I recognized the dark green coat that Jeremy had been wearing when he turned up on the doorstep of my mother's house. My attention was focused on another though, a pale, black-haired man who was huddled in a corner of the boat, separate and apart from the others as he gazed out over the ocean. His eyes were dead and cold, his face white, his expression so devoid of all emotion that it made his face terrifying and unfamiliar. He looked like he was in so much pain, his body could barely contain it. He was too pale, he stood too hunched, his face twisted into a permanent grimace. The sight of Sebastian like that shocked me so much that I lost my focus entirely. I lost control of the magic. Like a candle snuffed out, the magic was abruptly gone. The mist instantly vanished, the wind died mid-gust. I dropped David and Bridgette's hands and fell heavily to my knees.

"What, whoa!" Nathaniel mumbled. I heard several others stumble as they reeled beneath the backlash of my abrupt withdrawal from the ceremony.

"Grace, are you alright?" Bridgette asked me, gently placing her hand on my shoulder. I was trembling beneath her light touch, struggling desperately to keep my emotions at bay. What had they done to him that he would look like that? What torture and pain had he been put through that would make him look so broken, so dead inside? The icy fear inside of me was slowly morphing into a steadily building, passionate rage. It was so much easier to be angry than to be afraid.

"No. I'm not alright," I answered, my voice fierce. She took a small step back from me, letting her hand fall. Surprisingly, it was David who stepped forward and took my hand, pulling me to my feet without waiting for my permission. He looked unexpectedly disturbed.

"That was intense," Ella spoke up. "My hands are still shaking."

"Yeah," Red agreed, at a loss for words.

"I know that place, in the vision. It looked like the West Coast," Sylvia announced quietly. "Somewhere near Tofino or Ucluelet—maybe Long Beach?"

"That's what I was thinking too," Jai agreed. "It's 10am, we could reach the west coast of the island by 2pm if we leave now."

All eyes turned to me and David, waiting expectantly.

"Let's go," I agreed, my voice sounding rough and harsh.

Everyone immediately started walking back towards the trail but David paused, catching my wrist and pulling me back.

"Maybe we shouldn't rush into this. They're dangerous, Gracelynn, the spirit said so. I know you're eager to save Sebastian but the others have no experience with this kind of thing. You're leading them into a battle when they can barely hold a sword. I think it would be wise to take a little time to formulate a plan, to train the others more. Do you even know what you're going to do with Jeremy and his followers once we find them? And what of this 'darkness' that you're expected to destroy?" David demanded.

"I know exactly what I'm going to do," I answered. I tugged my wrist free from his grip. "I'm going to kill them all," I pronounced coldly. And with that, I marched away from David, stomping angrily over the wet, rotting leaves. For once, I left him in stunned silence.

Chapter Eleven – Carefully Laid Plans

"ARE WE GOING ALL THE WAY TO the west coast then?" Bridgette asked me as I tried to march past her.

"Yes."

"Too bad it's not beach weather," she sighed. She kept talking, before I could respond. "Are we all going in Sylvia's van? You'll sit with me Grace, won't you? I've barely had a chance to talk to you since I got here and now I've got even more questions."

Her smile was so innocent and friendly it made me hesitate. I had hoped to spend the drive in the front of the van with David. At least I could depend upon him for some silence. As I opened my mouth to say 'no', David caught my eye and gave me a significant look. His meaning was clear: I needed to spend time with these people, I needed to get to know them, as well as teach them. I could not shirk my responsibilities again, the results were sure to be disastrous.

"Sure, I'll sit with you," I agreed.

"Good." Bridgette beamed back at me.

David and Sylvia sat in the front of the van, David driving again. Jai, Ella and Nathaniel took up the second row, and in the very back sat Red, Bridgette and myself. There was just enough room for all of us with everyone's bags piled into the back and stowed under the seats.

Everyone was chattering almost excitedly as David pulled the van out of the parking lot. They were all still amazed by their first experience with the Lost Magic.

"My body's still vibrating with energy," Sylvia commented. She looked like she was buzzing, as if she'd drank too much coffee. In fact, they all did.

Bridgette held out her trembling hands and smiled. "Me too."

"That was amazing. The rush of power… I could get used to that!" Red grinned.

Nathaniel half turned in his seat, speaking to me over his shoulder.

"I've never experienced anything like that. The amount of magic you used… The things you could have done, if you had wanted…"

"But I didn't. I just wanted to contact the spirits, to get their help in finding Sebastian and the others. I don't think you could harness that much power unless your intentions were true. You have to want something with your whole unyielding heart and with only the purest of intentions."

There was a pause in the conversation as everyone considered my words.

"Tell us about Sebastian," Bridgette requested. She gave me a small, shy smile. "We all know you love him and you're supposed to be marrying him soon but… well, if we're going to all risk our necks to save him it would be nice to know a bit more about him."

Several others nodded in agreement. I hesitated. It was hard to talk about him right now. It brought up so many memories, making my chest collapse. I was so afraid and worried for him…

"He's strange," David spoke up from the front. "Always has been. He's a bit of a demented philosopher, takes some things with a grain of salt and looks far too deeply into others. But he can also be fun—Sebastian has always known how to have a good time. He can get broody though and boy, he has a frightening temper if you can push him that far. He's not at all what you'd expect from a two thousand year old man. Sometimes I wonder if his mental maturity was frozen at eighteen along with the rest of his body."

"What did ya say there?" Red called from the back. Bridgette openly gaped.

"Sebastian is around two thousand years old," David repeated. "Isn't that right, Grace?" All eyes turned to me.

"How old are you?" Ella asked curiously.

"Um, I'm nineteen. But I've known Sebastian since he was young, sort of."

"I don't understand," Bridgette whined. I sighed. I hadn't wanted to talk about this, to share this part of my life with them. But obviously I was going to have to. It was something they needed to hear, needed to understand and maybe it was something I needed to say.

"Ok, I might as well start at the beginning…"

And so I proceeded to tell them the whole story, starting with my life as the priestess Caoilinn, when I had first met Sebastian (or Seamus as he was called then) two thousand years in the past. I explained how Caoilinn had given Seamus his ability, how she was murdered and how Seamus/Sebastian, in his loneliness, later went on to create the Others. I continued with how he had eventually realized his mistake and left the Others, losing many of his memories and hibernating somewhere near the Arctic for several hundred years. Then I explained how we were reunited nearly two thousand years later in Victoria, how my powers were awakened and his memories returned, and we were forced to run from the Others together. I told them how the end of the Others came to be, how their magic had been permanently stripped from them and their memories erased. I did not mention the four of the Others who had the natural ability to access the Lost Magic or the ones whose memories I had restored. I didn't consider Lily to be a threat and Jai, Nathaniel and David were all under my control… more or less. I explained how I thought I had destroyed the Lost Magic in the Necromanteion last summer but then it had been reawakened just in those with the natural ability (as opposed to most of the Others who had possessed the magic unnaturally). The rest they knew, more or less.

"You've been through a lot," Sylvia commented from the front seat. She was gazing back at me with sympathetic eyes. There was an added element of respect to her tones, as if hearing my story had somehow elevated me.

Jai and Nathaniel were also turned around and looking at me differently, almost with admiration.

"I've never heard the whole story before," Jai announced in his crisp, precise way. He tilted his head to the side, his eyes considering me. "That was fascinating. Thank you."

"I've heard it all before, and I must say, it's just as uninteresting hearing it from you as from Seamus," David commented dryly. I ignored him.

"Well, that's enough about me. Please, tell me about yourselves," I encouraged and surprisingly, I really meant it. I felt lighter now that I had shared my tale, like I had gotten something off my chest. And now that I'd actually opened up to these people, I felt obligated to allow them to do the same in return. I wanted to get to know them, I realized. It had been so long since I'd had any friends, apart from Sebastian and perhaps Clarke.

"I'll start," Red loudly volunteered. "Well, I'm from Australia, in case you hadn't noticed. I just turned forty this summer, I got a girl-friend back home but no kids. She understood that I had to go on this trip, I think, I hope!" He laughed. "Well, hopefully she's waiting for me on the ranch when I get back home. That's what I do by the way, I'm a ranch owner and operator, a regular ole outback cow-boy…" And he continued to tell us all about his life back home and how he had ended up here, in Victoria, compelled almost against his will to search for a nameless young woman with an amber necklace from a recurring dream who he believed would guide him and in-stead, finding others like himself.

Everyone took turns sharing their stories. A few things surprised me, like that Sylvia, who wasn't much older then me, had two kids, or that Ella (who looked like a punk-rocker) was a high school teacher from Florida who taught Spanish and French but also spoke three other languages. I was also surprised to hear that Bridgette had been in an advanced program and completed high school over a year ago. She was now working on the second year of a Psychology degree through an online university. It was just another reminder of how little I knew about her and how much she had changed. The look on Bridgette's face when Nathaniel announced that he was nearly seven hundred years old was priceless, I actually had to bite the inside of my cheek to keep from laughing out loud. There were a few surprises for us all.

Finally it was David's turn. We all watched the back of his head expectantly as he continued to drive us through the winding roads that twisted up and over the mountains as we crossed the island, heading north and west. Unsurprisingly, he was not very forthcoming.

"Sebastian and I were once good friends. He gave me my powers. He betrayed me and when I tried to hold him accountable for his mistakes, Grace took my powers, erased my memory and tried to destroy the Lost Magic entirely. With our memories erased, Grace, Sebastian and myself became friends once more and were living together, here in Victoria. Grace returned my memories to me yesterday after Sebastian went missing but first she used magic to make me blindly commit to helping her. And so here we are."

"So are you friend or foe then, mate?" Red demanded, speaking the question that I was sure many others were wondering.

"I am an unwilling accomplice, for the time being," David replied, coldly. "Now if you've all quite finished with the group bonding, I'm going to put some music on."

And with that he cranked up the radio.

We stopped for gas and lunch in Port Alberni, a small, sprawling town in the center of the island. Everyone had split up for lunch, Bridgette skipping along after Jai and Nathaniel in the direction of a small Italian restaurant across the street. I remained close to the van, choosing to purchase my lunch from the gas station store and eat in the parking lot. To my surprise, David opted to join me. He sat in the driver's seat, chewing his sandwich and sipping from a cup of coffee. I sat in the passenger's seat, picking at a muffin and playing with my cell phone distractedly. I dialed Sebastian's number over and over.

"Why do you keep trying?" David suddenly asked, his voice unexpectedly soft. He nodded to the phone in my hands. "He's not going to answer. The number has been disconnected and even if it hadn't, the people he's with aren't likely to let him take calls."

"I know. I guess I just keep wishing that if I want it enough…"

"It won't work."

"What do you know?" I snapped. I dropped the phone back into my bag. We ate the rest of our lunch in silence.

By the time everyone had returned to the van, over forty-five minutes had passed. I felt like I could feel Sebastian slipping further away from me with every passing moment and it was driving me crazy. I couldn't sit still, I was overwhelmed with anxiety and fear. I desperately needed a distraction and chose to ride the rest of the trip up front with David.

"No music," I commanded as David fired up the engine. He glared at me as I hit the power button on the van's stereo, abruptly cutting off the tunes. I turned to face the other six people sitting behind me. "It's lesson time. If we're going to rescue Sebastian, I need you to be able to focus your ability and use the Lost Magic; even a little bit will go a long way. So let's start with something simple. I'll talk you all through it. Ready?"

"Yes," Bridgette chirped. Her eyes were wide with both excitement and awe. The others all nodded in turn.

"Alright, let's begin. The simplest desires can be the most difficult to fulfill as they are often the most whimsical. It will be much easier for you to use the Lost Magic if you are motivated by fear for your life, intense pain, hatred or any other passionate emotion. The challenge we face is that the best motivators are also the most dangerous. Allow me to demonstrate. Everyone start talking and don't stop, even if I tell you to. Go ahead," I encouraged when they all stared back at me in silence.

My companions slowly began chattering, babbling randomly to one another and laughing nervously. All except for David who remained stubbornly mute. I fixed him with a hard stare.

"You too, David."

"I'm not going to—"

"Stop," I cut in. My voice sliced through the air, the magic behind my words abruptly cutting off all conversation. The others all stared back at me in wonder, several mouths hanging open. David glared at the road ahead.

"How did you—?" Bridgette began.

"It was like you halted the words as they were on my lips," Sylvia wondered aloud.

"But how did you make us all stop when none of us wanted to?" Nathaniel quietly questioned. "I thought you couldn't manipulate another's will?"

"I can, if I truly want to, if I honestly believe that it is necessary. It still doesn't make it right, or easy to do."

"That was necessary?" David asked sarcastically.

"The lesson is necessary. That's how it works but we're going to have to start with a much easier motivator for all of you: pain. Now partner up. David, I'll work with you while you're driving. One partner is going to pinch the other—hard. Keep pinching until your partner uses the magic to make you let go. We'll switch every five minutes."

"Sounds like fun," Red chuckled from the back.

"Actually, it should be incredibly irritating, frustrating and borderline painful. Nothing less than that will motivate you enough to control the Lost Magic, at least not yet. Let's begin."

By the time we reached the west coast of the island it was nearly three o'clock in the afternoon. We had spent the rest of the trip practicing with varying degrees of success. Unsurprisingly, Jai and Nathaniel showed the most progress, managing to stop the other about half the time. Sylvia and Ella were both coming along nicely, occasionally finding success. Red was struggling and Bridgette wasn't able to make what she wanted to happen once, even when Ella and Nathaniel tried pinching her at the same time. Her pale skin was marred with bruises and red patches up and down both arms.

I had a new task for the group as we approached the end of Highway 4. We needed to make a decision, left to Ucluelet or right to Tofino? The road was about to split.

"Focus your desire," I encouraged the group. "We need to know which way to go to find Sebastian. I need all the help I can get."

The weather had turned stormy and wild the further west we had traveled. Sheets of rain, interrupted by blasts of wind were now driving down upon us. The wipers on the van were turned up as high as they could go. We were almost at the stop sign where the highway ended and met the main road that ran between Ucluelet and Tofino when I noticed there was a person standing in the middle of the road, waving to the traffic. I hoped that this was the sign we needed and we would receive the direction that we had asked for.

Hopefully our small group had enough control over the Lost Magic to at least manage that. I opened my window as we approached, shrinking away from the blasts of icy rain.

"I'm with the volunteer fire department," the man announced as we pulled up beside him. "We've had a bad accident just a few kilometers down the road. You'll have to head into Ucluelet for now—the road to Tofino is going to be closed for a few hours."

"Ok, that's where we were headed anyway. Thank you," I answered brusquely, already starting to close my window. Now that we knew exactly which direction to go, I was eager to get there.

"Wait!" Bridgette called from behind me. I left the window half open. The man peered into the van towards her, squinting through the rain. "I hope everyone's ok? We didn't want anyone to get hurt."

The man looked at her strangely. I winced.

"Actually, it's a miracle no one was hurt. A logging truck, two cars and a van are all piled up, blocking the road. The drivers should all be fine though," he reassured her.

"I'm so glad to hear that. Thank you!" Bridgette called back. The man smiled in response and we pulled away, making a left turn towards Ucluelet.

"Did we cause that accident to happen?" Ella asked quietly. An uncomfortable silence filled the van. The wipers swished noisily across the windshield.

"I don't know. It might have happened anyway, it might not have," I admitted.

No one spoke. David smirked.

"Or it might be Jeremy and the ones who've taken Sebastian using the Lost Magic to try to slow us down. They could have more control than us," Bridgette pointed out.

My heart sank, I hadn't considered that.

"Either way, we'll find out soon enough. Let's try and find the harbor. How far are we from Ucluelet anyway?" I asked, trying to distract the others and myself.

It took another half hour to reach Ucluelet. The small harbor wasn't difficult to find, nor was the information we were looking for; the Sea Spite had in fact been rented out to a group early that morning. We were on the right trail after all but now I was worried that it was too easy, that we might be following a false trail or walking straight into a trap as the spirit in my dream had warned. We were even able to find out where Jeremy and his 'friends' had gone: to a small island just off the coast, known for its wilderness camping. Unfortunately, no matter how badly we all wanted to set off that afternoon, no one would rent us a craft in the middle of a storm. The sky was black and rumbled with distant thunder, the wind whipped and tossed the waves that crested to white caps and crashed down upon the shore. The icy, winter rain poured endlessly from the sky. Perhaps I was the only one who truly wanted to set out but either way, it was obvious we would have to postpone our journey until dawn when the ocean was more calm.

"Where are we going to stay tonight?" Bridgette asked. "Please tell me we don't have to all sleep in the van!"

"There were a few hotels just down the road," Jai suggested. "It shouldn't be too expensive; it is the off-season and if we're going to be camping on that island for the next few nights, it might be nice to start out with a good night's sleep."

"Oh! How about the Rock Water Spa?" Bridgette's eyes lit up, her face hopeful.

"I can't afford to stay at a spa," Sylvia frowned.

"It's fine, I've got the bill. Let's just go," I sighed. I was drenched and frozen from walking around the harbor in the rain. I felt defeated and my exhaustion was finally catching up to me. I was dead on my feet. "Let's just go," I repeated tiredly. Bridgette clapped her hands together excitedly.

The Rock Water Spa turned out to be a ridiculously grandiose resort. It curved around a rocky peak that jutted out into the ocean. The oceanside face of the five story building was covered in large glass windows, ideal for storm-watching. The rooms were bright and modern with all the amenities, full room service, large flatscreen TV's and personal bars in each suite. We paired up, two to a room and I ended up with Bridgette. While several of the others headed into town with David to get the necessary gear and supplies for our journey, Bridgette remained with me at the resort. I had hoped to fall asleep but as soon as we were alone, Bridgette began chatting.

"I can't believe you know magic! Why didn't you ever tell me? Oh my God, Grace, I have so many questions. This is so unbelievable! Will I really be able to make whatever I want happen? Oh, I wish I could now. It's not fair that everyone else is more powerful than me. Will I always be the weakest? Do you think if I practice, my powers might grow? You'll help me won't you, Grace? Can we practice some more now?"

"No, Bridgette," I groaned. I flopped down onto the soft, cream sheets spread out neatly on my large bed. "Not now. It's been a really long day and night and week… I just need to rest."

"Oh right, sorry. I forgot." She giggled, shrugging apologetically. I closed my eyes but I could feel her still watching me.

"Grace… can I ask you something?"

"Why not?" I mumbled, eyes still closed.

"Why did you ask me to be your Maid of Honor?"

"I didn't. It was my mother," I blurted out without thinking. I was too tired to properly censor my thoughts.

"Oh. I see," Bridgette answered stiffly.

I sighed and opened my eyes. She was staring out the large window that stretched from ceiling to floor, watching the wild storm churning the ocean and the flashes of lightning flickering across the dark sky. Bridgette turned to me with accusing eyes.

"You know, I've tried so hard to get you to like me and it's like you don't even care. You've changed so much, Grace."

"I have," I agreed. "Sorry. But you're wrong, I do like you."

"No, you don't," Bridgette argued, her lips forming a pout. "You don't care about anything that you used to: fashion, boys, travel, parties. You barely even listen to me when I talk. I'm trying so hard, Grace. I just want to be friends."

"But, Bridgette, those things aren't important to me anymore because they never really were. Look, you don't have to try to impress me. I like you, I've always liked you. And I'm sorry if I haven't been reading all your emails or paying enough attention to you, I didn't mean to hurt your feelings and I still don't. I've just had a lot on my mind." Bridgette didn't look appeased. I continued on, hoping to distract her. "I can't believe I didn't know you'd graduated or that you were in an advanced academic program in high school! That's really special—I wish I'd read that in your emails."

"Yeah, well, I didn't actually tell you about that before today," Bridgette confessed. She gave me a shy smile. "I didn't want you to know what a nerd I am."

I rolled my eyes.

"Being smart doesn't make you a nerd. You should be proud. Graduating nearly three years early and being a straight-A psychology student at university is a lot more interesting than any party you might have been to in Paris or Milan. Or at least, it is to me."

"Really?"

"Really."

She giggled. "I made up half those stories anyway."

"Well, you didn't need to. I would love to get to know the real you again. Don't try and impress me anymore, please. I like you the best when you're just you."

"Ok. Thanks," she smiled. "Do you think Nathaniel likes me?"

I paused, considering.

"Why shouldn't he? You're nice and friendly, I'm sure he considers you a friend."

"But I don't want to be just friends," Bridgette objected. "I really like him, Grace."

"Bridgette… he's seven hundred years old," I reminded her.

"So? Isn't Sebastian nearly two thousand years older than you?" she shot back.

"Yes… but that's different."

"How?"

She waited expectantly, and when I didn't immediately answer she launched back in.

"I really like him, Grace. I've liked him from the moment I saw him; I just feel this connection with him and I know you said the Lost Magic draws people together but, it's different with him than anyone else. I've never had a real boyfriend or been in love before. When you were talking about Sebastian today in the van… it made me realize, that's what I want. I want someone to love me like that.

Do you think, maybe, there might be a chance Nathaniel could feel that way about me one day?" she asked hopefully.

"Of course it's possible," I assured her. "But, can I make a suggestion?"

"Sure."

"Sebastian and I were friends for months before anything ever happened between us. We were really good friends, and our close friendship is what our whole relationship is based on. Be yourself and really get to know him, take it slow. The rest will all follow. I do think he likes you though," I admitted. Bridgette grinned.

"Thanks. He's so… he's like no one I've ever met before," she sighed. She stared dreamily out the window, falling into silence once more.

I relaxed back against my mattress and closed my eyes.

"There's something else I need to tell you," Bridgette confessed guiltily. I slowly reopened my eyes. "I haven't been entirely honest with you. When I said in the van that I came here because I had a dream that I needed to find you, like the others all said, well… that wasn't entirely true."

"Ok. What is the truth?"

"I did have a dream but it wasn't just a dream. You see, I have this friend back in Berlin, or I should say, I *had* a friend. We were pretty close, she was like a big sister to me. I used to visit her all the time but then a few months ago she went missing. No one seemed to care that she was missing except for me. No one ever looked for her and they never found her body but… I'm sure she died. I know she did, actually because, well…" Bridgette took a nervous breath. I sat up a little straighter. "Her spirit comes to me in my dreams sometimes. She was the one who told me I had to find you, that you would guide me to my destiny."

My lips parted in surprise.

"Ok…"

"Yes, but that's not all. This is the part that's really crazy. But I think I can trust you, can't I?"

"Of course," I agreed, sitting all the way up now.

She slowly rose and crossed the room to where her suitcase sat on the floor. She began rummaging around in it.

"A few weeks before my friend went missing, she told me I had to leave town—she begged me to. She said her old boyfriend was coming back to Berlin and that she was pretty sure he was bringing trouble with him, dangerous people who were trying to hurt him and might hurt her too. She was afraid they'd hurt me if they found out we were friends so she made me promise I'd leave town for a few weeks. She was so insistent… I didn't want to but I couldn't say no. Before I left, she gave me something that she said would keep me safe. It was the last time I ever saw her," Bridgette added sadly. Tears sparkled in her large, green eyes.

I watched warily as she reached into her suitcase and pulled out a long, thin object. As I realized what it was, I jumped back on my bed, my hand flying to the necklace at my throat. In the same instant, I gathered the Lost Magic around me, ready to use it against Bridgette to defend my life.

Bridgette turned the ancient, ceremonial knife over in her hand, her eyes still sad and shimmering with tears.

"She gave me this knife and she told me that if a girl named Caoilinn ever came to me, I should use this knife to protect myself against her, that she'd be afraid of it and that when the time came, I'd know what to do. But then, David called you Caoilinn and you said yourself, in the van, that you used to be her… so now I don't know what to do. First she told me Caoilinn was dangerous but then she told me in my dream to go find you and that you'd help me. I don't know why but she must have been wrong. I know I don't need to protect myself from you; you'd never hurt me, would you?"

I stared at her in shock. I could barely process what she had just said. I swallowed hard, trying to find my voice. It all made sense. The spirit who had been visiting my dreams and Bridgette's mysterious friend in Berlin were one and the same. A girl who had hated and mistrusted Caoilinn while she was alive but desperately wanted to help me and to save Sebastian after her death. It was her, it had to be. I knew it deep down in my soul.

"You don't need to protect yourself from me. I would never hurt you like that but I'm afraid what I'm about to say now might hurt you, just in a different way," I whispered, my voice tight. Bridgette took a step back, her eyes wide. "I'm so sorry, Bridgette, but you're right, your friend is dead."

"How do you know?" Bridgette demanded. Her hand that held the large, ornate knife was shaking, her eyes were sparkling brightly with the tears that flooded them.

"Because I was there when Mags died."

Chapter Twelve - Last Breath

"How do you know her name?" Bridgette demanded. Her reaction was unexpected. Her whole body had tensed, her hand squeezed the large, silver knife handle tightly. She watched me through narrowed eyes.

"I used to know Mags," I admitted. "Her old boyfriend that she told you about, that was Sebastian but he wasn't really her boyfriend; he was actually her husband. And the trouble he brought with him back to Berlin… well, I guess that was me. Remember what I told you in the van, how the Others chased us across Europe until they finally caught up with us in Thessaloniki and took us to the Necromanteion? Well, Mags was with us when they caught us, she was actually trying to help us then. But… they didn't let her go." I left out the part about how I had completely erased Mags' memory so that she didn't even know who she was anymore beyond her own name. I had acted rashly, out of anger and it wasn't something I was proud of or something that Bridgette needed to know.

"Why didn't they take her to the Necromanteion with you?" Bridgette blinked away disbelieving tears. I noticed her grip on the knife still hadn't relaxed.

"She had made a deal with the Others, that she would turn me over to them and then they would let her and Sebastian go. Only, they had no intentions of ever following through with that plan. They wanted all three of us dead and they started with her. She was the one who helped Sebastian create the Others and they felt she had betrayed them. So they killed her."

Bridgette stared back at me, her beautiful face expressionless and devoid of all emotion. Her eyes hardened.

"How did they do it?" she asked quietly.

"Are you sure you want to know?"

"Tell me."

"She would have felt no pain," I lied. How could I tell her that Mags had been tortured for hours, perhaps the better part of the day, before they finally killed her? "One of the Others, he snapped her neck. They burned down the building that her body was left in: a hostel near the center of Thessaloniki," I tried to be as gentle as I could.

"Were Jai or Nathaniel involved in her death? Or David?"

"No," I lied again. David hadn't been there when Mags died even though it had occurred at his command. Jai was there but he had been acting under David's orders, and it was Darius who had actually killed Mags. Maybe one day Bridgette would learn the truth but for now, I didn't feel it was safe to tell her. I held her gaze as steadily as possible, until she seemed satisfied and dropped her eyes. She gently placed the knife on the bed between us.

"Mags hated Caoilinn and she hated me," I confessed. "She blamed me for everything that had gone wrong, she saw me as her enemy. But we had some common ground. We both truly cared for Sebastian, we'd both do anything to keep him safe. And though we were never friends, I think we had reached a mutual understanding. We were no longer enemies but allies, fighting the same battle."

Bridgette slowly nodded.

"Do you think if I tried to summon her, if I tried to call her to my dreams, she might come to me? I have so many questions."

"You could try. Maybe we could even try together but… not now. I really am exhausted."

"Right, sorry." Bridgette blinked away her tears. "I knew she was dead but to hear it confirmed… To know how… You're right, it was hard to hear. I think I'll go down to the spa now. I could use a massage and some time to think. What should I do with the knife?"

"Keep it. It was Mags' last gift to you."

Bridgette nodded. She slipped it back into her bag and walked over to the door, hesitating in the doorway.

"I'm glad we talked, Grace."

"Me too. I'm sorry about Mags. Are you sure you're ok?"

"Yes, I will be."

Alone in the room, I thought I would finally be able to rest but sleep eluded me. My head was swirling with thoughts and emotions, as dark and wild as the storm raging outside.

Why had Mags been spending time with Bridgette? What could her interest in her have been? She had obviously wanted to keep Bridgette away from not only the Others but also Sebastian and myself—but why? The dull, tired ache behind my eyes increased to a painful throb. I realized I wasn't going to sleep; what I needed was some fresh air. I grabbed my coat and headed downstairs. The storm looked like it might be lightening a little and a walk on the beach was just what I needed to clear my head.

The rain had eased off by the time I made it outside and though thunder still rumbled in the distance and an occasional flash of lightning cracked through the sky, it wasn't too bad outside. I made my way down a path on the rocky face of the point, carefully climbing down towards a small strip of beach below. The wind whipped at my face, freezing my skin and tangling my hair. As I climbed down lower, the rocks somewhat protected me from the wind and I was able to find a little shelter. I sat down on the smoothest part of rock I could find and gazed out over the white-capped waves. The water was almost as dark as the sky, the two barely distinguishable on the horizon as they blended into one another. Sebastian was out there somewhere, I realized. I prayed that he was safe, that he was holding on, that we would make it to him in time.

Tears danced in my eyes and a sob gathered in my chest. Cold, exhausted and finally alone, I no longer fought my tears.

"What are you doing?" David's voice demanded as he suddenly appeared, climbing down the path above me.

I quickly wiped the moisture from my cheeks, glaring angrily out at the ocean.

"Nothing. I just want to be alone."

"One of the sacrifices a leader must make: there's always going to be someone seeking you, Caoilinn. Get used to it."

"What do you want, David?" I had little patience for his games.

He jumped down onto the beach and took a seat on a rock near mine. I could feel him studying me.

"We got all the supplies we'll need for our little wilderness excursion tomorrow. The others are all inside, enjoying the restaurant and the spa and whatever else there is to do here. I came out because I wanted to be alone as well."

"Go find your own spot. This one's taken," I grumbled. "Why do you want to be alone anyway? I thought you'd want to spend time with Jai and Nathaniel, your old friends?"

"They were hardly ever my friends, and certainly not now."

David gazed out at the dark waters stretching before us, offering no further explanation. To my great annoyance he didn't appear to want to find his own spot, either. Maybe I should just get up and leave?

"You shouldn't worry so much," he suddenly commented to the air. "He's going to be ok, you know."

It took me a second to realize that he wasn't criticizing me, he was actually trying to offer some kind of reassurance. I stared at him in surprise but he still wasn't looking my way.

"What if he's not?" I asked quietly.

"He's a lot tougher than you realize and a lot more dangerous than they think. Even without magic, Sebastian is not someone to be taken lightly." There was a hint of admiration to David's voice. It made me think twice about him.

"Your perceptions of those around you are often quite naïve. There is more to a person than what you see on the surface, than what you think you know," David mused, his black eyes almost perfect mirror images of the stormy sky. "Sometimes assumptions can be proven false. You might think twice about those around you and find a change of heart."

"What are you talking about?"

"Take myself, for example. The time I spent with you and Sebastian, before you returned my memories to me, it has changed me in many ways, ways I could never have anticipated. Even though I can now remember my past hatred for Sebastian, I also have very clear and recent memories of admiring him, loving him even. And then there's you, Grace. My feelings for you have certainly changed."

We locked eyes and my heart skipped a beat.

"I'm not sure why you're telling me this," I said softly, suddenly nervous. Somehow he was able to hear me over the sound of the nearby crashing waves and the thunder rolling in the distance.

"You made me swear that I would give you my help," he responded. He moved slowly, his movements fluid and graceful, deadly and dangerous as he came to sit right beside me. His eyes never broke their lock on mine. "I'm being helpful."

"This is not helpful," I argued, hating myself for sounding so breathless, for not moving away.

He smiled, his eyes crinkling at the edges. It was the first time I could remember seeing him smile like that, full of such playful innocence. It was both charming and completely disarming all at once.

"Can't I offer you comfort when you need it? Tell me then, where do we stand, Grace? Not quite enemies, yet not quite friends? Our relationship has been complicated in a way I never thought to imagine. Everything about you is… unexpected. I'm not sure what to do about this."

"And what is 'this'?" I held my breath nervously as I waited for him to answer. I didn't know what I wanted him to say. I was so confused.

"This, us. It's complicated. I never expected you to be a good leader. I never thought you would be someone I could follow. I didn't anticipate the connection between us, this chemistry." His eyes lit up, he leant closer towards me. My whole body tensed.

"I don't know what chemistry you're talking about," I lied. I still couldn't lean away.

"You do," he murmured, his eyes staring deeply into mine. I'd never noticed how beautiful his eyes were, dark steely gray that I'd always thought of as hard but now they were pools of liquid silver.

"You should go."

"If you really meant that, wouldn't I already be gone?" His face was just inches from mine, his breathing shallow, his words surprisingly soft.

I felt so torn. I loved Sebastian, I knew I didn't want anyone else but I was so tired and felt so alone. I was afraid to do this by myself and here was someone who could help me, who was dangerous and exciting, and handsome. And he wanted me. I knew it was wrong but for some strange reason, I couldn't say no.

"Stop," I whispered back to him but my words were lost on the wind. Lightning flashed overhead as he brought his lips against mine.

The wind swirled around us, icy and bitingly cold. Goosebumps tingled all over my skin as his mouth slowly pressed against mine. Kissing Sebastian had always felt so right, so warm and passionate and heady. But this was different, this was entirely new. David was dark and exciting, his passion sudden and intense and exhilarating. His hand in my hair gripped hard, his mouth was cool, his lips hungry, moving slowly and torturously with calculated precision that for some reason, I couldn't help but respond to. The kiss only lasted for seconds, but when we broke apart, he had taken my breath away and left my heart pounding.

I blinked and found myself staring directly into his eyes. For a second, I thought I could see right down to his soul, to his true inner self. All the arrogance and pretenses that he usually hid behind were stripped away and I caught a glimpse of who he might truly be. His eyes abruptly hardened.

"Shit. Why didn't you make me stop?" he demanded, sounding angry. He rose to his feet, glaring at me. The wind rose to a steady howl all around us, large droplets of freezing cold rain splattered down from the sky.

"Why didn't you stop yourself?" I snipped back, feeling quite angry now too.

"It's complicated," he growled. He fixed me with an icy glare, much colder than the driving wind and rain. "Sorry," he spat out stiffly. "It won't happen again." And with that, he jumped to his feet and quickly climbed back up the path, disappearing at the top of the cliff.

What had just happened? What had I just done? I could barely believe I had just let David kiss me—why hadn't I stopped him?

And why the hell was David so angry now? He was the one who had kissed me! I should be angry, but instead I was just tired and confused. I felt so vulnerable. And in that moment, I wanted Sebastian so badly my whole body ached and trembled with my desire. I missed everything about him, his comforting presence, his calming words, his dependable advice. I just needed to hear his voice, to know that he was ok. I needed his reassurance and I desperately wanted his forgiveness for the stupid thing I had just let happen. Without thinking, I released a flood of magic as it swelled up within me, flowing out over the wild, stormy waves with a flash of lightning and a crash of thunder.

It was stupid and hopeless but I couldn't help myself. I automatically reached for my cell phone, dialing Sebastian's number without thinking. As soon as I realized what I was doing, I moved to hit the "End Call" button, but then I noticed that the call was connecting. I hesitantly lifted the phone to my ear, hardly daring to hope. Barely audible above the sound of the waves and the storm, the phone began to ring. There was a loud click, and then the ringtone cut off. I thought I could hear the wind through the other end but maybe it was just my imagination. Maybe it was just what I wanted to hear and not really happening at all. But then he spoke.

"Grace?" Sebastian's voice sounded different, lower and rougher, and disbelieving. It was definitely him. A jolt of adrenaline shot through me at the sound. My whole body instantly responded.

"Sebastian? Where are you? What happened to you? Are you ok?" I demanded. I couldn't believe that I was really talking to him.

"Grace, how did you get through? My battery was dead and there's no service out here. Not to mention that the number was disconnected. Is… is your magic really that powerful?"

I froze, my mind reeling as if I'd been slapped. It took me a second to form any words.

"You know?"

"About the Lost Magic? Yes. I can remember it now, Grace. Well, most of it."

I paused, losing my voice in stunned silence.

"But how? I mean… never mind, that's not important. Just tell me where you are. How do we find you? Are you alright?"

"No." I waited for him to continue but when he didn't I began to panic.

"Sebastian? Are you still there? Can you hear me?"

"I'm here." He sounded tired, even more exhausted than I felt. I could take no comfort in hearing his voice, not when everything about him sounded so wrong. "I'm sorry."

"What do you mean? What's wrong? Sebastian… what did they do to you?" Fear struck deep in my stomach, making me want to throw up.

"Nothing… Everything," he mumbled. "Look, you can't come after me, Grace. I'm sorry but you're too late." His voice was monotone, his words those of a stranger.

"No," I denied. "We're close, Sebastian. We're in Ucluelet. We chartered a boat and will be coming after you at dawn."

"No!" I flinched back from the harsh sound as he yelled into the phone. "You can't, Grace. Promise me you won't! It's too dangerous and you're too late. You can't save me now, Grace. I'm sorry. I'm so sorry," he repeated almost mournfully. "I wasn't strong enough. I couldn't fight anymore."

Tears flooded my eyes, panic overwhelmed me.

"I won't give up, I can't. You have to keep fighting them! What did they do to you? What did they do? I'll make them pay, I swear it," I declared, tears freely streaming down my face.

"No, don't. Please. Promise me you'll go home. Stay far away from Jeremy and all the others, stay as far from the Lost Magic as you can, Grace. It's dangerous: it'll kill you too. Promise you'll stay away," he begged weakly, the strength in his voice rapidly fading.

"I can't do that. I won't do that."

"You have to. It's too late, I'm beyond saving now. I'm so sorry… I never pictured it ending like this." His voice broke a little at the end. My heart tore wide open along with it. "At least I can say good-bye."

"Sebastian, don't. You'll be ok—you have to be ok. Please don't give up."

"I have to go. Please, just let me go," he told me, his voice beginning to break up.

"No! Sebastian—wait! Please!" I yelled into the receiver, begging and desperately wanting him to stay with me with all of my heart and soul.

"Go home, Grace, and remember me," he whispered into the phone. "Remember how much I loved you and all the beautiful memories we had. Move on with your life and be happy, do it for me. And whatever you do, stay away from the magic and stay far away from David; he's dangerous, Grace. And if you ever meet a girl called Caoilinn—run."

"What?" I gasped. I couldn't understand what he was saying. Had I misheard him?

"Stay away from David and Caoilinn," Sebastian repeated in that strange, flat voice. He didn't just sound like he was dying, he sounded like he was already dead.

"But... I am Caoilinn."

I was answered with heavy silence. I thought I might still be able to hear the wind through the phone.

"Sebastian? Please, don't leave me. Don't go! Sebastian!" There was no answer. My tears mingled with the raindrops that streamed down my face. "I love you," I whispered into the phone but the call had already been lost. It should never have gone through in the first place.

And that was when I felt it. A light inside of me, a part of my soul that I had always accepted even when I wasn't entirely aware of its existence, began to slowly fade. I could feel it slipping away. I could feel its light fading and the dark void growing in its place. My heart broke in half as I felt a piece of me die. And though I could barely believe it, I knew it was true. Sebastian was gone. Sebastian had died. The emptiness left behind was suffocating, my grief choking me, the pain unbearable.

"No!" I screamed into the wind, so loud and long my throat felt raw and bloody. But it made no difference.

I knew, without a doubt, that Sebastian was forever gone.

Chapter Thirteen – Journey

OW DO YOU LIVE WHEN A PART of you has died? How can you walk around with a gaping hole of grief and dark abandonment in your chest? Is it possible to survive such a loss? When the person who gave your life purpose and meaning is gone, what is the point in continuing? I was directionless and empty. I had been completely abandoned and left alone. I was nothing.

The crashing waves sprayed salty water into my face that mixed with the steady flow of rain and tears. The wind whipped at my body, the powerful gusts nearly knocking me down from the small boulder where I had curled myself up into a ball. By the time David and the others found me, I was soaked and chilled to the bone. I shivered violently, my teeth audibly chattering. The storm still raged around me but I was silent; silent and empty. I wouldn't respond to their words. They pulled at my arms, they snapped their fingers in front of my face yet I remained unresponsive and mute. Seeing but unseeing, alive but without any life left within me. It wasn't until David's face suddenly filled my vision, his molten silver eyes gently probing mine, that I was forced to respond. My traitorous body reacted without my consent, my heart rate minutely increasing, my eyes automatically focusing on his.

"Did something happen to Sebastian?" he guessed. He looked concerned, his voice soft, all traces of his previous anger had disappeared. How long had it been since he had kissed me? Hours? Days? It was dark out now, I realized, noticing the flashlights that the others carried. How many hours had passed since Sebastian…? I couldn't even think the word.

"He's gone," I whispered, my numb lips barely moving.

David blinked once. He looked completely stunned. I'd never seen him so discomposed. I knew he understood exactly what I meant. And I knew he didn't doubt me for a second. How could he? He suddenly cursed loudly; he sounded furious. He roared into the wind.

"What? What's going on?" I heard Red asking. No one answered him.

"We need to get you inside. You're freezing, Grace—your lips are blue. Maybe I should just carry you." David was back in front of me, his face so close to mine.

"No." His words brought me back to life, at least enough that I was willing to move on my own to avoid his touch. I couldn't bear the thought of David's hands on me right now. "I'll walk."

I slowly stood. It was difficult to straighten my legs, all my muscles had cramped up and frozen in position. I stumbled and hands caught me—Bridgette's and Sylvia's—their expressions so worried and full of concern. I stared back at them blankly but allowed them to silently help me back up the cliff and back to the resort, the others trailing behind or in front, I wasn't really sure. Word spread quickly. I could hear the whispers rippling through the group as they led me to the elevator.

"What happened? What's wrong with her?"

"Sebastian. He… she thinks he's dead."

"What? When? How does she know for sure?"

"Look at her—she knows."

I closed my ears and let my eyes fall blind. I retreated into the painful darkness billowing within my soul.

Bridgette, Sylvia and Ella took me to my room. I remained in a detached, trance-like state as they stripped me out of my wet clothes and sat me in a hot bath. After Bridgette gently washed my hair, they wrapped me up in warm towels and helped me dress in some old sweat pants and a shirt which had been one of Sebastian's. Hot tears instantly sprung to my eyes, fresh, piercing pain ripped through my heart. A sob escaped my lips before I could stop it. They all turned to stare at me; it was the first sound I'd made since we'd entered my room.

"This was Sebastian's," I whispered, hugging the soft, worn fabric against my skin.

"I'll get you something else," Ella offered gently.

"No!" I clutched the shirt to my chest tightly. "This is… fine."

Tears began to spill from my eyes, flowing steadily down my cheeks. Another loud sob escaped me.

"Go, please go," I asked them.

Ella and Sylvia both hesitated, surprisingly they looked to Bridgette. She gave them a small nod and they both quickly left, glancing back at me over their shoulders. Bridgette came to sit on the bed beside me. My shoulders were trembling with the effort of holding back all my grief for just a few moments longer.

"Grace, I'm so sorry. I know it seems like the end of the world now but it'll get easier—"

"What do you know?" I snapped, abruptly outraged. It was so much easier to direct my anger at her rather than face the pain and despair building inside me. "You're just a kid! A spoiled, rich, brat who's never known love beyond a pair of designer boots or a cute boy with a nice smile. Don't pretend you understand! Don't tell me that it'll get easier."

For a second, Bridgette looked shocked, then her wide eyes narrowed and her full lips pressed together tightly.

"I know how it felt when my best friend, the only person in the world who seemed to really care about me and understand me, suddenly disappeared. And I know how it felt today to hear you confirm that she's dead. But please, don't consider my pain over losing Mags at all, Grace. It's obviously nothing compared to yours! We're all nothing compared to you, right? The only thing that was important was saving Sebastian and now that you're too late, we're all just in your way. So please, allow me to leave."

She marched to the door, her back too straight, her movements stiff. I should have called after her but I didn't. I knew I'd hurt her. I hadn't really meant what I'd said but for now, I just wanted to be left alone with my pain. I was selfish and I was weak.

Hugging Sebastian's old shirt tightly against me, I curled up on my side and cried myself to sleep. But there was no peace, no escape. I would never find peace again.

Almost the moment I closed my eyes, I found myself in the middle of the now familiar dream. The soft, gray fog was swirling in, steadily billowing all around me. I wanted to run from it, to hide from the spirit trying to visit me and banish it from haunting my dreams. But then I was struck with a sudden, bright hope. What if it was him? What if he were able to reach me this way already? Wouldn't he be here now, in this strange place halfway between life and death?

The fog thickened, folding me into its soft, fuzzy warmth and trapping me within my own dream. I waited hopefully, praying with all my heart and soul. The fog in front of me began to solidify, taking human form. A bright light flared within the figure's center, momentarily blinding me. When I reopened my eyes, a spirit stood before me, an amused smile on its face.

"Not exactly who you were hoping for, I know, but really you should be thankful," Mags told me. Disappointment crushed my chest.

"Where's Sebastian? Is he with you? Why didn't he come?" I quickly demanded, focusing in on the only thing that I truly cared about.

"Sebastian can't come here, not yet," she quickly dismissed. "Now I only have a short time—you've got to listen."

"Where is he?" I repeated, my heart aching painfully at the thought of him, even in my dreams.

Mags sighed. She looked different as a spirit, her short red hair was now long and flowed half-way down to her waist. Gone was the harsh eyeliner and punk clothes she used to wear and instead she appeared in a plain, white dress that blended into the cloud around her. She looked beautiful and peaceful, with more patience and grace than she had ever expressed while alive. She smiled gently.

"He's waiting for you. That's what I'm trying to tell you."

"What? I don't understand."

"He's waiting for you, Grace. You can still save him, you can still bring him back to you. It's not too late."

"But he's already gone. I don't understand. The Lost Magic isn't powerful enough to reverse time like that, I can't really bring him back, can I?" I asked.

"You won't be strong enough alone," Mags agreed, her voice grave. "But there is power within yourself and the others that you've yet to fully realize; incredible power just waiting to be tapped. Together, you might be strong enough to bring him back but to do so will be extremely dangerous. You will all face death and not all will survive."

The soft fog around us appeared to darken as if the sun had gone behind a cloud. I shivered.

"I'll do whatever it takes."

"Good. Lead them against the ones who took Sebastian. Together, you must destroy the dark power at their center and then use your combined light to call Sebastian back to you. It might work, if you guide them." Mags' image started to fade.

"Wait!" I called. Her silhouette was wavering, blending into the cloud around her but her eyes brightened as they locked with mine. "Mags… I have to know. Is Sebastian dead because of the spirits and their meddling games? Has this all happened because you are trying to push me into a role that I didn't want to take? Tell me, Mags! Tell me the truth!"

The fire in her red-gold hair cooled and faded, disappearing into the fog. Her features blurred and evaporated until only her beautiful, bright eyes remained and even they were slowly fading away. She watched me sadly, reproachfully.

"Everything happens for a reason." Mags' voice came from all around me, whispering so peacefully in my ear. "Tell Bridgette I am with her still. And please… she needs you, Grace. Be her friend, earn her trust. You must guide her."

"I won't be your puppet!" I called out to the thinning fog. My words echoed back to my own ears. A breeze was rising, swirling and spinning the rest of the fog apart, allowing it to dissipate into the air. I could feel my physical body slowly awakening. "I won't let the spirits manipulate me and my life this way!"

"Save Sebastian," Mags' voice rode the wind, whistling in my ear. "He waits for you." And with the sound of her voice still in my ear, my eyes snapped open.

It was 4:30am, soon it would be dawn. There were already signs of the sky outside beginning to lighten. Despite my strange dream and the horrible events of the day before, I felt surprisingly energized and well-rested. Angry determination flowed through every fiber of my being. I would save Sebastian. How dare anyone, Death included, try to keep us apart? I knew that I was playing right into the spirits' hands, that this was all happening to force me to fully commit to a leadership role but I didn't care. I wanted revenge. I was focused and furious.

At some point in the night, Bridgette had returned to our room. I could see her sleeping soundly in the bed beside mine. I flicked on a lamp and sat down on the bed beside her. She stirred, mumbling softly in her sleep. I placed my hand on her shoulder, gently shaking her from her dreams.

"Huh…? What's going on? Grace?" Bridgette blinked up at me sleepily.

"I'm sorry," I said quickly, knowing I needed to get that out before anything else.

"Oh…"

"I shouldn't have said those things; they weren't true. I wasn't myself last night and I wasn't thinking straight. But really that's no excuse. I should never have spoken to you like that. I really am sorry, Bridgette, and not just for the things I said but I'm sorry that you lost Mags, and I'm sorry that I've been such an awful friend."

Bridgette sat up, her eyes looking bright and focused now that she had blinked the sleep from them.

"It's ok," she murmured but she didn't sound like she entirely meant it. I was almost glad she hadn't instantly forgiven me, it showed she had some backbone. I was ready and willing to have to work to regain her trust.

"What you said was wrong. Finding Sebastian is not the only thing that I care about: I care about you. You're my friend. You were once like a sister to me and I would love for it to be that way again. Will you give me another chance?"

She shrugged, attempting nonchalance.

"Sure, whatever," she dismissed but when I smiled at her, she slowly smiled back. "You seem... better," she commented cautiously. "Not happier but... determined?" Once again, I had forgotten how intuitive she could be.

"Mags' spirit came to me in my dreams last night," I told her. Bridgette's eyes lit up, her lips parting in surprise. "She told me that we could still save Sebastian, that we might still be able to bring him back from death."

"Is that really possible? You don't seem very hopeful." Her eyes were too knowing, bright with the intelligence that she often tried to hide.

"I have no false hopes. I know he's probably gone from me forever, at least in this life time. The spirits are playing games, trying to force me to go after the others, the 'dark ones'. They're pushing me to stop their rebellion and to put an end to the threat that they pose. For now I will go along with their plan. I will hunt them down and find vengeance in their deaths."

Bridgette stared at me, wide-eyed and pale. She slowly nodded.

"Ok. I'll go with you. Mags told me to trust you, that you would lead me along the right path and if this is it, well... then this is what I must do."

I wasn't sure that Bridgette was really ready for this or how much help she could really be but I decided to put some trust in her. She deserved to make the choice for herself and I would not turn her help away.

"Thank you," I told her quietly, my voice still harder than usual. "Mags asked me to tell you that she's still with you," I added. "She's here still, she's watching. You're never truly alone." Bridgette's eyes rapidly filled with tears.

"I know, but it's still nice to hear it." She brushed away her tears with the back of her hand. "She hasn't visited my dreams since the night she told me to find you... I wish she would but... never mind. Should we awaken the others? It'll soon be dawn."

"Yes, I'll gather them and let them know that I'm going after Jeremy and the others still, and that anyone who wants to fight can join me. Mags warned me that this is going to be very dangerous and not all of us are going to make it. Are you sure you want to come with me?" I warned.

"I'll come. The others will want to too. We all know this is what we're meant to be doing, whether it's what we pictured for ourselves or not. This is important. Jeremy and the others must be stopped. This dark side to the Lost Magic that they've discovered threatens us all. The others will see that too."

"I hope so." I rose and began pulling clothes out of my bag to dress in, keeping Sebastian's old shirt on underneath a thick, hooded sweatshirt. "Let's all meet downstairs in fifteen minutes. I'll tell the others."

I barely waited for Bridgette's nod before I strode out of the room.

Bridgette turned out to be right. Even after my warnings, the others all wanted to go with me still. Some were more enthusiastic than others. Red could hardly wait. Sylvia and Ella were both determined not to be left behind. Nathaniel immediately volunteered, as soon as Bridgette announced she would be accompanying me. Jai reluctantly conceded that it was our obligation to stop the others and put an end to the threat that they posed not just us, but potentially the world.

"We shall always follow you, Grace," Jai announced in his soft, accented tones. "We want to learn from you and we want to help you. Even after all this is said and done. You are our leader."

The others nodded their agreement. Bridgette offered me a smile of encouragement. David remained silent the whole while.

"And you?" I asked.

He narrowed his eyes at me. "Don't act like I have a choice."

"You swore only to help me find Sebastian. Sebastian is... gone. This is no longer about finding him, it's about stopping the people who took him from harming anyone else. I won't make you come with us, David. I'd like you to choose your own path."

He stared at me for several long seconds, his face totally expressionless.

"Come," he instructed, reaching for my arm and pulling me away from the others. They watched curiously as he led me across the lobby. He stepped so his back was to them, blocking me from their view.

"This is dangerous, Grace. It's suicide and you know it. This isn't about stopping Jeremy and the others from causing any more harm, this is about getting your revenge. I can see it in your eyes," he hissed. He stood close to me, his black eyes flashing with anger.

"My motivation doesn't matter, only my course of action. Will you help me or not?"

He stared at me a moment longer, his gaze heated, his chest heaving with emotion.

"Grace, you're being reckless; you're going to get hurt! Don't do this. You don't have to go after them. You can run away, forget about the Lost Magic and all of this—everything that's ever happened. We could help each other forget," he added, speaking with a sudden quiet intensity. My breath caught in my throat. "I will go wherever you lead me," he promised solemnly. I could see the passion building in his eyes and again, I thought I caught a glimpse of the true David Turner, for just a split second. But it didn't change anything.

"I can't," I whispered. My throat and lips were dry, my heart was hammering in my chest. The gaping wound that Sebastian's death had ripped open within me continued to bleed with fear and pain and rage. I could never forget. I could never just walk away.

His eyes hardened. He abruptly turned away.

"Fine. You'll need me to drive the boat then," he announced over his shoulder, his voice and expression both cold, his demeanor instantly changing.

"David, I'm sorry. I…"

"We should head out as soon as we can. The gear's all packed in the van and the boat will be waiting for us. The island they took Sebastian to will take us a good hour or more to reach. I'd like to be out on the water before seven when the tides begin to change."

I sighed. The cold, bossy, arrogant David was back. I wondered if I'd ever see the other side of him again.

"Ok."

"Good. Let's go." He turned away as he spoke, marching back

towards the others. I had no choice but to follow.

The only traces of the storm from the day before were the thick clouds and the chill breeze that still whistled through the air. It turned out to be a good thing that David had decided to come with us; he was the only one who had any experience operating a boat and navigating the ocean. He snapped out orders, treating us all as his incredibly inefficient and moronic crew. We did our best to stay out of his way and be helpful wherever we could but the voyage still took over twice as long as he'd expected. His foul mood increased the longer we were out on the water, his expression thunderous, his voice harsh. He glared out over the gray waves, his eyes fixed on the small sliver of land on the distant horizon.

"Sunama Island," he announced. He turned to me with hard eyes. "Last chance to turn back."

"There's no turning back," I answered quietly. He didn't even acknowledge my response. "Where will we anchor?"

"The map shows a small bay that we can anchor in. We'll have to take the dingy, four at a time, to the dock and split up the gear. From that point onwards, it's your show—we're all just along for the ride. The island's quite large and the trails might not be clear, it could take us days to find them. I hope you have a plan."

"Of course I do," I lied.

I stood beside David at the helm, both of us gazing out to the large island we were approaching. It rose up from the foggy, gray waters, a mass of low cliffs, rocky beaches and tall, thick pine and fir trees. We approached it slowly and steadily, moving along the island's massive coast. David steered the boat with a practiced ease, slowly navigating past the large rocks that occasionally jutted out of the water. Though the waters were fairly calm near the shore, the boat suddenly lurched and I lost my balance. For a moment I felt David's hands grab me, his strong arms supporting my weight and steadying me. Then just as suddenly, he let go. I crashed to the floor with a muttered curse of my own.

"What the hell, David?" I snapped, struggling to my feet.

He barely glanced my way.

"It's not my job to catch you when you fall."

His comment stung. It fueled the angry fire burning within me. I straightened my shoulders and stood tall, planting my feet firmly on the deck.

"I can take care of myself anyway," I announced in a cold, haughty voice of my own.

"I should hope so."

The silence swirled around us with the wind. The distant voices of the spirits whispered in the air but I pushed them away. I did not want to hear what they had to say, not now. Now, I needed to come up with a plan. And I thought I might know what to do.

"Are we going to park the ship in here?" Bridgette called, gesturing to the small opening to the bay ahead. David let out a low, growl-like sound.

"We'll *anchor* in the bay," I confirmed as patiently as possible. "Let's get the dingy ready. Is that alright, Captain?"

"Try not to fall in," David drawled, again without meeting my eye. I wanted to growl myself but instead I just walked away.

It was an hour later when we had all finally reached the island. David was amongst the last group to come over on the dingy. He leapt from the small craft to the dock with ease and quickly secured the little boat using a thick rope and a series of complex looking knots. The Sea Spite was nowhere in site. I wondered what they had done with it?

We all looked around. The air on the island was eerily still, mist hanging in the air, birds distantly calling, the cold damp of the forest and earth reaching out to us. There were no physical traces that Jeremy, Sebastian and the others had ever been here but they had, and I knew they were here still, somewhere.

"I can sense them," I announced quietly.

Jai pointed to the eastern side of the island.

"It's coming from over there."

"It's faint, but it's definitely there," Nathaniel agreed.

I turned to David, who reluctantly nodded.

"They're here."

"I don't sense anything," Ella commented. She was frowning in concentration. Red wore a similar expression as he strained to sense the traces of magic hanging in the air.

"How do you know?" Red demanded, his frustration evident.

"It's a vibration in the air," I struggled to explain. "There's an energy, a specific current that flows in that direction. Once you're more attuned to the Lost Magic, you'll be able to recognize it too. We've had more experience with it and so it's familiar to us. I'm blocking the 'frequency' we're putting out so that they won't know that we're here."

I noticed Bridgette was the only one who wasn't frowning, who didn't seem bothered that she couldn't feel the pull of the magic in the air. She was looking at the wilderness around her in wide-eyed disgust.

"It's so creepy here," she announced, shivering delicately. "Please tell me we can sleep on the boat tonight?"

"We'll be lucky if we're all still alive tonight," I answered flatly. All eyes turned to me. "We've got some hiking to do. Let's go."

And so we set out.

We had divided the gear between us with the strongest carrying the heaviest loads. We each had a large pack with various additional items tied onto it: sleeping bags, tarps, water bottles and food. Red and David bore the heaviest packs, Bridgette the lightest. My load fell somewhere in the middle. I forged ahead and set the pace for the group, a grueling march through the damp brush and overgrown deer trails that led us along the eastern shore and deeper into the center of the island. No one complained or even spoke. I had already threatened to silence Red with magic. He seemed like such a kind guy, and it may have been overly harsh but the way I was feeling, I meant it. Surprisingly, Bridgette never complained once and kept pace in the middle of the group with ease.

The island was much larger than it had originally appeared and with the rough terrain and heavy loads we were carrying, it soon became obvious that we wouldn't reach Jeremy and the others that day. Around mid-afternoon, just as the sun was starting to fade and a dim gray darkness was sinking in around the trees, we decided to set up camp for the night. It was David who found a small clearing in the woods, just off the trail with mostly level ground.

"Is it safe to light a fire?" Ella asked me as I finished helping string up the tarps to form make-shift lean-tos for the night. She stood in the center of our camp, a freshly dug fire pit at her feet, dug a foot deep into the ground and lined with large stones.

I nodded.

"We're still far enough away that they're not likely to see or smell the smoke, especially if we don't want them to. And we'll freeze tonight without a fire."

"Great," Sylvia grinned at me as she pulled a large knife from her belt with a quick flick of her wrist. "I'll round up some firewood."

"That won't be necessary," David announced. He appeared from the growing shadows with his arms full of thick branches. He tossed them down at the ring of stones at our feet, and snapped his fingers. The branches instantly erupted in flame, the fire flaring up so brightly it momentarily blinded me.

"How did you do that?" Nathaniel asked in the silence that followed. Everyone was staring at David nervously. I felt slightly apprehensive myself.

David shrugged.

"It's goddamn cold. It's all about motivation. Right, Caoilinn?"

I regarded him coldly. He spoke the name "Caoilinn" as if it were an insult.

"Yes, it is about motivation," I agreed slowly. I wanted the others' attention, I needed to remind them who was in charge here. I squeezed my necklace in my hand, focusing my magic on the crackling flames before me. I fed my anger and my pain into it, the raging emotions within me building the flames up higher and brighter as the fire stretched upwards into a crackling bonfire. Abruptly, I let go. The flames flickered and in an instant, they were back to normal. All eyes were now on me.

"Come, sit," I gestured to the logs that Jai and Nathaniel had dragged around the fire pit to use as benches. Everyone immediately stopped what they were doing and moved in close. Everyone except for David who was looking through one of the packs.

"Ella, will you help David start our meal, please?" I asked. "You can both listen while you cook. This is important."

I didn't take a seat myself, instead I moved around the fire, out of the path of the stinging smoke. I didn't look at the others as I spoke, instead I gazed into the flames.

"We will fight tomorrow," I announced quietly. "We will be up against others with magic like our own but they are not bound by the same rules that we are."

"What do ya mean?" Red demanded.

"They'll fight dirty. The spirits have warned us: there is a dark power behind their magic that is dangerous and must be destroyed, whoever or whatever that is. None of them can be permitted to leave this island alive, they pose too much of a threat to the rest of the world."

Bridgette opened her mouth as if to speak but then closed it again when she saw me looking at her.

"How will we fight them?" Jai asked. He tilted his head to one side. "We have not been taught how to fight with magic, let alone against it."

"You must know that you might die tomorrow, you must believe that this battle is life and death, as it is. Death is the strongest motivation possible. Focus on your fear and your anger, and you will find with it the strength to access the Lost Magic and the power to control it. It will come to you much more easily than in the tamer exercises that we practiced," I assured them. "You will know how to defend yourself when the time comes, of this I have no doubt. But to attack, you must really and truly want to attack. You must find the strength within yourself to fight back, and the courage to fully accept the magic within you and to use it. If you cannot do this, you will die."

"Great," Ella muttered.

David snickered.

"Well, that was quite the motivating speech. I'm sure we will all rest easy tonight," David drawled as he began handing out chunks of dried meat and fruit to the group.

"It's not too late for you to leave," I reminded them all, meeting each of their eyes individually. When David's eyes locked with mine, my heart again skipped a beat. I quickly looked away. "Anyone who doesn't want to fight tomorrow can head back to the boat and wait there."

"And hope that I survive to take you back home," David smirked.

I hesitated. I hadn't even considered that David might not survive the battle against Jeremy and the others. My gut twisted uncomfortably at the idea.

"If any of you want to turn back, believe me when I say you have the choice. I won't hold it against you."

There was silence and then Bridgette spoke.

"I'm not sure if I can do this, Grace. I'm not strong, or brave, and I barely have any ability to use the Lost Magic as it is. I'm not like you. Maybe… maybe I should go back."

My heart sank in disappointment. I should have felt relieved that Bridgette was removing herself from danger but I couldn't help but feel a flicker of contempt at her cowardice. Apparently, I had lied when I said I wouldn't hold it against anyone. I barely acknowledged she had spoken; I couldn't look at her just yet.

"Anyone else?"

My question was met with silence.

"Good. Let's finish eating and then set up a rotating watch for the night. Everyone should pair up. Bridgette, come with me," I added, abruptly walking away from the camp and back down the trail we had arrived on.

After a few seconds, I heard the crunching and snapping of twigs under Bridgette's feet as she hurried after me. I waited until we were out of earshot from the rest of the camp before turning and facing her.

"I need you to come with me tomorrow," I announced. Bridgette immediately began shaking her head.

"I can't, Grace. I thought I could do this but I can't. I'll just be in the way and besides… I'm scared," she confessed. "I'm terrified, Grace. I've been trying to play tough all along but I think it's time I just admitted it; I can't do this. I'm not like you, I'm not tough or strong or brave. I don't belong here. I just want to go home."

"Yes, you can do this if you want to," I argued firmly. "Stop underestimating yourself and saying you can't. I don't think you've ever really tried. Look, you don't have to fight tomorrow if you don't want to but I need you to come with me. I'll keep you safe, I promise."

Bridgette's lower lip trembled. It had become too dark to tell for sure but I thought I saw tears sparkling in her eyes.

"But why?"

"Because I need you. You are strong, Bridgette, and I need you to be strong for me. You're the only one here who cares about me and you're probably the only one I can fully trust," I confessed, regretting that it was true. "I'm not sure what will happen tomorrow or what we'll find but… I might need you there to reign me in. Not with magic but with common sense. I'm afraid of what I might do when I find the ones who… who killed Sebastian." I barely stumbled over the words. "I need your support and I need your friendship. I need to know there's someone with me who has got my back. I don't want to do something I'll regret. I need you there to remind me of who I really am. Can you do that for me?"

"I… I don't know if I can," Bridgette whispered miserably. She sniffed loudly in the darkness.

"Well, you need to figure it out," I told her harshly. "Stop behaving like a frightened child and find the strength to be the woman you're meant to be. I can see that there's something inside of you, something powerful and special and strong, and Mags saw it too. Now why can't you? Have some faith in yourself, Bridgette."

Bridgette didn't respond. In the darkness, I couldn't tell if she was still upset or just angry now. I shrugged it off.

"Let's head back to camp. Think about it tonight and let me know in the morning."

"Ok," she agreed, her voice sounded different, a little lower than usual. Maybe she was angry but that was fine. I preferred dealing with her anger than her fear and self-pity.

It began raining in the night and our fire went out. We huddled together under the lean-tos, trying to trap in some warmth. I wanted us all to stay warm and get a good night's sleep, but more than anything, I wanted to find the ones responsible for Sebastian's death and make them pay. I could think of nothing else and so my concentration continually wavered so that all I could manage was to use my magic to block some of the wind's gusts and to remove a little of the chill from the air around us. It still wasn't enough for anyone to be able to comfortably sleep but it was enough that we didn't freeze to death.

The rains started to lighten with the sky at dawn. There was a disturbance in the other lean-to as Red and Nathaniel returned from their shift on watch. I could hear their low voices speaking rapidly with David, when suddenly, David himself crouched under my lean-to, his eyes immediately locking with mine.

"You need to hear this," he told me, his voice hushed as the other girls were still asleep.

I quickly untangled myself from the thin, thermal sleeping bag I'd been using and crept carefully over Bridgette's sleeping form and out from under the strung up tarp. I pulled up the hood of my sweatshirt, protecting my head from the light drizzle that fell and trapping as much warmth as I could against my body.

David stood with Red and Nathaniel at the center of the camp, just beside the fire pit. The charred branches now sat in a small, muddy hole.

"What's going on?"

"Tell her," David instructed.

"I was bored of walking the same circuit around the camp while on watch so I decided to branch out a little further," Red explained. "I didn't go far. Just over the rise there, the trees start to thin out. The land slopes down to a bit of a meadow, some old cabins and whatnot down there. And then I saw people."

I blinked in surprise. I could sense the magic of the others to the east still but I hadn't realized they were so close. "How many were there? Did you see Jeremy?"

"I went back for Nate, here. Thought I should bring someone with a bit more control of the magic than I have, just in case." Red flashed Nathaniel a quick smile. Nathaniel didn't smile back. He turned to me, speaking gravely.

"It's definitely them. They all have the Lost Magic within them to varying degrees but all fairly strong. And there was one who was significantly stronger than the rest, stronger than David and almost as strong as you," Nathaniel declared solemnly.

"I'd bet good money that's their leader," Red declared.

"Jeremy?" I asked.

"I don't know, it was too dark to tell." Nathaniel frowned. "And something else. They appeared to be guarding something or someone in one of the cabins. I thought I heard a man moaning."

My breath automatically caught as I suppressed the quick flare of hope. It couldn't be Sebastian, Sebastian was dead, I harshly reminded myself. But who was it then? Had one of their own turned against them?

"How many were there in total?"

"We couldn't tell in the dark. Not many. I'd guess five to ten but I could be wrong," Nathaniel admitted.

David turned to me, a shrewd look on his face.

"So we've found them. Now what's the plan?" he asked.

"We'll send a small group to scout them out once there's enough light to see properly: myself, Bridgette, Nathaniel and Ella. We're the smallest and the fastest. You can wait here with the others," I instructed David. "Pack up camp and be prepared to fight."

Everyone nodded, even David. Today would bring me some form of closure, whether it be my revenge or my death.

Today was the day.

Chapter Fourteen – Black Fire

"There's a low ridge on the southern side of their camp. We should be able to safely observe them from the brush there in the shadows of the trees," Nathaniel explained.

"Alright. We'll hike around their camp to the ridge, get the information we need and then meet back here with the rest of you to form a plan of attack."

Everyone was gathered around me, the lean-tos already taken down and packed up. Sylvia was handing out rations of food and water. Everyone looked apprehensive; even David, which made me nervous.

"Shouldn't we have some kind of signal?" Red spoke up. "You know, in case something happens to the scouting group or if someone discovers us waiting here?"

"There's no point," I said, giving him a level gaze. "We don't want them to discover us yet. If they do, then their magic is already more powerful than ours, in which case we'll all be dead anyway."

"Wow. Good pep talk," Red tried to force out a laugh. No one else cracked a smile.

"We should be back well before noon. If we're not—run. David will lead you."

David arched an eyebrow at me.

"Will I?"

I grabbed his arm and leant in close, speaking softly in his ear.

"Would you prefer for me to leave Jai in charge?"

"No. I would prefer to be accompanying you myself rather than babysitting this group of children."

"I need you here."

"I know," he snapped, straightening up. "It doesn't mean I have to like it."

I took a slow breath, trying to focus my anger and my nerves. I could do this. I had to do this. It was time.

"Ok. Nathaniel, Bridgette, Ella—let's go."

I met Bridgette's eye. I could see her hesitating as the other two stepped forward. Something about her expression hardened as she looked back at me. There was a determined gleam to her eye, a proud set to her mouth. She walked up to me with her head held high following Nathaniel's lead into the forest and away from our camp. I thought I heard someone mutter "good luck" as we walked away though I wasn't certain who it was.

We moved as quickly and as quietly as we could, hiking the rough terrain up and around the campsite in the meadow that Red and Nathaniel had discovered. We had left our rustling waterproof jackets back at camp and our sweatshirts were soon soaked through from the drops of rain still clinging to the brush and branches, and the damp mist that floated through the air.

Soon we could hear the sounds of the other camp awakening just on the other side of the trees ahead. I signaled for the group to stop and then indicated that Bridgette and I would watch from one side of the ridge, and Nathaniel and Ella would go to the other. I tapped my watch and pointed to a large, bare maple just a few feet back down the trail we had made, reminding them we would meet back there in ten minutes.

"Be careful," I breathed softly, meeting each of their eyes. They all gazed back at me solemnly. Nathaniel's eyes flickered anxiously to Bridgette. Then he gave me a brief nod and tapped Ella's arm, leading her away.

"Ready?" I whispered to Bridgette. She nodded, her jaw set but her face a little too pale. She was actually doing much better than I had hoped, following along silently and quickly without complaining once. I was proud of her and would have to tell her so later, if I remembered, if we survived. I quickly pushed away the thought.

Beckoning with my hand for Bridgette to follow, I slowly began climbing up the steep rise ahead. I moved as carefully as possible, wincing every time we made even the slightest noise. There was a lot of talk and even laughter from the camp below so they shouldn't hear us. But still, I couldn't be too cautious.

We crouched down low at the top of the ridge. I slid down onto my belly and Bridgette followed suit. The wet leaves and mud stuck to my sweater as I slithered forward, inching myself towards the base of a tall pine while Bridgette positioned herself at the roots of another. Then very slowly and very carefully, I lifted my head just a few inches, to peek out around the rough bark and at the camp below us.

It was just as Nathaniel had described. A small muddy field stretched out below; I assumed it was a popular spot for wilderness campers to stay, considering how well set-up the camp appeared to be. There was a large fire pit, a small covered area and three small cabins each with glass windows and smoke billowing out of chimneys. It made me angry to think that the people responsible for Sebastian's death had been warm and cozy last night while we half-froze to death under tarps in the rain. My whole body began to tremble with fury as I silently observed the scene below.

There were people moving about, coming in and out of one of the cabins, preparing food and drinking hot beverages. Some were smoking cigarettes and laughing. None of them looked evil, but I knew they were. I tried to count heads.

Nathaniel and Jai had said that Jeremy and five others had gone missing the same night that Sebastian had first disappeared. There was one large man standing near the entrance to one of the cabins. No one was going in or out of that one but he definitely appeared to be guarding something. There were three other people who were also in view: a young man smoked while talking to a girl and an older woman who appeared to be tending to the fire. There must be at least two more, Jeremy and one other.

I glared down at them, the force of my fury so powerful, it left a bitter tang in my mouth and a quiver on my lips. Which one of them had killed Sebastian? Whose hands had been red with his blood? Should I grant mercy to the ones who weren't directly involved? These were the angry and violent thoughts that ran through my mind as I watched and waited.

Bridgette made a slight movement in my periphery, attracting my attention. I glanced at her and she tapped her wrist meaningfully. We were almost out of time and we hadn't learned anything useful yet. I gave a small shake of my head. *Just a few more minutes.* I was certain there must be something we could see here that would give us an advantage. And besides, I couldn't leave yet. I needed to confirm that Jeremy was here first.

As if summoning him by my thoughts, the door to the middle cabin swung open and Jeremy himself stepped out. He glanced around, waving at the others and then striding over to the woman by the fire and wrapping his arm around her shoulders. She grinned at him, the admiration and love she felt for him clear on her face, even from this distance. My heart clenched, the gaping void inside of me darkened and swelled. Why should he be happy and find love when he had destroyed any chance of happiness that I ever had? I grit my teeth together, seeing red, struggling to control the sudden dark anger that threatened to overcome my senses.

Two more men exited the cabin that Jeremy had come out of, bringing the head count to seven. My heart sank as two more people appeared, two blonde women who emerged from a trail on the eastern side of the camp and began striding across the field, their arms laden with firewood. This made nine people so far, giving them a one man advantage and with Bridgette's weak ability to direct any significant amount of the Lost Magic, her presence barely counted. The situation wasn't hopeless, we could certainly still come out on top, it just wasn't going to be as easy as I'd hoped.

The door to the largest cabin began to slowly open. All heads turned to gaze in that direction. People stopped what they were doing and stood straighter, waiting expectantly. I realized I was holding my breath.

"Aed!" Jeremy called in greeting. He slipped his arm from the woman's shoulder and began walking towards the cabin door. I could see a dark figure standing in the doorway but he was too far back in the shadows for me to make out any detail of his face. I could feel his power, the tainted magic flowing from him like a shadow seeping through the air. The pure force of it made me tremble, made my legs go numb and my stomach fill with dread. This was the dark force that the spirits had warned us about. This was the one that the rebels had found to lead them, to teach them the dark ways of the Lost Magic. This was the one I must destroy and not just because it was the responsibility given to me by the spirits but also, because I knew deep within my heart, that this dark, twisted soul was responsible for the death of Sebastian.

"Grace," Bridgette hissed, making me jump. She inched up on her belly right beside me. I had been so focused on the scene unfolding below that I hadn't even noticed her leave her post. "It's time," she whispered, glancing back towards the maple where we were supposed to meet Nathaniel and Ella.

"Wait," I mouthed. Fear and anger roiled through me as I glared down at the dark figure in the cabin's doorway. Whoever he was, I hated him so much that I knew I would have no qualms killing him myself. This death would be entirely justifiable and something I was eager for. I dug my nails into the moist, stagnant earth, breathing slowly through my mouth as I tried to calm my racing heart.

Bridgette pulled gently at my arm.

"Wait," I repeated softly. My whole body tensed as the cabin door opened wider and he stepped out into the light.

I stopped breathing.

The world came crashing down around me as his black, soulless eyes glanced up towards the rise and locked with mine.

His face was pale and drawn, his features hardened and twisted with a bitter fury I had never seen before. He was terrifying. He was a complete stranger to me. A stranger who wore Sebastian's face.

"Aed!" Jeremy called again as he approached him. My brain automatically translated the ancient Celtic name—*fire*. Aed broke his gaze from mine and turned to Jeremy, listening intently to whatever he was saying.

I began panting, my body trembling as my whole world fell apart. This couldn't be real. How was this possible? It couldn't be him. Was it really him?

"What? What is it?" Bridgette whispered, panic setting into her features as she took in my expression.

"Sebastian," I gasped. I couldn't stop staring at his greasy dark hair that had been slicked back or the purplish shadows that fell under his large, black eyes. Everything about him, the way he stood, the way he moved, the gestures he made as he spoke to Jeremy—it was all different, all wrong. How was it possible? "I think that's Sebastian," I whispered, my voice barely audible.

Jeremy finished speaking to Aed and began walking away, looking annoyed. Aed's head snapped back up, his eyes searching the crest of the ridge and immediately finding mine. He looked furious, he looked deadly. Any relief that I might have felt in discovering that Sebastian was still alive vanished with the look in his eye. Something was very, very wrong. This was not Sebastian. His eyes quickly moved from me to Bridgette, then over to the other side of the ridge where Nathaniel and Ella would have been hiding. He knew. He knew we were there and he did not look pleased. He looked ready to kill. My stomach clenched with fear.

His eyes flashed back to mine. Even from the distance at which he stood, I could clearly sense his intent, I could easily read his lips. He shook his head, barely perceivable across the great distance between us.

"Go," he mouthed.

Bridgette gasped. I shook my head back at him.

"I can't," I whispered, knowing that somehow he could hear me.

His eyes narrowed, his lips compressed. I was immediately afraid. I braced myself for what was coming, whether it be an onslaught of his black magic or a physical sounding of the alarm. But instead, he silently seethed a moment longer and then abruptly spun on his heel and marched back into his cabin, slamming the door loudly behind him. Several of the others in the camp looked up in surprise but Jeremy just shrugged, calling for them to go back about their tasks. He glanced suspiciously up at the tree line along the top of the ridge but was distracted by the return of the woman who he'd been sitting with before.

"Come on," Bridgette whispered. Again, she gently tugged on my arm. "We've got to go. Come on."

Slowly, I nodded. Together, we slid backwards on our bellies until our heads were hidden from view behind the bushes and brush. As we crept quickly back down the hill and towards our rendezvous point along the trail, I stared blankly ahead, moving automatically. My mind was somewhere else.

I couldn't believe Sebastian wasn't dead. I still felt that same empty void inside of myself, that pit of dark grief and rage that had begun festering at the moment that I had thought marked his death. My mind worked backwards, recalling the last conversation we'd had. Had he ever said he was dying? Had he ever said he was injured or had I just assumed? He had said that I was too late to save him and I could see that that might be true. What had they done to him?

"Good, they're still here," Bridgette said softly. I focused my eyes and realized that we were nearly at the maple tree. Nathaniel and Ella were waiting impatiently at its base.

"What took you so long?" Ella hissed but Nathaniel immediately silenced her.

"Wait. We're still too close to their camp. We'll talk when we get back."

Nathaniel looked to me for confirmation and I forced myself to nod.

We took a different route back just to ensure that we didn't leave a clear trail. The terrain was a bit rougher and it ended up taking us almost twice as long. We were all sweating and out of breath when we finally returned to camp, just minutes before noon.

"You're back!" Red called out, sounding relieved as we approached last night's camp. Everyone looked ready to move.

David glanced up. As soon as his eyes met mine, he seemed to know.

"Everyone! Gather in!" he called, without breaking his gaze from mine for a second. He looked concerned. "Grace, what happened?"

I paused, waiting for the rest of the group to gather in close before speaking. I'd had the whole trip back to organize my thoughts and I'd still come to no conclusions. I didn't know what to think or even how to start. Surprisingly, Bridgette stepped up to speak.

"Jeremy's there," she confirmed. "We saw him along with ten

others, and there could be more. There are three cabins. They seem to be guarding something in the smallest one that's off to the side; we still don't know what. Jeremy is staying in the middle cabin and," she paused, glancing at me quickly, "and the one who's been leading them is staying in the largest cabin."

"We don't know that he's leading them," I quickly interrupted, sounding far too defensive. David stared at me suspiciously.

"We do," Bridgette patiently argued. "Even I could sense the magic coming from him. He's very strong, perhaps as strong as Grace. And he was just radiating danger and death."

"Did you get a clear view of him?" David asked but I could tell he already knew the answer. I shifted uncertainly. It was time for me to speak, only I didn't know what to say.

"He… he looked like Sebastian." My pronouncement was met with stunned silence. I rushed to continue. "But it wasn't him, it couldn't have been. I know he's dead and Sebastian has no natural ability with the Lost Magic; he lost his ability after the explosion at the Necromanteion. Aed could definitely use the Lost Magic though."

"What did you just say?" Nathaniel asked me quietly, his voice steady and intense. Jai was also leaning towards me intently. David looked shocked.

"They called him Aed? Are you certain?" David demanded, exchanging glances with Nathaniel and Jai.

"Yes. Why? What does it mean?"

"Explain," David instructed Jai with a quick flick of his wrist. He looked distracted, his brows pulled down together low over his eyes.

"Before Seamus became Sebastian, he was Aed," Jai explained simply.

"I don't understand," I whispered but I was afraid that I did. Everyone was silent as we all listened to Jai's explanation.

"When Seamus was creating the Others, he forgot about Caoilinn, he forgot about his mission to reunite with her reincarnated soul and largely, he forgot himself. He was renamed *Aed Dubhan* after his fiery passion and his dark temper that emerged. It means *black fire*."

I stared at him disbelievingly.

"No."

"It's true," David confirmed. "He was the worst of us, the cruelest, the most volatile and the most powerful. He led us and we followed him because he brought us… the world. There was nothing that we couldn't attain under his guidance." David sounded almost bitter as he recalled.

"If Sebastian has died and all that is left inside of him is Aed, we are doomed," Nathaniel pronounced solemnly.

Everyone stared at me in silence. I ignored the feel of their questioning eyes and tried to concentrate, my mind and heart both racing.

"But that doesn't make sense. These are all aspects of himself; one can't kill the other. For whatever reason, Aed is now the dominant personality but that doesn't mean that Sebastian isn't still there too. We can still save him, the spirits told me so," I insisted. No one looked convinced.

"You said yourself that Sebastian is dead, that when he died you felt a part of yourself die too. Has that changed? Were you mistaken?" Ella gently probed.

I couldn't lie. I hated myself for not lying to them.

"No," I admitted. "But I have to be wrong. He has to be in there somewhere."

"Sebastian has been trying to suppress Aed for a long time," David spoke quietly to the group but his eyes were on me. "He has long denied and tried to forget who he used to be but those days and memories still haunt his dreams, they always have. It became much worse for him after the explosion, after Grace attempted to destroy the Lost Magic and left holes in all of our memories. He is Aed now—that is all he is."

"But he remembers me. I never knew Aed."

David's eyebrows briefly lifted in surprise, but he quickly hid the emotion. He paused before responding.

"When he was Sebastian, he could partially remember being Aed in his dreams, his subconscious retained the memories. Perhaps now that he is again Aed, he remembers being Sebastian but can no longer relate to those memories. Maybe it is you who now haunts his dreams." David wore the ghost of a smile. I glared back at him.

"So how do you know he remembers you?" David asked.

"He saw me, he seemed furious that I was there. He told me to go but he didn't alert the others. Doesn't that prove that Sebastian's still alive in there somewhere?"

"No. It proves you've put all of us in grave danger. We need to move now!" David barked, panic arising on everyone's faces.

"We will do nothing yet," I argued, speaking firmly and calmly. "If he wanted to capture or kill us it would have already happened. And it hasn't, so relax."

"It hasn't yet," David muttered darkly. The others still looked nervous but everyone settled back down.

"I thought you and Grace said Sebastian didn't have any natural ability to use the Lost Magic?" Bridgette asked David, offering a good distraction. "Aed obviously did."

Nathaniel nodded thoughtfully.

"I don't know how." David sounded annoyed. "The ability must have been inside him all along, so small, perhaps we overlooked it like Grace did with you when you first arrived. But he has obviously found a way to access a great amount of power since."

"He's dangerous," Red stated solemnly. He wouldn't meet my eye.

"We have to stop him," Sylvia joined in.

Several others murmured their agreement. This was getting out of hand again, fast.

"Stop," I interrupted, my voice instantly silencing their words and halting their movements. I would use magic against all of them if I had to. I wouldn't let them hurt Sebastian, or whatever there was left of him inside Aed.

"We don't have enough information," I argued, trying to sound as calm and rational as possible, even though my pulse was racing. "David, Nathaniel, Jai, you used to know Aed, do you think he'd welcome you to join his group? You could stay in the camp, earn his trust, try to find out what they're up to and if there are any signs that Sebastian exists still inside of Aed."

Nathaniel and Jai both immediately began shaking their heads. Surprisingly, David seemed to be the only one considering my wild plan.

"He would kill us on sight if he perceived us to be a threat in any way, which he most likely would. He never truly trusted any of the Others," Jai pronounced. "But David..."

David looked up and met my eye.

"He might kill me too, he might not," David shrugged. His steely gray eyes were locked with mine. "Would you ask me to risk my life on the chance that you might still save his? Would you command me to?" he demanded quietly.

"I would never force you to."

"But you would ask?"

"I would."

His eyes hardened, his expression went completely blank. I instantly regretted my words but I couldn't make myself take them back. Not on the hope that they might save Sebastian, however small the chance.

"Fine. I will go," he agreed.

I nodded, feeling a sliver of hope for the first time in days.

"And I will go with you."

"No," David immediately objected. Everyone began talking at once, all arguing over each other and telling me that I couldn't.

"Silence!" I snapped, cutting off their voices with magic again. I continued in a more reasonable tone. "We all agree that Aed and his followers must be stopped. And there is only one way to stop him and that is to kill him. I will not kill Sebastian and I will fight to the death to ensure that no one ever does. If he is still alive within Aed somewhere, I must know, I must see for myself. If Sebastian is truly and permanently gone... I will deal with Aed." I sounded confident, I hoped that I could trust myself.

"But how will you get inside their camp? They might try to kill you on the spot before you even have a chance to speak to Aed," Red questioned.

"I'll go with David, in disguise. We can use the Lost Magic to stop them from paying too much attention to me. I think I know a way that will work that they won't detect. I'm sure it'll work."

"And how will you get out of their camp again?" David asked, looking very displeased with my plan.

"If we're discovered, we'll fight our way out. The rest of you will be positioned around their camp, ready to attack. If not, we'll stay with them for two days, learn all that we can. On the second night, we'll sneak out and meet with you. If Sebastian is truly beyond saving, we'll form a plan and at dawn on the third day, we'll attack and end it."

Everyone slowly nodded.

"You're our leader, I'll follow where you guide us. I trust the spirits and if this is the way it's meant to be..." Ella raised her eyebrows questioningly.

"It is," I lied. I couldn't tell them that I had been pushing away the voices of the spirits all day, ignoring their mutterings in the wind. I was too afraid that they might tell me something I didn't want to hear. Something I couldn't bear to believe was true.

"Let's go then," David announced brusquely.

"Now?" Bridgette squeaked, her eyes going wide.

"As soon as Grace is in disguise. Why delay?"

"I agree," I joined in. "Bridgette, will you help me get ready?"

With Bridgette's help, I changed into slightly bigger and baggier clothes (provided by Sylvia) that helped to disguise the shape of my body. Bridgette did my makeup: heavy eye liner and dark eye shadow that made my eyes look quite different. I pulled up the hood on the sweater and let my hair fall loosely forward to try to disguise my face.

"It won't work," David objected. "Jeremy will recognize you the second he sees you."

"It will work. *See?*" I let the Lost Magic flow through me as I spoke, wanting others to perceive me differently, wanting them to believe that I was just another girl with David, no one special or overly interesting. Then I hid the traces of my magic, making the spell I was casting invisible to eyes that might detect it. It should be fairly easy to keep up, as long as I kept my focus.

David inspected me shrewdly.

"It might work after all," he admitted. "Shall we?"

"Yes." I turned to the others. "We'll approach from the other side of their camp, in case they're suspicious. It's a longer hike so that'll give you time to station yourselves around the ridge. If something goes wrong… I'll light the cabins on fire—not the one that they're guarding, not until we know what's in there. If you see the smoke, come ready to battle. If the sun goes down and all appears well, stay as far from the camp as you can for the next two days. On the second night, one or both of us will meet you here to form a battle plan. Then we attack at dawn."

"Grace… don't do this," Bridgette softly pleaded. She looked like she was holding back tears.

"I have to."

Her eyes began to fill.

"It's ok, Bridgette," I continued in a softer tone. "Just stay with the others and practice using your ability as much as you can. You're stronger than you think."

She sniffed and nodded.

"Be careful, Grace."

"I will. See you soon."

David had already started walking away. I had to jog to catch up to him.

"Slow down, we need to give the others time to get into position," I reminded him.

He threw me a withering glare and then slowed his pace to more of a brisk walk.

"You're making a mistake," he growled without looking at me.

"What do you mean?"

"You're assuming he won't hurt you and you're wrong. If he recognizes you, Grace, he'll kill you."

"He would never," I quickly denied.

"Sebastian would never hurt you. Aed would, and he will take pleasure in it if he does. Especially if he puts it all together and realizes that you're Caoilinn."

My brows pulled down into a frown as I recalled the last thing Sebastian had said to me. He had warned me to stay away from

David and Caoilinn, and I had told him that I was her. I was fairly certain he'd heard me which meant Aed probably already knew. I didn't tell David that.

"It'll be fine," I dismissed. "He won't recognize me and if he does… If I can just get close enough to him, I'm sure I can make him remember. I'm sure I can bring Sebastian back. The spirits said—"

"The spirits were wrong," David snapped. "Aed is beyond saving. Aed is beyond redemption. But you're too stubborn and stupid to accept that, aren't you?"

"Why are you acting like this? Why can't you just trust me, like the others do?"

"Because I know better. This is a deadly game you're playing, Grace, and I don't think anyone's informed you of the rules."

"What's that supposed to mean?"

David glared at me a moment longer before sharply looking away.

"Nothing. Let's go. No more talking—we wouldn't want to give ourselves away."

"No, we wouldn't," I murmured.

By the time we were close enough to Aed's camp it was mid-afternoon. I was growing tired from the hike and needed to rest before we revealed ourselves. We drank water and ate granola bars from David's pack. I was starting to feel increasingly nervous and uncertain but David appeared as cool as ever, calmly lighting a cigarette. He offered me one and I declined with a quick shake of my head.

"Ready?" he asked.

"Almost."

I reached for my necklace, feeling its comforting warmth against my palm. Slowly and certainly, I drew on the Lost Magic, focusing and directing it to fulfill my will and desire. I didn't want anyone to recognize me or to think twice about who I was. I just wanted to blend in. And I wanted to save Sebastian; I wanted it so badly, I felt sure it would happen.

Since we had arrived on the island, I had been using magic to disguise our presence but now that we wanted Aed's camp to know we were there, I released it, allowing our enemies to sense David's ability and just a small portion of mine.

"Now they know we're here. They'll be waiting for us. Let's go."

"Fine."

David slung his backpack over his shoulder and then walked straight up beside me, throwing his arm around my shoulders and pulling me tightly against his side.

"What are you doing?" I demanded, trying to ignore my heart hammering in my throat.

"Keeping you safe," he answered, pulling us forward as he spoke. We walked towards the gap in the trees that led out into the field. "You'll attract less suspicion from Aed if he believes you're one of my women. He was rarely interested in my castoffs."

"One of your women?"

"You heard me," he answered, his voice ice cold. I shrugged. Why should I care anyway?

We stepped out of the shadows of the trees, and together, began walking across the field, along a well-trodden, muddy path that led straight towards the cabin near its center.

"They're waiting," David murmured softly, his lips barely moving as he spoke.

I glanced up and saw he was right. Everyone, except for the one man guarding the smallest cabin, had quickly gathered in the center of the meadow. There were eleven of them in total. Eight stood in a slight half-circle, then ahead and slightly apart from the others stood Aed with Jeremy standing just behind his right shoulder.

I immediately dropped my eyes, my heart skipping a painful beat at the familiar sight of Sebastian. It's not really him, it's not really him, I chanted silently to myself. It was a challenge to keep breathing, to stay calm as we approached and I began to wonder if it was all a big mistake? Was I about to take a gamble that would cost me my life? And was it worth it for the chance to see Sebastian, to even touch him one last time? I was about to find out.

Chapter Fifteen – Lingering

NO ONE SPOKE AS WE APPROACHED THE group. I could hear myself breathing, along with the squelch of my shoes sinking into the mud, the distant calls of birds and the cracks and rustles of wildlife moving through the forest behind me. I imagined I could feel the eyes of my friends watching too; they had become my friends, I realized. It reminded me that I wasn't alone, that there were others willing and ready to fight alongside me. If it came to that.

"David," Aed called. His voice carried no emotion, no clue as to whether David was welcome or not. There was an expectation behind his words, a subtle command: *come*. David immediately obeyed.

He dropped his arm from my shoulders and passed me his nearly finished cigarette.

"You can kill that smoke for me. Wait here," he instructed. And then he stepped forward.

I let my hair fall in my face, peeking through it as I sucked on the cigarette, the bitter smoke stinging and burning my throat and lungs. I forced myself to hold it in and then blew out a thin, steady stream, attempting to look as casual and uninteresting as possible. It seemed to work. All eyes were on David, including Aed's.

"Aed Dubhan," David greeted, sounding amused. "You old bastard. It's been a long time, brother." He stopped before Aed, offering his hand.

Aed watched him emotionlessly, his black eyes cold and empty. Up close, it was nearly impossible for me to think of him as Sebastian, there were no immediate traces of him left. Slowly, Aed's pale lips began to pull up into a cruel and twisted smile. He reached out and he and David clasped one another's forearms in greeting, both smiling coldly at the other.

"It has been a long time," Aed agreed, his voice sharper than Sebastian's and without the usual lilt of an Irish accent with which Sebastian spoke. "What took you so long to join us? We've been waiting."

David shrugged.

"That bitch, Grace, tricked me into helping her. She bound me to my words with her magic and forced me to promise her my help. I also had to swear not to harm her, or Sebastian."

Aed laughed, the sound haunting and cruel, echoing off the trees and slopes that surrounded the meadow. I tried not to shudder.

"David, David, you've always been a fool around beautiful women," Aed chastised, shaking his head. "And how, pray tell, did you manage to escape the child's clutches?"

"She and the others are returning to the mainland to gather more followers and then move against you. Keira and I volunteered to remain behind, to observe you until their return in two days. They plan to attack at dawn on the third." David glanced lazily over his shoulder at me as he spoke. I tried not to frown. Why had he warned Aed that we were going to attack in three days? I began to feel uneasy. I watched him suspiciously through my hair, careful to avoid Aed's eye.

"Grace trusted you to remain behind?" Aed questioned. His face was expressionless but his eyes were piercing, locked on David's and demanding the truth. I could feel the Lost Magic flowing through him, twisting its way around David and squeezing the words from his lungs. There was no way he could lie or evade this question.

"She trusts me enough," he wheezed. "We have become surprisingly close."

A strange expression passed over Aed's face. His features momentarily contorted with what could only be called pure, murderous fury. A spark of madness brightened his eyes. Then just as quickly, it was gone. He smiled without mirth.

"Have you? How interesting. And what of this one?"

I quickly dropped my gaze, focusing with all my might to maintain my magical façade and to hide the true extent of my ability and the power I was currently using from all those around me. I could feel Aed's eyes burning into me.

"This one is mine," David growled, his voice suddenly threatening.

Aed laughed.

"Is she?" he smirked.

"Yes."

There was an audible pause, tension filling the air. Everyone seemed to be holding their breath, including myself.

"I'm surprised that you would take interest in one such as her," Aed commented quietly. Icy fear was rapidly expanding in my stomach, my legs already feeling too numb to help me if I needed to run. "I'm curious, brother… Call her forward."

"Keira!" David barked without hesitation.

I immediately began moving, my body responding before my mind had made the conscious decision. I was terrified but I forced myself to remain calm, to slow my heart rate and take deep, even breaths. I must stay in control. I glanced at Aed through my hair, thankful to find that his eyes weren't on me, they were locked with David's.

I came to a stop by David's side, directly in front of Aed. I felt his gaze shift onto me, the heat of it withering, the ice of it bitterly cold. I couldn't help myself; I looked up and found myself staring directly into his eyes. I was shocked to see all traces of the dark blue that used to swirl within the gray depths of Sebastian's eyes were gone. Aed's eyes were chillingly cold and hard, the gray of his irises so dark it seemed to almost blend into his black pupils. And as the crushing disappointment hit me, I realized that I had been hoping to see something else there, something familiar, something I could hold on to. But there was nothing. This was not Sebastian, this was a monster.

Aed considered me dispassionately.

"I would like to interview your friend before welcoming her into our fold," Aed suddenly announced. My stomach clenched in fear.

"Is my word not enough? I have vouched for her, what more do you need?" David asked slowly. He held Aed's deadly gaze.

"You're protective of this one—interesting. Have no fear brother, I only wish to speak with her… for now." His eyes gleamed wickedly. "Come!" he snapped, his eyes briefly looking my way and with that, he spun on his heel and marched up to his cabin, letting the door swing shut behind him.

Everyone else was dismissed and the group immediately began breaking up with a few curious and wary glances at David and thankfully, none for me.

"Go," David quietly instructed. There was a warning in his eyes.

I was terrified. I squeezed my hands together to try to hide their trembling. Why had Aed summoned me? He should have barely noticed me. Was my magic not working as it should? Was he too powerful after all?

"David, I've heard so much about you," Jeremy clipped in his clear, precise tones. He moved in front of me as if he hadn't even seen me standing there. "My name is Jeremy." He held out his hand expectantly; David just sneered at it.

"Make yourself useful, *boy*, and show me around this place. I'll need somewhere for my woman and I—that should suffice," David indicated the middle cabin that stood not far from Aed's.

"That's my cabin," Jeremy warned, his voice no longer welcoming.

"Not anymore."

I turned my back on their conversation and took a slow, steadying breath. It was time to face Aed.

The wind rose as I approached his cabin door, gusting so strongly that I had to hold my hood down with one hand. It was almost as if the spirits were trying to force me to reveal myself. Their voices whispered loudly in my ears, warnings and pleas twisted together in a howl of silent voices: *stop him… kill him… your destiny*.

Ignoring them, I took a deep breath and pulled open the cabin door.

I gazed around the room in wonder, almost forgetting to hide in my hood for a moment. I couldn't believe the luxury before me, so out of place in this rough, log cabin in the middle of a cold and muddy field.

The inside of the cabin was all one room with a cozy wood stove at its center. Closest to the door was a large dining room table, surrounded by eight chairs. A massive, throne-like, carved chair was positioned at its head and several maps and documents were spread out on the table before it. Beyond that, in the back corner of the cabin, a large flat screen television had been mounted onto the wall with two leather couches arranged at angles before it. There was a pool table and small bar squeezed into the closest corner to my right and the far right corner was partitioned off by dark, hung silks, cascading from the ceiling to the floor. Behind the silks, I could clearly see a massive, king-sized bed, draped in luxurious dark sheets. My mouth went dry.

"Drink?" Aed asked. He stood with his back to me at the bar, pouring a dark, amber liquid into a small crystal glass.

I was about to say no when I realized that any girl David claimed was his would probably drink. I was already pretending to smoke, after all.

"Sure," I answered as casually as I could manage. I lowered my voice slightly, hoping to disguise its usual cadence.

Aed expertly poured a second glass for me and carried them both towards one of the couches.

"Come," he commanded over his shoulder. I cautiously obeyed.

I was finally forced to meet his eye as I took the drink from him and sank down onto the adjacent couch. I glimpsed him briefly, attempting a quick smile that might have been more of a grimace. He was staring at me, a curious look in his eye.

"Do you know why I brought you in here?" he asked.

I took a sip of my drink while I carefully considered my answer. The spicy rum burned all the way down my throat like liquid fire. I swallowed hard, struggling to keep my face calm and stop myself from coughing and spluttering.

"You want to make sure that I pose no threat to you," I guessed, speaking slowly with my carefully lowered voice. I glimpsed up again through my hair and saw Aed watching me still, his lips twisted in amusement.

"How could a skinny, weak girl possibly be of any threat to me?"

he dismissed. He emptied his glass in one swallow. "I'll tell you why you're here: something doesn't add up about you and I want to know what it is."

I tried to stay calm and still even though my heart felt ready to explode. He was on to me. What should I say? What should I do? I clung to my magical shroud desperately.

"What do you mean?" I asked, taking another slow and deliberate sip of my drink. I felt like I should be breathing fire after the strong, spiced rum.

"I've known David for a long time, a very long time," Aed mused to the air. He leant back casually into the couch. "He was trying to hide it from me, but the way he looks at you. I've only ever seen him look at a woman like that once before, and she turned out to be an amazing, dangerous woman. A deadly, powerful woman." My mind flashed back to the night Sebastian had first disappeared, when David had asked me about a woman he had once loved; he had said he "worshipped her". I knew this must be who Aed meant but how could he possibly think David felt that way about me? He didn't—did he?

"There must be more to you than there appears." His eyes returned to my face, studying me with an unnerving cold, calculation. "You're weak and plain and demure; you're hardly remarkable and barely noticeable. There's no reason why one such as David should show any interest in you. So either you're smarter than you appear, or more powerful, or more beautiful and certainly more deadly... or all of the above."

My heart rate began to slow down. Aed had said I was "barely noticeable." Surely that meant my magic was working still? Perhaps there was a chance I could get away with this, if I answered carefully. I downed the rest of my drink, feeling emboldened.

"You call me weak and plain and uninteresting? What woman wouldn't be dangerous after that?" I purred, crossing my legs and leaning towards him flirtatiously.

Aed smiled coldly.

"Careful. You wouldn't want me to be too interested," he warned darkly. Goosebumps erupted all over my body. I couldn't believe how frightening he was, this dangerous man hiding in Sebastian's body.

"No, I wouldn't," I replied. "I'm with David and he's waiting for me." I boldly stood up and moved to leave, but Aed grabbed my wrist, twisting it painfully and pulling me back to him. I gasped in pain.

"Come here," he commanded, the magic behind his words forcing me to obey. I desperately wanted to resist and I could have, probably, but it would have given me away. I needed to appear weak; I had to try to keep up my façade. I turned and walked right up to him, stopping just an inch from his chest. My pulse was racing, my whole body trembling as the Lost Magic swelled in my veins, begging and demanding to be used, but I pushed it aside. I couldn't believe how close I was standing to this dark and dangerous man. I could hear him breathing, the rhythm so familiar that for a split second, I almost forgot that this wasn't Sebastian anymore. But his scent was wrong, his expensive cologne unfamiliar to me. And the way he stood, and moved, and spoke—and the look in his eyes as he roughly grabbed my chin and tilted my face up to the light—this wasn't Sebastian.

"What are you hiding behind those stunning, sapphire eyes?" he asked, peering down at me curiously. And then I saw it, the exact moment that it happened. A spark of rich, navy blue briefly flared within the black depths of his eyes, a momentary flash of recognition, and something else, something almost familiar, and then it was gone. Dark anger abruptly clouded his face and distorted his features. His fingers pinched into my jaw painfully, his grip tightening as if he were about to crush my face with his hand and I suddenly didn't doubt that he could.

"Caoilinn," he growled accusingly.

"No," I quickly denied. I could sense that he was barely in control of himself, that his anger was about to overcome him and he was about to do something very dangerous. I abruptly decided to make a bold move, it might be the only way to save myself now. I dropped my disguise, letting my magic evaporate into the air and revealing myself to him. "I'm Grace."

He didn't move to let go of me, he just continued to glare down into my eyes. His tight grip on my face slowly loosened.

"Is there truly a difference?" he asked.

I knocked his hand away, rubbing my sore jaw.

"You can call me Caoilinn, if I can call you Sebastian," I challenged.

Aed's lips twisted into another eerie smile though his eyes were still dark with anger.

"*Touché.*" He turned and casually walked over to the bar. He was still angry but he was in control of it now. I could sense that I was still in great danger. "May I offer you another drink?"

"No, thank you."

"Suit yourself." He refilled his glass and then slowly strolled back across the room, dropping down onto the leather couch. "You shouldn't have come here."

Slowly I sank down onto the far end of the couch from him, watching him warily all the while.

"I had no choice," I answered honestly.

"Yes, it's surprising how strong the connection between you and Sebastian was. Even now that he's gone, in some ways it still lingers," Aed commented, catching me by surprise. His comment stung, casting a dagger deep within the gaping void inside me while simultaneously, offering me a strange sense of comfort.

"It lingers?" I echoed cautiously.

"Must I repeat myself?" Aed snapped in annoyance. He took a long sip of his drink, downing half the glass in one mouthful, and then continued. "Some of Sebastian's memories still blend with mine, similar to how mine once blended with his. I can recall the strength of his emotions for you and though his feelings are not in any way my own, I can certainly see your… appeal."

He eyed me appreciatively, looking amused by my surprise.

"I can remember the way you smell, the warmth of your skin, the taste of your lips," he murmured seductively, "the torture of never having all of you, of always wanting more."

My mouth went dry. I licked my lips nervously, desperately trying to stay in control.

"I've decided I want you, Grace. And I always get what I want," he warned.

"But… I… David…"

"David and I have fought over women before. I always win," Aed smirked. "And so I'll make you an offer you can't resist—you *won't* resist—join me. Your power combined with mine… we will be unstoppable. Anything and everything we've ever wanted, the world at our fingertips, indulging all our desires, living each day with no regrets."

"I could never," I denied breathlessly though I was slightly tempted by his offer. "You're not Sebastian."

"Not entirely," he agreed. He shifted down the couch, leaning in close to me. "I'm the most dangerous parts of Sebastian, his deadliest sins, his darkest desires, his most carnal passions."

A thrill ran through me.

"Join me," he enticed, his eyes glowing. "I'll give you until sundown to decide."

"And if I decide against?"

"You won't."

"But if I do?"

"Then, I suppose I shall have to kill you," Aed answered, looking amused once more.

"Some choice," I murmured.

"I warned you to stay away, but you wouldn't listen, would you?" I didn't respond. He grabbed my chin again and tilted my head up so that I was forced to look into his eyes. "Yes, I see clearly now," he murmured, staring down coldly at me.

Without warning, Aed bent his head and crushed his lips against mine. He took me by surprise and I immediately tried to pull away, but he held me there with one hand in my hair and the other suddenly locked around my waist. And before I knew what I was doing, I wasn't fighting any longer. I closed my eyes and gave in.

He tasted like Sebastian. His lips were soft and warm, his arms steady and strong. The heat and warmth that radiated out from his body was the same that I had always felt. He gripped me tightly, kissing me with a hungry passion that was all too familiar. A desperate desire awakened inside of me and took control of my body as I pulled myself even closer against his. I forgot who this was, and my heart and soul rejoiced to be once more in Sebastian's arms. I had never thought I would feel this again. My head spun from the rum I had drunk and the dizzying desire that now overwhelmed me. Slowly, teasingly, his pulled back, leaving me breathless and charged. I opened my eyes, wanting so badly to believe that Sebastian had returned.

Hard, black eyes stared back at me and the pieces of my heart fell apart. Was it true? Was Aed really all that was left of Sebastian now? I had sworn before that I loved Sebastian, that I loved every piece of him, flaws included. Now that all that was left were his darkest most primal qualities, could I love him still? It wouldn't be as hard as it should, I realized. And it certainly might be easier than living without him.

"Leave me now. You may tell David what we have discussed, if you like, but no one else. And it would be wise to maintain your disguise until sundown. Jeremy still thirsts for your blood." Aed smiled his chilling, twisted smile. He hesitated, the first hint of uncertainty I'd seen from him so far, and then he cupped my face with both his hands, a gesture that Sebastian had done so many times. My heart pounded miserably and hopefully all at once. He spoke slowly and precisely, each word weighed heavily with magic.

"I want you to come back to me at sundown," he told me softly. I could feel his words being bound to me with magic, tying me to him irrevocably. Each word he spoke was like a barbed thorn, cutting and clinging beneath my skin and I was powerless to stop him. "You will wait for me there," he gestured to the massive bed behind the swaying silks at the back of the cabin, "and you will join me and my cause. I will not be disobeyed. I will have you, tonight and forever or until I tire of you," he declared, a crazed, possessive quality to his voice. I nodded mutely. "Now go, summon David for me; we have much to discuss and plan. I will see you at sundown."

I slowly walked out of the cabin, aware of his fiery gaze on my back. No one noticed me as I stepped outside. I took a deep breath of the cold, damp air, trying to clear my head. What was I going to do?

"Keira!" David called as he hurried towards me. Jeremy followed closely behind him. I quickly pulled up my hood and dropped my eyes to the ground. "Keira… did Aed approve of you then? You were in there for quite some time," he added, sounding almost suspicious.

"He approved," I answered softly. I continued on in a hushed whisper. "David, he *knows*. He's asked me to join him. He's left me little choice," I added speaking quickly and quietly as Jeremy had almost reached us.

"I see."

And from David's angry, clipped tone and thunderous expression, I could tell that he did.

"He wants to see you now," I continued.

"Who, Aed?" Jeremy asked as he came up behind David. "Did he summon me as well?"

"No. I need to speak with Aed alone," David answered for me. His face was expressionless but his words were sharp with anger.

"David… don't…"

"Don't tell me what to do," he snapped at me coldly. "Stay out of trouble until I return," he added and with that he quickly walked into Aed's cabin.

Jeremy and I were left standing there in awkward silence. I stared down at my hiking boots and the muddy grass beneath my feet, praying that my disguise would hold and that I could stay safe until sundown when I would… when I would what? What was I going to do?

"Come. Let me introduce you to my woman, Tessa. She'll make you something to eat and show you around," Jeremy offered in a surprisingly kind voice. It made me wonder, if I had met him under different circumstances or if I had not turned him away so coldly the first time we had met, if things might be very different for us all.

"Thanks," I answered quietly and followed him across the field.

Tessa turned out to be a kind and friendly woman, if a little rough around the edges. She made me a sandwich and a cup of tea; Aed's camp was amazingly well set up and supplied for having only been there a day longer than we had. When I asked Tessa about this she smiled mysteriously and simply replied, "We get what we want."

After eating she walked me around the camp, introducing me to the others who were there and pointing out the areas that had been set up: where the tents were erected at night time, the designated latrine-areas, the cooking area and communal fire, and where they all gathered each day, twice a day, for lessons in using the Lost Magic, taught by Aed himself.

The final stop on the tour was the small cabin that was positioned slightly back and apart from the other two, closer to the edge of the field. The daylight was starting to fade as we approached the old, log cabin, the sun steadily sinking behind the trees. I didn't have much time left before I had to return to Aed's cabin I realized, half an hour at most. And David still hadn't emerged.

"That's Harry," Tessa introduced. The burly man guarding the cabin door looked up at the sound of his name and waved. "He's on guard-duty right now. We all take turns, a six hour shift each. You'll be expected to do the same. The cabin must be guarded 24/7, no one in or out, apart from Aed."

"But why? What's in there?" I asked curiously. "And if there's something Aed wants kept safe… why should he need anything other than his magic to protect it?"

"I don't know and I don't ask. And if you're smart, you won't either," Tessa warned. "Now I've got to start cooking the evening meal. Why don't you come help out?"

"I've got to use the facilities," I lied. "I'll meet you over there in a minute."

"Sure," Tessa agreed and quickly began walking away.

I headed in the direction of where the latrines had been dug further into the woods but veered off the path just before reaching them and hid myself in the shadows. It was almost sundown, my time was nearly up. I needed to make a decision, whether I stayed and joined Aed or whether I attempted to run, and I needed to decide fast. But I knew I couldn't decide anything until I found out what it was that Aed hid in that cabin.

I watched the few people walking about the camp. No one had

noticed I was missing, but no one had even really noticed I was there today unless Tessa had drawn their attention to me. The beginnings of a plan were starting to form in my mind.

If I used enough of the Lost Magic, I could make it so that people didn't just look over me but so that they wouldn't even see me or notice anything I did, I could be invisible to them for a time. It would require a great deal of power: enough to influence another's perceptions and to some extent their free will. It would be difficult to hide the amount of power being drawn from the rest of the camp. The weaker, less-skilled ones might not notice but Aed and David were sure to, and possibly even Jeremy. They would know with that much power being used, that I was up to something. Aed would be furious with me, he might even kill me and it would mean exposing my true identity to the rest of the camp… but I had to risk it.

The light was fading to a misty twilight. I had no time left to solidify my plan. If I was going to do this, it needed to be now. I squeezed my necklace tightly in my hand, the gently pulsating warmth so soothingly familiar it brought tears to my eyes. My heart ached so badly for Sebastian. I couldn't afford to take the time to properly grieve yet, I had years and years of bleak mourning stretching ahead of me. Maybe one day, when this was all behind me, I could take the time to truly grieve his loss or maybe by then, the pain might have lessened in part. Maybe, just maybe, I could find a new happiness, a different life, with another who I might never have considered before, who would follow wherever I led him…

I pushed the thoughts aside and focused, letting a torrent of magic rush through me, filling me from my fingertips to my toes. My whole body vibrated with power and I directed it to fulfill my wants, disguising me from anyone who might look my way. I stepped forward from the shadows, marching quickly across the meadow, my head held high. The sun sank lower.

As I approached the cabin, the guard, Harry, didn't so much as glance my way even though I made no attempt to sneak up on him. I marched straight forward and placed my hand on his arm, he didn't even blink. With just the slightest amount of pressure, I gently guided him out of the way of the door. He moved easily, as if the decision to move were his own, completely unaware that he was being guided by another.

A large metal padlock held the cabin door shut. I didn't have a key but I didn't want it to slow me down. I was racing against the sun now. I reached for the padlock and tugged. The lock opened smoothly with a faint 'click' and I quickly pulled it free. My heart was beating fast, my pulse loud in my ears. I knew I only had a few minutes left before I was discovered. With the Lost Magic still raging through my veins, I pulled open the old cabin door and quickly slipped inside, pushing the door closed behind me.

It was dark within the cabin walls and it took my eyes a second to adjust to the low light. A dark shape loomed before me, strung up from ropes that hung from the ceiling above. The floor was sticky and scattered with straw, a foul scent hung in the air, reminding me of decay and death. A strange rattling sound seemed to come from all around me. The voices of the spirits hissed in my ears, their voices angry and incoherent. Terror gripped my throat but I knew I needed to see this. I needed to expose Aed's secrets to truly understand him, to know if this were really a man who I might join. I needed more light.

At that moment, a bright ray of golden light from the setting sun broke through the treetops at the horizon and shone down onto the field. The cabin glowed with a soft and eerie, dream-like haze. I gasped at what I saw.

A man was tied up before me, hanging from the ceiling by his wrists with his bloody feet just barely touching the floor. His head sagged down against his chest which was struggling to rise with each ragged and wheezing breath he took. His clothes looked like they had once been expensive but the fine material was ripped and stained from his own blood. Dark, dried blood caked his wrists which were raw from the ropes that bound them. His dark brown hair was matted and he reeked of blood and sweat. I stared at him in disbelief.

"Hello?" I whispered, my voice sounding as small and terrified as I felt. "Can you hear me? My name's Grace. I'm going to help you,"

I promised, yet I wasn't sure how.

The man stirred at the sound of my voice. He struggled to lift his head.

"Grace?" he mumbled. I froze at the sound. His voice was familiar. No… it couldn't be. "Grace, is it really you?" he asked hoarsely. He finally managed to lift his head and I found myself staring into his bleary, brown eyes.

"It's me," I whispered. My own eyes filled with tears. "Clarke… what's happened to you?" I gasped. "Why are you here?"

"Sebastian," he moaned, his voice both angry and afraid. "He's gone insane. We had just gotten back from Jamaica, he surprised us at the airport and offered us a ride. When we got into his car… I don't know what happened. I was knocked out. When I woke, I was tied up and Tanya was gone. I don't know what happened to her, Grace. Jeremy, the man who brought me here, says that Sebastian… he told me Sebastian killed her. He made me email my mother and say we were staying longer in Jamaica, Jeremy didn't want anyone to know where I was. At first I was left alone, I thought he had left me in this cabin to die but then Sebastian arrived. He tied me up and he's been… torturing me. It goes on for hours, I don't even know how long I've been here for. Why won't he just kill me, Grace? Why?"

It took me a second to fully process what Clarke had just said. My whole body went numb with fear and with the chilling realization of the truth. This is what Aed was capable of: this and worse. It was time that I face the truth, Sebastian was well and truly gone and if any parts of Sebastian still lived on inside Aed, it was his worst qualities: his anger, his jealousy, his possessiveness, the qualities that had belonged to Aed all along.

"It's not really Sebastian," I told Clarke as I began untying the ropes knotted around his wrists. They pulled apart like bows at my slightest touch. "Sebastian would never have done this to you or to anyone—ever. This was Aed."

"That's what he keeps calling himself," Clarke agreed, a crazed light gleaming in his eyes. "Why? Why is this happening? Are you going to kill me now, Grace?"

He was delirious. He sagged against me as I freed his other wrist. The stench of him was so putrid, I had to breathe through my mouth. I wanted to throw up.

"No, I'm getting you out of here—now."

"He's going to kill us. Just like he killed Tanya. Just like he killed our baby." Clarke began to sob, his whole body trembled violently. "You should run, Grace. Just run. Save yourself."

"It's going to be ok," I told him firmly. I wished I could believe it was true. "Come on, we need to get out of here."

Clarke didn't argue, he seemed to have lost the ability to speak. He was moaning and mumbling incoherently. I half-dragged him over to the door, kicking it open as I had no free hands. I froze as my eyes fell upon the still body that lay on the ground before us.

Harry lay motionless, facedown in the mud just a few feet from the cabin door. The handle of a knife stuck out of his back. I had no time to question how or why. I could see figures moving across the camp, coming towards us through the steadily lengthening shadows. I had no idea if one of them was Aed or if he was still waiting in his cabin; it shouldn't matter. I knew I'd been discovered by now, someone would have sensed the huge amount of magic that I had been channeling. Voices were crying out. It was time. A sob stuck in my throat.

"I want you to burn," I whispered and the cabin behind me— along with Jeremy's and Aed's—erupted into a tower of flames that climbed up high towards the early evening sky.

Chaos broke out all around us.

Chapter Sixteen – Battle

THE CAMP WAS FILLED WITH SHOUTS OF alarm as the cabins were consumed by flames. Someone must have known it was me, as a ball of fire about the size of a bowling bowl suddenly came shooting through the air towards us.

"Duck!" I screamed, tackling Clarke to the ground. The fireball narrowly missed our heads, exploding on contact in a spray of steaming dirt and rock.

"Get up, quick!" I urged Clarke, tugging on his arm. He stumbled to his feet, looking dazed. I felt the tingle of magic in the air and prepared myself for another fireball shooting at my head but this time, a ball of solid air shot past us from somewhere behind us in the woods and fired directly into Aed's camp. My friends were here still and they'd figured out how to fight back. Good.

"Let's go! We've got to move."

I half-dragged, half-carried Clarke away from the burning cabin toward the nearby trees. The sounds of battle were going on all around us, cries of rage, screams of pain, the earth exploding and trees bursting into flame. I was panting and sweating from the effort of moving Clarke and I was starting to panic. We were moving too slowly and with my head down like this and all my energy focused on getting Clarke to safety, we were vulnerable.

"Caoilinn!" Aed's bloodcurdling scream of rage echoed through out the forest and field, his voice bouncing off the rocky ridge and booming back down upon me. "Stop her! Bring her to me!" he screamed. My whole body began to tremble with fear but I forced myself to go on. We had nearly reached the trees.

"Leave me," Clarke wheezed as I dragged him along beside me.

"You can't save us both."

"No," I answered stubbornly through clenched teeth. And I was determined. I hadn't been able to save Sebastian but I would save Clarke if it was the last thing I ever did.

Just then, the sun's last rays started to disappear, winking out one by one as the sun sank below the horizon. The shadows deepened from gray to black. I took two more steps, then stopped.

"No, no, no," I moaned, panic setting in.

"Grace?" Clarke gasped.

I let his arm slide from my shoulders and gently set him down. We were only just at the edge of the forest. He wasn't very well concealed or protected here but it was going to have to do.

"My friends will find you here," I promised him. "They're close. They'll help you."

"Why? Where are you going?" Clarke sounded afraid. His face was ashen, his eyes large and imploring.

"I'm going back."

And as I said the words, my body began moving of its own accord, turning back towards the field. I fought it as much as I could but my legs began to move, my feet taking slow, reluctant steps back the way I had just come. There was a crashing noise behind me as something came charging through the forest. I couldn't even turn to see who or what it was.

"Grace! Grace! What are you doing?" Bridgette cried breathlessly from behind me. I could hear her footsteps thudding against the ground as she ran after me. She tried to catch my hand. "Grace, stop! You can't go back there, it's too dangerous."

"I have to," I tried to explain. "He's making me."

"No, you don't. Just stop!"

She tried to jump in front of me, planting her feet and holding up her hands as if she were going to physically block me from continuing. I pushed past her easily, nearly knocking her down even though I wanted her to succeed. I didn't want to go back.

"I'm sorry but I can't stop. He's too strong, Bridgette. I can't fight him."

"I won't let you go back!" Bridgette declared, grabbing my arms and trying to hold me. Again, I shook her off, my body moving as if another were commanding my actions. "He'll kill you, Grace. You'll die if you go back there."

"I know," I answered sadly. We were nearly back at the blazing cabin where Clarke had been held. It had almost burned to the ground. The battle was slowing down, only the occasional ball of fire brightened the thickening darkness. Any minute, we'd be discovered.

"Then fight it! Fight him. You're stronger than he is, Grace," Bridgette encouraged as she scrambled along beside me. "Please. Don't let him have this power over you."

Tears shimmered in my eyes making the shadows and bright orange flames dance in my vision.

"He's taken everything from me. I'm not strong enough to fight him," I whispered. My legs continued to move, my steps jerky as I weakly attempted to resist.

"No, he hasn't. You still have your friends, you still have your family back home and people who love you and need you. You still have me. Now stop!" Bridgette commanded firmly, a hint of magic adding strength to her words. My steps faltered then stopped but my muscles were coiled, burning as they fought to continue moving to take me back to Aed as he had commanded.

"You are strong. You can do this. Fight it—for Sebastian," Bridgette instructed, her eyes steady on mine.

Slowly I nodded.

She was right. Giving up was easy, but when was life ever easy? The easy choices were often not the right ones. I had to fight. I had to live. I had to escape. For myself and for the memory of Sebastian. I squeezed my necklace tightly and fought against the magic pulling at me.

"I can't," I grunted. It was too hard.

"You can," Bridgette argued. "You're doing it. Let me help you. Come on."

She took my arm and slowly began turning me back towards the woods. Her faint ability to use the Lost Magic was flaring to its full extent, offering me the small amount of strength that she could. It wasn't much magic but it was all she had. But it was they way she instructed me to rebel; I knew I had no other choice. I squeezed my necklace harder, focusing with all my might. I wanted to escape, I wanted to live and I did not want to go back to Aed. I loved Sebastian and I always would but Aed meant nothing to me. He was the enemy. He had killed Sebastian. And I must live so that I could make him pay. I must live so that I could destroy him. If I saw him again, I would kill Aed.

And with that thought, Aed's power over me was broken. I felt his magic crack apart, shattering with an almost audible sound that splintered through the night air. His answering scream of rage echoed across the field, making my blood run cold. He sounded outraged and insanely furious; he sounded like he wasn't that far away.

"Run!" Bridgette hissed in my ear, and we did.

"Where's Clarke?" I asked as we neared the edge of the forest. I couldn't see him anywhere but it was getting so dark that I might easily have overlooked him.

"Jai and Sylvia were close behind me. They would have found him, don't worry," Bridgette reassured me. I prayed that she was right.

A ball of fire as large as a beach ball suddenly hit the ground and exploded barely twenty feet behind us. We ran even faster, darting into the shadows and weaving our way between the trees, knowing that we were being chased.

The shadows were pitch black beneath the trees. We moved as quickly and carefully as we could, deeper and deeper into the woods. Bridgette led the way, surprisingly she seemed to have a better sense of direction in the dark than I did. I was only too happy to follow along without thought. I was exhausted.

It felt like hours later when we finally reached the rendezvous point; only five others were there.

"It's us," Bridgette called softly as we approached them.

"Who's us? Not Jeremy and Aed I should hope!" Red laughed, his voice just loud enough to make me wince nervously.

"Grace and Bridgette," I answered as we walked up. "Who's with you?"

"Nathaniel, Sylvia and the injured one, Clarke," he listed in a slightly softer tone.

"What about Ella and Jai?"

"Ella got hit by one of those fireballs," Sylvia answered. I could hear the tears in her voice. "She… she's gone. We had to leave her there."

"And Jai?" I whispered.

"We don't know. He's either dead or he's been captured," Red answered solemnly.

"Aed will show him no mercy. He's either dead already or he will be soon," I pronounced coldly. I couldn't afford to show any emotion; they had to understand exactly what it was we were dealing with. Bridgette gasped beside me. I felt numb, not allowing any sadness or regret to distort my thinking right now. "Where's David?"

"Down there." Nathaniel spoke for the first time and his voice shook with fury. I could just make out his gesture in the darkness as he pointed back down towards Aed's camp. "He fought *alongside* Aed. The fireball that killed Ella came from him."

"No," I denied, shaking my head in the darkness. "No, he couldn't have."

"It was him," Red confirmed angrily. "I saw it myself. He knew exactly where we were all supposed to be positioned and he made sure to tell the others. They would have picked us off if Bridgette hadn't suggested we reposition ourselves after you left, just in case Aed realized who you were and got the information out of you. I don't know why Ella didn't listen… if she hadn't been standing where David knew she'd be… but there can't be any doubt that David has changed sides now. He killed Ella; he would have killed us all."

"That's assuming he ever was on our side to begin with," Nathaniel added bitterly.

"Aed must have made him do it, just like he was trying to force me to return to him. He's powerful, more powerful than I realized. David would be powerless against him," I explained, not able to believe that David had betrayed us. He wouldn't. He couldn't have.

"Perhaps," Nathaniel answered softly, he sounded doubtful. No one else spoke.

"Grace?" Clarke moaned from the shadows nearby.

"I'm here." I rushed forward to reassure him, my fingers feeling for him in the darkness. As I blindly reached out for him, my hand brushed against his and his fingers immediately locked around mine, squeezing with a surprising strength considering his condition.

"I'm c-c-c-cold," he stuttered. I'd almost forgotten his grave injuries. Though we had managed to rescue him, whether he would survive or not was still uncertain.

"We need to get you back to our camp. We'll have to move to a new spot, just in case Aed gets more information out of David. We'll need blankets and some strong branches that we can make a stretcher out of; I don't think Clarke can walk far." Clarke moaned weakly in response. "We need to move quickly," I reminded them. I couldn't believe Aed would just let me walk away this time. Not after I'd taken his prisoner and defied his direct order to return to him at sunset. "How many of their numbers were left?"

"At least three were killed and two more injured," Nathaniel reported.

"Jeremy?" I asked.

"No." He sounded as disappointed as I felt. "Jeremy, David and Aed were well-protected."

"Next time," Red promised with a growl. It was the fiercest I'd ever seen him. I was surprised by the anger in his voice but then I remembered how fond he'd been of Ella. We all had scores to settle with Aed, but for tonight, we needed to retreat and regroup.

It took us hours to hike around to the other side of the island through the dark woods. Red and Nathaniel carried Clarke on the make-shift stretcher for the majority of the trip but Sylvia and I also took brief turns. When we finally found a level area along the island's coast that overlooked a small inlet where we could set up camp, we were all exhausted. Bridgette tended to Clarke's injuries by the low light of a small fire. She rinsed and cleaned his wounds, and carefully bathed his body with her gentle, proficient hands. She bound and covered his cuts and sores with fresh, clean bandages and a soothing salve from her own pack and found a fresh shirt and pants for him to wear that had been Nathaniel's. After forcefully making him drink some water and swallow a little bread—along with some pain-killers—she wrapped him in blankets beneath one of the lean-tos and watched over him until he fell asleep. A frown creased her typically smooth brow.

"What do you think?" I asked her when she came back over to the fire. Everyone else had gone to sleep except for Bridgette, myself and Nathaniel.

"Physically, I think he'll be ok," she answered, sinking down beside Nathaniel and leaning against him slightly. "He's dehydrated, exhausted and half-starved. He has some pretty bad cuts and burns, and he's covered in bruises but none of his injuries are life-threatening. He should heal and survive."

"But mentally?" I guessed.

She shook her head, staring sadly into the fire.

"I don't know. He's convinced that Sebastian killed his pregnant wife," Bridgette confessed, her voice a horrified whisper.

"You mean Aed," I corrected sharply.

"No, I mean Sebastian. Clarke says this started with Sebastian. That the people who first held him here said that they were acting under Sebastian's orders. And the first time Sebastian came and... beat him, he called himself Sebastian still. It wasn't until two nights ago that he started demanding everyone call him Aed."

"That was when you thought Sebastian died," Nathaniel commented.

"I know," I snapped.

Bridgette frowned at me disapprovingly.

"You can ask him about it yourself tomorrow if you like, Grace, but for now, I think we all should rest," Bridgette stated firmly. The fire abruptly went out, the scent of smoke left hanging in the air. I stared at Bridgette's faint silhouette in the darkness in surprise. The Lost Magic still lingered in the air, radiating out from Bridgette. I remembered how easily she had added her strength to mine when I had been trying to resist Aed's control.

"You've been practicing," I commented.

"You were right. When your life is on the line, it motivates you, makes the magic easier to reach and control. I think we all learned a lot today."

"I'm sorry you had to learn this way." I meant it too. I wished none of us ever had to fight or cause pain to another and especially to not have to take another's life. Unfortunately, the world just didn't work that way. This was our duty, this was our task laid out by the spirits themselves.

"It's fine. I'm going to take the first watch. Good night, Grace."

"Good night."

I heard Nathaniel quietly rise along with her. Against the distant backdrop of the stars, I thought I saw them walk away hand-in-hand, their heads bent close together as they whispered softly. I allowed myself one quick, sad smile.

Everyone was asleep. I was left all alone with my thoughts and they were dark and painful. I was faced with the truth that Sebastian was gone and Aed was a monster like I'd never imagined. Clarke was barely alive, Ella was dead, Jai was missing and David might well have betrayed us all. I suddenly could no longer bear to be awake, I could barely tolerate being alive. I crawled through the darkness over to the lean-to where Clarke was sleeping. He was snoring and rasping softly in his sleep. Needing some form of human comfort and warmth, I curled up against his side, pulled a blanket over my head, and fell fast asleep listening to the rhythm of his ragged breaths.

It felt like the moment my eyes were closed, the cold, gray fog started unfurling. I watched wearily as the otherworldly mist twisted around my ankles and thickened in the air all around me. In moments, I was encased in a cloud of soft, warm grayness. It was everywhere, it was all I could see, breathe and feel. An ancient voice whispered in my ear.

"We are displeased. Your ears are deaf to our voices. Your destiny is not fulfilled. You must guide them. You must destroy the dark power at their center," the voice hissed from everywhere and nowhere. I shivered.

"I know. I'm trying, I just... I needed to see for myself that Sebastian was gone before I could..." When I couldn't even say that

I was going to kill him, how could I possibly go through with it? I wondered.

"Sebastian is beyond saving," the voices chanted in unison, the sound strangely muffled by the fog. "Destroy the dark flame with light. It is your destiny."

"But how?" I demanded, frustrated and afraid. "I don't know how to defeat him."

"The Lost Magic must be bled from his veins at the tip of the ancient blade," the voices whispered back.

"What blade?"

"The dagger that once took Caoilinn's life. Pierce his heart and destroy the magic that bred in the darkness there. It is the only way to kill him and to stop him carrying his dark power forward into his next life."

"I don't know if I can do that," I whispered. The dark void inside of me felt like it was growing bigger, ready to swallow me whole.

"You must!" the voices hissed back at me, the shrill sound hurting my ears. "You will kill him or the whole world will be doomed, brought to kneel at his mercy. He must be stopped. You are the only one."

The weight of responsibility was crushing my chest. I could barely breathe, let alone answer. Instead, I offered a faint nod of acceptance.

"I will do what you ask of me," I gasped.

The fog started to thin and fade, the pressure on my lungs slowly relaxing.

"Mags?" I called out into the unfurling fog. "Mags? Are you there? Please, Mags, I need your help. Help me," I cried but there was no answer. "Mags, you once said David was the key but can he still be trusted? Has he really changed sides? Mags, please!" The soft, gray fog evaporated like smoke and before I could utter another word, my eyes popped open.

I was staring up at the underside of the lean-to I was sharing with Clarke. I could hear him snoring softly beside me, his breaths even and more regular than they had been last night. A flush of fever had crept into his cheeks but it might have been from the extra thick sleeping bag we had wrapped him in. Either way, I gently pulled the sleeping bag back from his face, allowing a little cool air to reach him before I wriggled my way out of the lean-to.

It was morning and the day was awakening crisp and cold. The golden sun was rising up from the ocean, its weak winter's warmth slowly melting the frost from the ground. It was still cold enough that my breath fogged up before me and I had to pull on my hat and gloves to stay warm. I was surprised to see that everyone else was already up, all five of them huddled around the fire and sipping from steaming mugs. Red waved as he saw me approaching.

"Look who's finally up!" he teased.

Bridgette smiled and quickly fetched another mug which she filled with piping hot tea. I took it from her gratefully.

"Why did you let me sleep so long? And why are you all here, shouldn't someone be on watch?"

"We couldn't wake you, we tried but you wouldn't stir. You were muttering in your sleep in a different language," Sylvia informed me.

"It sounded like an old form of Gaelic. We assumed you were consulting with the spirits," Bridgette explained with an apologetic shrug.

"Oh, I suppose I was," I admitted. "Not that it was much use."

"At dawn I went on watch by myself so that Bridgette could get some more rest. I decided to take a risk and head back towards Aed's camp, to see what was going on there and if they had captured Jai," Nathaniel told me.

"That was dangerous, you shouldn't have gone by yourself," I admonished.

He shrugged.

"I would prefer not to risk anyone's safety but my own."

I slowly nodded as I realized he had been worried that Bridgette would volunteer to go with him—which she probably would have— and then she might have been hurt. We exchanged a quick look, a mutual understanding. "They're still there," he informed. "Aed is directing the rebuilding of the camp. It was obvious even from a distance that he's furious. Seven of them still live including Aed, David and Jeremy. I saw no signs of Jai."

"Any signs of search parties out looking for us?"

Nathaniel quickly shook his head.

"No, Aed's not looking further than his own camp. All of his attention is on rebuilding the camp and preparing for… something. He seems confident either that we're not a concern, or that we'll come back when he wants us to."

"Or both," Bridgette whispered.

No one was meeting my eye. We were a sad group with little hope or enthusiasm. We needed a plan; we needed a leader. It was time to step up.

"David is supposed to be sneaking out of Aed's camp tonight and meeting us. We had planned to attack at dawn tomorrow but there's no longer any reason to wait. If he truly has joined Aed then he would have already shared the details of our plans. Any information he might bring us tonight—if he even comes—would be compromised and we'd be hard pressed to trust it, and him. I say we attack today, this very afternoon. We end it now before Aed has a chance to recover or cause any more harm."

"But how? We're outnumbered seven to four, and with David now on their side do we even stand a chance?" Nathaniel asked.

"Yes, we do. We have the spirits and destiny on our side, we are meant to defeat them and we will," I declared. "We'll catch them off guard and hit them hard. Their leaders will have to die. Aed, I will take care of; Red and Sylvia, I need you to go after Jeremy, and Nathaniel… if he truly has turned sides, then I'll need you to take David down."

"What about me?" Bridgette demanded.

"You'll be with me when I go after Aed," I informed her. Nathaniel's eyes widened and he immediately began to protest.

"Are you crazy? She'll die if she goes up against—"

"Thank you, but I can take care of myself," Bridgette snapped, glaring at Nathaniel in a way that should have made him want to curl up and hide. I was impressed and a little amused. I tried to hide my smile.

"I'm going to need that knife Mags gave you, Bridgette. The spirits said I must use it when I kill Aed. His death requires that ancient knife through his heart, to bleed the magic from his veins to ensure his power won't carry through to his next life," I explained.

"What about the others?" Red asked.

"The leaders must die, it doesn't matter particularly how Jeremy dies just as long as it happens. And David… if he is indeed a traitor then he must also die. The others we will try and spare. Once we've captured them all, we will ask them to swear not to harm any others, to live conspicuously and hide their abilities from the rest of the world, and to not abuse the Lost Magic in anyway."

"And you shall bind them to their words with magic?" Bridgette guessed.

"Yes."

"What if they won't swear?" Sylvia asked.

"Then they will leave us no choice but to kill them as well," Bridgette answered for me, her soft voice chillingly cold. It took me a second to realize I was gawking at her like the rest of them.

"You're forgetting one detail, Grace," Red spoke up. He squinted at me, looking apologetic. "How are we going to spring an attack on Aed's camp? We can't make the first move and he probably knows that. None of us have been able to gain any significant control over the Lost Magic unless there was a direct and immediate threat to our lives motivating us."

The others nodded their agreement. It was true enough.

"Don't worry about that. I'll make the first move and I can guarantee Aed's response will be immediate and enough of a threat that you'll all be able to fight," I assured him flatly.

"When do we move out?" Nathaniel asked, his eyes flickered nervously to Bridgette but he was wise enough not to voice his concerns. She was still glaring at him quite fiercely.

"Let's eat and break camp, we'll leave Clarke here, hidden safely until hopefully we all return. We attack at noon."

Chapter Seventeen – Vengeance

My heart was pounding in my throat. I tried to slow my breathing, but it was no use. Adrenaline coursed through my veins, making everything appear in vivid focus, all my senses heightened.

"Are you sure about this?" Bridgette whispered beside me.

I nodded. It was too late to turn back anyway.

"This is the way it has to be," I murmured back, my lips barely moving.

We stood at the edge of the field, watching the relaxed hustle and bustle of Aed's camp through the gently swaying branches. Aed either didn't suspect that we might attack or he didn't care. My eyes focused in on him. His back was turned as he walked away, stepping up into the new cabin that had been erected overnight. Without seeing his face, I could almost pretend that it was Sebastian, that I was seeing him one last time. But it wasn't Sebastian, Sebastian was gone and Aed had killed him. Aed was to blame for all my hurt and suffering, for all my misery, and he must now pay. Cold fury crystallized inside me, bringing with it sharp focus and complete calm.

"This is the end," I whispered as I unleashed the power of the Lost Magic down upon the field before us. The ground began to shake.

I closed my eyes and focused, directing the full force of my power like I never had before. It flowed through me, pouring through my entire being and threatening to sweep me away. My knees trembled from the force of it but I held on, I stayed in control. I clutched my necklace like a lifeline, using its steady warmth to focus my mind and the magic racing through me.

The earth beneath me began to heave. It shook and trembled, the trees groaning around us as their roots were pulled and torn from their shifting weights. Through out Aed's camp, people cried out in alarm and fear. I could feel the tingle of magic in the air coming from someone other than myself and I knew it was time to strike. I had to end this before he did.

The ground tore apart with a violent jolt, the noise of it deafening. I fell down upon the cold earth, Bridgette tumbling down beside me but still I didn't lose control. I ripped the field wide open in a line that led straight up to Aed's cabin. I opened my eyes just in time to see the logs of his cabin falling apart and crumbling down into the earth. The cabin was consumed whole by the large void that had opened beneath it.

For a moment, everything was silent and still as the earth quieted and resettled. It was like we were all stunned, in total shock. Had I really done it? Could I have defeated Aed that easily? Was it possible without using the ancient dagger, so carefully concealed under my clothes? A shadow of pain crossed my heart. Was all that had been left of Sebastian now truly gone?

"CAOILINN!"

Aed's bellow of rage echoed off the trees all around me. Bridgette clutched my arm in fear. I could distantly sense the Lost Magic gathering in the air, it was the only warning we had.

"Run!" I screamed.

We leaped apart just in time, the earth exploding all around us. I landed on my side, bruising my ribs and scraping the side of my face as I fell. My ears rang from the blast that echoed through out the field. I scrambled to my feet and immediately started running forward through the short, trampled grass of the muddy field as fast as my legs would carry me. It was like being in a war zone, balls of fire and invisible blasts of air were hitting the ground and exploding all around me. Everywhere I could see there was destruction and chaos. I zigzagged through the carnage, jumping over the torn, smoking earth and dodging the torrents of magic that whizzed by me.

The bright midday sun abruptly vanished, the world falling beneath a dark shadow. I risked a glance upwards to see that black, thunderous clouds had rolled in, swirling wildly as a magical storm brewed above us. The fine hairs on my arms and the back of my neck started to rise.

"Lightning," I gasped, realizing what was happening just in time. I threw myself sideways as fast and as far as I could while blinding hot lightning flashed down from the heavens with a crack that tore through the sky. I hit the ground hard, my ears ringing and my eyes struggling to focus as I blinked away the giant flash that had been burned into my vision. Slowly, I raised my head, hesitantly looking around.

I saw Red across the meadow, blood was trickling down the side of his face but otherwise he appeared unharmed. He looked furious, his face contorted with rage as he charged towards a slim, dark figure who stood unmoving at the edge of the large crevice torn into the earth.

My vision was still bleary, my head spinning as I struggled to pull myself back to my feet. I squinted across the meadow, blinking rapidly as I tried to focus. Red had almost reached the figure—was that Aed? What was he thinking? He couldn't stand against Aed alone. I had to help him.

I stumbled forward, lurching towards them at an awkward run. I could see who it was now, I recognized the proud set of his shoulders, the arrogant tilt of his head. It was David.

"No," I whispered as I felt the Lost Magic gathering within him. David was preparing to strike, to strike hard. The amount of power he conjured was impressive and terrifying, it was earth-shattering. "David—stop!" I croaked, but it was no use. I was too late.

The magic slammed into Red like a steam engine. I watched in horror as he tried to fight it, as he struggled against it, his steps faltering and slowly, his expression twisting with excruciating pain.

"No!" I screamed, my voice barely audible above the sounds of the exploding earth all around me.

Red briefly met my eyes and I saw the panic and fear in his expression, right before his eyes rolled back in his head, blood frothed at his lips, and he crumpled, lifelessly, to the ground.

"DAVID!" I screamed in anguish and fury. My hands shook. I was so angry, my whole body seemed to vibrate. I marched towards him, unable to get the image of Red's death out of my mind. It would haunt me forever. "How dare you kill him! Why did you do that? You didn't need to kill him!" I screamed, unable to reign in my anger.

He turned slowly to face me, an amused expression on his far-too-handsome face as I closed the distance between us. His eyes were cold as ice.

"Should I have stood by while Jai tried to kill me?" he asked calmly.

"You could have stopped him. You didn't have to kill either of them!"

"No," he agreed. He flashed me a vicious smile. "Their deaths were for my own satisfaction. This fool in particular has been getting on my nerves since Day One. You have no idea how many times I have fantasized about slitting his throat and drinking his blood. Almost as many times as I have dreamt about tearing open yours."

I gasped, unable to hide my shock.

"Traitor," I hissed. He shrugged.

"What are you going to do about it?" he taunted.

"I should never have trusted you."

"No, you shouldn't have," he agreed. "Now strike me down, if you can."

I started to react without thinking, preparing to direct the Lost Magic in a deathly blow that would wipe the smug smile from his face but just in time, I realized what he was trying to do. I slowed my breathing, forced myself to calm down and retain control.

"You're still bound by your promises to me," I realized aloud. "You can't hurt me or anyone else unless you think there's a threat to your life. But I can hurt you."

"The moment you try, I shall strike you down dead," he promised.

"But if I kill you with one blow, you won't have the chance to react, will you?" I pointed out, my hands flexing into fists by my sides.

"You don't have the will or the strength to execute me in cold blood like that. But please, I would love to see you try," he taunted again, his lips pulling up in a sneer.

"You asked for it," I growled, gritting my teeth together determinedly. But even then, I wasn't sure if I could do it. This wasn't in defense of my own life, this was a clear and deliberate execution, just as David had said. He saw me hesitate and began to laugh.

"Coward," he spat.

"Enough!" a voice snapped and we both turned towards the sound. It was only then that I realized the meadow had fallen silent, the only sounds were those of the resettling earth and the thunder that rolled distantly overhead.

Aed was marching towards us, dark, triumphant glory flashing through his eyes. I gasped as I saw who he dragged along beside him, his fingers ensnared cruelly through her long, dark brown hair as she scrambled to keep up.

"Bridgette!" I cried, immediately taking a step towards them.

"Stop!" Aed snapped and I froze in my tracks, silently cursing myself for letting him momentarily overpower me. Doing what Sebastian wanted was too much of an instinct for me to easily overcome it, even though this wasn't Sebastian anymore. "Come any closer or use any magic against me, and the girl dies." I reluctantly took a step back.

"What do you want?"

"Look around you," Aed gestured as he spoke. "You've lost. This foolish battle is over. Now it's time for you to beg for mercy. Depending upon how convincing you are, I might ever consider it."

Around the field, the earth and air was settling to reveal Jeremy, his woman and a tall, thin man, still standing. This time they had all survived. The tall man had Nathaniel, his arm twisted behind his back and his face ashen. One side of his face was badly bruised and covered in blood. His lip and cheekbone had swollen so that he was nearly unrecognizable. Sylvia was nowhere to be seen. It really was over. I looked down at Bridgette who steadily met my eye. She was surprisingly calm, accepting her fate with a quiet dignity that I hadn't expected. It was true, we had lost. What had I done?

"It wasn't supposed to end like this," I whispered under my breath. I hadn't meant for anyone to hear but David's eyes immediately lit up.

"Oh, but it was," he smiled, an evil, crazed light glowing within his eyes. "I have waited a very long time for it to end like this, Caoilinn, a very long time. And I shall enjoy every moment of your death, every drop of your blood that is spilt."

His words reminded me of the ancient, ceremonial knife still hidden in a leather sheath, tucked under my shirt in the side of my pants. I could feel the handle, warmed by my skin to the same temperature as my body. It glowed steadily, pulsating with a rhythm the same as my necklace, echoing my own heart's beating. It wasn't over. I could still end this, if Aed let me get close enough, if I was strong enough to do what was required of me.

The wind stirred my hair and a breathy voice whispered softly in my ear, "...*the key*..." A chill ran down my spine. I could feel Mags' presence in the air even though I couldn't see her. I knew she was there and I knew she was sending me this message for a reason. David was the key. It was important that before I took Aed's life and probably forfeit my own along with it, that I understood why David was the key to it all. Why had this happened?

"So this was your master plan? Befriend me, unsuccessfully seduce me and then encourage me to lead the others to a remote island to die? And for what purpose, David? Please, enlighten me," I drawled sarcastically.

David's face darkened with anger, his brows pulled down, his eyes flashed. Aed, on the other hand, looked amused.

"Yes, enlighten us, brother," he echoed. He tossed Bridgette aside by her hair, causing her to cry out in pain. She fell to her hands and knees in the mud, cowering before him. "Try anything, and you all die," he warned us, then he turned to David expectantly. "You've hinted that there was more motive to this 'plan' than your ancient hatred of Caoilinn, now is the time to explain."

David stared down his nose at Aed, obviously displeased to be commanded so dismissively in front of others. After a brief pause, he continued.

"As you well know, we all have good reason to hate Caoilinn: lying, manipulative, bitch that she is," David spat at me.

Aed laughed. The sound was humorless and chilling. "Careful, brother," he warned. "She's not Caoilinn anymore."

"At the core she's the same," David dismissed.

"And at the core, am I the same as Sebastian, the sap? Or Seamus, the coward?"

"No, of course not," David backtracked. "I was merely stating that this is not about just my hatred for Caoilinn. My revenge was against Sebastian, for stealing from me what was rightfully mine. I've now taken everything from him, including his life. And my revenge is not only against Caoilinn, but against you, *Gracelynn*. It was your actions that caused me to strike down the only one I had ever truly loved. And now, I will do the same to you."

"What are you talking about?" Jeremy demanded. He grabbed Nathaniel from the thin man and shoved him forward, where he fell alongside Bridgette at Aed's feet. I saw him search for her hand in the mud, his fingers twining through hers and squeezing tightly before his body appeared to go limp. Aed no longer looked amused.

"Mags," I gasped as I realized the truth. It all made perfect sense. "You were in love with Mags?"

"Magdalene was mine first and she should have always been," David growled possessively. "But Seamus stole her from me. I suppose he never shared that detail with you?"

"No," I whispered, disbelievingly.

"She found me first," he continued. "Mags was always drawn to those who had the potential for great power; she saw it in me before Seamus ever did. We quickly fell in love, a passionate and powerful affair. When Seamus came along, we were all drawn to one another by our potential to use the Lost Magic. For a time, the three of us were the closest of friends but as the years went on, a distance began to grow between Mags and I; she turned away from me and went to him. She couldn't help it. She was seduced by his power."

"By *my* power," Aed spoke firmly. He fixed David with a fierce and deadly glare. "Mags would never have held any interest in that weak and pathetic boy if it hadn't been for me. She saw the potential in him that was *me* and I stole nothing from you. She chose me."

David's lips compressed to a thin line.

"Seamus stole her from me before you ever existed. But yes, it was you whom she gravitated towards and it was at your side that she eventually stood. But after a time, Seamus's personality started to re-emerge, he started to question his choice to live as Aed Dubhan."

"A weakness that has long been destroyed," Aed muttered darkly but David seemed not to hear.

"That was when I told Sebastian of Mags' betrayal, how she had manipulated him, how she had lied about Caoilinn and used the Lost Magic to tamper with his memories. I helped him to erase his memories of her, of being Aed Dubhan, of everything. Her magic was too strong to let him entirely forget, to let him run from her, so instead, I helped convince him that she was dead. He wanted to believe, he wanted to escape her that badly. And so he did."

"Make your point, David. I'm getting bored," Aed warned, the threat in his voice clear. "I do not relish reliving the time when you tried to destroy Seamus' memories of me and drove Mags and I apart. It has been long forgiven but still, it would not be wise to spend too much time revisiting the past."

"All those years that Sebastian was missing, Mags searched for him and hid from me," David continued as if he hadn't heard. He ignored Aed now as he spoke rapidly, his eyes bright as he relived his memories of the past. "I knew she'd come back to me eventually but when she did, it was only to beg for *his* life. She was supposed to deliver Sebastian and Caoilinn to The Order, to make retribution for her past betrayal and abandonment of us and our cause. After yours and Sebastian's executions, I would have taken her up again as my woman, to let her stand alongside me in redemption and share in my glory. But she was so driven by her jealousy of you, *Grace-lynn*, that she endangered our whole plan. Then you wiped out her memory in Thessaloniki and destroyed the woman that I loved, and you left me with no choice but to order her death for her betrayal or appear weak and unfit to lead The Order."

I gasped as I finally understood. This had all been about revenge. David's revenge against me.

"So tell me, how does it feel, Grace?" David demanded. "Was it excruciating, watching your one true love slip away from you? To see Sebastian turn to confide in another, to watch the divide between you growing—did it hurt? It was all your doing, you know. When you erased his memories at the Necromanteion, you didn't know to erase *all* of his memories, like his memories of living as Aed. The memories from that life were too strong. It was all he had left; of course it overcame him—with a little encouragement on my part. Are you proud of yourself, Grace? To know your own part in Sebastian's death? I could never have done it without you," he gloated.

"You were so foolish, blinded by your own stubborn pride. It was easy to hide his ability from you once it had reawakened, small and dwindling as it was. You didn't want to see it, you didn't want to believe that the Lost Magic was back in your life. It only took a little extra push to awaken Aed's full ability which you provided yourself when you revealed to him that you were, in fact, Caoilinn, the woman he had hated for hundreds of years."

"How does it feel, Grace? To know that you are the one who killed him? To know that you are the one who pushed Sebastian over the edge? Tell me, how does it feel?" he raged. His jaw was strained, his hands were trembling. A vein bulged near his forehead.

Aed laughed, the sound hard and cold, echoing around the field. Everyone shifted uncomfortably. We were in the company of two madmen and it looked like Jeremy and his allies had only just realized it. Nathaniel still lay crumpled on the ground at Aed's feet, his fingers loosely holding Bridgette's. Bridgette herself now sat straight and proud, considering David emotionlessly. I briefly met her eye and she nodded. Her thoughts were so clear, I thought I could almost hear them in my mind. *Be strong*, she whispered in my mind's ear. *You can do this.*

Aed's laughter abruptly cut off as he noticed the unspoken communication between us.

"Well, you certainly know how to throw a party, brother," Aed remarked to David. "Your revenge is sweet but certainly flawed."

"Oh?" David arched a brow.

"You wanted to force Grace's hand, so that she would have to be responsible for the death of all that was left of Sebastian: *my* death. But Grace would never have been strong enough to kill me herself. There is only one weapon that might bring me to my knees, and even though she carries it on her person now, she makes not the slightest move to use it," Aed remarked quietly. He watched me the whole while that he spoke. My body tensed, my muscles froze. He knew.

"Don't fool yourself, Grace," he purred, stepping closer to me. I still couldn't move, I could barely breathe. I wondered if it was because he didn't want me to or was I paralyzed by fear? "You came back to me, just as I commanded. You deny it but you know it's true. You could never harm me, not when I wear your lover's face. Not when I am all that you have left of him. How could you be expected to destroy that?"

"I'll do it, I'll kill you," I warned, my voice barely a whisper. I slid one hand to my hip, gripping the warm hilt of the knife beneath my shirt and the other clutched at my necklace, desperately drawing strength from it.

"Do it then," he challenged. He held his arms open, his palms face out. "Kill me."

I pulled the knife out. In my peripheral vision I saw Jeremy move forward. David tensed but Aed didn't flinch in the slightest.

"Stay back," he commanded. His eyes glowed feverishly. "Not you," he beckoned to me. "Come closer. Show us all just how fear-less you are, how selfless. Let's end this, Grace, once and for all."

I moved closer, enticed by his words, hypnotized by his eyes.

He reached out slowly and clasped my wrist in one of his strong, warm hands. He squeezed tightly, the gentle pressure familiar and eerily reassuring. Without ever breaking eye contact, he guided the knife point to his heart, only releasing my hand once I held the knife directly over his chest, the point digging into the fabric of his clothes. I knew I should do it, I knew this would be my one and only chance but for some strange reason, I couldn't bring myself to push the blade in. I couldn't do this. I wasn't strong enough.

"Do it, Gracelynn. Kill me. You know I don't deserve to live. Kill me," he whispered, his voice no longer taunting and cruel, his words softened by his strange passion. I gazed back into his eyes and was shocked by what I saw there, a faint glimmer, a distant glow, a forgotten shade of blue. I nearly dropped the knife.

"Do it. Do it now," he urged. He grabbed my hand, pulling the dagger firmly against his chest. The tip pierced through his clothes and found his skin, blood began to well around it.

"No," I denied. "I can't."

From behind Aed, David laughed.

"You see! She is weak, she's a fool. This child is not fit to lead anyone. She has led you to nothing but your deaths at our hands."

"Kill…me!" Aed hissed through clenched teeth. Again a glimmer of blue flashed in his eyes. And I knew I couldn't go through with it, it was no longer even a possibility. I could never, ever harm this man because somewhere, deep inside him, Sebastian was still alive, at least in some form. A spark of hope flickered in the black void inside of me. A shadow of light crossed my heart.

Aed didn't truly want to die, but Sebastian did. Sebastian would rather die than live like this. Sebastian would rather die at my hand and save me from Aed, than risk living and seeing my demise. But Sebastian was not beyond saving as he must believe. I could no longer believe it. I knew what I had to do. I let the dagger fall from my hand.

"I love you, Sebastian," I said softly.

Aed's eyes widened. David snickered but I ignored him.

"Sebastian is dead. I killed him, you fool," Aed growled. All traces of blue had disappeared from his eyes and they were back to a hard and deadly black. "If you want to live, you will never, *ever*, call me that again."

"He's a part of you as much as you're a part of him," I argued. "You don't have to choose to be Aed or Sebastian, no person is all good or all bad, you can be both; you are both."

"You lying bitch!" Aed declared. "Stupid girl! How dare you insult me by implying that any part of that coward exists within me still?"

"Now that she won't move against you, what should we do with her?" David mused. "Do you still want her now that she has shown her true cowardice, or will you discard her and execute her as she deserves?"

"Do your own dirty work, David," Aed snapped. Jeremy and the others flinched at his harsh and deadly tone.

"She has bound me with her filthy magic not to harm her, might I remind you," David frowned. "You must kill her yourself, brother. Use the dagger and let her blood bleed out from her heart so that her magic won't carry forward with her into her next life."

"Very well. I tire of these games," Aed muttered as he bent to pick up the dagger. He straightened quickly and pressed the blade against my throat. I made no move to stop him.

"No!" Bridgette protested, speaking for the first time. A swift kick in the gut from David silenced her. Cold fury flowed through my veins. I squeezed my hands into fists. Though Nathaniel remained motionless, I thought I saw his muscles tighten and flex.

"Don't be afraid," I whispered fiercely to Aed. He frowned, obviously thrown off guard. "I see all of you now, I know all of your past. You never have to be afraid of the past again, once you accept it and leave it behind you, it will no longer haunt you. Aed will be powerless."

"Shut up!" Aed hissed. He pressed the dagger against my throat. I felt a trickle of blood run down my neck.

"Not her throat, her heart!" David instructed from behind him.

"Shut up!" Aed roared.

"I know you're in there still," I breathed as quietly as possible. I could tell Aed was listening to me, his eyes fixed unwaveringly on mine. Something stirred deep in the shadows of the gaping void within me. I knew I was close to breaking through to him. "Please, I love you. Come back to me."

Aed stepped even closer. He towered above me, the knife biting into my throat, burning with pain. He bent his head down to whisper menacingly in my ear.

"*Kill me*," he begged, the plea embedded with unspeakable hatred and self-loathing. His pain tore at my heart.

"I'm sorry, I can't," I whispered back. "Death might be easier but I'm going to force you to live with this, to live through this. That is the only punishment you deserve."

I heard Aed sigh, a familiar exhausted and exasperated sound. His breath tickled my ear, sending shivers down my spine. The void inside me shrank, a new, gently glowing light filling it, filling me.

"Do it! Kill her! What are you waiting for?" David screamed in frustration.

Aed immediately pulled away from me, turning with fury in his eyes.

"Do not presume to tell me what to do," he warned, the knife spinning in his hand with a flick of his wrist. I could no longer tell who was in control, Aed or Sebastian or were they now one and the same?

"Are you threatening me?" David demanded incredulously.

"Do I need to?"

"If you won't kill her, let me," Jeremy volunteered, his eyes eager. He held his hand out for the knife. "Or let me have the brunette," he suggested, his eyes lingering on Bridgette suggestively. "I'd love to have a little fun with her before we slit her throat. I wonder how many ways we make her scream?"

"Now!" Nathaniel yelled, suddenly coming to life.

The thin man and the woman who stood slightly behind Jeremy leapt forward at Nathaniel's command. They grabbed ahold of Jeremy, pulling him backwards and onto the ground before he could properly react. A blade flashed through the air as it swept across Jeremy's throat. His blood, scarlet red and steaming hot, sprayed onto the muddy ground.

With an animalistic cry of rage, Nathaniel charged at David. He threw himself at him with a roar of fury, his hands reaching for David's throat, a solid blast of air already forming before him. David moved so fast, he seemed to almost blur through the air. With an unshakeable, deadly calm, his hand clenched around Nathaniel's throat, crushing it with the added strength of his magic. A sickening crunching, gurgling sound escaped Nathaniel's lips as his windpipe collapsed, his hands loosely clawing at this throat as he lost all control of his magic.

"No!" I screamed, but Nathaniel was already dead. David cast his limp body aside, a smug, self-satisfied expression on his face. I couldn't believe I had ever thought he was handsome, that I had ever been tempted by him. He was pure evil.

"Stop!" I commanded to the tall, thin man and the woman, who were still attacking the lifeless and bloody form of Jeremy. I felt like I was about to throw up. "Just stop."

"Stop," Bridgette echoed, her voice barely louder than a whisper. Her face was white, completely bloodless. She looked like she was in shock. She crawled to Nathaniel's side, reaching for him with a trembling hand. She checked his pulse, but there was no need. Slowly and tenderly, she closed his unseeing eyes and wiped a splatter of mud from his cheek with her thumb. With the lightest touch, she swept his messy hair aside to press her lips against his forehead. Tears began to gather in my eyes.

"Too much for you to stomach, Grace?" Aed commented, sounding bored. He glanced over to Jeremy's mutilated corpse emotionlessly. "Nathaniel might have commanded them a little too enthusiastically. Mind control can be a dangerous game when you don't know the rules. You!" he snapped at the man and the woman crouched to either side of Jeremy's corpse, their faces now splattered with blood. "The one who attempted to command you is dead. You obey me now and only me, or you die. Understand?"

They both looked confused. The man hesitated, then spoke.

"Nathaniel bound us with his magic, but it was not him we were asked to obey."

"I don't care if he bound you to obey Grace or himself or even the pathetic child! He is dead, his magic dies with him, you are now mine to command." And with his words, David released a steady stream of the Lost Magic, twisting around and trapping the minds of the two people before him to do his bidding.

Their eyes glazed over, their faces blank. Slowly they both nodded, like mindless zombies.

"Look at all the bodies that can be piled at your feet," David accused. "All this death and destruction, all because of you, Grace."

"What have you done?" Bridgette suddenly growled. The sound of her voice was terrifying. The power commanded behind it immeasurable, and awe inspiring. I could feel the Lost Magic pouring into her like never before. The amount of power she was drawing on was limitless. I hadn't thought it possible to control so much of the magic. She slowly rose to her feet.

"Sit back down, child, before you get hurt," David dismissed. His eyes flickered nervously to Aed who was subtly shifting his body in front of mine.

"Careful," Aed warned, his voice low and soft and strikingly familiar. "You can't win against us. I don't want to kill you."

The wind began to rise, howling all around us. The sky darkened and lightning flickered at the edges of the field, striking the tops of the trees. Magic poured from Bridgette, filling the air, crackling with its own electric pulse and still she fed more and more into the air all around us. What was she doing?

"What have you done?" she screamed, her eyes wild with grief as she looked down upon Nathaniel's lifeless body, laid out on the mud before her.

As the wind swirled all around, wisps of fog began to stretch down from the sky, unfurling as they hit the ground, instantly thickening and solidifying into a dense, gray cloud. The boundary between the living and the dead blurred.

"Don't leave me!" Bridgette screamed, her plea echoing all around us. The fog continued to pour down from the sky. It was so thick now that the rest of the meadow had already disappeared. Beyond our small group of six, there was nothing but a wall of solid gray. A light began to grow in the distance, as bright and as warm as the sun. "Come back!" Bridgette screamed. "Nathaniel, come back to me!"

"What is that?" David asked, squinting into the fog. "Where are we?"

There was a blinding flash of light that made us all flinch. When we reopened our eyes, an apparition stood before us, bathed in warm, soft light. We all stared in speechless wonder.

"I'm here, Bridgette, it's ok now," Mags greeted softly. She smiled gently at Bridgette, her eyes full of pity. Bridgette sagged down to the ground, a loud sob bursting from her lips. "I'm so sorry about Nathaniel. I'm sorry about all of what you had to go through. But you have finally reached your full potential, you are about to finally meet your destiny as I once promised you would." Mags turned to me with a grateful smile. "Thank you, Grace. You have brought her here. Your obligation to the spirits has ended. And in return..."

She turned slowly to face Aed, her skin glowing with a warm, otherworldly light. She smiled at him, radiating such peaceful, pure joy.

"Hello, Sebastian," she greeted.

Aed frowned, his confusion obvious.

"I... who are you? Mags?"

"Yes, it's me. It's time for you to come back now, come back to Gracelynn. She loves you and she will continue to fight for you. She will never give up, Sebastian. Help her. Extinguish the dark flame in your heart and come back to her," Mags coaxed.

"No, I can't..." he moaned, the strain clear on his face. His eyes were clouded but the lines of his face were softening before my eyes.

"You've never been beyond saving, Sebastian. I love you. Grace-lynn loves you. The Jensons love you. Come back to us," Mags whispered.

Aed squeezed his eyes shut, his whole body shaking. Tears leaked out the corners of his eyes and began to trickle down his pale cheeks.

"I... can't..."

"Help him," Mags instructed me.

I ran to his side, my heart swelling with fear and hope. I tentatively touched his arm and he didn't pull away. My heart relaxed and melted; it felt so good to touch him again after all this time. He slowly opened his dark blue-gray, tear-filled eyes.

"Gracelynn," he whispered, his voice full of despair.

"It's ok. I'm here, it's ok," I rushed to reassure him, hardly able to believe it was true—he was back. I had Sebastian back.

"I can't... I've done such terrible things. If you only knew..."

"I know."

"No, you don't," he argued. He spoke so softly I could barely distinguish his words. "I… Clarke and…"

"I already know," I reassured him. I swallowed hard. "I know what *Aed* did to Clarke and I know about Tanya too."

"It wasn't just Aed. It was me too. Clarke will never forgive me, I'll never forgive myself. But not Tanya—I couldn't do it, even then, I couldn't hurt the baby. Jeremy arranged for someone to hold her for us, until I decided what I was going to do with her. She's in a cabin in Tofino."

Relief swept through me.

"Clarke will be so happy," I whispered in his ear. "I shouldn't have doubted you."

"But Gracelynn… it doesn't change a thing. The things I've done can never be undone, can never be forgotten."

"I know, but I'm still here," I repeated, wrapping my arms around him and holding him as tightly as I could. I felt him tremble, I heard him choke back a sob. The void inside me vanished and filled and swelled with light as bright and as warm as the sun. I swore that I'd never let him go.

"I love you," I whispered as I clutched him as tightly as I could.

"I love you too," he answered without hesitation, his voice thick with tears and sorrow.

"David," Mags' spirit turned to him. His face was ashen, his eyes full of panic. He shook his head, his mouth working in silent denial.

"You have fallen so far," Mags murmured sadly. "You have had so many chances to change your life but you do not ever take them. You almost let yourself love Grace, just as once you almost let yourself love me but then you pull back, you always return to the evil, hateful ways that are so familiar to your heart."

"Lies! Lies!" David cried, his face contorting with fury. "Don't fall for the girl's tricks, Aed! This is all a part of Caoilinn's game. It's not real. None of it's real. I'll put an end to this once and for all."

David began to gather the Lost Magic, preparing to strike against Mags. She stared back at him calmly, peacefully, while he gathered enough magic to quite possibly destroy her spirit so that her soul might never be born or live again. Panic overwhelmed me. I didn't know what to do. I couldn't move or think fast enough to stop him. But before David could utter the word, before he could release the spell from his lips, Bridgette stepped between him and Mags. With tears still fresh on her face, she drove the ancient knife deep into his heart.

"You…" he croaked accusingly, glaring at Bridgette with eyes full of hate. "It was you all along."

"One day you will be born again, but without magic, without power and with the chance to start anew. Until then, I hope you find redemption and forgiveness in the place between life and death. The place I send you to now to join the others whom you have sent there so untimely," she pronounced stoically. With one last thrust, she drove the dagger deeper into his chest, silencing the beating of his ancient heart forever. David's eyes glazed over, his body crumpled forward and hit the ground, a pool of dark blood slowly spreading from him. Bridgette fell weakly to her knees.

"It is not an easy path to walk," Mags spoke quietly, her voice blending with the wind as the image of her began to fade and the gray fog started to break apart in wisps. "But my spirit shall always be here to walk alongside you. Trust in your friends and trust in your heart. You shall lead them now and protect our secrets, along with the sacred magic that is now entrusted to you. I'm proud of you."

I stared in wonder at the two women before me, an apparition flickering in the wind and a young woman who I had thought I knew but now I felt like I was truly seeing her for the first time. All the pieces fell into place; it had all happened for a reason. Everything that had happened in my life, and in my lifetime two thousand years prior, it had all brought us to this moment. This was bigger than Caoilinn and Seamus, or me and Sebastian, or any one of us. For the first time in thousands of years, the Lost Magic had been truly awoken and a leader had risen strong enough to bring the magic and its practitioners into the modern world.

I glanced up at Sebastian and we shared a look that carried a thousand silent words between us. This moment was bigger than us, bigger than anything we had ever seen or felt. This was history in the making. The world was about to change.

"Don't go," Bridgette cried, reaching out to Mags just as she faded away.

"I will always be here," Mags' voice whispered upon the wind.

The sun suddenly burst through the stormy clouds overhead, a beam of light falling directly upon Bridgette, making her hair glow like golden fire. She radiated pure power and strength, looking like a young goddess. I clutched Sebastian's hand tightly as we stared in wonder at the woman Bridgette had transformed into before our eyes. A thousand ancient voices whispered together upon the icy wind.

"Rise, Guardian of the Lost Magic. Rise to your destiny."

With the wind in her hair and the sun streaming down upon her face, Bridgette turned to face us—and to lead us—into a new era and a future unknown.

Epilogue

THE TAXI SLOWLY MADE ITS WAY THROUGH the city, inching along the bustling streets through the late afternoon traffic. After traveling for so many hours and spending close to twenty-four hours awake together, you'd think we'd both be tired but Sebastian and I were full of excited, restless energy. Adrenaline rushed through my veins every time I looked at him, which was frequently.

I stared at him unabashed while he was looking out the taxi window, smiling slightly to myself. He had changed so much since the first day I had met him. I could still recognize the boy who I'd fallen in love with just a year and a half ago. His black hair was as wild and messy as ever, worn longer now but always clean and soft. His eyes still sparkled when he smiled and hinted at secrets and mischief yet to be revealed. His laughter was contagious, his wit quick and quirky. His smile still deepened by a dimple in his cheek. But there were changes too. He looked older, years older. He could no longer pass for a boy in his late teens: he now appeared to be in his mid-twenties, at the youngest. There was a look about his eyes sometimes, a sadness, a certain wisdom that spoke of many hardships lived through and horrors seen. He was no longer haunted by nightmares but he often muttered in his sleep and tossed and turned. He was still prone to brooding and sometimes had short, dark flashes of temper. He was different than he once had been but the same. He was broken and flawed, just as I was, and I loved him with everything in my heart.

He turned back and saw me watching him. A smile slowly spread across his face, that heart-stopping, stomach-dropping, bone-melting smile. I grinned back at him.

"We should be there soon." He spoke softly, almost shyly. It was so unexpected, I suddenly felt nervous myself. I had to fight a blush as I answered.

"I can't wait."

He smiled back, his gray-blue eyes sparkling as he reached for my hand. He linked his fingers through mine and lifted our clasped hands to his lips, gently kissing just below the small, silver wedding band that I now wore below my engagement ring. His lips brushed my skin as he spoke, his breath tickling the back of my hand.

"I feel like I'm dreaming. And I don't ever want to wake up. I can hardly believe that you're finally my wife."

"I'll live in this dream forever," I agreed.

He pulled me into his warm, waiting arms and I closed my eyes as I leant against his chest. The past twenty-four hours blurred together in my mind and seemed to stretch together endlessly. I hadn't slept yet for fear that this perfect day would come to an end, I never wanted it to. I could hardly believe it had been just yesterday afternoon, when we had exchanged our vows and become husband and wife…

"I CAN'T BELIEVE I let him convince me to walk down the aisle like this; down *this* aisle," I complained as I adjusted my dress nervously.

"Stop fidgeting, it makes you look twitchy. And don't slouch," my mother added.

"But I am twitchy—and nervous."

"It's not too late to change your mind," my father reminded me in his deep, gruff voice. He looked almost hopeful as he spoke. Whatever agreement or mutual understanding he and Sebastian had come to, I wouldn't take it so far to say that they had become friends. My father was not thrilled, to say the least, about the prospect of having a new family member to call him "Dad". Sebastian wouldn't be welcome to call him anything but a respectful "Mr. Stevenson" or "Sir" anytime soon. But I had hopes for the future.

"I have no doubts about marrying Sebastian, Dad." I rolled my eyes at him, the notion really was ridiculous. "It's the 'let's get married on a frozen pond' part that I'm questioning. Really, what the hell was I thinking when I agreed to this?"

"Well, this is all your own doing. I had a beautiful wedding planned for you: a wedding that they'd be talking about in Victoria for *years* to come. But no, that wasn't good enough! You had to go and make your own plans, breaking my heart and—"

"Really, Diane, that's enough," my father cut in. They glared at each other for several seconds, neither willing to back down. I winced; they'd been doing so well up until now, much better than I'd expected. As always, I felt it was my responsibility to keep the peace.

"No, you're right, Mother. I shouldn't be complaining when this is what I chose. I'm just nervous."

My mother hesitated and then finally unlocked eyes with my father. She looked upon me with a critical frown, reaching to adjust a piece of my hair which had come loose from the complicated knot of twists and braids that were piled upon my head.

"Don't be nervous. You look beautiful. I'm glad you still wore the gown," she added with a surprisingly gentle smile.

"Mom, are you crying?" I asked incredulously.

"I'm entitled to a tear or two. My only child is about to get married..." She sniffed, covering her mouth delicately with her hand. "I'll see you in a few minutes," she choked out. Then, with the help of Dr. Mackey, her new boyfriend, she awkwardly stepped down onto the slippery surface of the frozen pond and began slowly shuffling her way out to the center of the ice.

My hands started to shake; not from the cold, since I was draped in enough layers of expensive, ivory fabric that I couldn't possibly be cold, even with my bare arms. It was nerves and anticipation that caused me to tremble all over. It was almost time.

I fidgeted with my dress again, pulling up at the simple, straight neckline that fell across my chest and readjusting the satin bow wrapped high across my waist and gathered to one side. It was all unnecessary. Cassandra Battacenia had fitted and adjusted my dress to my body herself. It fit perfectly, hugging my curves at waist and hip and then flowing out from my just above my knee in a cloud of delicately embroidered lace, chiffon and silk that that seemed to float above the ground. The dress cascaded down behind me in a simple yet stunning train that would slide across the ice in my wake. Which I would be walking across any minute now, I realized.

"Your mother was right, you do look absolutely stunning, dear," my father complimented me brusquely with tears in his eyes.

"Dad… I…"

"I know. I love you too, sweetheart," he interrupted. He planted a quick kiss on my forehead, taking me by surprise. He loudly cleared his throat. "It looks like they're ready to start. Shall we?" He offered me his arm.

I opened my mouth to respond but couldn't find any words, I could barely find enough air to breathe. My father smiled understandingly and with firm, steady steps he guided me down onto the ice at the edge of the pond. I breathed a faint sigh of relief at the sturdy feel of it beneath our feet; it had felt sturdy last time too, I foolishly reminded myself.

I tried to focus on just breathing in and out as I waited for the signal to begin. And then I heard it.

The sounds of guitar strings being plucked echoed out over the ice. The notes were precise and crisp, hanging poignantly in the air and sending chills of pleasure down my spine. The music called to me with a magic of its own. A flush crept into my cheeks and excitement made my heart beat faster. I smiled, my soul soothed. I was ready.

Holding tightly onto my father's arm, I began to walk across the ice towards the sound of the beautiful, enticing music. It was late in the afternoon but the sun was still bright and unexpectedly warm, despite the winter's chill that hung in the air. It was an absolutely pristine and bright winter's day. Frost clung in perfect crystals to all the branches and bushes surrounding the pond. The ice sparkled in a beautiful, dazzling way, the day too perfect to believe with the golden sun and the bright blue sky above. I was filled with hope and wonder as we approached the old stone bridge that arched over the center of the pond.

A small group waited for us directly below the bridge, its underbelly lit by the reflection of the sparkling sun off the ice to reveal the faded but breathtaking mural Sebastian had created long ago, on the underside of the bridge. It was as awe-inspiring as ever to stand before it now. I was quickly distracted by the others who stood before me.

My mother was off to one side, looking absolutely stunning in a long, dark blue gown and faux fur coat, diamonds sparkling at her ears and neck. She clung to Dr. Mackey's arm, who smiled at me warmly and even offered my father a nod of respect. Beside my mother stood Bridgette, my Maid of Honor, who had bravely volunteered to stand between my mother and my father's new wife, Dahlia. Bridgette looked absolutely breathtaking. Her long, dark hair was pulled back from her face in a neat, braided knot, similar to my own and she wore a simple black dress, accompanied with a warm and stylish, short, black coat. Nothing overly fancy or special, but anything on her drew every eye around. She couldn't help it; it was part of her natural charisma and her magic that seemed to draw everyone in. She stood confidently, her head held high and a warm smile brightening her beautiful face. Tears of joy sparkled in her eyes. Dahlia stood beside her, plump and spunky with a ready smile and a short, red dress that was probably inappropriate for an outdoor winter wedding but made me grin anyway.

The Jensons were also there. Mr. Jenson had gone to the trouble of becoming a certified Justice of the Peace so that he could perform our wedding ceremony himself. He wore a fine, dark suit with a bright, royal blue tie. Mrs. Jenson stood back slightly, looking unexpectedly eye-catching in a matching royal blue dress with a lowered neckline and a beautiful sapphire necklace at her throat. Tears were already spilling down her cheeks—I had to quickly look away.

And then there was Clarke, who stood with Tanya, her belly starting to round enough that it was recognizable through her stunning, dark red dress. They stood just to Mrs. Jensons' right, both of them looking flawless. Clarke grinned at me, his eyes lingering just a little too long while Tanya frowned and elbowed him in the ribs. She flashed me a quick, apologetic smile which I readily returned. Somewhere along the line, in all that we had been through in the past few months, we had all become friends. I never thought I'd be able to tolerate Tanya's company, let alone occasionally seek it out.

And Sebastian had been so sure Clarke would never forgive him but he was surprisingly willing to accept the truth—or the closest version to it which we could allow him to hear—and to forgive. People change and life is never what you expect it to be. The world works in mysterious and wonderful ways.

And then there was Sebastian.

He stood at the center of the small, half-circle, wearing a simple yet superbly cut, dark gray suit. His shirt was ivory, to match my gown, his tie a steely shade of gray. He was clean-shaven, with his dark hair in familiar messy, black spikes. My heart skipped a beat as I laid eyes upon him, and then resumed in double-time.

He played his old guitar, his fingers gently plucking the strings and forming the complicated shapes of the chords without his eyes ever glancing down. He never looked away from me for a second. The look of wonder, love and adoration upon his face when he saw me… I knew I'd never forget it.

He played the last note as my father and I came to a stop before him. Sebastian grinned as he twisted his guitar around upon its strap and slung it over his back instead of handing it off to Clarke. I laughed delightedly to see that my groom was going to marry me with a guitar slung across his back; my father frowned.

The ceremony went by in a blur. Prayers and words and vows, tears and ice and our hearts beating in unison until finally our lips joined in a kiss, sealing our words and our lives together, forever. I was certain that I had never been happier in my life, in my existence. Had anyone?

"Mrs. Caldwood, have you fallen asleep?" Sebastian whispered in my ear, lowering his head to mine. I smiled sleepily, lulled by the hum of the taxi's engine and the comforting warmth of Sebastian's arms.

"I could never sleep—I don't want this day to end. I was just daydreaming."

"If you're tired, we can go to the hotel now so you can rest," Sebastian offered, immediately concerned. "We can always come back tomorrow."

"No, I'm not tired," I assured him. "Besides—look! We're here."

Our driver looked puzzled as he pulled into the parking lot. He glanced around, his eyes searching the large, empty lot, and the abandoned trail that led between the tall, swaying trees.

"I've never seen it so quiet! An' on a beautiful evening like t'night, you'd think there'd be more folks out. Ah well, enjoy havin' the Ring to yourselves."

"We will," I answered distractedly. I could already feel the magic in the air, prickling over my skin and putting my hairs on end. Excitement flashed through me, flushing my cheeks. Last time we had come to The Giant's Ring, I had felt so frightened, overwhelmed and full of despair and even then I had still somehow managed to forget it all enough to get caught up in the ancient magic of the place. But now, with my heart and soul ecstatic already from this morning's wedding and my spirits soaring high, the ancient magic of The Giant's Ring raced like adrenaline through my veins. I had never felt more alive.

Sebastian paid our driver and he quickly drove off, leaving us alone in the empty parking lot with just the wind whistling in our ears. Sebastian gave me his most heart-stopping smile, his eyes sparkling brightly.

"Can you feel it?"

I nodded, my own eyes wide.

"It's so much more intense than before. My hands are shaking."

"It's different," Sebastian agreed excitedly. "It's never felt like this here, ever. The magic has changed somehow. It doesn't feel that different from ours anymore. I feel like I could almost use it, harness it somehow."

"It's different, we're different. I can feel it pulling me forward, to the center."

Sebastian took my trembling hand in his.

"Let's go," he whispered.

My heart beat quicker with every step that we took closer to The Ring. As soon as we had landed in Ireland, we had both felt it calling to us. It was the first place we had wanted to come before we even began our honeymoon. We knew there was a reason, an ancient secret that perhaps this sacred place was finally ready to share.

The sun was just going down as we came out of the trees and the trail met the pathway that led around the circumference of The Ring, along its rolling bank. The sky was on fire along the horizon, burning up the clouds in a blaze of blood red, gold and hues of soft peach and blushing pink. The shadows stretched long before us, the boulders at The Ring's center glowing before the sunset's fiery blaze.

We hurried forward together, jogging down the side of the bank and striding hand in hand towards The Ring's center. The strange magic of the place pulled us forward, our lips rendered still. This moment was beyond words. This magic was stronger than us both.

We paused together, before the ancient tomb. The sun dipped lower on the horizon.

"It's coming from the stones," Sebastian murmured. The energy that filled the air, that vibrated and swelled all around us was radiating outwards from the smooth, five thousand-year-old stones. "What should we do?"

I reached out, as if to touch the weathered surface of the boulder before me but Sebastian immediately stopped me.

"Be careful," he warned.

"It's alright," I reassured him, feeling certain and sure of myself. "Trust me."

He slowly nodded, his eyes steady on mine as I reached out and touched the strangely warm stone. My breath caught in my throat as my fingertips lightly pressed against the surface of the large capstone. A powerful wave of magic rippled outwards through the air and throughout The Ring, causing us both to stumble backwards and the air to rush from our lungs.

Time stood still.

"What's happening?" Sebastian looked around in bewilderment. "How is this possible?"

I followed his gaze and took in all the astonishing details around us, impossible as they might seem. The sun had paused in its descent on the horizon, clearly frozen in time. The gentle breeze that only seconds before had been rustling my hair had abruptly stopped, a leaf caught in its path hung motionless in the air a few feet above the ground, several others hung in the air around us as if from invisible strings. The silhouette of a bird, paused in mid-flight above The Ring's bank, was just visible against the golden sky. The world was silent, the Earth was still. Nothing moved except us.

"Did you do this?" Sebastian asked, his eyes full of wonder.

"No," I shook my head slightly in denial. "But this moment, it's meant for us."

"What do you mean?"

"I'm not sure exactly," I admitted. "But it feels right."

His slow, returning smile warmed my heart and sent wild chills of anticipation up and down my spine.

"I love you," he whispered as he pulled me into his arms.

My heart swelled with love and joy, while desire flared deep within me. I held myself tightly against him, my lips finding his neck and kissing a slow trail upwards, searching for his lips.

"A moment outside of time, to be together in a way that time has never given our souls," I murmured.

His breathing quickened. I thought I could almost hear his heart beating or perhaps it was the sound of my own heart hammering wildly in my chest.

"Our own little piece of forever," he agreed, his voice hushed.

And then he kissed me, as time ceased to exist, as that one kiss stretched into infinity. We tumbled together to the ground, all thoughts erased from my mind as all I knew was him: his lips, his hands, his body against mine. Passion, desire and pure ecstasy thundered through me as our souls and bodies intertwined and joined together into one. The moment stretched into infinity, and all I knew—all that existed—was his passion and mine, and our love for one another. There was no beginning and no end, just us, together, forever.

A long time later, after days and weeks, years and centuries had passed, and yet no time at all, the amber fire that painted the sky along the horizon faded quietly away. Slowly, the blazing sun began to set against the sapphire sky.

ACKNOWLEDGMENTS

There are always so many people to thank at this point. This book would have taken me ten years to write (instead of two!) without all your help and support, and might never have become any more than an unfinished document on my laptop.

I have to start by thanking all my supporters and everyone who has read The Lost Magic books! This book was inspired by and written for you. It might not have been written if you didn't ask for it, so thank you. A special thanks to all the reviewers and book bloggers out there as well who have read, recommended and talked about my books. I really appreciate your hard work, professionalism and support. Thanks for helping to spread the word.

Mumma, ultimately you're responsible for absolutely everything that I do but thank you specifically for watching my monsters so I can get my work done, supporting me and listening to me whenever I needed a shoulder or an ear, and beta-reading my manuscripts. Thanks for your patience. Thanks for loving me. You're simply the best.

And speaking of the best, I'm so lucky to have the best friends in the world! Thank you for supporting me and my writing, for reading my books, coming to my events, listening to me vent, giving me great advice and making me laugh. Francoise, you're included under the "friends" category too before you ask where your name is! A sister is a friend for life, and your love and support are invaluable. Thank you Camille for being amazing, for keeping my website up-to-date, for beta-reading the book and being an incredible friend. I really couldn't do it without all of you.

My boys are my inspiration. I love you two so much, your smiles and laughs and sweet kisses and hugs make my world go round. Thank you for being patient with your Mummy whose head is often in the clouds or who sometimes has to send a "quick email" before she can play monster trucks. I would play monster trucks with you all day if I could. And hugs to my beautiful nieces who have their own adorable magic.

Jesse, my partner in crime, my biggest supporter and most valuable critic, my shoulder to cry on who is always there for me no matter what. I love you so much for the million things you do for our family and for me, for the wonderful person that you are. Thank you. I love you.

And finally, one of the best for last, thank you Michelle at Central Avenue Publishing! My books wouldn't be out there in the world if it weren't for you. Thank you for helping me translate the ideas in my head onto paper and wrapping them in such beautiful covers. Thank you for all the hard work you do for all your authors. Thank you for your support, your advice, your patience and your expertise. Thanks for being awesome.

www.ingramcontent.com/pod-product-compliance
Lightning Source LLC
Chambersburg PA
CBHW061529210726
48287CB00006B/1891